A Warrior's Path

J. A. GOGUEN

DEDICATION

For my wife, Denise, who patiently respected my "Work In Progress" sign
while I created a new world.

CONTENTS

Acknowledgments   i

Prologue   1

1   The East Lands   5

2   Divination   14

3   Precedence   18

4   Start of the Journey   30

5   Invocation   36

6   Discovery   47

7   The Aggressor   54

8   Progression   67

9   Ill Omens   75

10   Excitement   82

11   Lament   98

12   Plans   117

13   Perception   132

14   Awakening   151

15   Difficult Lessons   169

16   Change of Plans   190

17   Reunion   208

18   War   234

19   Aftermath   275

Epilogue   279

ACKNOWLEDGMENTS

Thanks to Chris List and Doug Lagemann for being willing to subject themselves to some of the earliest revisions of this book. Without their comments and insights, this story would not be nearly as good as I think it has become. A big thanks to Justin Walden for churning through multiple revisions and helping me refine this into something polished. His dedication and tips on the structure of the story and consistency of the characters were invaluable. And a special thank you to Denise, who was more than just a beta reader. She supported me every step of the way through this process and is the best wife an author could hope for.

PROLOGUE

The young boy padded silently into the dimly-lit room and approached the bed where his father was resting fitfully. Thick, black hair cascaded down his forehead, partially obscuring the full eyebrows and light brown eyes that he had inherited from the man sleeping just a few feet away. The balance and grace that had also passed from father to son was evident as the boy drifted to the bedside like a ghost. Despite the care he took in not waking the man, his father stirred. He seemed to sense the boy's presence.

"Urietsin," the man whispered with half-opened eyes. "Come closer, my son."

Urietsin saw the sweat glistening on his father's pale forehead. He should not have been in here. His mother had told him to wait until his father felt better, but the illness seemed to be getting worse each day. His father's skin had grown deathly white, and his eyes were rimmed with redness, and always there was the feverish sweat. It had been nearly two weeks since he had seen the man for more than a few minutes, but it seemed like an eternity to the son who looked up to his father as a hero.

"Hello, father," the young Urietsin whispered. "How are you feeling?"

The man's eyes opened a little wider to take in the sight of his boy's worried face, and it seemed as though his lip quivered for a moment, but then he smiled. "A bit stronger today," he lied.

A momentary look of doubt sculpted the boy's expression, but he bowed respectfully. When he stood straight again, he also wore a smile. "When do you think you will be out of bed?" Urietsin asked.

"Once I gain a bit more strength," his father replied. "Perhaps after another good night's rest."

The boy nodded and bowed again. "I shall let you sleep, then, father."

"Wait, Urietsin," the man called urgently. "Please stay a while. It has been too long since we have spoken."

1

"Yes, father," the boy said obediently.

The man regarded his son for some time in silence. Urietsin's father had done much in his lifetime, and he was proud to know that many of his countrymen held him in high esteem. But no deed or accomplishment gave him more pride than his son. He knew the boy would carry on the Retso family name and, more importantly, its honor.

"Would you like to hear a story, my boy?" the elder Retso asked.

Urietsin's eyes brightened and he nodded eagerly. His father told wonderful stories. He told of his days as a warrior, fighting beside his kin against the dragon Reisothin and of the days before, when the tribes were at war with one another. Though they were firsthand accounts, his father never overemphasized his own part in events, and he always spoke of the bravery and honor of his countrymen. The stories always made the boy proud of his father, his kin and his heritage.

"Long ago, when the soil was younger," the man began in the tradition of many of the old legends, "our land was the center of a great kingdom that spread from the mountains to the ocean. So rich was this kingdom, and so beautiful were its people, that visitors came from cities far, far away to trade with and admire them. Many different kinds of people came to this kingdom, even the elves, and went back to their homes with spices, art, exotic fabrics, and sometimes even our beautiful people.

"But the gateway between east and west was guarded by a great mountain, and on top of this mountain lived the Keeper of Erulin. He was a demon who would let no visitor to the east pass without an offering of libation at the foot of his mountain. If any walked by without at least a drop of cool water onto the ground, the demon would shake the mountaintop and cause the ground to tremble so that none could move their feet under them until he was appeased."

Urietsin stared at his father in fascination. So far, this was like no story his father had ever told him. He had heard some of the older legends from his mother about Emperor Teomin and his two cities, but none of those included a demon. The boy listened, enthralled.

"As generations passed," the man continued, "more and more people desired to visit the great kingdom, and the Pass of Erulin swelled with visitors. With so many people on the road, many thought they could slip by the mountain without the Keeper noticing. But the demon had a keen eye and many friends who could shape themselves any way they wished. Somehow, he always knew when someone had not paid the toll. The more travelers sneaked by, the harder he would shake the ground until they satisfied him."

The man paused for a moment and heaved a deep, wheezing breath. As he exhaled, he began to cough fitfully.

Urietsin's fascination became concern. "Are you alright, father? Would you like a drink?"

The man put up his hand and cleared his throat loudly. "No, son. I am fine," he said reassuringly. He turned away for a moment to take a few breaths and to wipe the sweat from his forehead.

"Now, where was I? Ah, yes. One day there came a wealthy merchant whose trade was beautifully-sculpted wax candles. When he and his son arrived at the mountain, they found that they had no drink to offer. They pleaded with the demon to let them cross, but he would hear none of it. As was his wont, he shook the ground, and the candlemaker and his son fled.

"When the two men stopped running, they looked in their cart and saw that every candle that had been so painstakingly sculpted was broken. The candlemaker was furious and vowed that they would cross Erulin without giving the demon so much as a drop. He instructed his son to go out and hunt pheasant for their dinner. Right away, the merchant began to melt down his wax and sculpt.

"His son came home later that night with two armfuls of pheasant, and the candlemaker and his son ate well. The next morning the son awoke to find his father placing the last pheasant feather on two sets of enormous wings. 'You see, my son,' the candlemaker said, 'if the demon will not let us walk across Erulin, we will fly.' So, the two men set out again for the pass. When they arrived, they donned their wings and took to the sky.

"Now, when the demon saw these two strange beasts flying past his mountain, he asked, 'What are these new creatures in the sky?' His demon friends answered, 'It is the candlemaker, O Keeper, and his son who denied you yesterday. They've grown wings like us!' At this the demon became enraged and began to shake the ground as never before, but it was in vain. The men flew over the quaking ground and laughed. The other demons shrieked, 'Quickly! They are escaping!' Then the Keeper of Erulin shook the mountain so hard that it broke apart and spewed forth fire from the center of the earth."

Urietsin's father heard his son gasp in surprise. He hid his grin and continued in a dramatic whisper. "The ground trembled in tumult, and fire rained from the sky. Ikiu'iu, the son of the candlemaker, could not keep up with his father, and so his wings caught fire and melted. When the candlemaker reached the other side of Erulin, he turned to see that his son was not behind him. He flew back again, searching for his son as he went. He finally found his son's body lying broken on the rocks at the foot of the mountain. His hubris had cost him his son's life, and the God of Fate collected the payment. The candlemaker wept and flew back and forth over Erulin until his wings caught fire as well. He fell to his death at the foot of the mountain.

"The demon was pleased that the candlemaker and his son were dead, but he refused to be tricked by humans again. He laid a mighty blow upon

Erulin with his fist, and half the earth fell into the sea. No more would people from the west visit the rich eastern kingdom," Master Retso finished, noting the look of awe upon his son's face.

"What happened to the demons, father?" the boy asked.

The man gave a slight shrug. "Some believe the keeper still lives in the crater of his mountain, far beyond the forest and over the mountains. His friends are rumored to have made their homes in the swamps that now grow on what remains of Erulin, beyond the mountains in the west named after the candlemaker's son."

Urietsin looked suddenly thoughtful. "Father, is it really possible to fly with wings of wax?" he asked.

While it hurt his lungs to do so, the boy's father couldn't help but chuckle. "I don't know, son. Perhaps."

The night wore on, and many more of Urietsin's curiosities were answered. His father told him a few other stories. Some of them were of his battles with the dragon. Others were much older stories that had been passed down from his grandfather. All of them captivated the young Urietsin until, finally, the hour drew very late and both of them could hardly keep their eyes open.

"I will go to bed now, father, and let you sleep," the boy said respectfully.

"Yes," his father replied in a hoarse whisper.

Despite his mother's warning about illness, Urietsin half-climbed onto the bed and gave his father a hug. "Good night, father. I hope you are well in the morning."

The man gripped his son as tightly as his weary muscles could. "As do I. I love you, Etsin," he said in a wavering voice, calling the boy by his nickname.

Urietsin climbed down from the bed and bowed. When he looked at his father again, he thought he could see tears in his eyes. "I love you too, father," he replied with a smile.

In the years to come, Urietsin would cherish this night as more important than any other he had spent with his father. He could not know, as he blew out the oil lamp and crept off to his own bed, that it would be the last time he would ever see the man alive. That night, in the darkness of his room, the head of the Retso family succumbed to his illness and passed into the halls of his ancestors, leaving his son and wife to care for themselves.

1 THE EAST LANDS

Kiusu Tho-Shoishu marveled at the majestic vista before him. For twenty years he had lived among the white-capped mountaintops of Ikiu'iu. Every morning he witnessed the sun breaking over the snow-covered peaks, bringing tantalizing hints of natural warmth with its yellow-tinged brightness. He never tired of the view. Even at his venerable age of one hundred and twelve, Kiusu felt the energetic rush of younger days return with the sun's warmth. He felt as though the years fell away from him, and a spring-like flexibility returned to his joints. And though there were few youths who could boast this old man's elasticity and dexterity, there was a time in his life when performing his daily physical routines was easier. Now, as he stretched his muscles in the warming but still crisp morning air, Kiusu began the combat training portion of his workout.

Time yielded to motion, and without seeming to, the old man shifted. It would have been easy to consider this one frail, considering his short stature and the long gray hair that surrounded his bald crown. His drooping moustache and the obvious wakes that time had left on his face with its passage made his instantaneous motion seem like an affront to possibility.

He was now in a lunge, as steady as if he were relaxing flat on the ground. His hands extended out slowly and began to move apart. In a blur, they swiftly drew back and shot out and up, ending in a double spearhand that would have relieved any opponent of his sight. Pulling back his palms, Kiusu advanced a step, now snapping out two fists with devastating quickness.

Falling into a broken rhythm, the deceptively fit man bounced on the balls of his feet. He took a few short steps forward and flipped into the air, twisting to land facing the other direction. His arm came up to block a strike from his invisible foe, wrapping his hand around an imaginary

5

deflected wrist. Shifting his balance, he snapped his leg forward in a straight kick to the midsection, then pulled the leg back in, pivoted on his other foot and shot out the leg again in a powerful sidekick.

Kiusu advanced quickly, imagining his invisible sparring partner stumbling backward. His front foot lifted into a low kick to the knee and then swung up and around, the tip of his toes easily exceeding his own height. Then, suddenly, the old man began to topple forward.

It almost appeared as if the he had pushed himself a little too far, not surprising, considering his apparent age. But just when it seemed that he had fallen beyond the point of recovery, his arms swung down by his side and up in the other direction. His front foot hit the floor and pushed his body up, providing impetus for a leap that brought Kiusu spinning into the air. In a single fluid motion, this small old man had lifted a full three feet off the ground, spun around in a complete circle, and swung out a kick that would have surely broken his opponent's neck. Back on the ground, as steady as if he had been standing there the whole time, Kiusu smiled. He was just getting started.

Jogging over to a nearby tree, the old man reached for his staff. As his hand went toward the smooth wood of the familiar weapon, a chill wind from the peak of the mountain blew through the trees and halted his motion. He turned into the wind and glanced around. There was something on that breeze. There was a familiar feeling that pulled the chill down into his core. Kiusu stepped away from the staff and hurried to his nearby hut.

Many years ago, before he had come to this place, he had known this feeling for the first time. It was a whisper on the wind that had told him a terrible truth. His old master had once told him that there would come a time when he would know of things that had yet to happen. He would hear the word carried on the wind in a primal language that only his deepest spirit could interpret. He would know that things were converging toward one great event that would shape his own life, as well as the lives of others.

Kiusu had hoped to never have that feeling again. Something was brewing in the amalgam of his destiny. The urgent whispers on the wind overcame his usually rational senses, and he began to feel frightened. The only other time in his life that he had felt the pull so strongly, it had shown him disaster. It had shown him things that he should have been able to prevent, if only he had been more attentive. Old memories within him welled up and struck at his center, imposing upon his balance and stability. Kiusu fought back, desperately grasping for control of his senses. He knew he had to compose himself and receive the messages on his own terms. It had not been this way the first time, but now he understood the nature of the premonitions. He would not be caught unaware again.

The old man made his way to the altar at the back of the hut and sat down on a little woven mat. He closed his eyes and began to go within. Down through the layers of his consciousness, Kiusu traveled to the core of his very being. He sat within a pulsating void that moved in time with his breathing. In this deep, meditative trance, the wizened master began to control the flow of the images that assaulted his mind.

The grayness of the blank canvas before him faded. He saw a rolling green hill, which blocked the setting sun. Suddenly, two silhouettes appeared up on the hill. One of them he obviously recognized as his own. The other seemed to be of a younger man. He could not make out many details from the black outline of the other man. The two shadows, one behind the other, went through a combat routine that was perfectly synchronized. The image faded to black.

His next vision was not one of sight, but one that attacked his other senses. He felt as though he were in battle. He vaguely felt the sensation of air passing quickly by his hands and feet, as it did when he was fighting. He felt a twinge of concern as he realized he had underestimated something. What was it? There was something close to him, something that exuded hatred for him. He felt a rush of adrenaline take over his actions, whatever they might be. A harsh metallic taste flooded the back of his throat, and he felt as though he were suffocating or drowning. Each of his hairs stood on end, electrified by the tension. He could hear the beating of his own heart. The sound grew fainter and slower as he felt the vision fade. When the sound stopped completely, he was left with a single thought.

'Prepare.'

Kiusu opened his eyes to find himself lying on his side, his legs drawn to his chest. He sat up quickly and looked around the quiet room. He suddenly felt very alone, something he hadn't experienced in more than twenty years. He brought himself to his feet and took a deep breath, shaking the almost alien emotions from his mind. After a moment's thought, he turned and got to work. His mind began to race with plans of the next several weeks. He had to hurry. There was much to be done. He had to prepare.

* * *

Beyond the mountains and to the east lay the small reunified city of Kesitul. The river Usinte'ikio, the Living Water, snaked lazily down from the glaciers in the far north, doing for centuries what its name implied, providing life. The decayed remains of an ancient aqueduct sprouted from the terrain here and there and cut a broken line from east to west through the city. It was the only visible remnant of the more ancient capitol after which this one was modeled. Widely-spaced stone houses dotted the landscape and converged up the sides of a low hill crowned by a grand palace.

The people of Kesitul knew very little about the history of their land beyond the great legends. Although accounts varied, every tribe agreed that Kesitul had once been the greatest empire in all the world and had riches beyond imagination. The people were fiercely proud and bound by tradition and had designed the palace in the style of their forefathers as told in legend. Their goal was to recapture the glory of the ancient days.

Home to emperor Geilo the Beloved, the palace on the hill was the finest edifice in the east lands. The people worked for over a decade to erect what they considered to be the greatest architectural achievement of the age. It was a tribute to Geilo for his triumph in reuniting the tribes of this land against an ancient evil that sought to destroy them and ever since ruling with peaceful benevolence.

Inside the Palace the empire's culture was reflected clearly in the artistic expression that shone from every explorable surface. Almost everything in sight was either inlaid with gold or sparkled with precious stones. The high, arching ceiling with its detailed carvings was covered in gold leaf, as were the walls. It was the floor, however, that was most breathtaking of all. On the shiny surface a colorful mosaic played out idyllic scenes and fierce battles from legends in a sweeping radial symmetry. In one place an old master and his younger student stood ready for combat in ruby, emerald, amber, and onyx. Across from them, a wise and wicked dragon twisted through the sky in gold, jasper, jade, and aquamarine. In the centerpiece of the whole mosaic, the eyes of Minotros, God of Fate, gazed upon Emperor Geilo, who was sitting astride the legendary horse that had carried him through the struggle for his people's survival. Around them a vast canvas of other stories was carved out and fitted together to make up this spectacular surface, and its reflective sheen never strayed from perfection.

The path leading up to the throne was flanked on either side by six rectangular spaces outlined in gold, on which knelt twelve of the emperor's most trusted councilors, mimicking tales from the days of the great Emperor Teomin. Each space was a different color, indicating its occupant's rank and position. The throne itself was solid gold inset with countless numbers of twinkling jewels. The back of the ruler's seat flared up and out in a shimmering fanfare that left onlookers breathless. Even the councilors, who knelt before the throne every morning, agreed that it was a sight to behold.

Seated back in the imperial grandeur of his throne was the emperor. His thin face was adorned with elongated features and accentuated by a black moustache and goatee that stretched halfway down his chest. Though the hair on his face was dark, that which showed from under his headdress at the temples was peppered with age. His broadly-swept eyes were dark, deep, and filled with wisdom. Clad in dress no less impressive than the throne room, he and his palace truly seemed to fit the role of his title borrowed from the deep, half-forgotten histories of his people.

Emperor Geilo surveyed his councilors. His look was firm but kind as his eyes moved from one to the next, acknowledging each one's presence before beginning the day's activities. It was a custom of his, out of respect for those men and women who helped him hold the empire together. Like the titles they carried, the advisors were selected as told in the only history known to Kesitul. Those legends that, like many tales that endure the ages, contained more truth than any could guess. But unlike their titles, their purpose was well understood by all, especially the emperor, who called upon their council daily. It was they, as much as he, who could be credited with the two-decade reign of peace.

Finally, his gaze settled upon the last man on his left, the head of the empire's military. His traditional title was *Uchilin*, but the emperor often called him general. He was solidly built, but not overly large, and his dark eyes seemed to demand obedience, though his well-tanned face was soft and, at times, kindly. Today, however, his smooth features were animated with anticipation.

"General Etrusin," the emperor acknowledged.

The Uchilin stepped out from his space to the center of the room and bowed. "*Ushisorein,*" he began, using the emperor's most honorable title. "It is my pleasure to report that over the past several weeks, the empire's youth has answered your call to join our ranks in the imperial *shiodu*. There have been over five-hundred new recruits."

Five-hundred. It sounded like so few to the emperor. He hoped that Etrusin's school could teach them all very well or that the school's numbers would swell to much more in the near future. Then again, Geilo conceded to himself, there might not be any need for them at all.

"Very good," the emperor said, hiding his disappointment. "Continue spreading the word to the furthest reaches of the empire."

"Of course, highness," Etrusin answered with another bow. He could not help but smile. It had been quite some time since the general had seen so many new volunteers in his army. His forces had dwindled over the past two decades, and even with the numbers he had managed to maintain, all he could do was train them. There did not seem to be much call for an army in this peaceful empire.

But Geilo's thoughts on this matter had been very different of late. The more he saw in his dreams and meditations, the more frustrated he became at the way the empire's defenses had been allowed to stagnate. He did not, however, want to let on that he was worried. It would do his empire no good to start a panic. The emperor was pulled from his musings by the motion of the general stepping back toward his space.

"Etrusin," Geilo called, halting the man's movement.

The general returned to the center. "Yes, sire?"

"I would like you to ready teams of scouts," the emperor commanded. "Gather some of your most promising recruits. Send them to survey the surrounding lands. It is time we looked beyond the confines of the empire."

Etrusin's expression was one of shock. When Geilo had told him to invite the empire's youth to train with him, he had assumed the emperor was merely being kind. He had guessed that Geilo was trying to engage him in his role once more after years of inaction and the onset of middle-age threatened to mire his remaining years in tedium. It had never occurred to him that the emperor might have further plans.

"As you wish, highness," the general replied, unable to keep the surprise from his voice.

"Send them westward, through the forest and beyond the mountains," Geilo continued, knowing that Etrusin must have been reeling with every new instruction.

Indeed, the general was stunned, though not because of the direction. It was obvious where they might explore. After all, the paths to the eastern ocean, the southern cliffs and the northern mountain range were all fairly well known. But the forest was said to be impassable and haunted. Not that Etrusin was frightened by spirits, but he knew of no one who ever made it more than a few minutes into the forest before either running away in fear or turning away in frustration at the impossibly thick brush that seemed to block every path. No, it was not where they would explore that had the general bemused, it was just that they were exploring at all.

Etrusin bowed. "However I may serve you, Ushisorein," he offered. When no other commands seemed forthcoming, the general stepped back into his space, noting the similarly surprised expressions of the other advisors.

The day's business continued, but Geilo was distracted for most of it. Many years had passed since the emperor had thought even beyond the borders of his own city. Once his people had joined together and begun to show that they were quite capable of sharing these lands in peace, the emperor was happy to finally sit back and turn his attention to Kesitul as a united nation, rather than a collection of warring tribes.

In some ways, though, those days of turmoil did not feel so long ago, and indeed, it was not in the reckoning of elders. While only twenty years had passed, the story seemed like some of the oldest legends. The empire had risen from the ashes of a great foe, the foe that brought about the reunification. Before this, many of the tribes had been enemies, fighting for control of the lands of their great empire of old. But the great evil, the *Seilen* Dragon Reisothin, had slinked through the countryside easily cutting down any resistance the tribes offered. The Abomination, as he came to be called, came on with his fiery breath and powerful magic, laying waste to entire families, entire clans. Divided, the pathetic creatures of Kesitul were no match for even a single Seilen.

But then, there was hope. Geilo's tribe had been one of the few that had perfected the art of combat on horseback, and the future emperor was a master cavalryman among them. His tribe joined with another and taught them their advanced cavalry tactics. Under his leadership, they had largely escaped the dragon's wrath for weeks and brought the creature much frustration. They rode through the land, beseeching other tribes to join forces with them to be rid of Reisothin forever. Badly beaten, some tribes' numbers frightfully thinned, the people joined with Geilo, the mounted warrior, and his brave young lieutenant Etrusin, wise beyond his years. Together they rose up against Reisothin, and with the help of the mysterious Grand Master Iou-Liu and his talented student Kiusu, trapped him and defeated him. It was no small task, but Reisothin, powerful though he was, could not stand against the united people of Kesitul.

Most of these memories played themselves out in the emperor's mind, but the advisors did not seem to notice his daydreaming. They did not even notice when those daydreams became something more.

There was a strange twinge deep within Geilo's chest. Sights and sounds that blurred just beyond his comprehension flashed in his mind's eye. He did manage to resolve a few glimpses, but none of them were pleasant. Old, wise, and terrible, Reisothin snaked through the sky and tore his people apart. There was something else, though. Something that was not a memory. Something that terrified him like the old stories they used to tell around the campfires when he was young. Whatever it was, it was not imagined, and in the fading image that remained he could see a massive army and blood on the hands of every soldier. They were all marching toward him.

* * *

As the sun sank below the white peaks of the Ikiu'iu Mountains to the west of Kesitul, a darkness swept like a cold wind across the plain of Ionotu. Positioned right on the western edge of the mountain chain, the plain supported Niele'itio, the Dark City. Harsh lines of smoke streamed from the soot-stained, broken chimneys on the western outskirts of the city. Toward the center, the disorganized jumble of ramshackle homes and run-down buildings gave way to plain, square, utilitarian edifices arranged in ordered lines. Near the eastern edge, a large stone castle stood beside a great temple. The temple's twisting spires stretched skyward, leaving a foreboding shadow upon the western face of Mount Thontur, cast by the low setting sun. The sprawling group of black and gray buildings, and especially the temple, almost seemed to emanate the darkness that might have given the city its name.

Deep within the walls of his drab castle, King Orbein conferred with his seer. The room was a dull gray and three dim candles threw a faint light around the room, casting long, flickering shadows upon the wall. The candlelight gleamed off Orbein's circlet, the only outward sign of his title. His simple military uniform, youthful round face and closely-cropped black hair did not immediately suggest his royal position.

"What see you?" the king anxiously of his seer, who was gazing into a bowl filled with an inky black substance.

"An army," the other man said through a thick accent. "They march through the mountains, bringing with them fire!" he exclaimed.

The seer Laernus was a man the likes of which the land of Ionotu had not seen in many, many generations. His graying blond hair and neatly trimmed goatee, which emphasized his angular features, stood out as obviously as his accent. Not only was he a foreigner, but a wizard as well. While the king and few others had acquired some limited ability in the magical arts after many years of laborious study, this stranger exhibited control over much more powerful magic. It was a very advanced arcane experiment that had left him stranded across the Gulf of Erulin almost twenty years ago. Since then, few ever saw him perform anything more powerful than divination, though this new laboratory that Orbein had granted him in the castle suggested he was still capable of much more.

"An army," the king repeated. "Is this my army?"

Laernus glanced up from the bowl and eyed his king uneasily. "I cannot be certain, highness," he said with a pause.

King Orbein scowled at Laernus threateningly. "Then devise a way to become certain, seer."

Laernus looked back to the inky blackness, disguising a slight rolling of his eyes. "Divination can be a complicated magic, sire. While the immediate future is often quite clear, the further from the present I gaze, the more difficult it becomes. My visions go..." A heavy sigh from the king cut off his explanation.

"Laernus," Orbein started calmly, "spare me your excuses. Return to your bowl, and tell me what I wish to know. Do not force me to reassess your value to my court."

Suppressing a sigh of his own, Laernus looked back to his scrying bowl, but saw only the wavering reflections of candlelight. Really, it had been Orbein's interruptions more than anything that had dissipated the visions. The king seemed to be quite foolish to the mage lately, almost childish since his coronation six months ago. Laernus had begun to more deeply regret his dabbling in the spellcraft that brought him to this land, for he knew it would be a long time before he would discover a way back to his home, especially with Orbein's incessant distractions.

He gave the king his best attempt at an apologetic smile. "Begging your most generous pardon, highness. The pool has gone black. You have seen many of these sessions end in similar ways. And what benefit would I reap from misleading you in this? Have I not proved my usefulness to you after all these years? Have I not helped to bring you this far? Have I not been rewarded greatly for this assistance to you? I understand the source of your frustration, but you must not let it blind you. It is fate that I cannot see all things. There is a reason that the gods do not wish you to know the outcome of all your endeavors."

"The gods..." the king snickered as his expression softened slightly. "Who needs their divine meddling? My army will once again serve me without question. I am the same man who led them as general to conquer these lands. I will lead them once more, this time as king, to conquer our ancient enemy."

Laernus stifled a smug grin at the king's verbal musings. He knew Orbein's crown carried with it new insecurities he had never had to deal with before. As a general, he had commanded the loyalty of his army with ease, but crowning himself king turned up more than a few eyebrows. The people of the city loved him, as his defeat of the surrounding lands gave them a sense of patriotism and had been good for business, infusing the local economy with new sources of revenue. To them it did not matter what he called himself. Orbein was a hero.

But the king cared nothing for that riff-raff. It was the army that mattered most. Only they had the power to uphold his reign, and likewise to tear it down. Laernus could not help but stoke this fear.

"But, how can you be so sure? What other enemies do you have to defeat? What else can you possibly do to quell their doubts?" he asked in a hushed tone.

Orbein smiled in a way Laernus did not expect. "You are not the only one with visions of the future," he said with some significance. "At night, in my sleep, I see an army as well. We march upon the ancient empire that sent us here and abandoned us. We rain fire down upon them from the skies!"

Laernus could not hide his surprise. "Indeed?" he asked. "That was generations upon generations ago. How can you be sure this empire still exists?"

The king's smile broadened. "We will know soon enough. I have a plan in motion as we speak."

2 DIVINATION

In the throne room, the emperor was pensive. "I want you to keep an eye on these warriors Etrusin sends out," he said slowly, considering each word that passed his lips.

Ninei, the emperor's mediator, raised her eyebrow. "Forgive me, highness, but do you mean you wish me to go with them?" she asked curiously.

Geilo nodded seriously. "Take some of your students to send with groups as they split up. We shall soon go places our people have not trod for generations, and we do not know who is out there. I need you to be there with them, to be the voice of the empire."

"Do you believe our services will be required?" the woman asked, intrigued even more by the emperor's request.

"It is merely a precaution," the emperor explained quickly.

Ninei pondered the emperor's words for a moment before bringing her almond-shaped eyes to meet his. "I see," she said as she bowed, though her brow furrowed as she did.

"Is there something wrong, *Giunin*?" the emperor asked, using the traditional title for the court arbiter.

"Nay, highness," the dark haired woman bowed again. "It is but a pleasure to serve you."

Geilo nodded, "Very well. When he sends out his scouts, you will accompany them. Make sure they take no...unnecessary measures. You are dismissed," he said briskly as he turned his attention to a scroll that sat in his lap.

Once the great doors to the throne room were closed, Ninei hurried to her chambers. She knew something was odd was afoot. There was something hidden in the emperor's request. She could tell that he was distracted. And what did he mean by 'unnecessary measures'? It was true that the empire was headed into the unknown, but she thought it unlikely that a scouting party would need a diplomat there with them.

So, why was the emperor silent about his true reasons? She could not begin to guess, but she trusted in Geilo's wisdom and knew of his gift of foresight. If the emperor wanted Etrusin's men watched, she would be the one to do it. The Giunin knew it was only a matter of time before the truth was revealed.

* * *

Emperor Geilo stood and looked around his throne room. His gaze fell upon the two guards at the door. He stared at them for a long while, half expecting them to shift uneasily, but these men had been well trained by Etrusin. They would not budge until the emperor commanded. After a long silence, he did so.

"You are both dismissed. Wait outside the door until I call for you again. No one is to enter unless it is at my bidding." The emperor's quiet voice sounded almost menacing, but again the men did not blink. They simply bowed, turned around and left, closing the throne room doors behind them.

The emperor looked to the scroll he had been holding since before Ninei had arrived. As a child his family had proudly announced that he possessed the gift of *Ohe Ren Utsouri*, Tomorrow's Eye. The priests of his tribe taught him how to more effectively apply this gift for the good of his people. He had used this along with his expert horsemanship to great advantage against the wicked Reisothin, but since the beast's destruction, the eye had remained dormant. Now, it seemed, his abilities were calling to him once more.

He stared hard at each of the words on the scroll, squinting and repeating each one. He had to memorize them all perfectly. He needed to perform this ritual meditation to confirm the fragments of disjointed time that played in his mind. If the disturbing visions that had been coming to him lately were true, then his empire was in grave danger.

Geilo looked up from the scroll. He dropped the arcane writings onto the throne behind him and walked slowly to the center of the room. There, the wise ruler raised his arms and began to whisper a chant. Gradually, as the volume of his chants increased, the usually bright throne room dimmed. The emperor's chants came from his lips faster and louder as the room grew darker.

Suddenly, the emperor's chant reached a climax, and complete darkness cloaked the room. Silence followed the absence of light for a few moments, after which a small pinpoint of shining blue pierced the darkness from the center of the room. The small light suddenly erupted to surround the emperor in a blue-glowing sphere. The surface of the bubble swirled and twisted around the leader, who seemed quite small within.

The emperor closed his eyes and began to move his outstretched hands slowly. His body turned slowly in a strange, sluggish dance. Eventually, the turning and twisting of the emperor's body matched that of the bluish patterns on the bubble. Almost as if he sensed this fact, Geilo opened his eyes and kneeled. He had attuned himself to this otherworldly sphere. Now he could make out the twisted images that played out upon the shiny inside surface of the large glowing ball. He hoped he could glean some promising information this time. Something that suggested a better course for his empire.

Deep within the subtle shades of every blue possible, the images began to take shape. The dark shadows and bright highlights coalesced into form and created a perfect scene. It was the line of the mountains against the sky. Almost-white blue clouds swept lazily across the darker azure skies. It was a peaceful scene, and for a moment, the emperor felt reassured.

Then he saw them.

A large, dark blotch on the ground far below began to stir. The emperor willed himself closer so that he might confirm his suspicion.

Soldiers. A number the like of which he had not seen since the days of Reisothin was gathered there in a field at the foot of the mountains. Black lines of smoke reached skyward from the scorched earth that seemed to reveal itself at their every step. Burning embers floated down among their ranks as though the dark clouds above were drizzling fire, and indeed, every so often the clouds blinked with lightning, completing the illusion.

The soldiers, whether dark by nature or simply smeared with soot, seemed inspired by the ominous thunderheads. Their mouths gaped wickedly with every flash, and their eyes glowed, either reflecting the show above or with their own evil light. They trudged grimly eastward, toward his home. These demon warriors with scarred and blackened faces marched for his empire!

"No!" Geilo cried out at the advancing force. Suddenly the vision dissipated, as did the globe and the darkness. The emperor found himself kneeling in his throne room alone, the image of fiery, wicked eyes burned onto his retina.

"There must be something that can be done," he said aloud, pleadingly turning his eyes to the ceiling. "I will ask for your guidance, Minotros."

The emperor made his way back to his throne and sat down. He told himself that his people would not fall before this demonic force that he saw in his visions. He would perform the ritual of Commune. It would take some discussion with his high priest, Shiu-Hi, but considering the urgency of the situation, he was sure this was the only wise course. A powerful sense of foreboding loomed from the west in Geilo's mind. That direction, he guessed, because of the mountains. Those cold, foreboding peaks and a pair of burning red eyes remained fixed in his mind for the rest of the day.

3 PRECEDENCE

Reniu, one of the veteran soldiers of the imperial guard, was in a surly mood. Many said that his natural expression was a scowl, but today there was a definite emotion behind the downturned corners of his mouth. For the most part, Reniu's reputation for having a bad attitude was exaggerated, but he was certainly not possessed of the coolest of tempers. Etrusin's newest trainees and their obvious inexperience reflected in the huge soldier's squinted eyes, bringing that temper to a point near boiling.

He sulked at all these children running around and swinging weapons that only grown warriors should be swinging. The sight of the whole lot of them irked him, and what irked him even more was the fact that he had been assigned to choose from the best of these poor excuses for warriors for the upcoming scouting mission. Most of them barely grew any hair on their chins! If they weren't even old enough to hold a shaving blade, how could they hold a sword, or even a staff? If that wasn't enough, almost a third of these trainees were little more than girls. These young women had little place among military ranks to his mind, even though on any other day he would openly concede that the best swordsman of the general's veterans was a woman.

Reniu watched the boys and girls swing their staves and bamboo longswords pathetically at the straw dummies that lined the training field. He seethed furiously every time one of them missed. He had a mind to go out there and show these children the difference between a straw dummy and a real warrior. He flashed his decaying teeth in a wicked grin as the thought momentarily distracted his attention.

His concentration returned suddenly as he saw a staff fly into the air and land on the ground several feet in front of him. The straw was placed and the camel's back broken. Reniu scanned the field for his victim and spotted the weaponless young man standing in front of his dummy with his fists raised. The angry soldier stomped off toward him.

"Hey!" he called out as he approached. "What're you doin'?"

The young man looked past his straw opponent to Reniu. He put his fists down and shrugged. "I am fighting my enemy," he said.

Reniu considered the young man. He was not very tall, but it seemed he packed a lot of muscle tone into the small frame. His *koje*, a small black jacket with white ties that lined the front, hung opened to reveal his well-shaped chest and rigid abdominals. He wore a tightly wrapped black sash for back support and light, loose-fitting black pants for ease of motion. The boy seemed ready to train, so Reniu decided to give him a quick lesson in what it feels like to be crushed by an enemy who fights back.

"Yer supposed to use the stick," the angry man sneered.

The young man pushed his straight black hair away from his forehead. "Why use only one weapon when my body is a weapon made of many?" he asked, sincerely hoping the large man could come up with a good answer.

The imposing soldier answered with a laugh, "Then let's see you wield yer weapon!" he bellowed as he rushed forward.

The young warrior stepped up, fists leading as though he had expected the charge. His shoulders turned bringing his right fist back ever so slightly. Reniu snickered at the obvious preparation; he knew he would teach this one well. And hard. The larger man went in for a counter attack before the young soldier even moved his fist forward.

Reniu had fallen for the ruse completely. The young warrior had purposely telegraphed the move, which he had no intention of making. Instead his foot came up from the ground and connected with the advancing man's kneecap. The experienced soldier howled, as much in frustration of his foolishness as in pain. He had underestimated this one; now it was time for the real lesson.

"Yer gonna pay fer that, boy!" the big man roared, swinging his hammer-like fist.

The young soldier merely ducked away from the heavy punch and shot his fist toward his attacker's gut. Reniu half doubled over, but recovered quickly. He may not have expected this young man to be this good, but he was a seasoned warrior himself. He knew the consequence of remaining vulnerable for too long.

From across the field, General Etrusin's trusted lieutenant, Komeris, saw the fight break out. He began to run toward the skirmish with the intention of breaking it up. He knew how temperamental Reniu was and expected that he would crush the young recruit where he stood. He stopped in his tracks when he saw the big man get hit once, then twice. The boy was good. Perhaps this might be worth watching.

"What's going on?" demanded Etrusin, returning from his duties at the palace.

Komeris turned to see his general stomping toward the fight, "Wait, sir!" he called after him.

Etrusin stopped, but did not turn away from the fight. "What is it?" the general asked impatiently.

Komeris nodded toward the commotion. "Watch him," he said, indicating the young man.

Trusting in his lieutenant's instincts, Etrusin watched the course of the battle, rather than running off to halt it immediately. He would let neither of the soldiers hurt each other too much.

The larger man had backed away and was considering his opponent. The young fighter sprang on the balls of his feet and waved his hands in front of him, looking ready. Reniu stepped up quickly and threw a fast punch. It was easily defeated by the quick parry offered by the smaller man. But that had been Reniu's intention all along. Even as his fist was being pushed aside he whipped his foot up to snap at the boy's head.

It seemed almost impossible to Reniu, but the young soldier reacted effortlessly to the move. As his first hand swung away the bulky veteran's fist, his next went up and grabbed at his attacker's ankle just as his foot came within an inch of his head. Before Reniu could free himself, the boy dropped to his haunches, twisted, and shot his first fist back around and straight into the large man's groin, letting out a high-pitched scream as he did so.

Reniu merely made a choking sound and slowly tipped over as the younger man let go of his leg. The large soldier fell like timber. The boy stood back at the ready and stared at the man lying still on the ground as if daring him to rise. The whole field was quiet as the other soldiers looked on.

"Who is that boy?" asked Etrusin, astounded that this young man had taken down Reniu, one of his larger men.

Komeris shook his head. "I don't know," he said, not fearing for the boy. The young warrior was not in any trouble. He had fought with skill and won against his superior, an action that earned warriors some distinction. He also knew that Reniu would leave the boy alone from now on. Reniu may have been quick tempered, but he wasn't stupid. Besides, it had been the surly warrior's own fault for leaving himself so vulnerable.

Etrusin looked to his lieutenant with sincere curiosity. "Well, then, let us go discover this young warrior's identity, shall we?" he said.

The lieutenant nodded. "Indeed," he replied.

Etrusin jogged up to the scene and approached the crowd that had gathered around the fight. He noted Reniu's wary expression as some of the other soldiers helped him up. The young man, on the other hand, seemed relaxed. His shoulders and arms were slack as he offered an apologetic bow to his fallen opponent, yet it also appeared as if he were ready to spring into action at a moment's notice. The boy looked over at Etrusin as he approached.

"What's your name, boy?" Etrusin commanded.

The young man bowed deeply to his superior and said, "Urietsi'in of Retso, sir."

"Urietsin," the general said, using a more common pronunciation of the boy's name. "I know your father, though I have not seen in some years. Is he well?"

"My father passed many winters ago from illness," Urietsin replied with a hint of sadness.

The Uchilin nodded solemnly. "He was a good man. I can see that he lives on in you. I am sure he would be proud."

The young man could not help but smile. "Many thanks," he offered, taking several dipping bows indicating extreme deference.

"*Usetsin*," said Komeris, translating the old tongue of the boy's tribe. "You are well named, Swift One."

"Indeed," agreed Etrusin, "and I believe we can find a way to make use of your speed. The emperor has commanded me to assemble a scouting party to explore the lands beyond our empire. I do not believe this party will be complete without your presence."

Urietsin bowed again, "Thank you, sir. You are most generous," he said, once more unable to hide his beaming smile.

The general nodded in acknowledgement. Not only was this boy a good fighter, he was also respectful. Etrusin had, indeed, known Urietsin's father. The patriarch of the main family of one of the larger tribes before the empire was founded, he was a skilled and honorable warrior. This boy had obviously inherited some of that instinctual essence. If only all the new soldiers showed as much promise as this one.

* * *

King Orbein smirked at the approach of the hooded figure. He took a step deeper into the shadows of the corridor within his dimly-lit palace. Unlike kings of legend, Orbein was not satisfied to sit on some glorious throne all day feeling pompous and venerated. Even after he had been promoted as an officer in the Dark City's Citizens' Army, he still frequently haunted the streets where he grew up, slipping from shadow to shadow, meeting with often mysterious and unsavory characters who would do his bidding. This hooded figure was such a character.

The cloaked form floated deeper into the shadows of the enormous hall and stopped a few feet from the king. "I know you are near, human. Your scent permeates the air," a crackling voice hissed beneath the low cowl.

The king stepped from the darkness. "Is my stench so overpowering?"

he asked.

The figure turned to him and slowly reached up to pull the cowl from its head. From underneath emerged a terrible face. The creature, for it was surely not a human, eyed the king. The blotchy pink skin, oozing with a clear slick liquid, seemed as though it had been glued unnaturally to the creature's face. The long, pointed nose flared, and the creased skin twisted dubiously in a lewd sneer. "On the contrary," the thing croaked, "you smell delicious."

King Orbein could not help but flinch at that comment. This creature was known as a Fiu-Het, a shape shifter. The ugly race of magical creatures was spoken of often in cautionary tales told to children in the Dark City. The stories warned of the dangers of wandering alone in the swamps, for the Fiu-Het thought of human flesh as a delicacy. These unnatural beasts were extremely clever and their shapeshifting abilities made them a formidable opponent or a powerful ally.

"You are the king?" it asked skeptically.

"Yes," Orbein said uneasily

The beast wasted no time. "Have you my payment?" it asked, flicking its large, sticky tongue over its lidless eyes to moisten them.

The king looked down to the money pouch he held in his hands, more to take his eyes away from the horrible creature than to confirm the presence of the heavy bag.

The beast followed his gaze. "Give it here," it hissed wickedly.

The king, who was not accustomed to being on the receiving end of intimidation and who was quickly adjusting to the creature's appearance, straightened. "A moment, beast," he said to its obvious displeasure. "I must be sure of my investment. Prove you are worth this substantial payment."

The Fiu-Het twisted its face into a scowl, which made it impossibly uglier. Within seconds, however, the misshapen face of the beast morphed into that of a beautiful, dark-haired woman with light, exotic eyes. Pinched and wrinkled skin unraveled into a silky white complexion, and the hunched form melted into the supple figure of a female with many endowments. Even the shredded rags that covered the shape shifter as clothing became a sheer, iridescent wrap that left little to the imagination. "Gayossha, highness," the woman said in a soft, melodic voice.

"What?" the king asked absently, for he was more concerned with the curves of the shapely woman before him than the breathy words she had just uttered.

"My name is Gayossha, human!" the creature screamed as it quickly assumed its original appearance. "If you dare to call me beast again, I shall begin with your feet so that you may witness the whole of my meal!"

Suddenly the king's mind flooded with images of being eaten alive. He saw the creature's lips covered in his own blood and heard his bones crunch sickeningly between those horribly deformed teeth. He felt bile rising in his throat, but swallowed it down. He didn't know where this uncontrollable wave of fear had come from, but he was determined to keep his composure before this disgusting creature.

"Very well, Gayossha," Orbein said, unable to keep the tremor from his voice completely, "You have proven your skill." He tossed the pouch to the creature.

Gayossha caught the moneybag easily and felt its considerable weight. "Good," it croaked almost uninterestedly.

"Indeed," said King Orbein, unsure if the thing was pleased. "And in return..." he let the statement hang.

Gayossha looked to the king with a gleam in its eye, "Ah, yes. What of these services you requested?"

Orbein nodded, glad to see the creature was still interested in business instead of dinner. "Yes, the services. I require...a scout of sorts," he said tentatively.

Gayossha's face twisted again, "A scout? Where? To what end?"

The king, likewise, frowned. "Of that I'm not entirely sure," he said.

The creature's pupils dilated quickly as they focused on the king, "I warn you, highness, waste not my time."

The king was beginning to lose patience with these threats. "I have paid you in advance, Gayossha, so you will find the time to listen to my requests. There are few who would threaten me so openly, for many know to do so brings about great consequence."

The Fiu-Het licked its eyes thoughtfully. "I see," the oozing creature reluctantly conceded. "Continue."

"As I said," the king began, "I am not sure where my request will take you. If you can truly assume any shape, then anywhere I ask you to go should not be beyond you. My first request will bring you over the mountains to the east. Go there and tell me what you discover," he explained in an eager tone.

Gayossha eyed the king curiously. "To what end?" the creature repeated.

The king took a breath. "That all depends on your findings."

"Am I looking for a something or a someone?" the creature probed for some clue to the king's intent.

King Orbein paused thoughtfully, closing his eyes to recall the details. "The stories of my city's founding tell of a great empire over the mountains from whence our forefathers came," his solemn voice echoed through the empty hall. "The main archway of my city contains an inscription that was written there after the empire conquered this place. It tells of how the original city's inhabitants were slaughtered and how the abandoned soldiers then had to rebuild here as their emperor had forgotten about them. Our city has always lamented the injustice of this empire's sins. To send an army to murder the innocent people living here, and for what? They did not even come to take their spoils. They left us here...forgotten."

Orbein leveled a purposeful gaze at the shape shifter. "I feel it is my duty as king to revisit the suffering of our ancestors upon this empire. The vengeance of generations of all those who suffered because of their bloodlust shall be ours. That should be more than sufficient an explanation for you."

Gayossha was silent for a moment, caught in the hypnotic effect of the king's story. Then, he burst into a gleeful giggle that sounded like a drowning cat. "Excellent!" the beast shrieked between gurgles. "Highness, I believe that doing business with you will be much more pleasant than I expected."

Orbein smiled and nodded, but within his mind he cringed. This creature's services were an unfortunate necessity. The king knew beyond all doubt that that this campaign of justice, if successful, would inspire the fervent allegiance of his army. And once he had their complete fealty, no force in the world would be able to stop him.

* * *

Kiusu sat on a large, flat boulder, legs crossed, body completely still. His eyes were closed, and he breathed slowly. Small stones lined the perimeter of a circle that surrounded his perch from three meters on all sides. At each quarter of the circle stood a tall, wooden pole that supported a disk made from a metal ring over which was stretched a small hide.

The man at the center of the circle fought to clear his mind. Never before had he experienced so much difficulty in his meditations. Usually, he could clear all thoughts from his head and focus on the air moving slowly in and out of his lungs. But now he could not push out the silent whispers of all the preparations that still needed to be made. He knew he was trying too hard. He had to stop for a moment and just relax.

Slowly, step-by-step, he made his way deeper into his true self. Each step brought him further from his noisy thoughts and closer to his inner spirit. Soon, the only sound he could hear was his breathing. It was a rhythm that offered him a hold deep within. In time with the rhythm of his breath, he could hear the symphony of all that sped infinitely through the multiverse. It was the rhythm of everything, the undeniable flow that sustained the multiverse and all its life. The energy knew no evil, no good; it set no expectations, yet it was the order of everything. It simply flowed, and Kiusu flowed with it. In a moment, he felt his connection with all of infinity and felt what it was like to breathe, and be the breath of, everything.

When he had started, a small part of Kiusu wondered if he would make it this far, for it had been a long time since he had meditated so deeply. To go within and become aware of the unseen realm and travel the vast interconnectedness was no easy task. Concentration was a word that implied an effort that was counterproductive to this type of meditation. What was required was to defocus on such a large scale that the entirety of existence would become visible while the relatively minor details of the perceived world faded away. Kiusu was no novice, but the last time he had truly attempted to transcend the limitations of the corporeal realm, his failure came at a steep price.

It had been decades ago. Kiusu and his master Iou-Liu were a part of the great struggle to save the people of the Kesitul plains from the evil dragon Reisothin. Then the old man had been a student of many years, and his master had been the elder sage. During the final battle that drove the beast's evil from the land, Kiusu had tried to harness the universal power, as his master had taught him. He tried to control the energy to save his master's life.

Kiusu had failed. He could not stop thinking of the physical world and of all the dangers around him and, especially, of his master. He had never forgiven himself for the events of that day. It was his one weakness; for all his wisdom, he still blamed himself for his master's death.

Today was different from that day so long ago. Sitting peacefully upon the large stone within the circle, he escaped the world's distractions. For a time, he relaxed peacefully on the winds of eternity and let them take him where they would. But this trip did have a purpose.

Subconsciously, Kiusu willed himself near his door to the corporeal realm, his own body. His spirit focused upon the area around the living vessel. He flowed with the energy through the stone upon which his body sat and felt the pulsing of the grass below as it breathed.

In this state, the essence that was Kiusu was capable of seeing all things, no matter how large or small, no matter how far or near. He saw the tiny things, imperceptible to the naked eye, which composed the wind, the earth and every other thing in this universe. He willed the flow of which he was a part to move the particles within his own body, to energize them with his very intent.

The response was immediate. The wind began to blow, and the area within the circle seemed to get a little brighter. Kiusu's spirit gave no thought to the physical intuitions of the world that made this seem impossible. In the astral realm, nothing was impossible, and through the astral realm, the impossible could be manifest in the corporeal multiverse. With the ultimate confidence that only a higher being could possess, Kiusu willed the flow of energy within and around him upward.

Almost imperceptibly, the old man's body moved. An onlooker would have thought that the man merely straightened up more, but Kiusu's spirit could easily see the open space between his body and the stone. With a little more force he urged the flow up again, and his body lifted noticeably from the rock.

Kiusu opened his eyes. The conscious part of Kiusu's mind that controlled his physical body celebrated briefly as he hovered over the big rock. His higher self kept such thoughts in check. He would have to finish quickly before he became too fatigued. Despite his strong connection with his higher consciousness, this feat was physically and mentally taxing. He unfolded his legs and stood ready in mid-air. The flow of energy swirled about him and shaped to his will. He took it all in. A yellow halo of light surrounded his entire body.

Kiusu shot out his left fist impossibly fast, but his spiritual eyes followed its motion effortlessly and used it as a conduit for the energy that now filled him. A bright yellow flash tore through the radius of his circle and demolished the disk that stood directly before him, ripping the wooden pole from the ground and flinging it several meters. His fist opened and came around to protect his ribs as he half turned and sent another blast of explosive energy to the disk behind him with a rolling right backfist. This disk was similarly annihilated, and the pole that supported it cracked in half. He destroyed the disk to his left with a burst that came from a devastating sidekick. He withdrew the leg, drove himself a little higher and snapped out a toe kick with his right foot. The ensuing blast hit with such force that the remaining disk momentarily lit ablaze and was launched, pole and all, into the sky only to come tumbling down the mountainside several seconds later smoldering as it went.

Kiusu saved his satisfaction for a time when he could afford to concentrate on it. Now the old man, almost completely exhausted, folded his legs and lowered himself back onto the stone. His eyes closed, and he slowly returned to his usual state of consciousness.

He had done it. Now he was confident that he would be ready to pass on his knowledge, no matter what other preparations were left undone. It was the finer points of this sacred lesson that were most important of all, for although such things may seem like magic, it takes an ultimately disciplined spirit to accomplish them without all the trappings of spellcraft. A truly disciplined warrior with a genuine understanding of reality could, in theory, call upon these abilities at a moment's notice during battle.

Kiusu opened his eyes. It was done, and he was tired. It was time for him to return to his hut. The old man pushed himself to his feet. Exhaustion overwhelmed him. He swayed and put out his arms to steady himself. It was no use. Darkness crept in from the edges of his vision, and the last thing he felt was the sparse grass against his cheek.

* * *

"You asked to see me, sire?" the aged high priest Shiu Hi prompted, bowing before his emperor.

Geilo looked up from his scrolls suddenly, completely unaware that the elderly cleric had entered. "Ah yes! Shiu Hi, my old friend. How glad I am that you came to me so quickly, we have much to discuss." He stood and motioned to his guards. "You are dismissed."

The guards turned and exited quickly, pulling the magnificent doors closed behind them.

Once the doors were shut, Geilo stepped up to them quickly to make sure they were secure. Satisfied, he turned to the high priest and offered him a grave expression. "I have news of the utmost importance to share with you."

"Indeed, sire? What is this news?" Shiu Hi asked with sudden concern.

"I have foreseen..." he paused, "I have foreseen terrible things."

The old priest grimaced. "Have you, sire? Please, continue," he urged, unable to contain his curiosity.

"I have foreseen the march of a wicked army over the mountains. They come with a black cloud that rains fire upon our people. Their eyes glow with a murderous contempt for all life. They are clad in blood-soaked clothes and armor. These creatures...these evil creatures march upon our empire!" the emperor shrieked as little droplets of sweat beaded upon his brow.

The priest nodded slowly, "Yes, highness. We too have seen omens warning of an impending danger, but none of us have had such detailed visions. We have been working feverishly to discover the source of this danger so that we may better advise you. It seems, however, that you have been given this information by God. Praise Minotros!"

"Yes," replied Geilo, "and with this knowledge we shall make ourselves ready!"

"How do you propose this? If your vision is to be taken literally, how can our small empire stand against such a foe?" the old priest asked.

The emperor nodded. "I have been giving that some thought," he said. He then leaned close to the priest and raised his eyebrows. "Magic," he whispered.

Shiu Hi's brow furrowed. "Magic?" he repeated.

"Of course! Magic!" the emperor shouted excitedly. "General Etrusin is well on his way toward raising an army. His forces will be invaluable if an enemy marches upon us, but there is only so much that swords and arrows will do against an army of such demons. If we had a force that could assist them magically..." he let the statement hang.

The old priest's eyes opened wide. "Sire, do you propose that I teach soldiers the secret ways?" he asked, incredulous at the emperor's suggestion.

"Of course not!" the emperor answered with a hint of annoyance. "I am suggesting that you raise your own force! Take men into the fold of your order, teach them your priestly ways, and share with them the secrets of your brotherhood."

The priest made a choking sound. "Highness, men are not recruited into the brotherhood! They join of their own volition. They come to us because their paths have led to our door. And even a man who truly seeks the path cannot know the secrets tomorrow. He must study. He must go within and discover certain wisdoms that are offered only by our cloistered life. Only when God has bestowed such wisdom is a man capable of channeling His power.

"This process takes years, decades even. So you see, highness, though our empire could benefit from such a venture, it would be impossible to achieve it in time. There is no man who can learn the secrets in mere days, or even weeks, or months, for they are bestowed by God in His own time," the priest finished, raising a hand to the heavens.

The emperor thought for a moment before speaking. "I understand what you say, old friend," he said finally, "and that is why I must ask you to beseech Him. We must ask for His benevolence and mercy. Surely there is some way that we can assist Etrusin's men when they march against these monsters."

Shiu Hi hesitated a moment. "There may be some things that we can do," he said at last.

"Go on," the emperor prompted eagerly.

"We could bless their weapons," the priest began thoughtfully, "so they may be more effective against these evil creatures. There is also the horn of Reisothin. It is a very powerful relic and can be manipulated safely by those who are instructed properly. It is the wicked Seilen's beneficent legacy. In this way we can, in essence, have powerful magic on the battlefield."

"Excellent!" Geilo cried, his eyes lighting up.

"But be warned, highness, this is not a matter to be taken lightly. It takes training and great strength of faith to work with the horn. It will take some time," the priest cautioned.

Geilo understood the priest's apprehension, but he was quickly growing weary of his constant hesitancy. "Get to work, then!" he yelled, "Gather your brothers and whoever else you need, and do what you must to protect our empire!"

Shiu Hi bowed contritely. "Sire," he said respectfully.

Geilo nodded. "I need more counsel," he said much more calmly. "I request conference with Minotros."

The old priest bowed his head. "Praise His name. We shall begin preparations," he said quietly, hiding for now his thoughts on the subject.

"You are dismissed," Geilo said.

The old priest bowed again, turned and exited, leaving the emperor with his meditations.

4 START OF THE JOURNEY

Ninei conferred with her two most talented students. Every day they studied with the advisor, and she put forth challenges that mimicked her responsibilities in the imperial court to watch them role play the part of the mediator. At any one time she had several students, as did many of the advisors, who were all eager to pass their trade on to the first generation born of the reunified empire, but none of these hopefuls had ever shown as much promise as the two before her. They knew how to be objective mediators and could improvise in any situation. It would be these two who accompanied her on the trek with Etrusin's group to the mountains.

Her first student, Ini'io, was a tall, handsome young man with fair hair and rounded eyes that were uncommon to the east lands. In fact, most of his features were in contrast to that of the society in which he lived. His sharp, high cheekbones stood out among the usually smooth curves of his people's faces. His anomalous features, however, were seen as exotic and quite attractive. He had a sharp intellect and a very charismatic demeanor, but truthfully, diplomacy was not his passion. He was a good student because Su-Ni was a good student.

Su-Ni, the Giunin's other pupil, was Ninei's adopted sister. She had been born in conflict, when the empire fought against the terror of Reisothin. Shortly after her birth, both of her parents were killed as the dragon torched their settlement, one of the last to fall to the beast before he was slain. Ninei was a distant family member from the same tribe and had insisted that her parents take Su-Ni in. When they died of natural causes only a few years later, Ninei finished raising Su-Ni on her own. It was only natural that the younger woman would follow in the footsteps of her adopted big sister.

Su-Ni was an energetic young woman with a quick wit and an almost mischievous sense of curiosity. She stood about chest high to Ini'io and slightly shorter than her teacher. Her features were more often seen among the people of the empire. Indeed, her dark eyes swept out and up delicately and flashed with a keen intensity. Her straight, dark hair lay against her shoulders reflecting the light with a sleek sheen. She was considered classically beautiful by the empire's standards, and it was the study of her that inspired Ini'io's study of diplomacy.

"Do you know why the emperor asks this?" Ini'io prompted.

Ninei frowned as she considered his question. After a long pause, she admitted, "I'm not entirely sure. There seems to me to be an element at work that the emperor is not sharing with us. But I trust that if there is anything the emperor is keeping to himself, it is with good reason. The duties of the emperor are monumental and we cannot begin to guess all of his intentions and motivations."

"Perhaps he knows of some hidden city beyond our borders," suggested Su-Ni, her eyes darting back and forth between her companions to gauge their reactions. "Perhaps he has evidence of hostility that may await us. It could explain why he hesitated to send out explorers for so long."

Ninei knew about the prophetic visions that had aided the emperor in his victory against Reisothin. She didn't rule out the possibility that the emperor had foreseen a new threat, but she wasn't sure why the emperor would hide this from her.

"Perhaps," she responded. "In order to explore beyond the lands we already know, we will have to trek through the forest. No one in living memory has gone very deep into that wood."

Su-Ni shook her head firmly. "Only because of stories told to scare children," she said with certainty, "and foolish adults."

Ini'io nodded, but he did add, "There are the people of the wood. Legends say that their magic protects the forest's borders from intrusion. Many such stories often contain a grain of truth."

"Yes," Su-Ni agreed with a quick nod, "though in those legends they are said to be a peaceful race. I believe if the emperor knows of something, it is beyond the forest. Perhaps the source of the emperor's trepidation lies there," she suggested.

Ninei raised her eyebrows. "The mountains," she said with a hint of fascination.

"Let's just make it through the forest first," Ini'io said realistically.

"Then from there we shall see what we shall see," agreed Ninei.

With that, Ninei dismissed them and all three went to prepare for the journey ahead. Nothing was any clearer than before the meeting, but it was no matter. They were all excited, and their excitement grew with each new theory about what lay ahead. No matter what they discovered on the road ahead, they were sure it would lead to exciting changes for the empire.

* * *

Etrusin stood eagerly before Emperor Geilo. He could hardly contain his joy, for his men were standing at the ready awaiting word from the emperor to begin. His eagerness, though intensified by years of almost dull routine and the wandering desire that seemed common of the people of his tribe, was tempered by the discipline he had forged over many years as a warrior. And while it was also significantly dampened by the fact that he would remain in the city training new recruits, excitement still coursed through his veins.

The emperor nodded to the general. "Uchilin Etrusin of Kilelu," he said.

Etrusin bowed and saluted Geilo. "Emperor, I come before you requesting permission for my scouts to begin exploration of these fine lands. Even now my men stand prepared to do your bidding, whatever it may be. What word do you have for them, Ushisorein?" he asked reverently.

Geilo pursed his lips as if in deep thought. Was this the first step toward that which he saw in his visions? Would inaction bring about that horrible end? He was nervous about what the next few months would bring to his people. He wished there were some way to be sure, but postponing the exploration might leave the empire unprepared for an attack. Even now the armies might be on the march. Deciding inaction his worst enemy, Geilo nodded.

"Send them forth, Etrusin," the emperor said with feigned confidence. "Send them forth that they may bring back news of how grand this land truly is and of how we may expand throughout it."

"Thank you, highness," the general said happily. "My men will not fail you."

"Will you not be joining this group in their explorations?" the emperor asked, though he was not really very surprised.

Etrusin frowned. "I will not, highness," he said sadly. "I have duties within the empire that are too pressing. My lieutenant, Komeris, has been named captain of the party."

Indeed, Etrusin's duties were too important for him to be away, but he was not as upset about it as he seemed. True, he would have liked be out in the unknown lands with his men looking for adventure, but his small force was turning into an army. Day after day since the word had gone out, more and more young men and women came to his barracks eager to become warriors. Yes, Etrusin had his hands full, but he gladly accepted that this was his destiny.

Emperor Geilo nodded, understanding and appreciating his general's growing responsibilities. "Very well then, in that case..."

The emperor clapped his hands twice, and the grand doors to the throne room swung open. Behind them stood Ninei and her two students. Geilo bade them enter. The trio approached the throne and kneeled.

"These three will accompany your men in case they should discover another city or kingdom. With their help, your men may perhaps return with word of new allies," the emperor said, and deep within, he hoped that there was some truth to that speculation.

Etrusin responded with a bow to the emperor and a nod to Ninei and her companions. "My men will welcome their company, highness," he said, though he was surprised at this last-minute addition. He trusted that Komeris could handle all diplomatic situations competently, and if diplomatic relations deteriorated, he knew that the captain could handle that even better. Etrusin would make sure, however, that the group was welcomed.

Geilo smiled. "Very well then," he said in a satisfied tone. "You are dismissed. I wish your scouts, Etrusin, and you and your group, Ninei, a good journey."

All of them bowed before their emperor and walked together out of the throne room toward their new quest, and he watched them go with no small amount of uncertainty. Though he had been preparing for this for months, now that the moment was here, he wondered if this was the right decision.

The ritual of Commune, in which Geilo would beseech Minotros, the God of Fate, for clearer guidance on the future of his small empire, was still undergoing preparation in the monastery. The emperor wished it were already done, for it may have made him feel better about this course of action. It could have at least helped him to choose a better one, if a better one existed.

Geilo grimaced. This was no time to start second guessing his decisions. If Minotros made it clear that this expedition was a mistake, then he would send out messengers to bring them back. The frustrated emperor heaved a great sigh. What difficult times these past weeks had brought him. What difficult times would these next weeks bring? He decided it was best not to think about it. He would choose his course and stay on it. He only hoped he could handle the inevitable consequences.

* * *

Kiusu stepped onto the floor from his tiny bed and stretched. He felt better than he had in more than a week. Ever since he had grasped the makings of the multiverse in his last meditation, he had felt overwhelmed by fatigue. It stole his strength from him and made him unable to complete his usual daily activities. For once in his life, Kiusu felt his age. He felt the soreness in his tired muscles and heard his joints crack and pop as he moved around his quiet little hut. A tiredness seeped down into his soul that called him always to his bed.

But not today.

After a few moments of basking in his regained strength, the spirited old man made for the door. These past several days had been difficult for him, lying in bed unable to do anything. Despite his usual good health and natural resistance to sickness and injury, Kiusu was suddenly acutely aware that he was old by any human measure. He knew his body was merely a temporary vessel that could not last as long as his immortal spirit. He was uncomfortable wasting his limited days in bed, especially now with so much to be done. He had no intention of letting another day pass him by.

As he stepped outside, Kiusu let the crisp, cool mountain air fill his lungs. It seemed so sweet and fresh compared to the confined air of his small shelter. He took in the mountainside panorama that showed through the sparse groups of trees that dotted the side of his mountain. It was another day in his long and full life, and he was going to enjoy it. This morning when he did his exercise, the old man focused on all the life around him and reveled in it. Always he had focused solely on his own motion during these morning workouts, but now he noted all the minute movements of the life around him.

Suddenly he stopped.

Something had caught his eye. It was a bird. A dark bird. At first Kiusu had thought it was a crow, but as he stopped to consider it, he realized that it was like no bird he had ever seen. It was very large and had a long, curving beak. It's stubby orange legs made it seem hunched over. Most striking, however, were its eyes. They were keenly intelligent and more oblong than the typical roundness of most birds' eyes.

It was clear to Kiusu that the bird was studying him. Knowing that birds were very curious creatures and always finding birds to be receptive to him, he took a step toward it. The bird straightened at his movement and ruffled its feathers. Kiusu paused. Never had he seen such a large, black bird. He decided to alter his approach.

The old man smiled and slowly extended his hands before him, palms up to show he meant no harm. He continued to advance slowly and tried to radiate an aura of friendly curiosity. He had often been able to soothe nervous and frightened creatures with such methods in the past. This bird was obviously not nervous or frightened. It cawed at Kiusu in a way that the elderly master could only interpret as threatening.

Kiusu's curiosity transformed into confusion.

* * *

Gayossha considered the old man warily. The Fiu-Het had seen the old man's meditation last week and knew that this small, elderly master was more than he appeared. Still disguised as a bird, the beast had easily followed Kiusu undetected after he awoke from his collapse. When it became clear to Gayossha that the man would not be coming out of his hut for a while, he flew out through the mountains hoping to spot some sign of this man's people, though not straying too far from the small dwelling. Gayossha flew back periodically, too intrigued by the powerful display on the mountain to dismiss the strange human so quickly.

Now, as the old man approached, the Fiu-Het wondered if it was so wise for him to be in such plain sight of the hermit, disguised though he was. The creature knew that the old man had noticed something strange about his plumage. Gayossha scolded himself for not knowing better. This human, living all alone, had probably studied every breed of bird on these mountains. Surely his own improvised bird form was out of place.

Gayossha ruffled again and cawed at the old hermit, who finally stopped. The creature considered the old man for a moment and flew off quickly, not wanting the human to let his curiosity get the better of him. The Fiu-Het decided to go exploring a bit more while thinking of a better disguise. He was definitely not through with this old man. Gayossha would return.

5 INVOCATION

Urietsin led the way beside Komeris and Reniu to the first line of trees that signaled the entrance to the forest. The trees were densely packed in most places with thick brush filling in the gaps. The way was hard enough for a single man hunting, but for the large group of soldiers, some of them leading horses, the way ahead would be difficult indeed. Urietsin stopped at the line and turned to consider the rest of the group as they caught up.

The veterans in the group wore the traditional armor of distinguished officers. A leather koje with densely and ornately plaited sleeves was covered by a bronze breastplate, bearing an animal of each soldier's choosing. Komeris had the face of a wolf carved in great detail into his armor. Reniu's animal, fittingly enough, was a bear. The younger soldiers wore mostly leather, but some added tunics of steel ring mail to this. Urietsin, who had been the general's first choice from among his growing number of new recruits, wore only his black koje made of simple fabric and matching breeches.

Urietsin glanced over at Reniu. At first he had been unsure of the huge soldier's presence in the group, given the outcome of their first encounter, but the Swift One found that the scowling visage that he often witnessed on Reniu's face was a permanent and relaxed state and not directed toward him. In addition, he found that he had actually gained a measure of respect from the towering man. A fact that relieved Urietsin, as he would much rather have the veteran's respect than his reprisal. Besides, he had found his own respect for the man on the rise as Komeris told him of Reniu's past deeds in service to the empire.

"Are we to set up camp, Captain?" the young man asked Komeris, hoping the answer would be no.

Komeris saw the eager gleam in the Swift One's eyes. "The afternoon is still young, and we only started this morning. It may take us many days to

36

reach the other side with this many following, so we should make as much progress as possible."

Urietsin nodded enthusiastically. "Indeed," was the young man's quick response.

Komeris looked back to the rest of the group as they approached a short distance behind. "Although, a short rest might be in order before we press forward," he admitted.

"It'd be a good time for lunch, I say," Reniu agreed.

"Perhaps," Urietsin conceded, "but the sooner we begin, the sooner we shall be through it."

Komeris chuckled. "Patience, Swift One, you will find your adventure soon enough," he said with a pat on the young man's back.

Urietsin looked to the dense forest before them, not even hearing Komeris as he instructed the group to take a short rest before continuing. The young warrior felt as though his destiny was calling to him softly between the thick tree trunks and beyond the forest. His first step into that forest would bring him into a world that he had dreamed of so many times as a child.

Wanderlust and adventure coursed thickly through his veins as his heart began to beat faster. He began to envision the stories his father had told him about how he had fought beside Emperor Geilo in the battle against Reisothin. He imagined himself in his father's place then, swinging a shining broadsword, slashing and chopping at the vile beast as it breathed fire and poisonous smoke all about.

Suddenly, Urietsin's vision changed. Instead of a sword, he held a staff, and instead of a great dragon, the young warrior found himself against another vile creature of a much lesser stature. The beast, whose features the young warrior could not make out, made threatening moves toward him and emitted a horrible gurgling sound. Despite Urietsin's lightning quick reflexes, the smaller creature kept him on the defensive, never allowing him enough time to attack. The Swift One knew he needed a distraction if he was to be at all effective against this creature, but what could he do? As soon as the beast withdrew, it was back again with another wet slap in his direction. Urietsin swatted defensively with the bottom of his staff and flung the dripping appendage to the side. Then, for some reason he did not understand, he flung out his open hand toward the creature. This action did not invoke the reaction that the young warrior expected at all. Instead of the beast moving forward to grab Urietsin's outstretched hand, it went backward, as if it were afraid. It took the young man a moment to realize that he had pushed the beast away somehow.

Never one to miss a sudden advantage, Urietsin shot forward, staff leading. His weapon snapped downward with an overhead swing that connected with a loud crack on top of the creature's head. The young soldier took another half step forward and twirled the staff back up, swinging it back up to hit the slimy beast with the other end. Urietsin pulled the leading end of the staff under his arm and forcefully twisted his upper body, whipping the staff out and sending the creature spinning head over heels sideways.

The voice of Komeris violently shattered the vision. "Urietsin?" he asked, flinching when the young man jumped at the sound of his own name. He looked at the captain, eyes wide, sweat pouring from his brow. "Urietsin?" the captain asked again.

It took Urietsin a moment to realize that he should respond. "Yes, Captain Komeris," he said distantly.

"Are you alright?" Komeris asked, a concerned look crossing his face.

Urietsin nodded slowly. "Yes..." he said uncertainly. The young man looked around him and smiled. "Yes," he said again, "just daydreaming."

Komeris watched as the young man walked away toward the group, his look shifting from concern to confusion. The captain was sure that Urietsin had experienced more than just a daydream, but what it was eluded him. He shrugged and told himself to keep an eye on the young man for the time being. Somehow, Komeris didn't see that as a problem. A lot of people would be keeping an eye on the impressive young warrior.

* * *

King Orbein walked casually into his dimly lit, sparse throne room. Unguarded by soldiers, unescorted by an entourage, the monarch strode toward his usually vacant seat of power. He glanced around briefly, stepped up to the platform flanked by grand pillars upon which sat his fairly new, yet neglected throne, and lowered himself onto the giant black chair. He leaned back and gazed up along the stretching black talon-shaped claws that made up the back of the throne and became lost in thought. Orbein let his mind wander back through the years that brought him to this point in his life.

He had been a pauper wandering through the streets, robbing from the pockets of the less skilled thieves in the less orderly parts of the city. In that time not so long ago, the city was controlled by the army, the only real source of authority. The abandoned soldiers that resettled the area brought with them a strong military tradition. That tradition had been upheld for generations.

But there were, of course, parts of the city where the watchful eye of martial law did not care to look for very long. These were the slums on the western outskirts of Niele'itio. If young people living in these areas had not been marked for impressment by the age of sixteen, then two other options opened before them.

The men nearly dominated the category of thievery; it was hard to find a female thief. Most of the women gave themselves over to prostitution. In this city, it was the closest to an honest line of work a civilian woman could find, not that people in the slums cared too much about honesty.

Orbein recalled the day he had been thrust into the world by himself. His only guardian as a child had been a prostitute who might have mothered him, but he never knew for certain. This day the old woman had brought home yet another man. He was a large and imposing soldier in uniform. The young boy had shrunk away into the shadows when he saw the man walk by. His mother had led the man around the corner to the place that served as her bedroom in the ruined building that was their home. Orbein heard some strange noises coming from the woman's room. It was not unusual to hear the old woman moan or scream in pleasure, but this sound was neither of those. Orbein had sneaked around the corner and peeked into the room.

There stood the man, his breeches around his ankles. He was standing behind the woman, holding her up by the hair and pressing against her in an odd fashion. The look on his face was one of animalistic ecstasy. It was then that Orbein noticed the flash of silver against his guardian's chin. Fresh blood gushed from the newly opened wound onto the tattered bedroll below. The young boy gasped audibly, and both the man and the old woman looked in his direction. The old woman, who had served Orbein as a mother, tried to whisper his name, but sputtered up blood instead. A single tear traced the edge of her cheekbone. It was the first tear she had cried in many decades, and was the last tear she would ever cry again.

The man dropped her now lifeless corpse, and the sound of her dead flesh and bones hitting the floor shattered the silent trance that held the young boy. He tore his eyes from the body on the floor and looked to the huge man standing over it. The man tossed his bloodied dagger aside casually and pulled up his breeches. Orbein stood frozen as he witnessed every motion, and he still did not move when the man stepped calmly up to him and swatted him viciously on the head.

When he came to, the young Orbein looked around cautiously, fearing the soldier's presence. He was relieved to find that the looming man had disappeared, leaving him alone with the dead woman. Orbein got unsteadily to his feet and stepped slowly toward the bloody crumpled bedroll. Within its ragged folds lay the woman who had taken care of him since he could remember. Orbein looked down at her sadly, suddenly feeling very lonely.

Loneliness.

It was the first and last strong emotion Orbein ever remembered feeling. From that moment on, the future king swore that he would never feel that way again. He wandered the streets, supporting himself, stealing and doing what he must to survive. When he was fifteen he was arrested for theft from an officer. As was the tradition, after serving his sentence of one year's imprisonment, he was impressed into the ranks of Niele'itio's proud army. Ironically, it was at this point that Orbein's life began on his own terms.

It seemed a pathetically simple life to him. March where the officers told you, exercise here, repair this, clean that. And for your mindless obedience you were rewarded with clean living conditions, regular meals, and best of all, power over other soldiers after a time of distinguished service. Biding his time, Orbein did all he was told. He was a good soldier and advanced quickly. It was not long before he found himself the commanding officer of the very same man that had made him an orphan. Needless to say, that man met with an ill fate on one unfortunate recreational trip to the seedier side of the Dark City. These years were the beginning of Orbein's struggle to the top of this city's now newly reformed hierarchy.

A slight motion at the back of the throne room snapped the king from his reverie. His eyes narrowed as he looked for the source of the motion. All was still.

"Who's there?" Orbein asked sternly, quickly rising to his feet.

A shuffle over in one of the rooms many dark corners revealed a hunched creature that was slowly making its way toward the throne.

"Halt, shadow, and make yourself known," the king commanded.

A telltale hiss from the creature's direction made Orbein smile. "Gayossha?" he asked eagerly, hoping for good news.

"No, highness," a raspy whisper replied. "I am one of Gayossha's...associates."

The king straightened and narrowed his eyes. "How did you get into my throne room unnoticed? What is your business?" he asked, the stern tone returning to his voice.

The cloaked Fiu-Het slowly changed shape. Its posture straightened considerably. Its tattered cloak became a tightly-fitted suit of hide scale armor. The uniform of a castle guard. "In answer to your second question," the creature said in a deep, calm voice, "I am here as an emissary of my people."

King Orbein raised an eyebrow. "Your people?" he asked sarcastically. "Well, what business do your people have with me?"

The tall form of the guard shrank back to that of the hunched Fiu-Het. It approached the throne slowly, its wide, bare feet making a wet slapping sound on the hard floor. The king watched suspiciously through slitted eyelids. The emissary stopped a few feet from the throne and brought its own bulging eyes up to meet Orbein's. The monarch averted his gaze at the sight of those two bright yellow orbs. He shuddered internally as he thought how hungrily they stared at his flesh. But this was not the time for him to be intimidated by this creature. Orbein recalled the legends that said the Fiu-Het could smell fear.

"Businesss..." the beast said, trailing to accentuate the serpentine hiss in its voice. "Our business with you, dear highness, is the well being of our...of Gayossha."

The king did not miss the slip. It sounded as though this creature had almost referred to Gayossha with some kind of title. Orbein became intrigued. "Of what importance is his well being to you?" he asked, accentuating the rudeness of the question with a superior look.

The creature's face twisted into an expression resembling a frown. It paused uncertainly as though it were trying to form a response. "Highness," it said at last. "You seem to underestimate Gayossha's position in our society."

The king snickered at the Fiu-Het's use of the word society, but the beast continued, casting a dangerous glare in Orbein's direction. "I assure you, highness, our society is quite advanced, and our culture is more complex than you can imagine. I will not waste our time by trying to describe it. I will say, however, that my people would be very...distressed should we happen to lose Gayossha while he is in your employ."

King Orbein noticed the not-so-hidden threat in those words. He was very curious as to Gayossha's true position among his own kind. He was also annoyed with the thought of this creature standing in his throne room threatening him on behalf of its people. Orbein wondered how many warriors Fiu-Het society had and how well his own men would stand against an army of those warriors. It suddenly struck the ruler how glad he was that his quest for power was starting in the east. To the west lay the deep forests, bogs, and marshes. Home to the Fiu-Het. They were not a race the ambitious king looked forward to conquering any time soon.

"I see," Orbein said finally. "What is it that you want, exactly?" he asked bluntly, wanting to get this meeting over with.

The creature's head tilted back slightly as its tongue flicked out over its lidless eyes. "What do I want?" it repeated blankly, as though surprised Orbein even had to ask. "I want to know where, exactly, is Gayossha."

The king sat back down on his throne. He was not sure what to make of this. When he had hired Gayossha, he did not know that the beast held any sort of position among his people. He didn't even know that these creatures had any sort of positions that could be important. He had simply sent out a messenger into the bogs who, to the king's mild surprise, returned alive with word of Gayossha's eventual arrival. Now he was sitting in front of an emissary who was throwing not so vague threats at him. With all these thoughts running through his mind, king Orbein made a decision. He decided he was angry.

He turned to the emissary and plastered on a smile. "My, you are eloquent for a Fiu-Het. I can see why they sent you."

The creature's pupils dilated quickly as he considered the king. "I think you will find, highness, that we are not so stupid a race as you may think. Among other things, I am an excellent linguist."

The king made no effort to hide another snicker. "Any fool can learn to speak," he replied, waving his hand and looking away as though bored with the conversation.

"I warn you, highness, you will gain nothing..." the Fiu-Het began, but was cut off by a sudden rush from Orbein. The king jumped up and grabbed the creature by its neck, lifted it easily off the ground, and slammed it into the nearest pillar. Agucho tried to melt over the king's viselike grip, but his head spun from the impact. He began to understand the danger he was in as his throat was constricted.

"No," the furious king said calmly. "I warn you. You will listen well to my words, you putrid, sniveling beast, for if you do not, I will ensure they are engraved upon your tombstone. You will not threaten me again. I do not fear you, or your people, and no matter what the legends say or how much truth they contain, you would never be able to match the atrocities my armies can inflict upon you. So, say what you will, but I would watch my words in your place, filth, for they may be your last."

As Orbein stood there choking the Fiu-Het emissary, he realized for the first time that the creature was afraid of him. Its body shook with fear, and its pupils were so wide that its eyes seemed almost black. The king stood there and soaked up the feeling of power that emanated from that fear and the knowledge that he had caused it. This was how he had risen to his position. He was rather skilled at instilling fear.

A rasping sound snapped the king's attention back to his victim. The emissary's fearful shaking had transformed to a twitching, and its pupils began to shrink quickly. Orbein realized that he was close to killing this beast. He almost let himself continue, but a thought came to him. Perhaps this Fiu-Het could be of some use. Orbein let his arm go limp and the emissary clattered to the ground but came up quickly to gasp desperately for air.

The king looked down upon the pitiful creature. "Are we understood?" he asked.

"Of c-course, your highness," the emissary stuttered frantically between pants. "My apologies. I am your servant. You have but to ask, and..."

"Enough," Orbein said. "Enough groveling. No doubt your precious Gayossha will be returning soon. If you wish to know his fate, wait for him. Now, leave me...but do not go far. I shall require your presence again when you are not so..." he paused, looking for the right word. "Pathetic," he decided finally.

The Fiu-Het bowed its way backward out of the throne room slowly, not wishing to anger his new master. Orbein watched it go with distaste. It turned out that the Fiu-Het were not such fearsome beasts after all; at least, this one wasn't. The ruler chuckled to himself when he was alone once again. "Pathetic," he repeated in a whisper.

* * *

Shiu Hi donned his clerical vestments with great care and ceremony. The ritual was only beginning, but already the temple was vibrant with the energy from the past few days of preparation. The altar was set up with a cloth bearing the well-muscled form of the bull-headed Minotros. The image portrayed Minotros with a decided look of power, bearing a magical rod with which he carried out his duty of fate. The god, however, did not actually decide fate; rather he bestowed it upon each person as an inevitable result of his or her actions. People decided fate; he simply ensured its manifestation.

Small images of the horned head of Minotros appeared all around the altar room. Great tapestries hung with scenes of the god bestowing the gift or curse of fate. Each clerical vestment bore a tiny bull's head. Even the long carpet leading up to the altar showed complex entwined patterns made from simple lines, signifying the many possible paths of fate. Each line was of equal length, the divine length of the mystical rod that channeled the god's power.

Despite the god's startling appearance and the sometimes unwelcome consequence that He bestowed, the people accepted it and Him as the natural way. Without Him there would be no order to the multiverse. There would be no cause and effect. Minotros carried the encumbering duty of keeping the natural balance that was inherent to existence. He was a busy god, and busy gods had better things to do with their time than converse with humans.

Shiu Hi walked solemnly toward the altar. He realized the emperor's desperate situation. Indeed, it was a situation that involved the whole empire, but he wondered at the wisdom of such a ritual. As a priest, one of the first things he had learned was that great rites such as the one he was about to perform were not to be taken lightly. Though he knew each and every ceremony in detail from his studies of the temple texts, he had only ever participated in a ritual this powerful once, and that well before he had become high priest. That important title made him feel no less nervous. He knelt before the altar and began a prayer.

Behind him the side doors of the altar room opened and the other priests shuffled in quietly, single file. The last priest on each side closed his door silently and stood in place, as if guarding the portal. The rest of the priests lined up side by side, flanking the aisle leading to the altar. They all stood silent and still for several minutes while the high priest finished his prayer.

Shiu Hi ended his prayer in a whisper and sat in a meditative silence. Quite abruptly, the priest rose up and shouted out the beginning of a chant. The priests behind him echoed in answer. Shiu Hi turned to face the men standing before him as he continued to lead the chant. The priests' voices rose in unison toward the temple's high roof. Their chant was so perfectly synchronized that they sounded as one powerful voice.

This was merely the cleansing chant. This part of the preparation was meant to fill the air with the pure sound of holy words that would drive out any energies contrary to their current purpose. It was only the beginning of another purification ritual that would take the entire day. And although this was but a small fraction of the ceremony, it was just as essential. Each piece of the ritual had an important function and had to be performed to perfection. The gathering of priests was more than up to the task, but it was hard not to be nervous.

Shiu Hi's only other experience had been part of a plea ritual for divine intervention. It was among the more powerful of ancient rituals, though nothing like this. No one was even entirely sure if it worked, though the vanquished Reisothin was good evidence. The ritual of Commune was much more interactive and, thus, less practiced. There was little mention in the culture's history of it. What information there was seemed foreboding. Most stories tell of wrathful gods of old punishing their weak followers for disturbing them. Of course, these stories were part of the culture's myths, and few attributed much truth to them. But it was difficult not to think of such things at a time like this. The high priest looked at his men and up to the heavens as he began the next verse of chants. He pushed the distracting thoughts away and tried to concentrate on the ceremony.

That next morning the atmosphere outside the great temple tingled with excitement and a twinge of fear. A crowd was gathered several meters from the front of the grand dome that loomed above the great arching doors. The people seemed to want to be as close as possible, but none of them would breach the semicircle that they had formed around the temple. All were excited because they knew that the ritual that had been under preparation for the past three days was culminating today, but they were apprehensive about the effects of this ritual. They knew the old stories too, and none wanted to be too close in case things went tragically awry.

The buzzing of the crowd silenced and gave way to curious whispering. The people parted and bowed as the royal guard, led by Uchilin Etrusin, made its way to the finely-carved majestic doors. Behind them came the imperial carriage, covered in gold leaf and shimmering in the morning sun.

The emperor's remaining councilors followed the carriage with clasped hands and bowed heads. The entourage stopped before the temple, and the door to the imperial carriage opened.

Out stepped the emperor, shining as brightly as his carriage. The look on his face, however, dimmed the shimmering gold of his robes. This was serious business, and the emperor looked painfully aware of the consequences. Slowly he marched to the doors, which were pushed open by two large guardsmen. Only when the doors touched the inside wall did the emperor step in. Once he was clear of the doors, the guards pulled them closed again, leaving him to join the ceremony alone, as he had requested.

Geilo stepped nervously down the dimly-lit corridor. The emperor had pushed eagerly to have this ritual performed, but now he wondered if it was justified. He clenched his teeth and quickened his pace. Geilo would not give up now, not when he knew that his people needed him. If his visions had any validity at all, this ceremony was necessary. The emperor paused briefly before the door, bowed his head, took a deep breath, and stepped into the altar room.

As the door closed behind him, Geilo suddenly felt overwhelmed by the energy suspended in the atmosphere. He watched and listened as the priests' chanting reached a climax that reverberated throughout the temple and deep within his chest. As the priests fell silent and the last echoes of their chant died down, Shiu-Hi waved the emperor toward the altar. As Geilo approached, the priests followed behind him and formed a semicircle around the altar.

Shiu-Hi nodded and smiled reassuringly at the emperor and said, "Come you in peace, mortal man, lest you leave this circle and know naught but strife for the rest of thy days in this world."

Emperor Geilo nodded reverently. "I come in peace, friend of Minotros, beseech Him that He might hear my words today," he replied ceremoniously.

The high priest bowed his head to the emperor. "Nay, friend, for if you come in peace then you are brother to us and, therefore, a friend to Minotros. Beseech Him thyself, for thine own purpose."

The emperor returned Shiu-Hi's bow and turned to the altar. "O Great Minotros, God of Fate, God of Consequence, hear my call. I, emperor Geilo of Kesitul, your loyal servant, have seen that which you have sent to me through my gift. A frightening vision of destruction. A wicked landslide of evil that advances down the mountainsides. Minotros, I fear for my people. This is my purpose in asking you to appear today. How might my people fare in this seemingly terrible fate?"

The echoes of his heartfelt plea hung in the air for quite some time before silence overtook the acoustics in the temple. And it remained silent.

This was the worst part. Now the emperor would have to wait for a response from above. It could take all day...or all week. No god was at any mortal's beck and call. So, Geilo would wait. If it was the will of Minotros that he know the fate of his people, it would be made apparent sooner or later.

6 DISCOVERY

Gayossha soared over the mountains north of where he had seen the old man. He relished the cool feeling of the wind rushing past his face. He knew that to fly directly east would be the most efficient use of his time, but he was enjoying the freedom of this sensation. The Fiu-Het, still in bird form, pitied the pathetic humans, who would only ever know one shape throughout their entire lives. The avian form was definitely his favorite, as nothing compared to the feeling of flight. It was the one time when he almost felt at peace with the world.

He was fortunate among his race. Gayossha was born with an unnatural endurance, a trait held very sacred to his people and a fitting gift for one of his social status. For days he had flown without rest, combing the mountains north to south, only partially interested in finding where the old man he had seen could have come from.

The bird-shaped creature dove toward the ground near the eastern edge of the mountain chain. Although he was enjoying his flight, Gayossha decided to get to work. The Fiu-Het were a busy race. They were very dedicated toilers. Always doing, always accomplishing, always busy. Unfortunately, this work was primarily for the individual's benefit, rather than the good of the whole. Most of the shapeshifters were fiercely competitive, constantly trying to outdo one another, and treachery was not unheard of among them. The Fiu-Het didn't really consider themselves wicked because of this, just very determined.

Gliding a few hundred meters above the ground, Gayossha spotted a dense forest ahead, east of the mountains. He flapped his wings a few times to pick up some speed. His instinct told him that he would find something in that direction. Perhaps just another hermit living in the wilderness, but Gayossha hoped for more. The eastern lands had been at peace for as long as he could remember. It would be nice to stir things up a bit.

To the west of the swamps of the Fiu-Het, a thriving civilization had eventually risen from a depressed population plodding through a dark age as though it were the debris of some apocalyptic disaster. Unlike the people of the east lands, the people of this culture spread far and wide, populating the continent of Riijahn. Huge cities sprang up, and wars raged through decades. It was the stuff of childhood stories for a Fiu-Het. Massive armies of humans clashing together and slaughtering each other in great numbers. Much like the people of the east, the people of the west left the Fiu-Het to themselves, fearing the shapeshifters' mysterious abilities and dubious natural appearance. Humans were all the same.

As Gayossha glided ever east, he mused upon the unimpressiveness of the people on this side of the fen. Compared to the civilizations of the west, these people seemed as mere tribal folk, wandering the hinterlands in search of a home. Even Orbein, with his small army and gray castle, was but a chieftain to these poor pathetics who would most likely be wiped out within the century. Not like in more ancient times, before the Fiu-Het had diminished to the bogs.

At one time the men of the east had been superior, and most of Riijahn had been uncivilized. Such was the way of things. Kingdoms great and small rose and fell since the beginning of time in these lands. Gayossha loved the thought of it. He cackled at the scenes that played out in his mind's eye. These wretches battling for control of hillocks and glens just before some greater foe arrived to wipe them from the history books. And he would be there to see it all. He would be there to lend a helping hand to the destruction of these gentiles.

As he glided over miles and miles of trees, Gayossha maintained this fantastical meditative trance until his daydreams were interrupted by something. It was a feeling, an instinct that told him to investigate. He adjusted his course and veered downward toward the treetops. Now he could smell it more clearly. The remnants of a campfire, extinguished fairly recently. The bird-shaped creature let his keen senses guide him to a clearing where he fluttered to the ground for a closer look.

There had indeed been a campfire and a fairly large camp as well. Continued investigation revealed that a large group of humans, for no other race would leave such obvious signs of its presence, had chosen this spot to rest. Furthermore, it appeared as though the group reentered the forest heading west. Backtracking to the point where the group had emerged from the forest into the clearing was not difficult either. They had come directly from the east. This left Gayossha with an interesting choice.

East or west?

If Gayossha flew back the way he had come, he might be able to spot the group through the trees and find out who they were and where they were headed. On the other hand, if he flew east, he might find out where this group had come from. The Fiu-Het decided that the bloodthirsty, would-be-conqueror King Orbein would probably be more interested in where they came from, especially if it was this empire he spoke of. Besides, he could catch up with the group on the way back and have a little fun of his own.

Gayossha spread his wings and prepared to take flight when he caught a slight movement out of the corner of his eye. He looked in the direction of the motion curiously, cocking his head much like a bird would, but saw nothing unusual. Folding his wings closer to his body, he stepped forward and peered into the forest.

There was nothing, and yet, despite the fact that he could see only trees, the Fiu-Het was certain there was something there. He could smell something unusual, but familiar in the air. So intently was the shapeshifter staring into the forest that he almost did not notice that something had sneaked up directly behind him. Jumping quickly into the air and fluttering his wings in short, rapid flaps, Gayossha ascended quickly to a high tree branch and looked down.

Looking back up at him from the ground was a man-like creature, slightly more compact than most humans. He had long, dark hair and bright eyes that meshed unusually well with his tan complexion. His face was delicately angular, like a marble sculpture. The most telling feature, however, was the creature's ears. They were elongated at the top and came to a rounded point. Gayossha could tell from this and his forest camouflage clothing that he was looking at an elf.

The shapeshifter had never actually seen an elf before, but he had heard many stories about the mysterious people. He also knew that his disguise would not fool this one, especially if this forest was his home. Gayossha was uncertain of what to do next. He could fly away, leaving this elf to wonder what strange creature had entered his forest, or he could stay and talk to him. His curiosity got the better of him, and he hopped off the branch and fluttered back to the ground.

"What manner of creature are you?" the elf asked in his own tongue, which was unknown to the shapeshifter.

Gayossha looked the figure before him over and recounted all he had ever heard about these creatures. He closed his eyes and envisioned an elf: lithe, fair, pointy ears, and all. When he looked again at the elf, he looked through shimmering emerald Shionen eyes. The elf raised an eyebrow inquisitively.

"I do not speak your tongue, good sir, perhaps you speak mine?" Gayossha asked, shuddering internally at calling the human language his own.

"A human that can change shape?" The question came back in a dialect almost identical to the one the shapeshifter used.

"Please, friend, forgive my deception. I am an emissary, a magician from the court of King Orbein the Benevolent," Gayossha paused, unsure of where to proceed from here.

"Are you a part of the group of humans who were camped here a short time ago?" the elf asked suspiciously.

"Yes," the Fiu-Het lied again. "Yes I was. I was scouting ahead, and I seem to have lost my way. I was trying to backtrack to see if I could find them. Could you tell me which direction they went?"

Shionen lips curled to amused condescension. "Were I blind and lame I could still track them. They left an obvious trail heading west."

Gayossha feigned relief. "Ah, excellent. Thank you, friend," he said beginning to walk in the direction indicated by the elf.

"Tell me, magician..."

The shapeshifter halted and turned. "Yes?" he replied.

"Why do you appear to me as an elf?" the elf asked.

At that, Gayossha faltered. It wasn't as though he was particularly afraid of this elf; the Fiu-Het could probably easily break him in half. But he also knew that appearances could be deceiving, and where one elf was out in the open, a host of others could be waiting in the trees. Gayossha's mind raced to come up with a lie, something he was normally good at.

"Ah yes!" he said finally, trying to put a hint of pride in his voice. "I'm glad you noticed my attempt. You see, as a magician, shapeshifting is my specialty, and I always enjoy a good challenge. I have never been an elf before."

"Nor will you ever be," the elven stranger said calmly.

Gayossha was taken aback. He had always heard that elves were a prideful people, but this one's last response seemed tactless. Unsure of what a human would do in this situation, the shapeshifter decided to be respectful.

"Of course not," Gayossha said reverently. "There is much more to an elf than just his shape."

The elf nodded, seemingly ignoring the compliment. "Go then," was his simple response.

Gayossha needed no further prompting; he abruptly turned and headed back into the forest. Once he was deep enough in the foliage, or so he thought, he transformed back into his bird shape, altering it as much as possible from his usual avian form. He decided to continue west toward the group of humans that he knew was ahead of him. He could always fly back east fast enough for his own liking. Besides, he might be able to learn some valuable information from the group and pinpoint exactly where they had come from.

* * *

Tilon Enshei watched the Shionen-shaped creature quickly enter the forest. He stood in the clearing for a while until he could only hear faint footsteps. This creature, whoever he was, could never be an elf. No elf would make such noise walking through the forest. Shaking his head, Tilon followed the sound into the trees hiding amid the tall trunks as he went. He did not walk far before the sound ceased. The elf listened intently, thinking that his target had stopped for a moment to get his bearings. After a period of silence, Tilon decided to go on, tracking to the place where the sound had stopped. He didn't expect to find anything there.

It did not take him long to reach the spot where the trail ended. Tilon knew every inch of the forest, and the creature did not choose a difficult path. The elven warrior looked around curiously. There was no sign of where the 'magician' had gone. Tilon was not surprised, but he was interested in discovering just where the deceiver was going.

"He took the shape of a bird again," a feminine voice behind him explained.

Tilon turned. "Marui," he said to the Shionen female as she emerged from among the trees. "You saw him?"

"Yes," she replied. "He assumed a new bird shape and took wing heading west. Perhaps to quicken his reunion with the humans?" Doubt was obvious in her tone.

Tilon shook his head. "I don't think our magician friend was completely honest with us," he said.

Marui raised an inquiring eyebrow. "Another stranger in our forest. Do you think he was even human?" she asked.

"I don't know," he answered thoughtfully, "but I'm not sure what else he, or it, might be."

"But he is heading back toward the group," Marui said.

Tilon nodded in agreement to his partner's instinct. "He is not with the group, but I am also sure that he is heading for them. Whoever or whatever he is, he must be watched. Go home and tell the others what we've discovered thus far. Bring them to Oak's Expanse in two days time. The way will be difficult for them, but they should make it by then. I will meet you there. It's time we addressed the sudden unwelcome interest in our home."

* * *

The elderly master Kiusu sat in a kneeling position on the soft leaf and pine needle-covered ground of the mountain. His palms were flat and relaxed upon his lap. His eyes were closed, and his breathing was slow and steady. He was motionless but relaxed. It almost seemed as if he were in a seated slumber. This was quite far from the truth. Kiusu was keenly aware of his environment, even more so than most conscious people. On the ground before him was a curved shortsword that glistened its perfection.

Kiusu was not one to use weapons. He was a peaceful man who preferred any means but violence to solve his problems. Of course, some problems brought violence with them, and Kiusu was no fool. Should he have to defend himself against such violence, he could do so more competently than any other warrior he had ever met, aside from his own master. And despite the fact that he preferred to use his hands when doing so, he also understood the benefit and enjoyed the challenge of working with weapons.

The shortsword lying before him was his favorite weapon after his hands and feet. It had been his first and only sword his entire life, and though he had carried his share of staves, knives, throwing daggers, and a host of other weapons, it was this sword that had seen him through countless battles. There were many times in his youth that he had been called upon to defend himself and others, and during those times he had forged a strong relationship with his sword. Whenever he drew it, the sword became an extension of him, and he could handle it more deftly than any swordsman.

None of these things passed through Kiusu's mind now. Early on in his training he had learned to empty his head of thoughts, but it had taken him many years to learn how to keep those thoughts out, he could now sit for hours, even days, in this meditative state. This time, however, Kiusu's mind was not completely empty. He was focusing. Though his eyes were closed, he could see as well as if they were open. More accurately, he could feel every detail of his surroundings. The leaves, the trees, his sword, he could feel each of these in relation to his position, to the point where he knew the tempo of the branches swaying in the breeze.

His hand came up, and his fingers reached. In a flash his sword was there, held firmly by his now closed fingers. But Kiusu had never actually touched the sword. The weapon had just shot up as though propelled by some unseen force. The old man opened his eyes and smiled. This was an easier task than the one that had stolen his strength for a week. This time Kiusu had decided to start out more slowly. Reaching out with his concentration, the powerful master had coaxed his environment to bring the sword to him.

Kiusu gently placed the sword before him again and straightened. He reached again, and again the sword flashed into his waiting palm. Satisfied with his progress, the old man nodded and stood. Sheathing his weapon, he headed back toward his hut. He would have liked to celebrate and congratulate himself, but he still had some work to do.

Not wanting to wear himself out again, Kiusu decided he would get some manual labor done over the next several days. He had always kept up on his meditation, but he had not performed such feats in a while. He would have never believed that using his mind in this way would prove so difficult after so many years. He realized that knowing the process of these preternatural abilities was not the same as putting them to use. He understood now the mind's muscular nature. It had to be worked out and exercised every day, just like the rest of his body.

These facts did not come as much of a surprise to Kiusu, but they were things he had never paid attention to in his younger days. Manipulating the environment with his mind had always come so easily to him all those years ago. After he had come out to the mountains, though, he never found much use for these talents, so he let them go unpracticed, believing that his daily meditations would keep his mind sharp enough should he ever need to call on them again. It never ceased to amaze Kiusu that, despite his age and all he had learned and seen in his lifetime, he still discovered new things every day.

As he approached his hut he reminded himself that such was the nature of life. From birth to death everyone learns and grows every day. Kiusu was certain that this must be life's purpose, as it was the one defining constant of living. No matter what any man or woman does throughout life, no matter what day or season, there was always something to be learned. The old master grinned to himself at this. It was an idea he had carried with him throughout many years. He felt it was a secret inspiration passed to him from nature. He would gladly tell any man who asked him about it, but he believed most would be confused by it. His fellow humans seemed to him too eager to find the quickest answer, and so, if they felt they had to ask what the purpose of life was, then they were doomed to fail to understand it.

Kiusu arrived at his door and, instead of going inside, bent over and picked up his two buckets in one hand and his staff in the other. Sunset would be approaching soon, and he wanted some water to clean up and make supper. He headed off toward a nearby mountain stream, musing as he went about his success today and about life in general.

7 THE AGGRESSOR

Thontur, the largest mountain of the Ikiu'iu chain, cast a looming shadow over the field in the morning sun. It was under this shadow that the soldiers of the Ionotu valley trained for battle. King Orbein stood sweeping a steely gaze over his troops, casting a different kind of shadow over the valley. He watched the men as they sparred. From what the king could see, the soldiers appeared to be holding little back against their comrades. Closest to him, one man let his fist fly, dagger clenched in hand. It connected with his opponent's jaw, and blood flew several feet. Fortunately, most of them practiced in full armor, a thick hide arranged in overlapping scales.

Orbein chuckled. As he turned to view a different match, he noticed the general making his way across the field toward him. Orbein smiled to himself and looked the field over again, making a note to congratulate him on his good work. As he did so, he caught sight of Laernus shuffling toward him from the other side of the field. The king saw that his seer skirted around the fighting, giving the soldiers a wide berth.

Orbein shook his head in amusement. The mage had always been that way. Even when he was assisting the then future king as he made his way through the upper ranks, Laernus had avoided other soldiers as if they carried some sort of plague. If ever confronted by one of these soldiers, Orbein was sure the wizard would die of fright before a sword could be stuck into him. This amused the king greatly, and he found himself snickering audibly as his general approached.

"Highness," The general acknowledged, snapping Orbein a salute. "You seem in good spirits."

Orbein waved off the salute and raised an eyebrow. "Do I?" he asked, amused.

"Yes, sire," the general said seriously.

Orbein flashed a conspiratorial smile. "General Vethisir..."

The general knew that smile. It was the same smile he had seen years ago when Orbein had vowed he would rule this city. "Yes, highness?" he responded firmly, trying to hide his curiosity.

"You have done quite well in taking over command of these men. I am genuinely impressed."

Vethisir brightened considerably at this, but his pleased expression quickly transformed to concern as he looked out to his soldiers with a furrowed brow.

"Is there a problem?" the king asked flatly.

The general looked back to the king with a frown. "To be honest, sire, the men are a little...well, that is to say, they're quite challenging," he decided finally, choosing the most benign adjective he could think of.

Orbein raised an eyebrow. "Pray tell," he said in an inquiring tone.

"Well, sire, the men don't seem to understand the definition of training. As you can see around you, they do not spar; they fight. Every day more and more injuries are treated. Some men have almost been killed, so grievous are their wounds. This is what happens when the bulk of our soldiers come from prison," the general muttered before he could catch himself.

Orbein glared dangerously at the general, but answered in an indifferent tone, "What is the problem?"

The general looked confused and strangely timid. "Sire, as I'm sure you remember, one of the most important lessons the men are to learn from their training is how to act as one cohesive unit. They must be able to work with each other, not against."

"Indeed," the king nodded, but he also grinned again in that chilling sort of way. "Have you done nothing to deter this behavior?"

"Of course, highness!" the general said, trying to keep the surprise from his voice. "I have punished the worst offenders, but still they defy me. I think they take my command as seriously as they take your..." The general trailed off, silently scolding his inability to let his brain control his mouth.

The king scowled suddenly, and Vethisir felt a sinking in the pit of his stomach. He paled visibly, fearing the worst. The general was a strong man, physically and emotionally, but after years under Orbein's command, he knew well to fear his unpredictable moods and whims. Orbein did not seem to notice his change in complexion, however, and as the king's seer approached, the general recovered quickly.

"Laernus," he said, a bit relieved.

Vethisir knew that the king was not fond of the foreign wizard, and realized that this was the source of his scowl. The general often wondered why his king kept the seer in such a high position if he disliked him so. Granted, there were not many magicians in the kingdom, but Orbein was rumored to be a great magician. Surely he possessed enough skill to make this man's presence unnecessary. Then again, Vethisir was not really all that well versed in magic, so he was not entirely sure.

Laernus bowed before the king. To the general, who always prostrated himself sincerely, the move seemed to lack deference. Apparently, Orbein agreed because he rolled his eyes before speaking, "Rise, Laernus."

The seer stood and showed his teeth in an artificial smile. "Highness...General," he greeted each of them with a nod.

"What is it you want, Laernus?" the king asked, clearly irritated.

Again came the smile. "Your highness requested my presence," he said with his strange accent.

Orbein flashed his teeth as well, but in more of a sneer than a smile. "You may wait here. I am having a discussion with the general," he said. Then, an idea seemed to occur to him and he added, "In fact, why don't you train with the soldiers while you wait? I'm sure they would welcome your company."

The sudden flush of Laernus's cheek showed a moment of humility. "If it makes no difference to his highness, I will wait to the side."

The king's expression darkened. "It does make a difference to me...but you may wait," he said. Laernus sulked away, having suddenly lost his sarcasm. Orbein turned back to the general. "What was I saying? Ah yes...Vethisir, I will talk to your men. I believe I can take care of the problem."

"As you wish, sire," the general said, stepping aside.

Closing his eyes, King Orbein lowered his head and began to whisper a chant. When he looked up again, those eyes glowed with purpose and a decidedly red tinge. He somehow seemed larger and even more intimidating. When he spoke, his voice boomed from the sky and echoed all across the valley. "Soldiers of Ionotu! Heed me, your King Orbein of Niele'itio!"

A deafening silence overtook the soldiers as they cringed in fear of their monarch, forgetting their bravado of moments ago and the snide comments they regularly uttered since his coronation.

Now that the king was certain he had everyone's undivided attention, he continued, "I have come to speak to you about a very grave matter. Once, many generations ago, this was a fair and rich city. We were the pearl of the east and an essential ally of a selfish neighbor. It was this neighbor who sent an army to destroy us. But those who come to this city do not find it so easy to leave, and the army had no home to which it could return.

"Thus is our call to vengeance twofold! For not only was our beautiful city perverted, but also the army that destroyed it was abandoned here. We are the legacy of that terrible past, and the time has come for us to reclaim the home of our ancestors and recapture the former glory of the once bright city. Most importantly, it will be our chance to have justice for the wrongs done to our ancestors. It will take all of you working as one to achieve this goal. You are, as I once was, men of humble beginnings, but together we may rise up and become the founders of a new empire!"

The king raised his hands triumphantly, and after a moment of silence, a deafening cheer went up from the field. His soldiers cowered before him no more. They were energized and inspired by his short speech, and now that he had them inspired, he delivered his command.

"Warriors! Heed well your general. Heed him as you heeded me in his rank, for he will guide you on the path to victory. And we shall have victory; I will expect nothing less. And if I find that any of you will be an impediment to that victory, you will surely wish you had the chance to die on the field of battle..."

His speech over, Orbein turned back to his general to find him staring back with a wide-eyed, bemused expression. He was as much in awe of the man's ability to motivate the crowd as he was shocked by his message. The king smiled. "Vethisir, you look surprised. Surely you cannot deny that this is our duty, to ourselves and to our ancestors," he said, though he was not explaining himself to the general, rather he was enticing him, as he had the crowd.

General Vethisir blinked away his surprise. "Far be it from me to question your wisdom, highness, but do you know for certain that the empire still stands?" he asked. Then he added, "What if they do? Do you not think they could amass a considerable force as they obviously have in the past?"

Orbein laughed. "Do not worry, my friend," he said. "We will not be without allies, should we need them."

A look of confusion washed over the general's face. "What allies, sire?"

Orbein patted Vethisir's back reassuringly. "All in good time, General. All in good time," he said, flashing his scheming smile once more.

Vethisir was still perplexed, but he would not press the king any further. "Yes, highness. Now, if I may, I have much work to do," he said, indicating his troops.

Orbein gave a slight nod, sending his general off. He watched the general go for a moment, then he turned to look pensively at his seer. Laernus stared back, one eyebrow raised in doubt. The king returned it with a scowl. "Surely you, of all people, cannot be surprised," he snapped.

The seer shrugged. "No, I simply think you are too ambitious."

King Orbein stepped up to Laernus with an unpleasant grimace. "I do not employ you to give me your opinions, seer," he said threateningly.

Again came a shrug. "Perhaps not, but I must tell you that your plans are dangerous."

The king narrowed his eyes suspiciously. "Have you seen something?"

he asked.

Laernus nodded gravely. "All too often, highness. A man with absolute power over his people always falls before them. Especially when his ambitions are so high."

Orbein pushed the seer away forcefully, throwing the man to the ground, then leveled a menacing finger at him. "I also do not employ you to tell me silly parables, you fool. If you attempt once more to perform duties beyond your position, I will remove your tongue!" The king turned his finger upward to emphasize his point. "Once more..." he concluded, turning and storming off.

Laernus opened his mouth to ask the king how he could serve him better. He had, after all, sent for the seer. The fallen man closed his mouth, however, deciding instead to get off the ground and get back to his laboratory. If the king needed him again, he would surely send for him.

* * *

Creaking sounds echoed throughout the temple. Emperor Geilo looked up from his prayers and glanced around. All was as it had been since he entered a day and a half ago. The priests still stood on either side of the aisle. Shiu Hi still sat next to him in prayer. Yet the creaking persisted and grew louder. It seemed to come from everywhere around him.

The emperor stood up and peered at every corner, hoping to find the source of the unnerving sounds, though his tired eyes had difficulty focusing. Suddenly, there was a clang as one of the altar candles toppled over, setting the main tapestry alight. Geilo jumped back, mouth agape at the flames slowly consuming the figure of Minotros. Shiu Hi, however, remained kneeling before the cloth, flames flickering dangerously close to his face. Geilo was about to reach for the tapestry to tear it down and beat out the flames when a voice caused him to freeze.

"Geilo of Kesitul," the deep timbre resonated, and all the glass in the temple shattered with explosive force.

Emperor Geilo fell to his knees and raised up his hands. "Oh, Lord Minotros, I am here," he said reverently.

The voice came again, shaking the ground upon which the emperor knelt. "Hear me, Geilo. I have heard your plea and have come to answer."

Geilo bent and touched his forehead to the floor before the altar. "I, your servant, humbly await your word, Great One."

"Go forth, Geilo. Brandish your sword. Your enemies cannot stand against you. Know this: the aggressor will fall..."

Geilo looked up just as the flames rippling over the tapestry went out, and in that last moment, he saw fire in the eyes of the god's image. The emperor shuddered as he was reminded of another set of burning eyes; the power behind them inspired the same feeling of insignificance. He looked about, bewildered. "Lord Minotros...." An eerie silence followed his call, and he knew that they were again alone in the temple. He glanced at the high priest, who was returning his look with one of confusion. The emperor's eyes darted around and he noticed with shock that the windows were not broken, and the tapestry showed no sign of fire.

"What is it, highness?" the priest asked as though nothing had happened.

"I...I heard Him," the emperor explained pointing a shaky finger toward the cloth.

"He spoke to you?"

Geilo could only respond with a nod.

"Praise Minotros!" Shiu Hi called. In response the other priests rose up in song. The ceremony was over.

Geilo stood and looked long and hard at the unsinged tapestry, hoping to find some clue to better understand the message that had just come to him. He was awash in a jumble of confusing emotions. In four words the deity had confirmed Geilo's worst fears. An attack was coming. Although the emperor was very displeased to learn this, Minotros had said that the aggressor would fall. The implications of all this left Geilo feeling very tired and old.

The emperor had been a young man in the days before the empire, but now he felt it was beyond his time. His empire had known nothing but peace under his rule. Thoughts of how unprepared they were for these circumstances made him feel even worse. What could they do?

But the aggressor would fall. Geilo clung to this part of the message in the hopes that he would be reassured. As he slowly exited the temple, he repeated it over and over in his mind like a mantra. As they had done for weeks, images flitted just beyond his vision.

As he exited the temple, the emperor found Etrusin waiting impatiently. The general rushed up to him, concern clearly visible on his face. "Are you well, highness? You were in there for quite some time."

Geilo raised a reassuring hand. "I am fine, Etrusin," he said.

"What happened?" the general asked.

The emperor considered his military advisor for a moment. There was much Geilo needed to tell him, but he was too tired to arrange his thoughts coherently. "Meet with me tomorrow, Etrusin. There I will tell you everything, but now I must rest. Take me back to the palace."

Etrusin bowed and led the emperor back to his carriage. Although he was eager to learn what the emperor had discovered, he did not press him. From the emperor's state as he left, the general did not feel that he was very pleased with what he had learned, or perhaps he was simply tired from the night of missed sleep. Whatever its cause, Etrusin was sure that Geilo's weariness was warranted and would not disturb him further. The general would hear all tomorrow, for good or ill.

The emperor stepped up into his carriage, and Etrusin ordered his men to march back to the palace. Inside the carriage, Geilo sat with his face in his hands. Through the weariness he could hear the voice of Minotros playing in his mind. Along with the deep timbre came a feeling of dread. He sat up and shook the feeling off, clearing his mind as he did so. He would not let this affect him so. The emperor knew that he had to be strong for his people. This would be a great test for them. In the past the empire had known peace, and this conflict was to be its first since the unification. If his people emerged triumphant, as the God of Fate had implied, it would be a testament to their ability to survive. In the end they would be stronger.

Geilo let these thoughts bolster his confidence as the carriage rode on. He would have Etrusin ready his troops. The general seemed sure of their abilities. The emperor hoped that confidence was not misplaced. Shiu Hi had also claimed he could make the military force stronger with the aid of magic. With what had transpired in the temple, the emperor was sure that the high priest would be completely cooperative, even if he had not seen it himself.

Tomorrow Geilo would meet with the two men, the high priest and the general. Together they would determine a plan of action. The emperor nodded, feeling a little better that he had things, especially his emotions, under control. He had apparently been thinking for a while, though, as he was surprised to feel the carriage slow and come to a stop. Looking out the window he could see the palace looming before him in the sunset. A wave of fatigue washed over him, and all his previous thoughts were replaced by a strong desire to get to bed. The emperor exited the carriage and started making his way to his chambers. Tomorrow would bring another day and a new future for his people.

* * *

Urietsin sat staring into the campfire intently, meditating on the random motion of the flickering flames. He found that when he had something to concentrate on, he could focus his attention completely and wash away all the thoughts that constantly raced through his mind. It was something that he tried to do every day since he was a child, when his father had taught him the technique. It left him feeling refreshed and alert, as though shutting off his senses somehow heightened them. He felt at one with his surroundings.

A snap shattered his concentration, and at first he thought it was the fire that had made the sound. He looked up to see one of the diplomats the emperor had sent with them looking down at him curiously. "Hello," she said amicably, smiling down at him. "I'm not disturbing you, am I?"

Urietsin nodded blankly, surprised for a moment by her approach, but then caught himself. "Oh, I mean, no," he said returning her smile sheepishly.

She laughed and sat next to him. Urietsin knew of Giunin Ninei, but before they had joined this expedition, he had never seen the one who sat by him now or the tall man who was with them. This woman was the youngest of the three, possibly closest to his age.

"Tell me, warrior, are you interested in diplomacy?" she asked.

Urietsin raised his eyebrows and blinked. "Diplomacy?" he repeated blankly.

The young woman giggled, looking away and covering her mouth as she did so. "I'm sorry," she recovered quickly. "What I mean is that most of the soldiers don't pay us much attention. They nod when we greet them, they give us food at meal times, but all in all, they act as though we're an inconvenience. You, however, seem to have taken an interest in our small group."

The Swift One flushed. He had been keeping a watchful eye on the diplomats ever since they had set out. He was curious about their presence, not to mention drawn by this young woman's attractive features. Now that he was being confronted about it, he wasn't sure how to respond. "I...I, ah," he stuttered.

Again, the diplomat hid her giggle behind a delicate hand. "I'm sorry," she repeated, shaking her head. "Please, let me start over," she stood and bowed deeply. "My name is Su-Ni."

Urietsin likewise stood and bowed as deeply as she. "Urietsi'in," he said.

"May I call you Urietsin?" she asked politely, bowing again, though not quite so low this time.

Urietsin nodded and returned the bow. "Most people call me Etsin, but you may use whichever you prefer," he grinned.

She nodded. "Swift One," she repeated, hiding a chuckle.

Urietsin flushed slightly. He decided to bring the focus back to their conversation. "In answer to your original question, I am more interested in you than in diplomacy," he explained.

Su-Ni's expression abruptly changed; she looked surprised. "Me?" she asked awkwardly.

Urietsin's mind raced backward quickly. He reviewed his last statement and realized his error. "Oh! No, no. What I meant was I'm interested in your group of diplomats. Specifically, I'm curious as to why the emperor thought it necessary to include you in this scouting mission," he explained evenly, his tone belying the bright red burning in his cheeks.

Su-Ni nodded, apparently oblivious to Urietsin's embarrassment. "I imagine that's what all of you are wondering," she said. She grew pensive for a moment. "In exploration like this, it's probably best to have people like Ninei around. If we come across another city out here, the best interest of the empire would be to start up peaceful relations right away."

She fell silent for several beats while she stared into the fire. She finally added, "We think the emperor knows something."

"Hmm..." Urietsin acknowledged. This conversation was just getting interesting, and he wanted to say more, but something else had caught his attention. Su-Ni noticed his gaze and looked behind her into the darkness. Urietsin stepped by her saying, "I'll be right back."

The young woman watched him, noticing how gracefully he moved. He approached the trees on the balls of his feet and was both silent and ready. Su-Ni could see nothing through the darkness of the forest, but Urietsin apparently did, for his head turned suddenly to peer someplace else. As he padded forward, the darkness engulfed him, and the diplomat could no longer make him out. She suddenly started to feel very uncomfortable and looked back toward the main camp. She saw several soldiers sleeping and a few up and walking the perimeter of their campfire's light. She looked back to see if Urietsin had emerged yet. He hadn't. Su-Ni ran quickly back to the main camp to find Komeris.

Tilon looked to Marui as the woman ran off. He didn't understand how the boy had seen him in the darkness. He hadn't expected to make an appearance quite yet, but it seemed as though it might be inevitable. Marui agreed, apparently, because she leaned close to him and whispered, "What are we waiting for?"

Tilon nodded wordlessly and stepped away from the tree where they had been conferring. The young soldier from the camp stopped his progress. The elf held up his hand and spoke in the human's own tongue, "Hail. I mean you no harm."

"Who are you?" Urietsin demanded.

"My name is Tilon Enshei. We who live in this forest wish to speak to you and your party."

There was a slight pause as Urietsin thought about his response. After a moment, the young warrior's posture changed. "You will want to speak with Komeris. He is our captain."

Tilon nodded before recalling that the human probably couldn't see such a slight motion in the darkness. He apparently did, though, because he turned around and gestured for them to follow. The elf thought to himself that this human must have exceptional eyesight. Tilon followed the young man, nodding to Marui to join him. There were many more hidden in the forest, but Tilon had ordered them to wait.

The group exited the tight copse of trees to find themselves surrounded by Komeris and his men. The flickering shadows cast by the nearby fire made their stern expressions seem otherworldly. Each soldier had a weapon drawn and looked ready for action. Urietsin scanned the crowd and spotted Su-Ni and her companions huddled toward the back, whispering to one another excitedly.

The Swift One held up his hand. "Please, sheath your weapons, men. These two you see behind me are our forest neighbors. They come to speak with us. They are unarmed," he said.

Again, Tilon was impressed by the young warrior's eyesight and awareness. He did, however, refrain from alerting the human as to the many bows that were doubtless drawn on the group from the trees. The elf wasn't sure if this warrior had seen them, but either way, he thought it wise not to mention it. He was pleased to see that one man, apparently the leader, was the first to put away his sword, gesturing for the others to do so as well; this, Tilon assumed, was Komeris.

As if he sensed what the elf was thinking, the captain stepped forward and bowed. "I am Komeris, captain of this scouting party from Kesitul. We welcome you to our camp."

Tilon stepped up to Komeris and returned his bow with a simple nod. "I am Tilon Enshei of the Shionen people, and I welcome you to our forest, although I am curious about your presence," he said, looking around at all the warriors. "This is an impressive scouting party."

Komeris chuckled. The sound instantly broke the air of tension radiating from the soldiers around them. The elf gave a sincere, if tight, smile.

"Yes, I know how this must look," the captain conceded. "I assure you, though, our intentions are quite peaceful. We come from an empire just to the east of these woods, and we are not very accustomed to exploration."

Tilon nodded as if he knew all this. He let his focus shift to the large campfire in the middle of the clearing. "Shall we?" he asked.

Ah yes," Komeris said, smiling. The captain turned and ordered his men back to their posts and led the way to the fire. He sat a few feet from the flames. Komeris indicated to Tilon and Marui to do the same. The elves sat rather stiffly and stared expectantly at the captain. Urietsin hurried over and sat near them while Ninei and her party gathered by Komeris.

The captain looked around and noticed his company. "Ah, Tilon was it? These three here to my right are our diplomats: Ninei, Ini'io, and Su-Ni."

He gestured toward each one respectively.

Tilon gave them an appraising stare. "Diplomats?" The question sounded doubtful.

Komeris flinched at this and cleared his throat. "And you have already met Urietsin."

The look that the elf gave the Swift One was considerably different than the one he had shot at the diplomats, more respectful. He nodded. "This is Marui," he said, indicating the female beside him. "She is something of a diplomat herself, and the finest archer of our people."

Marui bowed her head. "Captain, we apologize for sneaking up on you and your group, but we have much to ask you and were not sure how to approach. We are a quiet people, and we do not seek much contact with outsiders. You can imagine how surprised we were to find a large party of humans traveling through our territory."

Komeris glanced at Ninei, expecting her to speak. When she did not he shrugged and turned his attention back to Marui. "Had we known the extent of your ownership of this land and a way we could contact you, we would have asked your permission. We mean no ill will. These things are the reason we set out. To come in contact with others and perhaps work toward the mutual benefit of our peoples."

Tilon looked unimpressed. "We're quite familiar with how humans work to benefit themselves."

Komeris raised a confused eyebrow.

"Tilon is quite outspoken in his opinions of outsiders," Marui spoke quickly to salvage the conversation. "You must understand that our lives are very different here in the forest. We have lived in peace for many centuries, and in our entire history we have never fought with other elves. There are many old stories, however, about people who inhabited your land long ago. Many things happened in those times that are painful to remember. We do not hold you responsible for your ancestors' actions, despite Tilon's attitude."

Tilon appeared unruffled by Marui's subtle reproach. Ninei took this opportunity to speak. "We do understand, Marui. Our cultures must be very different, and we have not had the opportunity to share them. This is possibly the most important part of our work. We hope to learn from one another and make our lives richer through peaceful relations. It would be a great honor, indeed, if we could consider ourselves allied with the noble Shionen."

Marui raised her eyebrows, impressed by Ninei's flattery. Tilon, however, was scowling. "Allied? Against whom?" he snapped.

The female elf turned to scold Tilon sharply in their native tongue. Komeris shot a glance at Ninei. She nodded reassuringly. "You must forgive Tilon," said Marui contritely. "We have seen many things recently...well, it is difficult to explain."

"Ask them about the magician," Tilon said in a commanding tone.

"Magician?" asked Ninei.

Marui nodded. "We heard reports of your presence shortly after you entered the forest. It was very surprising as we had believed all paths into the forest were blocked. We came to investigate. When we found one of your campsites two days ago, there was a strange bird there. This bird turned out to be a magician in disguise. He transformed into the shape of an elf and spoke briefly with Tilon. He claimed to be part of this group and then returned to bird form and flew in this direction."

Ninei looked confused. She glanced at Komeris, who seemed similarly perplexed. "We know of no magician," said the captain slowly. "The only people I have ever seen perform magic are the emperor and the priests."

Tilon gave a derisive sounding snicker. He said something to Marui in their own language. She clearly ignored him. "Hmm, that is puzzling. Tilon and I suspected he was not part of your group. In fact, though I hadn't noticed it before, he spoke in a tongue that sounded older than your own, if similar. I would guess that he was not even actually human."

Puzzled looks continued from Komeris and Ninei. "What else could he be?" asked the captain.

The patronizing grimace on Tilon's face deepened. He opened his mouth to say something insulting, but Marui quickly cut him off. "There are many races in this realm, captain. And shapeshifting comes easily to only a select few. It is possible for a strong magician of any race to learn to do it. It is difficult, though."

"If such a spell can be learned by a human, what makes you think this magician wasn't one?" asked Ninei.

Marui pondered her answer for a moment. "Our race has a deep bond with magic. It gives us senses beyond those of most other races. Sometimes we can feel when another magical creature is near. It is also difficult for magicians and wizards to cast spells without chanting or using ingredients. This makes it difficult for them to cast a spell without drawing attention to themselves. Whoever this magician was, he could shapeshift apparently at will."

"Did you sense that he was a magical creature then?" asked Ninei.

At this Marui turned to Tilon. "It certainly appeared so," he said.

"Hmm," was Ninei's only response.

Whatever it was that Tilon had said to Marui before, he said it again. This time she did not ignore him. Instead she began to speak quickly in Shionen, seemingly rebuking him. He seemed annoyed, but did not speak again. When she finished, she stood and looked at Komeris. "We must go now. There are some things we must discuss. We will speak again soon."

"How will we find you?" asked Komeris.

Marui could not repress her smirk. "Do not worry. You should reach the western edge of the forest by about midday tomorrow. Assuming, of course, you get an early start. We will find you before then."

Komeris stood and gave a slight bow. "Tomorrow, then."

Marui nodded in return. Together she and Tilon left the clearing and disappeared into the darkness of the forest.

Komeris looked to Ninei, eyebrows raised. "Well, we'd better get some sleep, then," he said.

Ninei rose, nodding in agreement. They walked separately to their respective resting places and prepared to sleep. Urietsin looked over at Su-Ni, who had been nearby listening to the conversation. He got up and walked over to her.

"Interesting, isn't it?"

"Indeed," she replied. "They don't trust us."

"Marui. She has yet to make up her mind about us."

Su-Ni looked up at Urietsin with a measure of respect. "You are quite observant, for a soldier."

He grinned at her broadly. "Thank you."

* * *

Through the foliage, and as part of it, Gayossha watched the camp with fading interest. So, the elves had seen through his deception. No matter, the Fiu-Het doubted they could catch him if they tried. Even if they did, the members of his race were hard to kill if they were expecting death and even harder to keep captive. Gayossha felt it would be a good idea to disappear for a while. He had enough information to tempt Orbein. He would go back and tell him of the empire from which these scouts claimed to have come. Undoubtedly the king would be furious that he hadn't actually gone to investigate this empire, but the shapeshifter would enjoy the game. He would rest here for the night and in the morning fly back to Niele'itio, making a little stop in between.

8 PROGRESSION

"Tell me what you see, wizard," the king's eager voice urged.

That voice, hoarse with anticipation, made Laernus the seer flinch and almost broke his concentration. "I see an army," the wizard replied shortly.

"What is this army doing? Is it mine this time?"

"I know not. It appears to be...yes, I believe."

"You believe? Mage, if you want to live another day, you will be sure this moment. Now, is it my army or not?"

Laernus shot him a look, but quickly returned to his gazing, as the king was clearly very serious. "They are beneath clouds that rain fire upon the mountains."

"Damn them to the underworlds..." the king muttered in frustration. "Do the gods ever see fit to show you anything else?"

"Highness, we are lucky to see what we have seen thus far. Not everyone..." the mage began to explain.

Orbein interjected angrily, "Do not make excuses! I tire of your ineffectiveness."

"If you would but be a bit more patie-"

"Do not!" Orbein warned, one threatening finger stabbing toward Laernus. Much more silently, but no less angrily, he continued. "Do not...speak out of turn again. When I ask you to speak, then you will speak. I do not wish to know your opinion, or anything else you have to say, unless I ask you."

Laernus looked warily at his king. How he hated this. If the king disliked him so much as to refuse his counsel when he gave it, he should let him leave. In fact, as the thought occurred to the mage, he realized how perfect the idea was. Maybe Orbein would just let him leave. As nice as his laboratory was, he truly did not need it. Perhaps he could find another way to get back to his homeland.

"I will go," he said aloud, more to himself than to Orbein.

The king cocked an eyebrow. "Did you say something?" he asked.

Laernus drew himself to his full height and nodded. "I will leave. You have no use for me, and it is clear that you cannot bear my presence. Perhaps it would be best if I just left."

Orbein nodded slowly, but a look in his eye told the wizard that he had not heard a word of it. "I thought you had spoken..." he said, almost wistfully. The king walked by the seer's table, brushing it as he stepped. The table shuddered strangely as he passed, and Laernus believed some magic was afoot. The mage began to mutter defensively, preparing to cast a spell, but something suddenly shot out of the table and into his mouth.

It was a slippery tentacle that quivered in the air between him and the table as it wound itself around his tongue and halfway down his throat. Using the mage for support, the table pulled itself forward shooting out other tentacles that wrapped around his hands and bound his feet. Terror gripped Laernus as he gagged. Losing his balance, he toppled to the floor. He heard Orbein laugh.

"Why did you speak?" he asked with mock wistfulness. "Did I not warn you?"

Somewhere close by Laernus could hear a voice agreeing with the king, but he couldn't possibly begin to understand what was happening to him. Even if it weren't for the suddenness of these horrific events, the pain that he now felt prevented him from any rational thought. The tentacles that were holding him down squeezed him until he felt he would be crushed. And that one slimy limb probed his throat and wrenched his tongue until he thought he would suffocate.

Then, suddenly, it ended. There was a deafening silence and Laernus opened one eye slowly. He saw before him a short, trollish creature groveling before king Orbein.

Orbein half-grinned and said, "You performed well, my new friend. A shining example of your race. Gayossha will be angry I have taken your services."

The last comment was a dig for information, not the first since the Fiu-Het had arrived and hinted at Gayossha's importance, and probably not the last. The king was more concerned with other things, however, and did not wait for a response. He glanced over at the crumpled form of Laernus and knelt to have a closer look.

"And as for you...what shall we do with you? I suppose we could let you go, but then you would be free to return and be a nuisance whenever you liked. No, I don't believe I like that option. I could kill you, but then, your foresight has proven to be a useful gift on rare occasion, though less so the past several months."

He looked to the shapeshifter, "What do you think? The dungeon, perhaps?"

"If I may be permitted..." the creature spoke. Orbein made a gesture and the Fiu-Het continued, "I think he will be of much greater use to us within the ranks of the Ionotu army."

There was a long pause. Laernus could not tell what the king was thinking, as he was facing the shapeshifter. After a few moments, Orbein burst into peals of hearty laughter, obviously very pleased with the suggestion. That was it. Laernus knew he was doomed. When the laughter finally ceased, the king rose and indicated the restrained mage. "Take him to his new home. I'm sure it will be an educational experience."

The tentacles that bound his limbs gripped tighter and forced him, painfully, to rise. Thankfully, though, the one gagging him had gone away. Every step was agony, but he dared not pause for a moment, fearing worse pain awaited him if he showed the slightest sign of resistance. The shapeshifter and the mage left the king to his thoughts as they made their way to the training grounds of the Ionotu valley. Laernus was unsure of whether or not it was safe to speak to this creature that now held him. As much as he dreaded the soldiers, he had a better chance of surviving the army than the dungeon. Well, maybe not so much 'surviving' as 'escaping'.

"Why did you help me?" the wizard ventured.

The shapeshifter made a hissing sound. "I said what would please my new master the most. It had little to do with helping you."

"Little...but something?"

"You are a fool!" the creature scolded. It sounded oddly sympathetic. "You do not understand. When you are in the service of someone like King Orbein, you do not speak against him...not openly at least. I saved you from your own ignorance."

"But, why?"

This question seemed to fluster the Fiu-Het, whose features twisted to extreme angles. "You speak too much!" And with that he shot out another tentacle, but this time it merely covered the mage's mouth. It wasn't the answer Laernus was looking for, but it did bring him a step closer to understanding.

* * *

Kiusu climbed over a rocky incline that led to a more wooded part of the mountain. He seemed to be searching for something specific. He studied each tree he came across with great intensity, especially those that appeared dead and rotting. Each time he discovered some sign of life within the tree, he moved on to the next. Finally, he came to a great dead hulk of a tree. The branches had long since decayed, and all that was left was a great trunk standing straight into the air. The dry roots still held the ground firmly, but in a death grip that hadn't changed for possibly decades.

Kiusu slowly scaled the trunk knocking here and there, searching for some indication of living matter. The tree itself was completely dead. The old man could tell as soon as he touched the rough bark that the life force had left some time ago. It felt empty. But nature hardly ever let a thing like death break the cycle of life, and dead matter such as this was often home to many creatures. Of these, however, Kiusu also found no sign. There had at one time, perhaps, been several colonies of ants and other insects all over the tree, but they had gone leaving the bulk of the trunk still standing. He had also found signs of nests or holes long ago lived in, but long since abandoned.

Satisfied that this was the perfect specimen, Kiusu lowered himself to the ground. He opened the sack he had left lying at the base of the trunk and pulled out a long black sash, which he wound tightly around his waist, tying it there securely. He then stood facing the tree, studying every rough and cracked feature. Several quiet moments passed in which Kiusu meditated on the tall trunk before him. His breathing was slow and steady, and his expression was relaxed and serene.

With surprising swiftness, the old man sprang into action. His fists were a blur and bark flew violently in all directions. In that span of a single second he had pelted the dead trunk six times with each fist. Pausing only long enough to shift his weight to one leg, he lifted the other to the bare spot created by his devastating punches. The foot landed, and a crack rang out over the mountainside. More bark was propelled off the opposite side of the trunk, and before it landed, the old man came forward with his elbow, leaving a deep dent in the old, thick wood.

It suddenly seemed, as he pulled away from the tree, that gravity lost its hold on him. With the barest of motions he propelled himself off the ground, easily six feet into the air. At his peak, where he hung for a seemingly unnatural span of time, he swung his other foot out, connecting with the wood with another shattering crack. The tip of the trunk wobbled, and a large crevice appeared diagonally along the middle of the dead tree's length. As the old master fell, he loosed two fierce punches that broke the dry wood fibers holding the now cracked trunk together. Some twelve hundred pounds of dead wood flew free and rolled several meters, crushing grass and bushes as it went.

Kiusu landed and froze. Quickly he ran down the path that the huge timber had made, checking the bent plants as he went. He hadn't meant for this to happen. He had checked the trunk so meticulously to ensure nothing was hurt or killed as he practiced. Luckily there had been no animals in the path of the flying wood, but the bushes had been bent. He knew they would grow strong once more, though. Turning back to the remaining trunk he looked past it to see what lay behind. Nothing.

The old man took off running. Ten feet before reaching the tree, he launched himself back into the air. Leading with his right foot, he slammed into what was left of the tree. A reverberating pop issued from the ground and dead wood groaned under a rising cloud of dust. The air eventually stilled and silence fell. Sand and dirt particles headed slowly back to the ground. When the dust finally cleared, Kiusu was standing triumphantly upon the rest of the uprooted trunk barely out of breath.

He could have continued to chop this wood into kindling with his bare hands, but the work was mentally tiring. It took incredible concentration to do what he had just done. Fortunately, Kiusu found that such things were coming easier to him as he practiced day by day. Besides, he had a hatchet in his sack that would do nicely. It would be another day or two before he could clear the area entirely of the trunk while he saw to other tasks as well, but this kindling added to his current store would last him well through the winter.

* * *

Geilo awoke that morning with a great sense of purpose. The decisions he made today would determine the future of his people. He sent a message for Etrusin to meet him in the field behind the palace and made his way to the stable. He spent a lot of time while waiting for his military advisor to arrive thinking about the time before the empire when Reisothin briefly rule this land by terror. He recalled how he united his people to fight against the dragon. Hope seemed bleak then, and the emperor hoped to draw some insight from those times. When Etrusin finally galloped up beside him on the field, Geilo felt somewhat reassured by his time alone. They rode together in silence for a while.

The emperor barely pulled on his reign, bringing his horse to a stop. He smiled at the Uchilin. "I am glad you are here, my old friend."

The greeting caught the military advisor off guard. "I am glad to be of service, emperor."

"Please, Etrusin, time has made us forget the past. We were once good friends, you and I," the emperor said quietly. He seemed almost sad.

Etrusin wasn't sure how to react to this. It was true; they had once been close friends. They had fought side by side against Reisothin and the general had been at Geilo's right hand during the formation of the empire. Time had changed things, though. His friend had become his emperor, and ever after things had been different. It filled Etrusin with hope that Geilo remembered their old friendship. "Yes...yes, we were. And I should like to think that we still are...but, you are emperor."

Geilo waved the thought away. "A poor excuse for forgetting those who stood by me during such trials as we saw. And time is not kind, for I fear it is all too soon that we face those trials again."

The general's eyes widened. "What do you know?"

Geilo's horse suddenly began to shuffle as it felt his change in posture. "Come. Let us go back to the palace," the emperor said, taking off across the field before Etrusin could answer.

When they got to the throne room, the emperor composed himself briefly before proceeding. "Etrusin, my friend," he began, "I fear that war is upon us. Please! Do not speak! I must tell you everything." With that he explained all that had happened in the past month, from his first visions of a demonic army, to the message that Minotros had given him.

The entire time Etrusin watched silent, but wide-eyed. A realization dawned upon him. "That is why you gave orders to rebuild our forces."

Geilo nodded. "Yes, I had done it in the hope that, should anything happen, we would be ready. I only hope we are not too late."

"We will be ready," Etrusin assured him. "Since you commanded me to train new soldiers, I have amassed a force!"

Geilo looked pleadingly at his general, hoping against hope that his last statement was true. "Is it enough to defeat an army?"

Etrusin thought about this for a moment. "I will not mislead you, sire. I don't know if we are quite ready for a war, but the ranks increase daily. Many strong young men and women add themselves to our number, bringing us closer every day. It will not be long now."

"I hope it will not be too late," the emperor repeated. He sighed deeply, exhaling all the negativity he had built up since recounting his story to Etrusin. He had to bring back his earlier confidence. Just then a knock issued from the chamber doors. "Enter," Geilo called.

The doors opened and the guards escorted in the high priest. Shiu Hi walked in and bowed low before the emperor. "Sire...General," he nodded to Etrusin in acknowledgement.

Geilo bade him rise and dismissed the guards. "Welcome, Shiu Hi. I was just informing Etrusin of the situation."

"I see. What, exactly, is the situation?" the priest asked calmly, curious about what the emperor learned from his communion with God.

"Minotros has confirmed my fears. We are in danger. We must be ready to defend ourselves," Geilo explained.

Shiu Hi nodded. "What are our plans?" he asked.

"If I may," answered Etrusin. Geilo gestured for him to speak. "I believe our best option may be to move some of our forces away from the empire."

"And leave it unprotected?" asked Shiu Hi.

"No...not completely. We would leave enough men here for defense and to take on more for training. But I believe we should set up our main barracks away from the empire, beyond the forest. Emperor, you said you saw the army marching from the mountains. If that is where they will come from, then we would be ready for them as they approached," the general explained.

"And if they come from the sea?" the emperor asked, though he knew that was unlikely.

Etrusin's brow furrowed. "I don't know. I've only just learned all that is happening and will need more time to plan out the finer details. Though the reefs surrounding the eastern shores and the cliffs on the southern shores are likely to give us all the protection we'll need, perhaps we can set up sentries to keep watch," he paused, sighing. "I hope the scouting parties send word soon. They might have information that would help our plans."

Geilo nodded. "Indeed, the mountains have played a prominent role in my visions. I think it might be best for you to set up a barracks closer to them. Not too close, though. If the enemy is empowered as I have foreseen, the high ground will give them a distinct advantage."

"The enemy will not be the only one who is empowered," commented Shiu Hi significantly.

"Ah yes!" Etrusin cried suddenly, a different light in his eyes. "The emperor mentioned that you would be able to assist us with...magic?"

Shiu Hi nodded solemnly. "We would indeed. If you could gather all your men's weapons, we could bless them with a sharpness that would smite the enemies of Minotros." The light in Etrusin's eyes glinted as the priest continued. "We also have a weapon. A device carved from the remains of our slain enemy, Reisothin. With a bit more practice, the men of our order may learn to wield it with deadly consequences to our foes."

"Magic," Etrusin repeated in a fascinated whisper.

"Great care must be exercised, however," Shiu Hi went on. "Only those who are strong of will and true of purpose must wield such power. For it can control forces of nature for both good and evil. Because it comes from a wicked creature, it has a maleficent will of its own. A weak will might falter and use it for ill deeds."

"That is why priests will be on hand to manipulate this magic," explained the emperor.

Etrusin nodded. "A wise decision."

"If Emperor Geilo has seen correctly, this power will be of utmost importance to us," said Shiu Hi.

Geilo nodded. "With the ability to control nature...they may be able to alter the clouds that rain fire that I have seen in my visions."

"So, how shall we proceed?" asked the general.

"It may be too soon to tell...or too late to act," Geilo said.

Etrusin nodded. "I will send a messenger to the scouting party. Surely they should be through the forest by the time anyone can catch up with them, and hopefully they have not yet split up. If we send out a rider to meet them, we can have them set up a permanent camp in preparation for our arrival. This will give us some time to plan, if it is, indeed, not too late."

Geilo slapped Etrusin's back, pleased with his suggestion. "Very well. Go now and send out the rider. Shiu Hi and I have some things yet to discuss."

Etrusin bowed to Geilo, and although he had done it many times before, this time it was as much as an old friend as it was a loyal subject.

9 ILL OMENS

The sun was near its zenith as the scouting party approached the edge of the forest. Tilon and Marui stood just beyond the line of trees watching the mountains and conversing in their native tongue. Komeris and Urietsin were the first to arrive, followed closely by the diplomats of Kesitul. Urietsin knew that the elves had long since detected their approach, but their focus was now held by something else.

Tilon gestured to the mountains and spoke quickly in Shionen while Marui gazed west toward the closest peak. Urietsin looked west also and saw the distant mountain, its base still at most two day's walk away. It was a crystal clear day, and the young warrior's eyes easily scanned up to the lightly snowy cap when he noticed a thin trail of smoke coming, apparently, from somewhere on the opposite face. This appeared to be the source of Tilon's excitement as his continued gestures followed the trail of smoke up into the sky.

Finally, Marui interrupted her companion, putting a hand against his chest to calm him. "Good day, friends," she said to the party. "Please, give us a moment." She then turned her attention back to Tilon and spoke to him calmly for a few moments.

Komeris waved and nodded, pleased to give the remainder of the party a chance to catch up and rest. Noting the keen look on Urietsin's face, he moved closer and whispered, "What do you see?"

Urietsin pointed to the mountain. "Smoke," he replied, "as do they. It seems to be worrying our friend here." He gestured toward Tilon.

"Indeed, young warrior," Marui said, startling Komeris and Urietsin who thought their conversation private. "Forgive me. We have very keen hearing." She indicated her ears.

Komeris nodded in comprehension. "I see..." he said, although with regard to the thin tendril of distant smoke, he really couldn't see. "Why is this smoke so distressing?"

"It is an omen!" cried Tilon. "A bad omen!"

Marui admonished her companion in Shionen and turned her attention back to Komeris. Her expression was apologetic. "It seems that the meeting of our peoples has come at a time that seems more than coincidental. We have many stories that tell us of signs, some subtle, others less so, that presage certain events. Recently we have seen much, subtle and otherwise, which foretells of bad fortune for our people. Such portents have not been so strong or pressing in many years. Until several days ago, we were not quite sure what the warnings were about. Since your party somehow managed to enter the forest, there has been much speculation..."

As her voice trailed, Komeris smiled reassuringly. "I understand. Our emperor too can see signs of the future. As for the speculation you speak of, I don't blame your people. You don't know us, and so you are being cautious. But let me assure you, we mean you no harm. Indeed, we wish to work with you in peace, or leave you in peace if that is your wish."

For the first time since they had met him, Tilon seemed pleased. "Believe me when I say that we would be happy with either situation. You must understand, however, that your arrival is an omen in itself, and for our race, which has had little contact with the outside for centuries, it is seen by many as a bad one. In our last dealings with humans, long ago, our friendship was spurned and our home here, almost lost. Until you entered our forest, the way was blocked to all of your race, a step that had been intended for the protection of both our peoples."

Komeris was taken aback at the sudden tact that was employed by the elf. Urietsin spoke before the silence became uncomfortable.

"Perhaps our coming is a good omen," suggested the Swift One. "Perhaps we can help you with the trouble that lies ahead."

Komeris interjected, "Yes! We have come to investigate the lands beyond the forest. That peak seems as good a place as any to start. We will send some scouts up there to see if they can find the source of the smoke."

"And what if they do?" asked Tilon. "What if they climb over and find only a scorched tree, what then?"

Komeris shrugged. "Even if they do not find some unnatural source of the fire, it is exploration for my party. It will be no waste of our time. If we do find something, it may be for the better of all of us."

Tilon simply stared off thoughtfully.

With that they all agreed to send some men to meet the elves at the same location once they had finished their exploration of the mountain. With little fanfare, they left the edge of the forest behind them. The warriors and diplomats all headed for the foundation of the first peak.

* * *

Gayossha stood before the blaze, enticed by the flames that licked hungrily at the dry wood hut. He hadn't intended to burn the old man's home, but now that the fire consumed the tiny cabin, he watched with glee. The Fiu-Het had been investigating the area where he had seen the human before and found the kettle steaming over some hot embers out in front. He had only wanted to have a little fun...but now it seemed as though he was going to have lots. He stood cackling while he watched the devouring flames of the fire.

Unexpectedly, he was grabbed from behind, and before he could react, a strong forearm was wrapped tightly around his chest. "Who are you!" the old man's voice asked. Gayossha cackled again and began to shift. His throat melted over the old man's arm, and when the dribbling flesh touched his chest, he had dissolved through the restraining hold. The shapeshifter stood facing Kiusu, giggling maniacally. The old man was shocked but recovered quickly and launched at him, fists leading.

Normally Gayossha could dodge such an attack, shifting his flesh away from the blow. This human, however, was different from any foe he had yet faced. Kiusu struck as fast as lightning and no less powerfully. The shapeshifter took the double front punch fully on the chest, flying back toward the burning hut. Perhaps this would not be as much fun as he thought. Before Gayossha could compose himself, the two fists moved away to reveal a foot already en route to his chin. The kick connected solidly, and he stumbled backward again, this time against the burning flames.

Pain erupted upon his back as his ragged cloak ignited. Panicked, the Fiu-Het dropped to the floor and began to writhe. The old man ran up and began to roll the shapeshifter away from the fire, meanwhile attempting to extinguish the flaming cloak. The acrid smell of burnt flesh emanated from the shapeshifter as he panted unevenly. Never before had he known such pain!

Kiusu turned to appraise the situation. It did not look good. At this point the flames were well out of control and already licking at a nearby tree. He cursed his foolishness at leaving the embers unattended. The only logical course was to move clear of the fire and wait for it to burn out. His hut was in something of a small clearing; only a few trees stood nearby. The air was also unusually calm, and embers were not flying toward the denser wood. There was little chance of the fire destroying much more than his little space. He turned back to the creature, thinking to drag it away as well, but in its place was a bird. Smoke curled from its singed feathers, and much blistered flesh peeked out.

Gayossha flapped briefly, but could not leave the ground. Excruciating pain racked his body with every motion. It was clear that he would escape nowhere in this form. He limped away, shifting once more. He took the shape of a small rodent and bounded away toward the woods. Each jump, and worse each landing, sent waves of agony along his spine, but he could not stop. He had to get away. He would not be killed by this old man. He would not die alone on this forsaken mountain peak.

Kiusu ran after the creature, but quickly lost him in the underbrush. A larger creature he could have tracked easily, but a field mouse was much more challenging without more preparation. He rushed back toward the clearing to monitor the fire. If the wind picked up and embers floated to the trees, he would be the only one to prevent a worse disaster.

It was at least an hour before the flames finally died down, but by then his hut was reduced to a pile of ash and embers. As the sun sank low in the mountains, Kiusu walked over to what was once his home. Nothing remained save his kettle, which had been outside, and his sword and hatchet, which he had taken with him to cut wood. As he sifted through the remains, he was surprisingly optimistic. He could build another hut. Perhaps some of the wood from the great trunk he had felled could be used to start rebuilding. It would mean a bit more work come winter, but he had a feeling that would work itself out sooner or later. As for the shapeshifter...

Kiusu wasn't quite sure what to think of that. In all his time he had never seen anything like the Fiu-Het. There were stories, of course, but those were just legends, or so had he thought before today. And why had the creature set fire to his hut? That question was even more perplexing than the creature itself. Kiusu hadn't had outside contact for almost twenty years, and now this strange creature appeared to destroy his home?

Just then, a feeling came to him. A whisper on the wind, very quiet and mild. It told him that it was all a part of his destiny. He would know the answers to his questions someday soon. This was unlike any premonition he had experienced before. He had a strong sense that things were happening at that very moment which would set events into motion. It left him feeling heady and euphoric.

'Yes,' he thought, 'I will sleep under the stars tonight and begin rebuilding tomorrow. Everything will be fine.'

* * *

"You called for me, highness?" The creature's voice sounded as though it bubbled through the slime that oozed from its skin.

Orbein considered the hunched shapeshifter before him. Since he began his dealings with Gayossha and, through him, the Fiu-Het, he never ceased to be amazed at their ugliness. They all appeared as though they had been through some grisly battle and had lost badly. Their skin hung from them as though it were not securely attached and looked bruised and battered. Now, as he regarded Agucho, disdain for the race swirled in Orbein's mind.

"Yes," the king replied after a pause. "I have something to discuss with you."

The creature bowed humbly. "I am here to serve you, my lord."

The king nodded absently. "My kingdom is about to expand," he said.

"I see," said the Fiu-Het, not really understanding, but wishing to keep his master content.

"No, you don't," Orbein said plainly. "You cannot begin to imagine my designs. But that is aside from the point."

Agucho shifted uncomfortably for a few moments before venturing, "Of course not, highness. How may I, your humble servant, be of assistance in this plan?"

Orbein's eyes narrowed as he dissected the response, searching for a hint of sarcasm. "It would be foolish of me to assume the world is so uninhabited that I will not meet resistance," he said.

The Fiu-Het looked at the king blankly. He suddenly feared that the monarch was hinting at invading his home to the west. If Orbein was planning such an attack, it would be a harsh, bloody fight with no clear advantage to either side. Although the swamps were an unfamiliar place to these humans, the sheer number of men in the king's army would make defending a difficult endeavor. Could Orbein be that ambitious?

The creature's long pause made Orbein continue. "Many generations ago this city was rebuilt from the ashes of one much older. It was a bitter reconstruction, borne out of desperation. The empire of the east that massacred and abandoned us must submit to us or perish."

Agucho understood from Orbein's tone that he would prefer the latter. "You know for certain that this empire has survived the generations? Did no one ever try to return?" he asked.

The king's brow furrowed. "They did. The soldiers sent here to destroy the city found all the paths to home closed. Since then, we have heard nothing from the east, but I know they are there. Waiting for us. Fearing our return. This is why I have sent forth...a scout."

The careful manner in which Orbein selected that word made Agucho uncomfortable. "A scout," he echoed. "Yes, a very wise move."

The king chuckled to himself as though he were recalling some joke. "I believe you know him," he said.

Agucho's eyes widened. "Gayossha?"

Orbein now laughed aloud, "Yes. I sent Gayossha out, knowing that he could fly over the mountains quickly and investigate the lands undetected by any who might inhabit them."

Stunned, Agucho stood before the king, mouth agape. The creature's thin, slick tongue stretched out and slowly licked his eyes. "When were you expecting him back?" he asked, voice monotone.

The king shrugged. "When he is finished. I do suspect he shall return quickly, though. He knows my intentions and seems quite pleased."

The shapeshifter nodded slowly, the information still sinking into his brain. Everything was becoming clear to him now. The seer Laernus, Gayossha's absence, the king's frequent visits to his army and the temple. Orbein was readying for something massive. The air seemed so very dry, and again the Fiu-Het's tongue rolled over his bulging eyeballs.

Orbein reclined in his throne and eyed the shapeshifter closely. He knew that this news was very enlightening to Agucho. After a time, the king spoke again, "If Gayossha returns with word of inhabitants, I intend to ask him to rally your people that they may help us in the battle."

Agucho's sticky eyes dilated. He seemed more alert. "I do not think you understand how serious the situation really is," he hissed slowly.

"What do you mean?" said Orbein curiously.

"Gayossha, highness, is the son of our queen," the shapeshifter explained.

Orbein straightened suddenly at the revelation, but recovered quickly. "How is this possible? Why would your people send a prince on such a mission?" he asked incredulously.

"Gayossha was hunting," Agucho sighed. "He came upon your messenger. He alone heard your request. I found him sneaking away, as he often does. He would not tell me much, but it was enough to lead me here."

Orbein raised an eyebrow. Increasingly amused at the situation, he let out a laugh from deep within his chest. It was some time before he calmed enough to see Agucho shifting nervously and licking his dry, lidless eyes. "And what, pray tell, is your position in relation to prince Gayossha?" he asked mockingly.

"I am a distant cousin to the prince and, therefore, I have my place in our court," Agucho explained with great humility.

Chuckling once again, Orbein nodded. "I see. Perhaps you can find a more noble post here," he suggested.

Agucho was not amused. "Highness, as I have told you before, my people will be very displeased should something happen to our prince. I am sure now that you can appreciate why and what consequence it might bring."

Orbein fixed a steely gaze upon the Fiu-Het, his sense of humor spent. "That sounds like a thinly-veiled threat," he said.

The shapeshifter remembered what happened last time he delivered such a threat. He also knew what kind of man Orbein was, and this calmed him. "No, highness, it is not a threat. I simply have an obligation to my people to ensure that their prince is safe."

The king scowled. "And now you are in my employ and have obligations to me," he answered.

The shapeshifter stared at Orbein for some time before bowing low. "Of course, highnesss," he hissed.

"I grow weary," the king stated. "Off with you."

Agucho bowed again. "As you wish, highness."

With that he left the king alone in his throne room. The Fiu-Het had some thinking and, perhaps, planning to do. What would all this mean for his people? For so long they had lived alone in the swamps, hardly ever interacting with humans, of whom they were very wary. Now there was a possibility that they would be summoned to fight alongside this wild king and his army, assuming that Gayossha returned safely. And if he didn't, the Fiu-Het would likely still be going to war. War against Niele'itio. Agucho shuddered and wished Gayossha would just appear so that the both of them could return to the swamp and pretend none of this had ever happened.

10 EXCITEMENT

The easternmost mountain loomed before the new explorers as they stood at its base. Two days travel had drawn them from the forest to the foot of this rocky mount, and here they rested once more before venturing up it. Eager eyes rose toward the thin, white-speckled cap atop the peak that today held fast the sky's mist. It seemed magical to them as they stood admiring the grandness of the jutting landscape that they had only heard about in stories. Despite the relative closeness of the mountains, no one alive today in the empire had ever actually seen them aside from standing on a hill and glimpsing the very tallest peaks just rising over the treetops. Now, as they camped beside the majestic stone heights, their imaginations flowed like the stories from their lips and the celebratory libation from their flasks.

Komeris strode toward Urietsin, two goblets in his hands. He greeted the young warrior and handed him a drink. "Wine, my friend?" he asked jovially.

Urietsin graciously took the goblet and swallowed its contents. "It is beautiful, is it not?" he stated more than asked.

Komeris looked up, nodding as he did. "Indeed, and tomorrow we shall scale it."

Urietsin smiled enthusiastically. "It should prove interesting. At least, I hope it does," he said.

"Don't worry, young warrior. Your life is long ahead of you. Adventure awaits," the captain reassured him with a grin.

The Swift One responded with a nod. "I feel it too." His expression shifted, and he regarded Komeris curiously. "Are we all to go up?" he asked.

Komeris looked back to the rest of the soldiers and shrugged. "No, only a few. This would be a good place to split into smaller groups. I want to get some scouts riding north and south as well to see how far this range extends."

Again, Urietsin nodded. "That sounds wise. The slope is not too steep, but there are places that would hinder a large group. The more of us that go will be the more of us that could slip on a pile of loose rocks..." he trailed gazing toward the peak.

This time it was Komeris who was nodding. "I'll decide who is to go tomorrow morning," he said.

Urietsin looked back to his captain. "Shall we go all the way to the top?" he asked.

Komeris shook his head slowly, thinking of a route of exploration for tomorrow's assignment. "No, not to the peak. Maybe scale little more than halfway, and then make your way around the mountain to see what, if anything, can be seen from that height. We'll see if we can find the source of that smoke from the other day. If needs be, we can explore higher. I would prefer that we not climb too high just yet. Not until we get a feel for the terrain on the way up."

The young warrior listened, but his gaze was inexorably drawn back to the mountain. He felt something there. Something pulled at his being, telling him that his destiny lay just beyond. Yes, this journey was only the beginning, he knew. He hoped. He accepted another generous helping of wine from Komeris's flask. The Swift One gulped the wine and joined his fellow soldiers in the night's festivities. As he drank his imagination soared with the possibilities of the next day's adventure.

* * *

Etrusin paced before his soldiers, looking to each one as he passed. The fire and hope that gleamed within his eyes struck every warrior as significant. The general was sizing up his troops and wondering if they were ready for the road that lay ahead. He had confidence in the empire, and he knew that these men were receiving the best training he had to offer. He hadn't expected to be tested so soon and hoped that he and his soldiers could pass this test. The empire would suffer for their failure.

"Warriors!" he called to the ranks, stopping to gaze over all of them. "A time may come soon when we are called to defend our glorious empire. It has been only two decades since we united for this cause. Many of you were infants, and a few were not yet born. For those of you who are too young to remember the days before the empire, it was a harsh time of war and struggle. You are fortunate not to have known such times. I fear, however, that it is all too soon that we are called back to action! A new enemy threatens, unknown and far from here. Now, you young warriors are called to fight!"

A low murmur ran through the ranks as the soldiers began to understand their general's speech. After a short pause, Etrusin continued, "You, like those warriors years before, are called to defend the peace and security you have thus far taken for granted. You will follow in the steps of your great emperor and your parents and make our home safe for future generations. Children who will grow up to know the same freedom you have enjoyed. I know this news is unexpected, but I assure you this is not merely a precaution. I have conferred with the emperor, who has heard the voice of Minotros Himself! An enemy approaches, and if we are prepared, the aggressor will fall!

"Now, I ask you all to stand with me and the other distinguished officers of the empire to fend off this aggressor. As you are all men and women of free will, I shall permit you to go if you wish. You may go back to your homes and rest comfortably until the enemy comes to conquer you. If you do wish to go, do so now, for should you choose to stand with me today, you will stand with me until we fall in battle or die of old age."

As his eyes scanned the faces of each soldier, the general noted the confidence and bravery in their features and postures. His momentary silence was clearly the pause to allow those who would not fight the opportunity to leave.

No one left. Every man and woman who stood on the training field before Etrusin, stood tall and did not budge. These warriors knew their responsibilities to the empire and would fight alongside the general. The possibility of death did not frighten them, for they understood that it was sometimes the price of freedom.

General Etrusin smiled approvingly, and his heart swelled with pride. This, he knew, was their first step toward passing the approaching test. Which brought him to the next round of business for the day. Standing just outside the boundary of the training field was a line of priests headed by Shiu Hi. Etrusin now waved these men over.

"These men are here to aid us in the coming task. They are the priests of the great temple led by Shiu Hi. I ask that you now draw your weapons and present them to a priest when he approaches," he instructed the soldiers.

The priests filtered into the ranks and collected each soldier's weapon. Many of them carried censers that smoked and filled the air around the field with a heady aroma and lent a mysterious quality to the setting. The holy men carried the weapons through the purifying smoke and brought them to a cart that would carry them to the temple for a week long ceremony.

Even though the real magic hadn't started yet, Etrusin could feel power in the air. It strengthened him and his faith in their victory. He could see his soldiers waving their shining weapons in the air, loosing a battle cry that shook the earth. He could see them charging headlong into battle. He could see them vanquishing the enemy through the raw power of faith and freedom.

* * *

Geilo felt a cool breeze gently sweep past him. He could hear the rushing sound as that wind blew by his ears. The emperor opened his eyes and found himself sitting on his horse in a wide open field. Fear gripped him as he realized he didn't remember how he had gotten there. What frightened him more was that he was alone. Even though he didn't recognize his surroundings, he felt sure that there should be at least one other person with him.

The breeze stopped, and the air was suddenly still. Silence ensued. Geilo called out, but the silence seemed so encompassing that it engulfed his words even before they left his lips. Slowly, he urged his horse forward. Surely there was someone else here, and if so, he would find this person and ask how to get back to the palace.

The emperor began to feel less fearful as he trotted though the grass, noting that the moon was bright in the sky, and there were no clouds to block it out. He pressed on, quickening his pace. Something inside him told him this was the right way. Indeed, it must have been because he could see a light up ahead.

He drew his horse to a stop. Something was there, blocking his way. He suddenly realized that there was a huge web before him. As he focused on the sight, an enormous woven symmetry became visible. It was a silk web, as made by a spider of some sort. Geilo was puzzled as to what was supporting this web. It seemed to stretch up to the stars.

As Geilo dismounted, he became aware of something hanging from the center of the web. It was a gorgeous bejeweled dagger, and it shimmered and sparkled in the moonlight. He reached for the blade, thinking to use it on the web. As his hand moved close to the gem-encrusted handle, the metallic edge suddenly stirred, apparently of its own accord. It twisted fluidly toward the emperor's hand and the point darted forward, deeply piercing his palm.

Geilo withdrew his hand and looked at the wound. Blood flowed freely and dripped to the ground. Stunned at first, he simply watched as the red fluid moved down the single rivulet, then fell inevitably to the dirt. Blinking away the shock of what had happened, the emperor pulled at his long sleeve and balled the cuff into his fist to stem the flow of blood.

He looked up from his bloody hand to find that the web was gone. In its place, a pair of fiery eyes stared back at him. A monstrous laugh echoed through the air. Geilo jumped back, adrenaline surging into his veins. Then everything disappeared, and he was no longer in the field with his horse. He was back in the palace, standing before his throne. It looked so empty to him, and as he stood there pondering the significance of all this, his hand began to throb. He looked down and noted that his sleeve was soaked with blood. But the life-giving liquid was not red; it was green. He opened his palm and drew back the sleeve. His hand was swollen and gray and covered in the thick green goo that oozed from his wound.

As he watched the curious sight, his hand began to shrivel at the fingertips and curl up grotesquely. Horror washed over him as the deformation crawled up his arm. He began to cry out, and pain racked through his entire body. The shriveled hand slowly disintegrated, and the dust floated into the air and disappeared. All the while Geilo screamed.

He sat up with a start, his scream dying in his throat, his arm held up in the air. The room was dark, but from what little he could see, his hand was still there and intact. The emperor looked about, bewildered at the sudden change in surroundings. He was in bed in his chambers and was drenched in sweat, shivering with cold.

A dream. It had all been a dream. Geilo wiped his dripping brow, then brought his hand down to examine it in the dim light of the early morning. There was no mark, and he found he could flex his fingers normally. Naturally, as it had all been just a horrible nightmare. Now that he thought about it, he couldn't really remember everything that had happened. He just knew something had been terribly wrong with his hand.

The emperor chuckled to himself nervously in the safety of his own bed. This had not been a good month for sleep. As disturbing as this nightmare had been, at least it was a change from the normal fare of marching demons. He shifted uncomfortably as he noticed again the dampness of his clothes and bedding. Early though it was, Geilo decided now was as good a time as any to start the day. He would be able to sleep no longer in his sweat-soaked nightclothes.

* * *

Deep in the mountains, the rodent Gayossha scurried through the snow. Normally the extreme cold would have bothered the shapeshifter, but the icy drifts on the mountain peaks were the only relief he found from the searing blisters that lined his back. For more than two days he had run, half blind from the pain that the fire had left. When he found himself on the next peak, the hard, icy snow began to sooth the horrible burns. He had slept fitfully through the night, as he could not go another step without rest, but he had woken up early to begin running again.

He was weary, and the insidious injury on his back sapped his strength, but fear kept him moving. He got up the energy to transform himself to a slightly larger and faster creature and ran straight on to the next mountain.

He badly wanted to assume a bird shape and fly quickly back to Niele'itio, but he knew the constant flapping of wings would only agitate his already agonized back.

Without consideration to food, drink, or rest, the shapeshifter ran on toward the west. It did not take long for delirium to seep into his already half-crazed mind. He kept thinking of the old man that had done this to him and of the horrible, torturous ways he could make him pay. He thought also of the empire that supposedly existed beyond the eastern forest and of the elves that would no doubt ally themselves with the empire's army to crush Orbein's soldiers. After that they would come, with the old man leading them, to dominate the swamps where his people lived. They all had to die, the shapeshifter decided.

And so they would. Gayossha would make his way back to the king and warn him of the sly cunning of the mighty empire. He would tell him to mount a massive attack, to destroy these wicked people and the old man who did this to him. Perhaps he could get his own shapeshifting people to fight alongside Orbein's. Together they would make an unbeatable force.

Fantasy became indistinguishable from reality to the Fiu-Het prince as he scurried along the snow-capped peak. He could see the glorious battle engaged before him. Orbein's army, united with the Fiu-Het, beat back the imperial forces from the east. They laid waste to the countryside and left not a soul alive. In his fantasy he became a bird and flew overhead surveying the destruction.

Unconscious of his actions, Gayossha's large, scurrying rodent form sprouted wings that began flapping wildly. Blisters popped, and blood and pus spattered on the snow, melting small circles and sending up tiny tendrils of steam. The half rodent, half bird form lifted from the ground and shot ungracefully into the air. Wobbling and shuddering insanely, the deformed creature set a fast course to the west. Gayossha was oblivious to it all. His dementia blocked out all the pain, and he continued on with one single-minded purpose.

* * *

Kiusu brought his hatchet down onto the thick trunk, cutting it more deeply than most younger men could with such a small edge. His work was going quickly, and he was pleased to find that much of the wood from this old tree was still sturdy enough to make a good beginning for his new hut. The hulking mass of dead wood would have been ideal for fire over the long winter that would chill the mountaintop for months. But winter was still more than a season away, and he would need to gather a bit more wood than this to complete construction of his home and heat it during the cold season.

Several more chops in an unbelievably straight line brought the hatchet more than halfway through the trunk. Wanting to save some time, the old man slipped the tool into his sash and stood straight before the cut in concentration. With a quick upward then downward snap of his leg, Kiusu's heel cracked through the rest of the wood with minimal splintering. Now he had several long sections that could be dragged back to the spot where his hut had once stood.

While he worked this morning, Kiusu thought a lot about the creature that had set the fire. What was it, and where had it come from? Why would it set his hut ablaze? It was obviously somewhat intelligent, as he had heard it cackling as it watched the fire, and it wore some kind of clothing. The old man then remembered the strange bird he had seen watching him as he went through his routines. When the shapeshifter had tried to transform into a bird during the fight, it had looked oddly similar.

So many questions about that incident raced through Kiusu's mind. He continually reminded himself, however, that all would be revealed soon. Fate had assured him of that. His goal now was to rebuild and await the circumstances that were to come. He decided to shake away the curious thoughts and focus on his work. The wooden section was large, and it would take him some time to drag it back to his clearing.

Bracing himself, the old man lifted one end of the chopped trunk. His dense musculature tensed and corded, but did not strain. Kiusu began to drag the huge piece with the strength of a man twice his size. His hands were locked firmly into the holds he had made, and his feet made their way surely without slipping once.

* * *

The next morning Urietsin awoke to the sounds of the sunrise. Soldiers were ambling about on their way to cook up some breakfast, birds were chirping, and someone was singing merrily. The young warrior had never heard such an awful ruckus in his life. Every pounding, sonorous utterance pulsed through his brain and bade him rise to look around blearily. He felt terrible. For the first time in his life, he didn't remember what time he'd gone to sleep or the events leading up to that point. The last thing he remembered was joining in the chorus of a boisterous song of which he only knew a few words. Confused, the normally dexterous youth stumbled toward his captain.

"Good morning, Swift One!" Komeris cried cheerfully, slapping his young friend on the back.

Urietsin groaned and swayed at the hit. "Never have I awoken to such a horrible feeling. I think I was clubbed in the head last night."

Komeris chuckled heartily. "Yes, my friend, clubbed by a flask of wine,

I think. Perhaps next time you'll not accept a drink so readily, or so often."

"Or ever again," the Swift One croaked groggily.

"Here, drink this," the captain offered a liquid-filled skin to the young warrior.

Urietsin eyed the object warily, but accepted it and hazarded a sip. It was cool water, and it felt so good moistening his lips that he gulped at it greedily.

"Careful," warned Komeris. "Drink too quickly and you'll feel worse than you do now."

Not wanting to even imagine that possibility, Urietsin pulled the flask away, slowing his consumption to intermittent sips. "So, what is the plan for today?" he asked, already feeling a bit better.

"Well, I was just about to go and gather some soldiers and tell them what we discussed yesterday," Komeris replied.

Urietsin nodded. "Who did you have in mind?" he asked.

Komeris looked to the warrior with a smile. "Well, I was hoping you would offer your assistance in that...unless, of course, you're not feeling up to it?"

The Swift One's posture straightened suddenly and he shot Komeris an incredulous stare. "Of course, sir, I'm feeling fine now," he said eagerly, ignoring the dull ache that lingered in his head.

Chuckling, Komeris nodded and motioned for Urietsin to follow him. Together the young warrior and the captain selected nine soldiers from the group and brought them away from the camp to discuss their plan for exploring the mountain. "It may be to your advantage to travel up together, then form two groups of five to go in opposite directions. That way you cover more ground quickly," Komeris explained after giving the men a general idea of the assignment.

A hand went up in the group. It was the surly looking warrior that Urietsin knew all too well. "Yes, Reniu?" the captain asked.

"Yes, sir, who'll be leadin' this party?" Reniu asked with his traditional scowl.

Komeris smiled at this and stepped aside to indicate Urietsin. "I believe we'll let the Swift One have the honor."

Urietsin's head turned slowly to look at his captain. The young man bowed deeply.

The captain nodded and gave a slight bow in return. "I have complete confidence in your abilities, soldier." He turned a firm gaze to the rest of the group. "As should you all. Urietsin is a fine warrior, and you should all be honored to serve under his first command." His tone left no room for comment. With that he turned to Urietsin, bowed again, and walked off, leaving the young warrior to his assignment.

The Swift One turned to regard his party. He looked to each one of them looking for some sort of protest; there was none. All of these men were trained soldiers, and they all trusted Komeris's judgment. Urietsin shrugged. If Komeris had faith in him, then he would have faith in himself. He waved toward the campsite and said, "Okay, men, gather only what you will need for the climb. Meet me back here when you have everything, and we will begin the journey."

The party dispersed to retrieve the few things they would need that they were not already carrying. Urietsin stepped slowly, but confidently, toward the campsite. As he approached, Su-Ni came to meet him. "Are those men going to explore the mountain?" she asked.

Urietsin nodded. "Yes, we will climb halfway and split up to investigate both sides on our way to the opposite face," he told her.

"Is Komeris going with them?" Her tone suggested more than just casual inquiry.

Urietsin paused to regard her. "No, he has placed me in charge."

"I see," the young diplomat responded with her hands placed impatiently on her hips. "And which one of us will you be taking with you?"

The Swift One understood now. Su-Ni was afraid that the exploration would continue without a diplomatic representative. "None of you will be going with us. You can see there is no thriving city on the mountainside. Likely it will be more dangerous for one of you to be there. The mountain is no doubt crawling with vicious creatures, and a bit of loose rock may prove more hazardous than any animal."

Su-Ni turned an appraising stare at the mist-shrouded peak. "We can take care of ourselves," she said determinedly.

Urietsin grinned. There was more to this young woman than her looks. "I don't doubt you," he said, "but I assure you it will be unnecessary. With just this group of warriors we will be able to more quickly scout out the area. If we find any situation that requires your special prowess, we will return to escort you there safely."

The woman returned Urietsin's smile with one of approval. This warrior was skilled in many more ways than just fighting. He was proving to be very well spoken. Su-Ni was sure he could handle many diplomatic situations almost as skillfully as she. While she was just as curious as everyone else about the new lands they were exploring, she decided to be patient...for now.

She bowed to him and placed her hand on his arm. "Thank you. We will stay here and patiently await some word that we are needed."

The young warrior placed a hand on hers and grinned again. The silence that followed was immediately awkward. The pounding from earlier returned to Urietsin's head. He stood there for several moments trying to wipe the foolish smile from his face and to somehow remove his hand from hers in a way that seemed casual. A call from behind him broke the moment and he looked back to see a few of the soldiers waiting with their equipment.

Urietsin put his hand down and bowed quickly. "I must go now," he said with a serious expression.

Su-Ni nodded once and took a step back, indicating the path to the campsite. The warrior wasted no time and set a quick pace in that direction. "Swift one!" she called after him. Urietsin stopped and turned. "Do be careful," she said with a smile.

Urietsin gave a short nod and returned quickly to his walking. He was grinning again. On the way back to the campsite, and then to the meeting point with his equipment, the young warrior wondered at his behavior with Su-Ni. Of course, the Swift One was not so young and naive that he couldn't recognize the reactions of a man toward an attractive woman. And there was no doubt that Su-Ni was an attractive woman, but Urietsin had always prided himself on being in control of his emotions. The inability to rid himself of that grin proved otherwise.

The young warrior met up with the other soldiers and went over the plan once more. Thoughts of the exchange with Su-Ni were quickly lost as the men headed toward the mountain. It was not a very large peak compared to the rest that stretched out to either side as far as the eye could see. It would still take some time, and they were prepared for the possibility that they would have to camp on the mountain overnight.

As the morning went on, the group quickly saw that they were making good time, and it was just after midday when the party had reached the halfway point. Urietsin instructed the men to follow him just a little higher before they split up to either side of the mountain. He was thinking of the smoke he had seen rising from behind and made a guess at the elevation of the source. They climbed for another twenty minutes before going in opposite directions.

Four warriors were to follow Urietsin around the south face of the mountain, while four went north, led by Reniu. The surly but respectful warrior accepted the responsibility with pride and immediately began barking orders to the men. Urietsin turned the other direction and led his men southward along the mountainside.

Urietsin was ecstatic. Excitement pulsed through his veins as he expected something to pop out at them at every turn. The men grew hungry and suggested they stop to eat, but Urietsin urged them on. "Just a bit further," he said. A few quiet grumbles were heard, but the men pressed forward. In actuality, they were as excited to be there as Urietsin was.

Before long the small group of warriors came to an area of very sparse growth. Here the dirt was very dry and only a few small bushes grew. The most noticeable feature, however, was a large broken trunk lying on the ground. Urietsin brought his group to the trunk and they began to prepare their late lunch. Salted meat and bread was passed around, and each soldier took a healthy swig from his full water skin.

Urietsin was chewing slowly, peering around. He seemed much more intent on surveying the area than eating. Something seemed unnatural to him in this clearing. His instincts pulled him to investigate. He got up to start looking around, but then his eyes fell upon the enormous log that most of the men were resting against. It suddenly became very clear to him that this trunk had not simply fallen on its own.

The young warrior pointed to one of the ends. "Here, look at this," he said. The men looked around curiously. "Someone, or something, has brought down this tree recently."

His companions gathered around him. Perhaps not quite as quickly as their leader, the men began to see evidence that the tree had indeed been forced down and cut shorter. Urietsin pointed to a long trail in the dry dirt. It looked as though something heavy had been dragged that way. "Should we follow it, sir?" asked one of the men.

In answer the young warrior began walking in the direction of the trail. He did not get but a few steps away before he froze. There was something else. Urietsin could hear a quiet rustling in the trees ahead, and he felt as though he were being watched. The rest of the group stood a little behind him and exchanged confused glances. They knew something was amiss as well, but only because of Urietsin's change in posture. They could not hear anything apart from the wind rolling through the trees. A motion from the trees' edge in front of their commander, however, caught their full attention, and now they stood frozen as well.

A huge creature lumbered out from the foliage. It had the mass of a bear, but its wide snout and sharp, forward reaching tusks clearly identified it as another creature. Urietsin and his men remained still, not only because of the excessive size of this beast, but also because they knew what it was. When they were children they had all heard stories of the *gotori*. It was said to have eaten whole hunters alive and gored others to shreds.

It had been many years since any of the men had heard or even thought of those stories, but now, with the beast's bloodshot eyes rolling over them hungrily, every chilling detail returned to them. The gotori stepped toward the group slowly, sniffing the air as it went. Several steps short of the men, the creature pushed itself up on its hind legs and rose to its full height. The men's eyes followed the beast's head up, and they suddenly felt very small as this childhood nightmare towered over them. Unprovoked, the creature threw its great claws wide and let out a deafening roar as it charged straight for Urietsin and his men.

Up until this point, the Swift One had not been too sure of any course. Now, as this monster's tusks thrashed inches from his body, he sprang into decided action. Rolling to the left, the young warrior narrowly missed certain death as a tusk sailed over his ducked head. The rest of the men behind him were frightened, but they were no cowards, and similarly dodged the beast's initial attack without fleeing.

Urietsin came up from his roll just as the gotori's rear flank sailed past. He launched a kick that would have staggered a man much larger than himself. But this creature was many times larger than the largest man, and the kick only served to aggravate it. It turned quickly, blasting out another roar. Urietsin ran up, jumping right in front of the beast's face, his foot sailing toward its lower jaw. The gotori's roar stopped short as its mouth was slammed shut painfully by the Swift One's flying foot. The beast reared back to snatch the young warrior from the air, but Urietsin fell past the swatting claw back to the ground and dove through its legs. As Urietsin left his sight, the gotori's murderous glare shifted to the rest of the group, which was now advancing menacingly with spears. Instead of roaring this time, the beast let out a low, threatening growl. Behind it the Swift One stood silently, thinking that everything was now under control. Between the five of them, four with weapons, they should make short work of this creature.

The gotori had other ideas. It sprang forward in a flash, raking two of the men with its deadly claws before they could even raise their weapons in defense. The other two men dove to either side to avoid the beast's dangerous claws and tusks. When they rolled back to their feet, they saw their two comrades being gored mercilessly by the insane thrashings of their mad foe.

Urietsin was shocked by the speed with which the creature had finished off the two men, but he wasted no time lamenting their deaths. Not yet, when his life and the lives of the other two men were still in danger. He ran up behind the still thrashing beast and hit one of its rear legs with a low sweeping kick. The gotori's leg slid only slightly, but it stumbled low enough for the young warrior to plant his fist firmly into the thick fur of its haunches. The creature leapt forward to get out of Urietsin's reach and began to turn so that it could meet its enemy head on. The young warrior darted forward as the beast turned and jumped into the air for a flying sidekick that connected with rib thicker than his own leg. A satisfying crack echoed from the gotori's chest, and a howl of pain echoed from its throat. It finished its turn, revealing its blood-soaked tusks.

Urietsin winced at the sight, but prepared to punish the creature without mercy. From behind he heard one of the men yell, "Aside!" The Swift One skittered right, keeping a wary eye on the beast as he went. The young warrior watched incredulously as the gotori reared back and swatted a spear out of the air. He glanced back to see the man who had thrown it wearing a similar expression. Urietsin rushed back up to engage the monster, but the creature simply swung out with the back of its claw and charged the spear thrower. The hit clipped the Swift One's head and sent him flying away from the charging beast. He landed painfully against a tree and slumped to the ground, the air knocked from his lungs. Blackness crept into the edge of his vision as he shook his head stubbornly to clear it away.

Through the haze, Urietsin could see the fast moving form of the gotori crashing into a human shape. The whole scene was shifting in and out of focus, but the young warrior knew well enough that another of his companions had fallen. The situation was hopeless, that much was clear. Urietsin only hoped that the last man would be able to flee to safety. He pulled in a deep breath of air, his first, he realized, since being hit by the creature. The world came back into full focus with shattering intensity. The Swift One put his feet under him and attempted to rise. Balance, however, was still something of a challenge. His side hurt whenever he inhaled, and the entire left side of his head was numb where the creature had hit him.

The creature.

In trying to stand, Urietsin had somehow forgotten about the gotori. His head was still spinning and he felt almost giddy. The young warrior tried to blink his thoughts back into order. He looked up to see the beast several feet away staring back at him. For several moments all was completely silent as the two foes stared into each other's eyes. Then the gotori began to stalk its prey. The Swift One knew he was not in a position to defend himself. His vision was beginning to fade again, and his legs pleaded with him to sit down or a rest. He slumped against the tree and slid to the ground.

Gazing forward, Urietsin thought he saw something drop down behind the gotori. He disregarded the blur as the hazy fog that was reentering his vision. He now defocused, relaxing his eyes to stare at some nonexistent point far away from his present location. He could still see the gotori in his peripheral vision, low to the ground, getting ready to jump. A sudden quick motion from that direction made Urietsin close his eyes in defeat. This was the last second of his life.

As the thought dissipated throughout his body with a sad acceptance, he became painfully aware of how interminably long this second was lasting. Fate, it seemed, had a cruel way of manifesting itself. As the Swift One sat there, eyes shut, pondering the last moment before his vital flame was extinguished, it seemed ironic to him that this moment was very enlightening. A great understanding came to him all at once, but was lost as the swirling thoughts and harsh wounds dragged the young warrior mercifully into numbing unconsciousness.

* * *

Agucho stepped out onto the hard-packed earth of the Ionotu training field. Soldiers were everywhere, practicing their macabre skills with various edged weapons. They would have been quite a frightening sight to an innocent onlooker, but the shapeshifter had lived much too long to still be innocent. In fact, his own appearance on this field of mock battle and real blood caused the soldiers to pause in their tasks. The sight of this thing of childhood nightmares, the Fiu-Het, sent chills down the powerful backs of Ionotu's soldiers. They had seen him only once before, when he brought the seer to train with them. Now, as before, the men parted from his path as he headed straight for the same man he had brought with him during his previous visit.

The mage was encircled by a group of soldiers who had been 'sparring' with him. The circle of men opened as Agucho approached, and the shapeshifter could immediately see the cruel fun that the Ionotu army had been having with their newest recruit. Several old and fresh slash marks crossed his once smooth face. Bruises and welts covered almost every inch of exposed skin. He stood among the broken circle of soldiers weakly holding a longsword. Even if not for the obvious severity of his beatings, it was clear from the way the seer held the blade that he was not an experienced fighter. The Fiu-Het almost pitied the poor human.

"You," Agucho pointed a crooked finger at the mage, "come with me."

Relief softened the hard squint in Laernus's eyes, which had grown accustomed to flinching over the past week. The seer stumbled forward and dropped his heavy sword, almost cutting himself as he tripped over it. Not unexpectedly, one of the nearby soldiers sniggered derisively at the sight, drawing a threatening hiss from the shapeshifter. Just to further unnerve the now cowering soldier, Agucho sent his long sticky tongue out to twist over each bulging eye, staring at the man all the while. A visible shudder ran through the coward's body, and he turned away.

"Shouldn't you all be training?" the Fiu-Het gurgled.

Were general Vethisir there whipping them all with a spiked scourge he could not have motivated the soldiers more effectively. The men fell over each other trying to look hard at work for the creature who might sup on the unenthused. At least, that's the image that popped into most of their heads. Agucho grinned as only one of his race could, and fortunate were the men who were not looking, for that grin would not visit them tonight in their nightmares. The shapeshifter plodded away with Laernus in tow, leaving the soldiers to their own devices.

"Why have you come for me?" the seer asked after they had left the field behind. He drew a shaky breath. "Has the king..."

Agucho spun on his shadow. "You should know better than to ask that. The king has no interest in your well-being. I'm sure he believes you to be dead already. My business with you is my own."

The two walked a bit longer in silence before Laernus asked, "What, then, is your business? Shall I be free to go when it is done?"

A guttural chuckle issued from the Fiu-Het. "You shall be free to go on one condition...that you survive."

The mage stopped and watched the shapeshifter as he trudged on. "Survive what?" he asked.

Agucho stopped as well and turned to walk back to the seer. "I seek knowledge. Knowledge only you can provide to me. There is much that I am sure your skills can tell me, and I have an intuition that I will need the help. I will reward you for any assistance you give me, but do not mistake this...if you cross me, you will beg for your death long before I am finished with you."

"Very well. What would you have me do? I will do anything you ask if you take me away from those fiends!" Laernus looked over his shoulder, back the way they had come, back to the training field.

"You will do anything I ask anyways. You have no choice. But I will not take you from your training," the Fiu-Het responded assertively.

A look of terror washed over the seer's face, and he fell to his knees. "Oh, please do not send me back!" he pleaded, gripping his new master's cloak. "I will surely die!"

Agucho pushed the groveling human away in disgust. "You will not die, fool. If you do as I say, I will ensure your protection. The soldiers of Ionotu will not treat you as they have, but that does not mean you shouldn't train while you are with them. I want you to learn how to wield that weapon you were holding when I arrived today. You should make sure you are strong enough to wield it. Although you are the seer, I have a premonition of my own. I predict it will not be long before you are called upon to test your skills with that blade."

"Am I to go with the soldiers on their mission of expansion, then?" Laernus asked, picking himself up off the ground.

"Yes," replied the shapeshifter with an absent stare. "In fact, I think many of us will be joining you."

"Many of us? What do you mean?" the seer asked.

The Fiu-Het shook his head. "Nothing. Well, perhaps nothing. This is why I need you. You must use your gifts to advise me. I must keep one step ahead of Orbein. Many lives may depend upon it, for my people as well as yours. Follow me; we must leave the road for a more secret place. We don't want to arouse any more suspicions than we may have already."

* * *

General Vethisir stood just beyond the edge of the training field. He watched the unlikely duo step off the road and into the woods nearby. He was certain this was not Orbein's doing. He would be even more certain later when The Fiu-Het returned to send Laernus back into the ranks. Regardless, the moment the general had spied the king's new assistant on the field, retrieving the seer no more than a week after his induction, he knew something was amiss. And a secret meeting away from the castle? Orbein was bound to find this interesting. Vethisir chuckled as he imagined the shapeshifter's expression when the king administered his retribution upon the conspirators.

11 LAMENT

Komeris stared through the fire at the dark silhouette of the mountain against the starry night sky. The anxiety grew within him as the hour drew near midnight of the second day, and still no sign of the small scouting party could be seen. He had expected them back earlier this evening at the latest and thought that if they were on their way down, he would at least see a torchlight or two slowly descending. There was nothing, though, and the veteran soldier was seriously considering going up to look for them himself. He stood with this in mind and stepped around the fire, away from the rest of the soldiers. Many of them looked up at their captain, knowing the thoughts that creased his worried brow.

Out beyond the flickering light of the campfire, a noise issued forth from the darkness. Komeris crouched low and drew his sword quickly at the sound, ready for whatever might reveal itself. The rest of the warriors tensed, their hands going toward the closest available weapon. All held their breath as they peered into the darkness for the origin of the sound. Again it was heard, a sort of thump on the dirt ground. Immediately the other soldiers were standing, weapons drawn.

A shadow swayed just beyond the camp perimeter, catching the eyes of all the startled onlookers. "Show yourself!" Komeris called into the darkness. Shadows drew back as several figures stepped into the light.

Six figures, five men supporting one other, stumbled toward the campfire. It was Reniu and half of the party that had scaled the mountain. At first Komeris was relieved to see the men, until he realized that no more than these six had been approaching in the night. "Where are the others?" the captain asked sternly.

Reniu shook his head. "Don't know, sir. We found this man crawlin' down the mountain and mutterin' gibberish. He seems to have been beat somethin' terrible," he answered.

The captain walked up to the bruised warrior and tried to catch the attention of his wandering eyes. "What happened up there?" he demanded of the seemingly oblivious man.

Several such inquiries were made before the man began to tremble visibly. Finally, he shouted, "Gotori! The gotori lives...it killed them. It is real...I must flee!" He shrieked incoherently and struggled briefly with the soldiers who were helping him stand, then went limp and slouched to the ground, apparently unconscious.

Ominous whispers of the word gotori rippled through the crowd of warriors in the camp. Half-remembered childhood legends stirred up old fears in them, and many knuckles shone white as their grips tightened over their weapons.

Komeris's jaw twitched in frustration as he thought about those victims, if that was indeed what they were. He wasn't sure if he entirely believed in the gotori, though he didn't doubt that they had been attacked by something. He wouldn't give up hope on his four lost warriors until he found irrevocable evidence that they were dead. By daylight tomorrow he would lead a larger group to search for the wounded man's companions. He had an intuition that there may be at least one other who could have escaped the clutches of the mysterious attacker, even if it was the dreaded gotori.

The large Reniu had a scowl for every occasion, and he now wore one of perplexed unease. "Don't worry, sir, we'll be ready to find 'em when the sun's first ray splits the night sky," he said as if he had read his captain's mind.

True to his word, Reniu was awake to see the morning's sleepy yellow eye peek over the horizon. Beside him stood Komeris, who was grateful to see the beginnings of this sunrise but was not about to waste time admiring it. The two gave each other a hopeful look and set about waking the other tired warriors. It had not been a restful night for many of them as they tossed and turned thinking of their lost comrades and their probable fate in the claws of the gotori.

Komeris carefully, but quickly, selected the group that would follow him up the mountainside. There were nine strong men, four of whom had followed Reniu two days before, one woman whose skill with a blade was yet unmatched in the empire, and Reniu and Komeris made twelve. Twelve warriors set out from the camp that morning, heavily armed, to journey up the mountain and find the men who had not returned.

With the larger group of people and much more gear, mostly weaponry, there was a noticeable difference in progress up the mountain compared with the group from the previous day. It was very late in the afternoon when the search party reached the point where Reniu and Urietsin had gone in opposite directions. The group did not stop to rest or eat, however.

Instead they continued on in the direction that the Swift One's group had chosen two mornings ago. From that point on, the terrain was not too rough, and it took little time for them to reach the site of the gotori attack.

Signs of the struggle were clearly evident all throughout the area. Blood was caked upon the ground where it had pooled after the fight. Dirt and grass had been gouged out of the ground in several spots. Footprints and claw marks circled each other and crossed here and there. Komeris scrutinized the evidence and tried to piece together the battle in his mind. The conclusions he was coming to were not very pleasant.

"They never stood a chance," he said sadly. "From the looks of it, this creature would be a challenge even for the twelve of us."

Pei-Shi, the female blade master, pointed to the long trail of blood that stretched beyond the surrounding trees. "It looks like the bodies were dragged this way," she said.

Komeris shook his head. "I'm not sure. Look how wide the grooves in this path are. This seems a bit more than what would be left by men's bodies."

"There's no way we're knowin'," remarked Reniu thoughtfully. "'Till last night we never thought of the gotori as anythin' but a myth."

The captain nodded, but doubt still sculpted his expression. "If this was even a gotori. The man who survived might be mistaken. They may have been attacked by a bear or some other common mountain creature," he said.

"If the creature is real, it may be just as common in these mountains as a bear would be," suggested Pei-Shi. The comment drew many apprehensive looks from her fellow fighters; they looked as though maybe they had enough exploration for one day.

Reniu, big though he was, looked around warily. "I'm fer bettin' that whatever it was that attacked the men left nothin' of them to find, and I don't think I want to be around when it gets hungry again."

Komeris gazed into the trees beyond the clearing, uncertainty on his brow. It was clear that even though there were twelve of them, no one was looking forward to coming face to face with the creature that had done this. Still, he did not want to leave without being certain that the lost men were indeed lost forever, and if they were, he wished to find their remains and give them an honorable burial.

Conflicting thoughts battled each other in the captain's head as he watched the sun approaching the horizon. Dusk would be on them in a couple of hours, and though he desperately wanted to find some clue to convince him of the group's fate, he also did not want to make the other soldiers stay up here in the dark of night if they did not wish to. He looked back to the east and noticed a thick plume of smoke rising into the sky from where he knew the campsite to be.

He pointed and bade his soldiers to look. "Either there's trouble or they are signaling us. Let us hope it's the latter, for there's already been too much trouble for my liking," he muttered.

"Are we goin', then?" Reniu asked.

Komeris thought for a moment. "Yes, you may go. I will stay and look around a bit longer."

"Captain, are you sure that's wise?" Pei-Shi asked.

"I must know what happened to my men," he said firmly.

"Then I shall stay with you," the blade master said.

"As shall I," Reniu echoed the sentiment.

"No," Komeris said, holding up his hand before anyone else could join in.

"Pei-Shi, you may stay with me, if you like," the captain said. "The rest of you go and make sure everything is well at the camp. If they are in trouble, they will need your strength. We will follow shortly."

Reniu and the other warriors stood and looked at the captain for a long while. "Very well, sir," Reniu answered finally. Then he added, "Be careful."

"Don't worry," Komeris reassured them. "If we come upon serious danger, we will flee."

Reniu nodded his agreement with that logic. With a quick bow to the captain and Pei-Shi, he turned and ordered the rest of the warriors to follow him down the mountain.

As soon as they were out of sight, Komeris began to inspect the ground.

"What are we looking for?" asked Pei-Shi.

"Any sign of Urietsin and his men," the captain replied without looking up.

Pei-Shi nodded. "Well, whatever made that track in the dirt, we should probably follow it," she suggested.

Komeris nodded and began to step along the path into the trees marked by the gouge. Pei-Shi followed quickly behind. They tracked the markings easily for most of the way, but as the sun edged closer to the western peaks, and the ground became firmer, their task became more difficult. As the shadows grew to cover almost everything, the two came upon a clearing. Komeris hurried quickly toward the middle of the open area.

"What is it?" Pei-Shi asked, staring at the low, flat grouping of stones.

"A hearth," said Komeris.

"Here? In the mountains?" she asked in disbelief. "It must be old. The dwelling has deteriorated around it."

"No," the captain answered. He wiped his fingers along the surface of the hearth and held them up. Even in the dim light he could see that they were black. "Soot," he said. "This was the source of the smoke seen by the elves at the forest's edge."

"But...who could have lived here?"

Komeris shook his head. "More importantly, did whoever it was come across Urietsin's men?" he asked.

Nearby, a pair of wide eyes watched from a hiding place. They looked from the man to the woman, then down to the warrior who lay unconscious and, likewise, hidden. The eyes closed in concentration. Theirs was as much a hiding place of the mind as it was a physical location. He could not risk being discovered. Despite the longing he felt at seeing the two familiar warriors, Kiusu could not let them come between him and his destiny.

"Captain, it's getting dark," Pei-Shi said hesitantly, though the sunlight was already almost completely gone.

Komeris continued to look around. Quite suddenly he called out, "Urietsin!"

Other than the echoes that reverberated across the valley, there was no answer.

Komeris looked to Pei-Shi and nodded resignedly. "Let's go," he sighed.

Together they strode off as the stars multiplied.

Dusk had long relinquished its hold on the sun's lingering light, and night had overtaken the sky when the two warriors strode back into camp exhausted, their torches announcing their arrival well in advance. Reniu ran up to welcome them back.

"It was a messenger from the empire," he explained to Komeris. "Said he had urgent news from the emperor and the general."

Even through his tired eyes, Komeris looked surprised. "What was it?" he asked.

"First," said Reniu, "did you find anything of 'em?"

"I wish I could say that we did," he replied, grief evident in his tone. "We did find the remains of a dwelling of some sort, burned down recently."

"But no one around ta claim it?" the big man asked.

Komeris shook his head. "We shall have to go back tomorrow, when it's light."

Reniu looked away and sighed.

"What?" asked Komeris.

"It'll have ta wait, captain. There's more pressin' business. General Etrusin is makin' his way ta the edge of the forest with a thousand soldiers," Reniu explained.

Komeris reeled back at this, shaking off his weariness. "A thousand!" he exclaimed. "Moving with the general outside the empire? What has happened?"

"I don't know fer certain, but the rider said somethin' about an enemy comin' from the west. We're buildin' the army ta defend the empire!" Reniu shouted.

"One thousand soldiers makes for a pitiful army, although it is the largest force we've had since the days of Reisothin. Etrusin will have to recruit a lot more warriors to compete with the numbers it took to defeat that beast. Hopefully the current threat is not so great," said the captain.

Reniu nodded. "The general's sendin' out more requests through the empire. Any who're fit ta train and fight are welcome and needed. The messenger said he needs us ta return and help with the trainin' at the new camp."

Komeris's gaze shifted to the black shadow of the mountain against the sea of stars. The silhouette, which had held much promise three nights before, slashed the sky in two and seemed to the captain a blight upon the horizon, reaching for the fully-risen moon. "Good men were lost up there yesterday," he said after a moment of thoughtful silence.

"Yes," agreed Reniu. "Wish we could've found 'em."

Something about that wish pulled at the back of the captain's mind. It didn't seem right that he should have found nothing of the men except for footprints and blood caked in dirt. No warrior gave any argument or question to the orders to break camp. Though they did not wish to go without knowing what had happened to their brothers in arms, they knew it was more important business that called them east. The diplomats, one specifically, did not seem to be so understanding.

"How can we leave before discovering their fate?" implored Su-Ni.

"I do not wish to leave this matter unsolved either, but we have orders from the empire," Komeris explained.

"Your orders, not mine!" she stated firmly.

"Su-Ni! Know your place," rebuked Ninei, then to Komeris, "Forgive her, sir, she is saddened by the loss of those brave men."

"As are we all," was the captain's reply. "As are we all." He looked one last time to the westward looming shadow, and a grim expression descended upon his face. He did share Su-Ni's grief, especially for the talented young Swift One. Although none of the warriors were expendable, it was he for whom Komeris felt the most sorrow. Such energy and promise, stolen from the world. Again he thought of the clearing near the south face of the mountain where he could find no remnant of the men but the markings on the ground. So unusual it seemed to him that there remained no gear, little though they took, and no weapons, just blood and footprints and a gouge in the earth that lead to a burned down shelter.

* * *

Niele'itio. Urishenutoi'isonu.

Orbein read the words as he had countless times before. They conjured up a whirlwind of images in his mind. Dark City. The fruitless victory. The stark spacing of his city's title accentuated the hopelessness felt by the men who erected this monument. They had carved it on a massive slab of smooth stone and hoisted it upon two colossal pillars. An overhang protected the deeply-carved relief from the elements and had been kept in perfect repair for generations by the military. It was visible to all in the city, a constant reminder of its abysmal beginnings.

Scanning down the columns, Orbein could see more references to those beginnings. The left column contained carven imagery of lines of soldiers marching upon the bones of their fallen victims. The right depicted men searching desperately along a forest's edge for some kind of path, any opening at all. It was the story of how the city came to be as it was. It was the story that fueled Orbein's pretense for war and made his people so easy to manipulate.

It was also the entrance to the grounds of the city temple, and Orbein stood there studying the pillars for several minutes, as he had many times before. Finally, he turned his attention away from the frozen history and made his way to the temple doors. They opened, as all the doors in the temple appeared to, on their own, and the king hurried down the main corridor to his destination.

An otherworldly glow filled the main chamber of the dark temple of Niele'itio. It was not the natural light of the sun. Even if the sun's bright rays could penetrate the haze-choked sky over the Dark City, they would do little besides emit a dim, purple shimmering through the windows that did more to confuse sight than to help it. The light came instead from blue orbs that protruded randomly about the walls of the chamber. What powered them only the priests of the temple could say, but they never shared such secrets with any but the men of their order. No priest was present, however, and the lights now sent out their eerie illumination for only one person.

Orbein stood before the sacrificial pit that dipped in toward the middle of the room. He looked into its empty shadows. It seemed to him as though it had become a hole into eternity. Staring into its depths, the king's eyes moved as he followed motion that only he could see. The shadows parted, and he saw a great army marching down the slopes of Thontur. At first he thought this was a vision of his army arriving home from a victorious campaign. He soon realized that this was not the case. The men were stern-faced and road weary, but not battle worn. Their uniform was not that of his own army, but a light colored leather with a golden leonine device emblazoned on a segmented breastplate.

These men marched toward Orbein, and he saw their ranks, so thick that when the front line stepped beyond the roots of the great mountain, more still flowed over its jagged peak. Their expressions were grim, and their advance was strangely silent. Tens of thousands of soldiers walked over the soil where, even now as the king had this vision, his own men were training. In this waking dream, though, the field of Ionotu was empty, and the army from the east came ever on unimpeded. They marched right up to a massive gate set in a great wall.

Orbein knew that this was not his city, but it was certainly the ground upon which Niele'itio was built. In place of his plain, square dwellings, there arose a noble city, clean and beautiful. White buildings reached for the clouds, several of them capped with gold. A majestic bouquet of palatial towers trumpeted itself as the crown jewel of this peaceful setting. The brightness of all that assaulted his eyes was contrasted by an all-encompassing silence. This did not appear as a city that was about to find itself besieged by a massive army.

The charge was called out over the ranks, and a crest of shining helmets swelled against the wall, a raging stormy sea against stark stone cliffs. Great sharpened rams were heaved at the gate, and towers were pushed up against the battlements so that soldiers could pour down into the city. Men soon filled the streets. Then the real carnage began. Women and children were dragged out of their homes and slaughtered; their bodies were left to lie in the gutters. Houses were set ablaze, and a thickening circle of smoke crept inward toward the palace. The streets were soon filled almost to overflowing with the bodies of the innocent and the fell soldiers from beyond Thontur. An enormous contrivance, the like of which Orbein had never seen, was rolled up to the palace gate.

The king looked on with amazement and great interest as a mass of pitch was loaded onto this contraption and flung ablaze over the gate and into a great colored window that adorned the palace like a big glass painting. Glass exploded, and he actually ducked and threw up his hands in defense.

Orbein wondered at his reaction and scoffed at being startled by a vision that existed only in his mind. His curiosity grew further as he realized that he felt shards falling on him from above. He ventured a peek and saw something fall into the pit among a pile of shattered glass. He was again in the main chamber of the temple, and a great gaping hole in the dark glass let in a breeze that cooled the beads of sweat on his brow. Looking back into the shadows of the pit, the king saw something stirring ever so slightly, and tiny curling fingers of steam brought a terrible stench to his nostrils.

Shaking off the lingering remnants of his trance, Orbein stepped cautiously into the pit. Glass crunched under his boots, which made it impossible for him to move down silently. After several tense moments, he had eventually crept up to the steaming shadow as best he could. He could not see well enough to make out what it was, and he prodded it with the toe of his boot. It hissed in a way that seemed all too familiar to him. He bent down and began to feel in the shadows, looking for some way of holding this thing so he could bring it into a more well-lit area and confirm his suspicion.

Orbein's hand wrapped around something leathery that was sparsely covered with either fur or feather, which it was he could not say for certain. A long and low whimper issued from the shadow as the king tried to lift whatever it was out of the glass. Though he could tell this thing was small, at most the size of a wild dog, it was also deceptively heavy. Still, he did not put forth any great effort in carrying it; rather he dragged it unceremoniously through the broken shards and out of the pit. Much sputtering and whining could be heard from the creature, for it was surely a living thing. The sounds did not bother Orbein, and he was only careful enough to make sure he didn't kill the thing outright.

He sighed as he approached the wall. He could see no better near the strange blue lights than he could away from them. He pulled the creature toward the door, which opened as he came near.

Light poured into the chamber from the vast hallway beyond and the many candles that adorned it. There in the doorway, Orbein stooped to get a closer look at his burden. His breath caught as he beheld it in full light. It was hideous. The creature seemed very bat-like, but malformed in the most horrible way. Its lips were curled in a feral expression, and a line of pus streamed off its back.

As Orbein examined this strange perversion of a beast, its eyes opened and blinked wearily. It stared at first, as if blind, but then it focused on the king. A whine sounded out as the creature attempted to withdraw from the king's grasp. It struggled for only a moment before a gleam of recognition sparked in its eyes. A shudder ran through its body, and a sickening crack echoed through the hall as Orbein watched the creature's face contort in a way that did not seem possible. The leathery skin and tufts of fur twisted and reorganized, and when they finally settled, the king recognized the face of his scout Gayossha, prince of the Fiu-Het.

An astonished gasp came out of the shadows not made by either the king or the prince. From behind a column stepped Agucho. He ran up and looked upon the face of his cousin and former master and became sad to see it, though he would later be thankful to Laernus for making this reunion possible. It was clear to Agucho that his prince was in great pain and very close to death. The wounds on his back were grievous enough to wonder why he was still alive.

"Oh, my prince," Agucho sobbed. "What terrible fate has befallen you?"

At the sound of this familiar voice, Gayossha turned to behold his kinsman. "My cousin," he croaked sickeningly. "You must help...my revenge. Our people...mussst fight. Old man and...the empire. Fly! Fly over the mountains! Kill the enemies of our people! Especially the old man of Eastmountain!" These last screeching statements seemed to be too much for the prince, and he slumped limply in Orbein's hands.

"Oh, Gayossha!" lamented Agucho as he knelt with his face in his hands. The Fiu-Het began muttering other things, but whether it was because the words were in his own tongue or completely muddled by sobs, the king could not understand them.

Orbein released his hold on the lifeless body of the Fiu-Het prince, and as he did it began to twist and grow. Within moments the grotesque, bat-like shape was replaced by Gayossha's original form. Agucho paused in mid-sob to watch as the prince's corpse seemed to deflate, as if it had been a skin filled with only air. It was said among the Fiu-Het that the bones were the house of the soul, because after its departing, the body becomes nothing more than a bag of flesh, and when the flesh decays and turns to dust, no remains are left behind aside from a pile of ragged clothing.

The king watched Gayossha's corpse dissolve without so much as a blink or raised eyebrow. He knew that his scout had just died before his very eyes. His wonderful marvelous scout. Joy welled up within him even as his newest, and now only, Fiu-Het agent despaired at his feet. Though this scenario had been unexpected, it was better than he could have ever hoped for. Now he had the perfect purpose for dragging the Fiu-Het into his war. He guessed that they would be unable to resist offering their assistance.

* * *

Urietsin saw a light piercing the darkness, but as from far away. He felt like he had been wandering through a dark cave or tunnel. Voices whispered his name, some inviting, some desperate. He felt as though things were reaching for him, and whether it was for help or to pull him deeper into the impenetrable darkness, he could not say. It all frightened him. He could not tell if he was walking or swimming or flying, and he never knew which way was up. But he was moving, and whatever his orientation, he refused to go near the wall of the cave. He was not sure how he accomplished this, as he could not see anything, but he somehow remained just out of reach of the hands that grasped and the voices that whispered.

He couldn't tell how long he wandered, for time seemed to have no real meaning in this place. At times it felt like he had been there for an eternity and others only minutes. It was a place where five seconds ago seemed further away than the hour that had just passed. Not a moment went by that he didn't hear a voice whispering for him or feel a rush of air as something tried to grab him. He was beginning to believe that there would be no end to this dark tunnel of lost souls.

Unexpectedly, the light had come tearing through the black shadow and showed Urietsin the way. It was like the sun was shining on his face after a dark, cold winter, and he basked in its energy. The grasping hands shrank back, and the whispers fell silent, giving way to a strong voice that called clearly to him. This new voice did not frighten him, and he sped along the tunnel toward the light. Although he did not know where he would end up, he knew it would be a place where he belonged; it would be home.

The Swift One emerged from the obscurity, and the light closed around him as the tunnel disappeared into nothingness. At first it seemed as though his world was just one white brightness, but colors slowly separated themselves from the light until he saw a blurry collage of familiar vibrance. As he remembered how to see through his eyes once again, the world came into focus.

He was under a tiny hide shelter that opened out to a small clearing in sparse woods. The hide over him was covered with a dense fur. He reached up and caressed it gently, but as he did a pain shot through his head. His hand went to the pain, and he felt a deep bruise throbbing under his scalp on the back of his skull. Memories flooded back to him of his last conscious moments. He marveled at his apparent survival of the horrific events that had befallen him and his companions.

Crawling out from under the lean-to, Urietsin suddenly felt sore and much battered. His muscles ached, and as he examined himself, he saw many cuts and bruises, though they had been cleaned and well-tended. It took much strength and a moment of deep breathing before he could stand without swaying. He regained his bearings and looked back on his little shelter. The side that pointed out toward the elements was still fairly fresh and curing. Something within told the Swift One that he was looking at a gotori skin. Beyond the shelter, in the center of the clearing, stood a scorched, but sturdy-looking stone foundation and a hearth with strips of meat hung and drying over cooling embers.

The Swift One headed toward the hearth to investigate a bit more closely. The sound of a crunching leaf from somewhere behind sent him into a spinning crouch. His vision blurred as intense pain spidered throughout his ribcage from the sudden tensing of bruised muscle around fractured bone. He was not yet strong enough to have made such an intense motion. His mind struggled to hold onto consciousness as his body urged him to give into the sweet darkness again. This time it was his mind that won out, and he forced his eyes into focus.

The world looked strange to him, and he had trouble regaining his bearings. When he finally did, he realized that he was lying on his side. His chest was very tight from the sudden shock, and his breath came in short, intermittent gasps. He waited for a moment, trying to relax his lungs and let the air just flow. As his breathing returned to normal, he became increasingly aware that he was not alone. Something was moving toward him from behind the foliage, and whatever it was, it was about to step into the open. Urietsin, determined to look into the eyes of his oncoming fate, forced himself to sit up. With pain-clenched teeth, he peered intensely at the brush that blocked the advancing target from his sight.

"You should be resting."

The clear, stern voice that had sounded from beyond the clearing nearly caused the startled young warrior to leap from his seated position. Pain, however, kept Urietsin grounded, and he squinted in the direction of the voice. "Who are you? Show yourself!" he called, managing to sound quite confident, despite his vulnerable state.

An elderly figure stepped around the brush and stood for a moment staring at The Swift One appraisingly. At least, the figure looked elderly at a glance, but upon closer inspection, Urietsin realized that this was only because of the long gray beard and bald crown. In all other respects, this man appeared much younger. Dense musculature rippled slightly as he shifted his weight and dropped the very large section of tree trunk he had been carrying over one shoulder. In a symphony of graceful balance and dexterous posture, the strange, ageless man stepped over the uneven ground to where the young warrior sat. "You should not have risen. Your wounds are still quite serious," he said.

"I feel fine," Urietsin lied with a tensed jaw. "Just a few bruises."

The elder man smiled. "Yes, a few very serious bruises. The kind that require rest to heal."

"How long have I been resting?" the Swift one asked.

"Just about three days, and it is good that you have awakened. Had you slept much longer, I would have feared you lost in the dark forever."

Those words chilled Urietsin's very spirit, and he shuddered visibly. It made him feel very tired. He looked to the bed of soft furs upon which he had been laying only moments before. The old man followed his gaze and smiled, offering the Swift One a hand. He understood what the young warrior had seen in his brush with death and how it could seem frightening to one so inexperienced. He helped Urietsin to his feet and supported him as he walked back to the lean-to.

Sitting upon the piled furs beneath the shelter, the Swift One looked up thoughtfully. "I wonder," he prompted, "how did you find me?"

"In a bad way," the older man replied, sitting on the bare ground next to the shelter. "The gotori had slain those other men you were with. It was about to finish you when I arrived."

"So, the other men are..."

"Dead, yes. I buried the three of them and their weapons in a spot not far from here," the man replied.

Urietsin's brow furrowed. "The three of them? Where was the fourth? There was a fourth man with us."

The young warrior's caretaker shrugged. "I know not. Perhaps he was able to flee before my arrival, as you all should have done. The gotori is a deadly foe, able to take out many more than just five men at once."

"But you defeated him alone?" the Swift One asked doubtfully.

"A warrior's mind is his greatest weapon. With it he can defeat even the strongest foe."

At that Urietsin fell into a contemplative silence and did not respond for several moments. "Well, once again I ask, who are you?"

"I was called Kiusu Tho-Shoishu when my name was still called by men of the world. A warrior sometimes and a seeker of wisdom always, but most simply, I am just a man living in solitude in the mountain wilderness."

Urietsin's jaw fell open and he bowed his head. "You're name is well known in the empire. My father told me stories of how you and your master helped to defeat Reisothin. It is my greatest honor to meet you."

Now it was Kiusu who was silent. The young warrior spoke of the past as if it was so distant, but to the long-lived hermit, the time of the dragon was not so long ago at all. After a moment of reflection, he looked back to Urietsin and smiled. "Rest again, young one. Tomorrow you can tell me more of the empire. Long has it been since I last heard another human's voice. Now that I have heard yours, I long to hear more. Rest and rise healthier tomorrow."

Urietsin wasn't sure if he was truly tired enough to sleep. His body was wearied from the effort of rising today, but his mind raced with thoughts that he felt sure would keep him wide awake. As this hero of the empire spoke to him, though, he felt his eyes closing of their own will. It seemed to him that this Kiusu was lulling him to slumber with his soft words. Unable to keep a hold on his usual alertness, the young warrior slipped into the folds of a deep sleep. As he succumbed to his subconscious, several images flashed through the haze of his resting mind. Each one never came into full focus, but he could see the faces of the men who had fallen to the gotori staring back at him sadly.

Urietsin had rested a few more days at Kiusu's urging, but eagerness and quick healing found him out of bed within a week and exploring the area that had been his host's home for two decades. So frequent were his explorations that Kiusu had rarely any time to hear much about the empire he had left so long ago. The old man noticed the Swift One's curiosity with no small measure of satisfaction. This inquisitive, intelligent, and observant young warrior would make the perfect pupil. Of course, Urietsin knew nothing of Kiusu's intentions, but the time was quickly approaching for this information to be revealed. For as he healed, the Swift One seemed closer and closer to the conclusion that he would eventually have to rejoin his companions and report the outcome of his mission.

"Swift One!" Kiusu called, fond of Urietsin's nickname like so many others seemed to be.

Urietsin bounded over to the old man and helped him lift a large section of timber closer to the already nearly completed hut. The young warrior strained slightly at the weight, but Kiusu hardly even breathed heavily. He suspected that the unceasingly amazing man didn't truly need his help, but he seemed to ask for it more and more as the days went by. The two laid the wood down by the gaping front section of the hut, which needed the most work. Urietsin stood up and adopted a pensive pose.

"What is it?" the perceptive old man asked.

"I shall be leaving you soon. I must get back to my party and let them know that I am still alive and that the others are..." the young warrior trailed off, unable to finish.

Kiusu's brow furrowed. "Hmm..." was his only response.

"Of course, I thank you for saving my life, and for tending to my injuries. For that I owe you an enormous debt. Know that you will see me again so that I may repay it," the Swift One amended quickly, fearing he had hurt the old man's feelings.

Kiusu simply raised an eyebrow and nodded. Now seemed as good a time as any. He looked down at the trunk sitting before him, then closed his eyes.

Urietsin flinched, suddenly startled at the seemingly impossible event that manifested before him. Somehow the old man was crouching low with his fist pointing downward, though the young warrior hadn't actually seen him move. Even more startling was the loud crack that echoed over the mountainside as the two now cleanly separated halves of the trunk flew away from each other with incredible momentum.

Urietsin moved his mouth a few times, looked from one half of the trunk to the other, then finally found his voice. "How?" was all he could manage to say. He had seen the old man perform amazing feats of strength over these past several days, but nothing that seemed so implausible as this.

Kiusu smiled. "There is no explanation I could give to you that would provide a true understanding of what I just did. You would have to do it yourself."

The Swift One shook his head. "I can't even believe you did it. How could I possibly do it?"

"You don't believe I did it? Why?" the old man asked.

"Because it is not possible for a man to do that. Even if he is as strong as you appear to be," Urietsin replied.

"You believe it is not possible for a man to do what I just did, and yet I did it. What does that tell you?" The question was wrapped in expectation and filled with hope.

Urietsin was silent for several moments as a jumble of thoughts fought to converge into one simple answer. "My belief is incorrect."

Kiusu beamed. "It would be better to say that your perceptions are limited. Here is a secret truth you should always remember, Urietsin: although the world would like you to think differently, your reality is a slave to your perceptions."

Urietsin turned this over in his mind quietly. Eventually he said, "But how can that be? Reality is what it is."

Kiusu chuckled. He remembered the days when he asked that very same question. He now understood the amused expression on his master's face. "Allow me to demonstrate," he said. The old man bent over and moved the dirt around until he found a small piece of rock. He placed it in the palm of his hand and held it up for Urietsin to see.

"Are you going to tell me this pebble only exists because I perceive it?" the young warrior asked.

"Not quite," said Kiusu with a smile. Slowly, he closed his hand around the rock, his fingers completely concealing it from view. His other hand hung passively by his side. "Now tell me," he said, "does the stone still exist in my hand?"

"I do not see how it could be otherwise," the Swift One replied.

The old man smiled mischievously and opened his palm to reveal nothing. The stone was gone.

Urietsin's expression, however, was one of skepticism. "A simple trick," he said. "My father used to produce coins and trinkets from behind my ears when I was a child. That was no different."

"Really?" asked Kiusu. "And yet you were convinced that the stone was still there only moments ago."

Urietsin shook his head stubbornly. "A trick," was his only response.

"Perhaps," the old man replied, "but even if that is so, where is the stone?"

The Swift One's brow creased momentarily, but then he shot Kiusu a triumphant look. "If reality was a slave to my perceptions, as you say, and I perceived the stone to be in your hand, why wasn't it?"

His retort did not have the effect he had expected. Instead of realizing his folly, the old man seemed even more amused at Urietsin's debate. "Your reality, Swift One. Only your reality is such a slave. You may have thought the stone was still in my hand, but I knew that it wasn't. This demonstrates the difference between existence and reality. Reality is perceived by an individual; it is an abstraction of existence. In many cases we are taught to limit that abstraction, but by broadening our perceptions we can get a better idea of what existence truly is and the infinite ways in which we may interact with it."

Urietsin wore a blank expression. It was clear that he had no response, and after several moments of blinking, it was also clear that one was not forthcoming. Kiusu walked over and patted his shoulder. "Do not worry, Swift One, you will understand. I will show you, if you wish."

"You will teach me how to do the things you do?" Urietsin asked, waving to one of the trunk halves.

"No," replied Kiusu, "but I will teach you how to discover them for yourself." He gave the young warrior one more pat on the shoulder and walked back toward the foliage.

Urietsin watched him go with no small measure of intrigue. He was fascinated by the possibility of being able to do the things he saw Kiusu do. He absently walked over to one of the trunk halves that the old man had punched through, debating with himself about whether he should stay or leave. He sat down on the wood, which was easily two feet in diameter, but jumped up quickly rubbing his backside. There, on the smooth bark where Urietsin had tried to sit, was the stone the old man had held, unmistakable in shape. He saw no way that Kiusu could have placed it there without him seeing, trick or no. Now his mind was made up.

* * *

Captain Komeris had led a tired but determined march from the base of the eastern mountain back to the forest. The journey was a bit longer than it had been in the opposite direction, as the party had moved more slowly through weariness and sadness. Many more torches had been lit at night than was necessary, and the group had stayed close together, many of the scouts fearing the gotori, or perhaps some other beast forgotten to all but legend, would pounce upon them from the shadows.

But rest did not come when they arrived. Many of the captain's men groaned internally as they were sent out to collect whatever would assist in the building of a semi-permanent camp for the general and his forces. Some went to work felling a small group of trees for the necessary timber, while others hunted for food. Komeris had small groups sleep in shifts as the majority of the camp readied the site for the imminent arrival of the imperial soldiers. By the ninth day, the camp was beginning to take on a more finished look, and the captain eased up on the workload.

It was just after midday, and many exhausted soldiers were resting and waiting, when a startled cry rang out from the edge of camp. Though they were tired from the labors of the past several days, every warrior rushed, weapon in hand, toward the sound. As they approached the line of trees that marked the entrance to the forest, they slowed cautiously and fanned out.

The young diplomat Su-Ni lay motionless on the path into the wood. A figure, cleverly camouflaged in forest colors, stood over her, shifting purposefully as if to make itself noticed. It was the Shionen elf Tilon, and as the warriors realized his concealment, so did they also see a line of elven archers stretching out as far as could be seen on either side of him. Though they stood as still as statues under the overhang of the canopy, their intent seemed clear as they held every arrow-cocked bowstring taught and took aim at a human.

While all of his warriors stood tense and ready for a fight, Komeris stepped forward, weapon down. "What is the meaning of this, friend? Have we offended in some way?" he asked pleadingly.

"Friend?" came the cold response. "I think you use that word too lightly, or perhaps you do not know its meaning. Friends have need for deception?"

"Tell me, Tilon, in what way have we deceived you? I do not understand."

The elf shot him a dangerous scowl. "Do not feign ignorance with me, human. It is a game your race plays all too well, but I am not fooled. A thousand warriors now approach our location from the east. They come to join with you, no doubt, trampling the forest as they go, causing almost as much destruction as you have here." He waved angrily at the fresh stumps that had once supported healthy trees. "Do not say you know nothing of this."

Komeris nodded and sheathed his weapon before he answered. "Yes, Tilon, I did know of their approach, but only after our last meeting. A rider was sent to us with a message to return here and arrange a camp for the arrival of the soldiers led by our general. I say to you truly that I was as surprised as you to discover this."

The captain's voice was sincere and Tilon's scowl softened for a moment. He was now not so much angry as cautious. "Why do they come?" he asked.

"Why do you not ask them yourself?" a melodic voice called from deeper in the forest. Marui emerged from a grouping of trees and stepped down the path toward Tilon. "As you should have done before you took this action." She indicated the archers with a look of disappointment.

Tilon turned to look at her, then back to Komeris. The air thickened with a tense silence. The elf's face was blank, his expression washed away in a wave of uncertainty. It was he who broke the spell, holding up his hand and calling out in Shionen. Many of the humans flinched at this, but it became clear that the order was to withdraw as the archers dissolved back into the forest. Tilon knelt. "Do not be afraid," he said quietly to Su-Ni. "You may rise."

Komeris heaved a relieved sigh when he saw the diplomat rise unharmed. He noticed that Tilon glanced at him as he did so. The captain had momentarily forgotten how well elves could hear and realized that his sigh had likely been interpreted for what it was.

As if he could hear the captain's very thoughts, the elf nodded. "Yes, captain, she is not harmed. I am not as hasty as you might think, merely wary. I know you are not equipped with the ability to hear them, but your countrymen approach. They shall arrive momentarily, and then we shall find out what your true purpose is."

"I assure you, Tilon, it will be as enlightening to me as it will be to you," Komeris replied.

Men and elves stood silently in their places as they waited for the general to appear. Minutes dragged on uncomfortably while the human warriors strained to hear what the elves already could. Eventually, the rhythmic sound of armored feet marching in time seeped through the light rustle of the leaves in the gentle wind. The sound grew steadily until it drowned out all else.

To Komeris, who had been straining to hear like the rest of his men, each echoing footfall became a deafening boom. He almost despaired to hear it. It had been many years since that sound had been heard by any in the empire, and all of the warriors who were old enough to remember stood in apprehensive awe of its implications. Any who had not wondered at the purposes behind their mission before, wondered now.

A call rang out over the thunderous march, and at once all was silent. Tilon turned to face the forest, presumably to wait for the appearance of the general, but Komeris noted how he cocked his head sideways and looked up to the trees. The captain knew that the elven archers were still watching, hidden among the boughs of the forest. Boldly, he stepped across the grassy space between his men and the opening from which the elf watched the foliage. Next to Tilon stood Marui and behind them, Su-Ni, who was not watching the forest, but the approach of Komeris with eyes full of trepidation. The captain nodded to her reassuringly as he passed and looked to the path for the first sign of movement.

He did not have to wait long before that sign came. Around the bend came the reflection of the sun off a well-polished bronze helmet. Etrusin and two other soldiers stepped their way toward the awaiting party. He and his two men trod unflinchingly on until they were not more than a meter from where the captain stood and quite abruptly halted.

"Hail, captain, report," the general said, not acknowledging the elves' presence at all.

Komeris bowed. "General, it is fortunate your messenger caught up with us when he did. We had not yet sent riders to the north and south. But..." he trailed.

"But?" Etrusin prompted.

The captain looked away. "We sent a small party up one of the peaks.

Not everyone returned. We've lost four good men," he said with sincere disappointment.

The general gave an understanding nod. "Well, now we have a new mission. Do not worry yourself with the events of these past days, for much larger concerns await us," he ordered.

"Indeed," cut in Tilon with an inquisitive tone. "What sort of concerns might you be referring to, general?"

The general glanced briefly at Tilon, then back to Komeris. "Captain, introduce me to our guest."

Tilon stepped in front of Komeris who stood open-mouthed to answer the general. "I will introduce myself, general. I am Tilon Enshei and a warrior as well among my people, the Shionen, who have been your patient hosts for these past several days. While you are in our forest, you are a guest of the elves, and it is only because you are guests that you have not all already felt the bite of an elven arrow."

"Tilon!" snapped Marui.

Komeris took this opportunity to step in front of Tilon and stretch out his hand, indicating that Etrusin should walk with him. As Marui and Tilon argued in Shionen, the captain and the general headed down the path from whence Etrusin and his men had emerged. "General, do not take Tilon's seemingly threatening nature to heart," Komeris began to explain. "He is terse, but not without reason. He is simply concerned for the safety of his people and his home. All of this activity is leaving him a bit shaken. Honestly, sir, I cannot say he is the only one. I am not one to question you or the emperor, but what is going on? I believe we all should know."

The general nodded. "Yes, Komeris, I will explain everything, but for now I have many tired warriors who are in need of a decent camp. Let me move them out of the forest. Then, I will brief you all on the situation."

12 PLANS

In a small room hidden away in the corner of the castle in Niele'itio, three figures sat around a small table with meals set before them. On the center of the table lay a drawing of some mechanical invention. Though the food was hot and sent twisting tendrils of delicious scent into the air, those at the table seemed more intent on a collection of carefully placed lines upon paper.

General Vethisir gave a perplexed grimace to the large parchment on the table and looked back at his king. "What is this thing called again?" he asked.

Orbein looked over to Agucho. "A catapult," the shapeshifter answered with some measure of annoyance.

"Cat-ah-poolt..." the general repeated intelligently. "And how is it supposed to help us?"

The king frowned at Vethisir, drawing an apologetic stare. "It is a weapon, you dolt. A weapon of the grandest scale. Upon this catapult you may place a mass of flaming pitch and hurl it into the ranks of your enemies, or heavy stones to topple their towers."

"I see," Vethisir said, though it was plain that he didn't. His confused expression was replaced quickly, however, by one of surprise as a piece of food flew into his face from across the table. He glared dangerously at the Fiu-Het, who was loading another morsel onto his fork to further demonstrate the physics of siege weaponry.

Orbein grimaced. "Enough!" he yelled. "This weapon will be instrumental in our victory. I have explained our plans to your men, and they are eager to carry them out. They may start by working with my assistant on the construction of this catapult."

Vethisir held his breath for a moment. "Sire, will it be necessary for him to be present? My men are frightened of him. I fear it may interfere with their ability to work," he said, speaking of Agucho as though he were not even present.

King Orbein laughed. "What sort of womenfolk are you training out there? If they are scared, all the better. The sooner they complete this project, the sooner they will be done dealing with him, for a time. Contrary to what you think, I believe Agucho's presence will be an excellent motivation!"

The general responded by scowling resentfully.

"I advise you and your men to grow accustomed to the shapeshifter's appearance, else I fear you will all be in for a rude awakening," he said threateningly.

Vethisir swallowed nervously. "Yes, sire," he sulked.

Orbein nodded. "You are dismissed."

The shapeshifter and the king watched general Vethisir rise ungracefully and give a flustered salute before hurriedly making his exit. Orbein watched him go with absent amusement, then looked back to the scroll with the catapult design drawn upon it. He brooded quietly for several moments, and Agucho simply watched him, waiting for words that he knew would come. Eventually the king blinked and looked over to his shapeshifting servant.

"Agucho."

"Yes, sire," The Fiu-Het replied.

"I know that this has been a difficult time for you. I would like to give you the opportunity to take some time to go back to your people," Orbein said.

Agucho cocked his head, and the folds on his brow deepened in the closest thing to a skeptical expression for a Fiu-Het. "Sire?" he asked, feigning ignorance.

The king looked to the shapeshifter with seemingly sympathetic eyes. "They do not know of the death of their prince, and you have yet to report back to them. They are likely getting concerned about both of you."

Agucho's sticky tongue curled around his eyeballs absently. "Yes. Yes, I suppose I should go and tell them what has happened."

Orbein smiled. "Yes, you should. And how it happened. Your poor prince. I shudder to recall it. The shape he was in just before... I can't imagine what they did to him." He shook his head as though forcing the image away.

The distant stare in Agucho's eyes left, and his pupil dilated as he refocused on the king.

"Ah," the king continued, "but I am sorry. It must pain you even more to think of it. The horrible things that must have befallen him. I am sure your people will be very saddened by his loss."

The Fiu-Het's features began to twist dubiously. "Saddened and angry, highness. I assure you, they will not look well on the circumstances of his death."

Orbein nodded. "Yes, nor should they! The death of your prince has not only proven that there are violent savages beyond the mountains, it has also given us further inspiration to go conquer them, destroy them, grind them beneath our heel."

"This you already wanted to do," Agucho stated matter-of-factly.

"True, but now there is more, and not just for me. You heard Gayossha. He said you must fight. Kill the enemies of your people. You can fill your bellies on the entrails of our mutual foes," the king explained.

Agucho looked away, hiding his amusement at the king's misconception. If a Fiu-Het had ever actually filled their bellies with human entrails, he would become violently ill, perhaps even fatally. The race of shapeshifters was mostly herbivorous, but their unique ability to radiate fear, to emanate waves of horrifying imagery, propagated the myth that the Fiu-Het liked to feed on the other intelligent races. But Agucho was not about to tell the king that.

Orbein smirked, mistaking the turned head for embarrassment. "Do not be ashamed. Does it make your mouth water to think of all the men you will kill?"

The Fiu-Het nodded as convincingly as he could. "Although we prefer to watch you kill each other, as you seem to enjoy doing so frequently," he added.

Orbein nodded. "I see," he said, pausing for a moment to think. "Listen, Agucho, your people are going to be angry about this, as you have said. I think you should heed your prince's advice and lead them here to stand beside my army. March together with them to claim our vengeance upon the murderers of Gayossha and of my own ancestors many generations before. Our two peoples will comprise an unstoppable force. Separately we will be an easy victory, but together...together we will conquer."

Agucho nodded slowly. "Perhaps."

"Go, Agucho. Go to your people. When you tell them what has happened they will want retribution, and you will see that my proposed solution is the only way." The king's voice lowered and he muttered something imperceptible, then, "Go, Agucho. Tell them."

The shapeshifter's focus suddenly shifted again, and he was staring to some faraway place. When he responded, his voice sounded monotone and as distant as his gaze. "Yes, highness, I will tell them." He then rose mechanically and exited the room.

"Indeed," the king muttered to the empty air. With this he reached into his pocket and pulled out a small patch of fabric that closely resembled Agucho's rags and twisted it onto his little finger with a piece of cord. He chanted quietly and waved several gestures over the makeshift ring. Upon finishing, he looked back to the catapult scroll. "The circumstances of my victory have been set in motion," he whispered.

* * *

The lone candle cast a dim light within Etrusin's dark tent. It was midday, but the thick canvas blocked out most of the sun's brightness, leaving the general to sit in the faint glow of the flickering flame. He stared silently down toward the table before him but not at it. He seemed to be deep in thought, perhaps even meditation. On the table lay an incomplete map of the area, but its details, few though there were, could not be made out in the shadows. Etrusin, however, saw them all in his mind's eye. He even saw some detail that was not there. Always his attention was drawn west, to the mountains. He was filled with apprehension at the seemingly endless line of peaks, though he could not say why. He simply sat and stared, hoping the map would reveal some great secret to him.

The brightness within the tent suddenly increased dramatically, and Etrusin squinted toward the source. One of the flaps had been pulled aside and in stepped Komeris. "Hail, general, you wanted to see me?" the captain asked.

The general nodded. "Please, come in," he said.

Komeris closed the flap, plunging them into obscurity until their eyes readjusted. Etrusin began lighting some more candles and a lantern, which brought the ambient light to a comfortable level. When he was done, he leaned back in his seat again and adopted a reflective pose. "Is everything alright, sir?" the captain asked.

Etrusin looked up at Komeris and indicated the seat across from him. "Sit," he offered. Komeris did so and watched his general attentively. After several moments of silence, his commanding officer spoke again. "Captain, what do we know about the mountains?"

Komeris stared blankly for a moment, then responded, "Nothing much, really. To my knowledge we have never explored them successfully." He looked down soberly, thinking of the terrible loss from his previous mission.

"Komeris," Etrusin began gently, knowing the captain's disappointment, "you must not dwell on the events of the past. It was not your fault. You could not know the fate those men would meet when you sent them up there."

Komeris nodded. "I know that. I do, but it has been a long time since I have been called upon to serve the empire. I feel like I have failed the emperor and you...I especially failed those men who were lost."

The general gave a sympathetic smile. "Yes. Unfortunately, that is sometimes the cost of leadership, but you mustn't let it interfere with your duty."

Komeris nodded. "Yes, sir. You are right, of course," he said sincerely, understanding his commander's wisdom.

"Are you ready to go back, then?" Etrusin asked.

"What do you mean?" Komeris replied cautiously.

"According to the emperor's visions, the threat to our people comes from the mountains, or somewhere beyond. With this knowledge, we would be foolish to remain ignorant about those areas. I need you to continue your exploration, Komeris. Take some soldiers, a small contingent. Go out and see if you can spy our enemy. Go quickly, but the moment you encounter danger, run. Leave the fight for our army. You must survive to return and tell us what is out there," the general explained.

Many uncomfortable minutes passed silently as Komeris processed the general's request. After much shifting, the captain finally spoke. "I will do as you command, sir, but should we be engaged I will not leave without all of my men."

Etrusin stared at Komeris for several minutes, and then nodded. "You are a man of honor, my friend. This is why you've always been at my side. Know that your service to the empire shall never be forgotten."

Komeris bowed his head respectfully. "When shall we go?" he asked.

"At dawn's first light," the general replied. "Take to the low ground whenever you can. The peaks are treacherous, and stealth will be your ally."

"Yes, sir," said Komeris, bowing again. "I shall assemble some of our best warriors today. We will begin at dawn, as you have ordered."

Etrusin bowed his head in response. "Yes, but take only a few. There is much to do here, and I need skilled warriors to continue training the newest members of our army. Make sure you return, my friend, for we could not do without you as well."

"We shall," replied the captain with a determined nod. At that he gave one more bow and exited, leaving his general to his thoughts.

Alone again, Etrusin looked back down at his map. He grimaced at its incompleteness. "Why have we stayed so secluded?" he muttered. "Foolish men. Now we are put to the scramble. To be defeated would be no less than we deserve for such stagnation.

"No," he tried to say firmly. "We will not find defeat. Loss perhaps, but not defeat I pray..."

* * *

Outside the tent, Komeris heaved a big sigh. With that exhalation he expelled any doubt he had left about himself. He walked toward the largest tent in the camp, where he knew he would find most of the soldiers, the mess. As he approached, he could smell something delicious being served. He stepped in and saw a large boar on the table surrounded by a sea of rice and vegetables. Several soldiers were gathered around, piling savory meat upon their plates. Those who were in line for the food drank heartily from mugs filled with rice wine and talked and laughed boisterously with their comrades. He was pleased to see how well they all got along. The captain spotted Pei-Shi standing with a group of men, all of them laughing over some anecdote. He smiled and walked over.

"Hail, Pei-Shi," he greeted her.

"Ah, captain, well met," she replied, bowing awkwardly as she balanced her food and drink.

"I must speak with you," Komeris said in a low, serious voice.

She noted his tone and the look on his face. She put down her dinner and walked with him outside. "What is it, captain?" she asked dutifully.

"Pei-Shi, we have served together many long years," he began with a deeply respectful tone. "In that time I have come to trust in you and your abilities more than any other soldier aside from the general himself. I come now to ask you again to serve by my side in a possibly dangerous mission."

Pei-Shi bowed humbly. "You have but to command it, captain."

"No," he said quickly. "No, I will not command you; rather I will ask you to do this of your own will. And I would ask you to help me to select three other warriors who would volunteer to come with us on this assignment."

"By my own will I would follow your command into the very mouth of doom. I will help you find those brave enough to join us. Shall I tell them the nature of our mission?" she asked, curious about it herself but still willing regardless of the details.

Komeris nodded. "Yes, we are to continue exploring westward. The general wants us to see if we can spy the home of this mysterious enemy the emperor has foreseen."

Pei-Shi raised an eyebrow. "Is that all?" she asked jokingly.

"Yes," Komeris replied, "but do not be deceived. It will be a difficult journey. The terrain through the mountains is unknown to us. We must take great care to return safely with whatever information we can find."

The blademaster nodded her head solemnly. "Very well, captain. When should we be ready to go?"

"First light tomorrow," he answered.

Pei-Shi nodded again, then bowed and turned to reenter the mess, though she did not go to finish her meal. Komeris watched her disappear into the tent and turned to walk to his own. He paused as he looked toward the forest and noticed someone was standing by the path into the wood. He walked over, and as he approached, he recognized Marui, the female elf that always seemed to accompany Tilon.

"Hail, captain," she said.

"Hello," he replied with a smile.

"Where are you going?" she asked.

"I was heading back to my tent. I only came this way because I saw you here."

The elf shook her head slowly. "Nay, captain, I mean where are you going tomorrow?"

Komeris gave her a perplexed look. "How did you..."

She laughed. It was a musical sound, much like elven speech was, magical. It lifted the captain's heart to hear it. "You never seem to remember our excellent hearing. While it is much better than yours, it does have its limits. I overheard some of your conversation with that soldier, only enough to know that you are going somewhere dangerous at first light tomorrow."

The captain turned back and looked to the mess tent, which was easily seventy paces from where they now stood. "I wish my ears were so limited," he grinned. His expression became serious as he looked back to Marui. "It is true that we are to leave tomorrow. We are to explore the mountains and beyond to find where our enemy, or any ally, may lie."

Marui gave him an appraising look. "Captain, do your people really know so little about their history?" she asked.

Komeris frowned. "We know no history before Reisothin aside from tribal conflict and our bedtime stories."

The elf nodded after a thoughtful pause. "Very well," she said at last. "Captain, I shall accompany you tomorrow when you and your group head off into the mountains."

The captain didn't know what to say.

"If there is some enemy in or over the mountains that is coming to attack you, then they threaten us as well. Such an enemy would have to enter the forest to get to your empire. This would not be the first time this has happened. We live much longer than humans do, thus our memories are much better. I think some of our memories would be very helpful to both of our peoples right now. Let me guide you along the paths of your ancestors so that you may better avoid their mistakes. Perhaps together we can avoid a conflict entirely," Marui explained.

Komeris nodded slowly, though he did not entirely understand. He guessed that the elves had likely kept a more detailed history than his people had, so perhaps they could indeed be very helpful. "Your presence would be welcomed," he said gratefully.

* * *

Inside the mess tent, Su-Ni watched as Pei-Shi returned, not to eat with the rest of the soldiers, but to whisper to Reniu and point to some of the others. Ever since the loss of the Swift One and his company on the mountain, the young diplomat kept a close eye on captain Komeris and the soldiers he regularly associated with. She had watched with interest as he walked outside with the blade master and now as the female warrior had come back alone to share some secret, it seemed. Su-Ni was an observant one, and she knew something was happening. So, when Pei-Shi, Reniu and two other soldiers exited the tent together, the curious young woman was not far behind.

The four warriors quickly crossed the campsite, oblivious to their living shadow. They came to a small tent and filed in. Su-Ni crept up from behind another tent close by. She looked around cautiously. Fortunately, it seemed that most of the soldiers were gathered in the huge central tent around their lunch. The diplomat tip-toed up to the tent flaps and strained to hear the conversation happening inside.

"...dawn tomorrow our path goes back west, back to the mountains," a feminine voice said, obviously Pei-Shi's.

"We're goin' ta find the Swift One?" the northtribe brogue clearly identified the speaker as Reniu.

Su-Ni's eyes widened as she heard Urietsin's nickname and almost fell through the tent flaps as she strained to hear Pei-Shi's response.

"If the young warrior is still alive, I am sure he will find his way back to us," she said hopefully, "but our journey will take us well beyond the place where he and his men fell to the gotori. We go to find our enemy..."

Su-Ni was momentarily disappointed to hear that their secret mission did not involve searching for Urietsin, but her heart leapt when she heard Pei-Shi's last statement. The Swift One was all but forgotten at hearing what they were really up to. Her ear was practically pressed to the hide of the tent, and she began to wonder if her silhouette might give her away. She was trying to position herself more inconspicuously when suddenly Komeris came from around the corner.

The young diplomat straightened slowly and looked straight at the tent. Then she turned and stepped away, looking at the other tent directly across from this one with what she hoped looked like puzzled expression. Inside her chest her heart was pounding like a blacksmith's hammer, but she kept her motions slow and casual. She walked up to the other tent and tilted her head toward its opening, as if listening for some sound.

Komeris approached her with a cocked eyebrow. "It's lunchtime and you are far from the mess tent, young diplomat. Are you not hungry?" he asked suspiciously.

Su-Ni put a finger to her lips and stepped away from this tent as well. "Have you seen Ninei and Ini'io?" she asked conspiratorially. "I know I saw them come this way. I'll not have them making any plans without me.

Sometimes I feel like they leave me out because I'm the youngest." She pouted prettily and folded her arms across her chest, though in truth she knew that both the other diplomats respected her talent and maturity beyond any doubt.

Komeris fell for the ruse, especially when he saw that undeniable pout. He grinned. "I am sorry, I did not see them. Perhaps they were simply walking around the campsite and turned back to the mess for a meal."

"Perhaps," she responded, but she managed a disappointed look.

The captain reached out and patted her shoulder. "Do not worry, my friend. I am certain they respect you very much. I cannot imagine why you would be here with them otherwise."

Su-Ni smiled broadly at this and bowed to Komeris. "Thank you, captain," she said. "I will try to go find them in the mess tent."

Komeris nodded and watched her walk off quickly. He chuckled to himself and began to walk toward his own tent when the flap of Pei-Shi's tent was pushed aside and four soldiers stepped out.

"Hail, captain," said Reniu with a bow.

The soldier's bow was met with an absent nod as Komeris considered the four before him. The captain turned to look the way the young diplomat had gone. For a moment, he almost shook away the coincidence as just that, but his better judgment told him differently. After witnessing the physical prowess of the young Urietsin, he reminded himself not to underestimate the diplomat because of her age. He would have promised himself to keep an eye on her too, were it not for the fact the he was to be away from the camp and the empire for some time starting tomorrow. He clenched his jaw as he turned back to the soldiers who stood before him with quizzical expressions. He bade them to follow him back to his tent where they would make plans for the next morning. All thoughts of the strange encounter with Su-Ni were soon forgotten.

* * *

Thick fog clung heavily to the ivy-choked branches of dead trees spotting the moist ground from which the haze seemed to emanate. In some places, the soil was just damp from the constant humidity that permeated every layer of the bog. In others, it was completely soaked to produce a slimy, stagnant mud. Puddles of standing water pooled everywhere, and each swam with the bottom-feeding life one would expect to find in such a place. Frogs chirped instead of birds, and toads croaked in seeming chorus. Dozens of other nameless creatures occasionally threw in their moans and gasps, topped off by the disturbing call of a loon. In a word, it was home.

Agucho relished the feel of thick mud around his webbed feet. Every so often he would snag a small toadstool or patch of moss and gobble it down greedily. He never realized how much he could miss his home. He licked his eyeballs, though mostly out of habit, as the moist air of the bog made this action somewhat unnecessary. His pace quickened as he neared Edogh, the royal court of the Fiu-Het.

Edogh was a dense circle of cypress with twisted roots entwined above and below the deeper water of this part of the bog. The effect was a veritable fortress of interlocked wooden limbs, through which only one of the Fiu-Het's ability could navigate. Agucho stretched and squeezed his biology in a way unfathomable to the other intelligent races of this land. As though he had simply walked through an open path, he emerged on the other side to stand on a wide mound of peat and clay. The area would have looked empty to one of any other race, but Agucho recognized many that he knew watching from behind the guise of a branch or a stone. He promptly knelt and prostrated himself before the court.

From out of the bark of a cypress, a tall Fiu-Het assembled herself. Her height seemed to be derived from the lack of the hunch present in the males of her species. Her skin did not hang quite as loose as well. On the contrary, it seemed to be drawn quite tightly over her form and made her appear more amphibian than trollish.

"It has been some time since we have heard from you, Agucho," she said in a soft voice, a stark contrast to the harsh gurgle of the males.

"My humblest apologies, highness," Agucho groveled.

"Never mind that. We have been quite worried about the disappearance of Gayossha. Tell me, have you encountered him in your absence? I hope he is well." Her tone was icily suspicious.

At this Agucho choked, his face still to the ground.

The Fiu-Het queen looked down at the groveling shapeshifter before her. After a long pause she spoke. "Rise."

Agucho stood slowly, though he still kept his eyes pointed downward. He did not need to look to feel the queen's stare boring into him. He knew she would not speak again until he did.

"A horrible fate has befallen our great prince!" he admitted finally. Again, without looking he knew that several more Fiu-Het shapes emerged from the surroundings at this statement. Ambitious siblings wanted to get closer to hear every detail of their brother's demise.

"Go on," commanded the queen in a gentle tone that belied the sneer upon her lips.

It suddenly seemed very cold to Agucho in this dank circle of trees. He began to tremble slightly, shivering as though it were deep winter. His skin began to ooze its thick liquid so profusely that it dripped off in great gobs. He was nervous, but something else contributed to his condition. Something inspired him to look up and shout suddenly, "Murdered! Our prince was murdered! A foul race of barbarians across the mountains killed Gayossha. Enemies of the benevolent King Orbein, our neighbor to the east. We must seek retribution and destroy these murderous wretches!"

"Humans?" the queen asked doubtfully. "They are not our concern. If Gayossha interfered in their struggles, then his death was unfortunate but necessary. Let this be a lesson to all of you." She looked to the rest of the Fiu-Het of the court. "Humans are dangerous. Let them be dangerous to each other. They will kill themselves off before they have a chance to attack us."

"Not true!" Agucho screeched, drawing a daggerpoint gaze from the matriarch. "These barbarians are bloodthirsty and powerful. They spread west, an infestation of massive proportions. Alone Orbein's army will be defeated, and we will be the only thing keeping them from the rest of the world. I care not for the humans. I care for us! For our people! If we do not stand with Orbein, we will fall as he will. This is how your Gayossha died, dear family, protecting our way of life! You should be ashamed for licking your lips at his corpse when his death may have helped ensure your continued life!"

With this exaltation, Agucho threw the late prince's ragged cloak to the floor. The mood was immediately solemn. The Fiu-Het may not have usually cared whether or not one of their brothers died, but if he died defending their way of life, it was shameful to disrespect such a brave citizen. Presently, the siblings approached and retrieved their fallen brother's livery and faded with it back into the surroundings. Agucho was left alone, truly alone, with the queen.

"You seem to have grown quite bold in the short time you have been away from us, Agucho," she said.

"Perhaps, highness. I only say what is true," he replied, panting from the effort of his outburst.

"Do you?"

Agucho looked at her for the first time directly. His expression carried a message of its own. One that only she could understand.

"I see. And do you truly believe these barbarians are a danger?" she asked.

"I believe the ambitious humans must be stopped before they reach the swamp. Standing beside Orbein will be the best chance to prevent this and avenge our prince's noble death," Agucho explained.

"And this benevolent Orbein...he and his people are not repulsed by our appearance or by the legends that humans have conveniently fabricated for us?"

The question gave Agucho pause. There was so much he wanted to tell the queen now, but one burning focus obscured everything else. "My queen, I have seen to all of this. You must trust me when I tell you: we must be by Orbein's side when he is engaged in battle. To do otherwise would bring great peril to our race."

The queen glared at him darkly. "Although your answers have not completely satisfied me, that is one thing I do believe. It will take some time to gather our warriors together. How soon will you need them?"

"I shall return for them," Agucho said.

The queen nodded and stepped toward him, studying him closely and sniffing the air with purpose. "This I will do, Agucho, but only because I fear great danger to our race regardless of our action, not because you tell me to do so."

Agucho nodded. "I understand, highness," was his reply.

She turned and walked away, but before she disappeared into the cypress, she called back to him, "Agucho, you bring the smell of humans with you. You are not welcome back here until it has been washed away."

With that, she disappeared, leaving Agucho to ponder her meaning. It did not take long for an understanding to come to him, but he sat for some time afterward in deep thought. Finally, he got up and ambled toward the cypress and began his return journey back to the Dark City.

* * *

A hot breeze blew from the west, bringing no comfort to the sweating backs of the soldiers of Niele'itio. It was noon, and even the high mount Thontur could not block the sun's scorching rays. As the men burned in the late summer sun, slaving over large foreign contraptions, they worried at the direction of the wind. It was not wholly uncommon for this season, but in general the air moving through Ionotu rolled off the cool peak of Thontur, keeping the summers mild. But when the air blew from the west, the hot, sticky air carrying moisture from the wetlands, it always made the weather interesting. Now it was simply hot and miserable. Later in the day, however, the clash of hot air from the west and the cold mountain air would throw the sky into upheaval. The wretched men of the Dark City's army would be left trembling in their leaky, drafty barracks, if the wind and hail even left any for them to cower in away from the lightning.

Vethisir watched his men assemble the third catapult and noted their speed. Not only were they getting quicker with each assembly, but they also hurried because of the weather. He looked up and, though he saw not a cloud, he knew they would come. He almost felt sorry for the wretches. When the wind and the rain came, the general would be resting comfortably in his palace quarters. But Vethisir had not gotten where he was in life because of pity, so he let the feelings pass. These were soldiers. Miserable experiences like the one they would have tonight only made them tougher. With this thought, the general focused his attention on one man in particular.

The light-haired, light-eyed foreigner was familiar with the design of the catapult. His lack of surprise at the announcement that the western technology was to be used in this mission of expansion seemed suspicious to Vethisir. Of course, he was a seer and had likely already known that the contraption would be introduced. The general kept a close eye on Laernus. Since the strange meeting with the shapeshifter, the seer's demeanor had completely changed. No more did he cower before the other soldiers and play their victim. Now he partook of the zealous sparring, actually learning how to use a sword in the process. He became intimately involved in the project to build the catapults, as he knew more about them than any man native to Ionotu. He seemed to grow stronger and more confident with each passing day now, and his fellow soldiers' attitudes shifted from disdain to fearful respect. It had not taken them long to learn that this seeing traveler knew magic, and he had learned to use it to his advantage quite well in a fight.

Vethisir had noticed all of this and would have encouraged this kind of development in any other recruit, but with this one it just made him nervous. If it weren't for the sudden absence of Agucho for reasons known only to Orbein, the general would never have allowed this situation. He watched the foreigner shout at the men in his strange accent and point to important sections of the catapult. He supervised the building of the siege weaponry with a sharp tongue and a harsh glare. He seemed completely dissatisfied with the whole process and made sure the entire army knew about it. When the men finished with the third engine, he called for them to test it.

The general was happy to avert his attention for a little while and watch the catapult in action. He had seen the other two tested upon their completion, and the effect had not yet worn off. It was one of the most incredible sights he had ever witnessed. The men tightened the winch and pulled back the arm. Two soldiers lifted a heavy stone into the bucket and stepped back. Another man swung a heavy hammer and knocked out the slip hook. A perfectly-performed symphony of motion reflected in the eyes of every onlooker. The arm swung upward, and at the appropriate angle, the stone came hurtling out. The arm continued up to the vertical where it slammed against the crosspiece. All eyes were on the stone, though, as the crosspiece cracked and broke from the catapult's mobile base. Before the rock had finished its flight, the broken piece of the siege engine toppled to the side and nearly crushed one unfortunate soldier's skull.

"You fools!" called out Laernus.

The soldiers paid him little mind as they rushed to drag the dazed man away from the wreckage. Laernus stalked over to scold them some more. This irked Vethisir, and he went to intercept when he heard a much more important call.

"General," Orbein addressed him.

Vethisir turned and saluted abruptly. "Your highness."

"Impressive machinery. Does it break every time?" the King asked derisively.

"Of course not, highness, clearly there was some flaw in the construction of this particular machine."

"Clearly," Orbein answered. "Is the seer in charge of this particular operation?" he asked, watching the foreigner circle the broken engine and yell at anyone who came near. He watched in much the same way Vethisir had done.

The general shrugged. "Somewhat, sire. He does know the machinery better than any of us, and the men seem to prefer him to the shapeshifter."

The king nodded. "Your training seems to have grown him a spine."

Vethisir grimaced. "Actually, sire, I've been meaning to speak to you about that."

Orbein turned and looked at the general with a raised eyebrow. "Go on."

"Well, shortly after the seer joined our ranks he was visited by your, uh...the shapeshifter."

Orbein's other eyebrow joined the first. "Really?"

"Yes, sire. They stole off to the woods by the road and came back several minutes later. Ever since then, the seer seems to be much more interested in his training," Vethisir explained.

"Why did you not tell me of this sooner?" the king asked.

"Your forgiveness, sire, I was so busy with the new assignment, and you seemed so focused upon this. It seemed secondary." Even for such a hot day, the general was sweating profusely. More than the weather was causing the beads on his forehead.

Orbein grinned. "Vethisir."

"Yes, sire?"

"Never overlook something so simple. Should you notice anything unusual, I want to hear about it immediately. I will not correct you again." With that the king turned and marched off the field.

Vethisir sighed heavily and shakily. He looked back to the catapult to see that there were men gathered around it removing the broken crosspiece. Laernus was not watching, though. Instead he stared at the king's back as he left, and then over to the general. The seer shot him an insincere smile and plodded over to him.

"Sir, the men will be removing the crosspiece and replacing it with one that is properly reinforced," Laernus explained.

The general squinted at him suspiciously, then nodded. "Let them do it tomorrow," he said. "Your day is over." He pointed toward the mountains.

Laernus looked over his shoulder and saw a dark thunderhead rolling quickly toward the field from several miles away. Thunder rumbled subtly at first, softly knocking at the sky to announce its presence, a mockingly gentle fanfare for what would become a tumultuous summer storm in less than an hour. The seer did not need to call to the men to pack up the catapults, they had already begun. It would take at least twenty minutes, and the rain would already be falling before they were done, but finish they would for fear of losing all their hard work to nature. Laernus stood and watched them scramble, and over his shoulder, Vethisir watched him. He could feel the general's eyes boring into him, but he ignored it. The seer knew that someday soon, he would be free. Free from the prying eyes. Free from the condescending glares. Free from the burden of taking orders from somebody else. Free.

13 PERCEPTION

Blackness. Occasionally the light would shimmer through the clouds and the canopy to play upon his closed eyelids, but for the most part he saw only blackness. Kiusu had described gleaming sheets of transcendence and sparkling streams of existence, but Urietsin saw none of these. Instead, he saw black and sometimes red. He found it difficult to concentrate with his eyes closed. Although he meditated regularly, the Swift one found himself becoming frustrated at his inability to focus and see the things Kiusu saw. Part of it was this new method, but more than that, behind his eyes he could only see fresh blood dripping off the tusks of the gotori and the crumpled bodies of the men that had followed him up the mountain.

"I see..." Urietsin spoke.

"Yes?" Kiusu asked eagerly.

"The back of my eyelid," he responded dryly.

Kiusu chuckled. "Patience, Swift One, it will take time. You must first release the firm grip that a proposed reality has upon your mind. Also, do not look with your eyes. That is why they are closed. Do not expect to 'see' these things as you would with those limited organs. You should simply feel existence, and your perception will give it a form that you can only describe as sight."

Urietsin sighed and opened his eyes. "How can I release the hold of this proposed reality when it is the only thing I know?"

"By recognizing that the reality you have been taught to perceive is not completely true. It is merely an illusion to describe our interaction with existence to our physical senses," Kiusu explained.

"But is not existence merely another word for reality?" the young warrior asked.

"Perhaps for some, but there is a difference between reality and existence. Reality is that which exists to us because we perceive it.

Existence is everything that is regardless of our perception of it. Reality is encompassed by existence, but does not define it. Reality is defined by form and measurement. Existence cannot be defined because it has no specific form and cannot be measured. It is the cause and consequence within itself."

Urietsin looked a little confused.

Kiusu nodded. "Think of your home. You are not there now, so you do not perceive it, but does it still exist?"

"I certainly hope so," the Swift One sighed, feeling a slight pang of homesickness.

The older man grinned. "I'm sure it does. That is how existence is. Existence is contained within a vastness that we are incapable of perceiving in its entirety. We do, however, perceive parts of it. The other parts still exist, even when we are not there to perceive them. What we happen to be perceiving at any point in our existence is our reality. Understand?"

"I think so," was the reply.

"Do not worry, Urietsi'in, you will understand more completely in time," his master reassured. "One time all men understood this, but as they have grown away from nature and the true consciousness, it has slipped from their grasp. The last men to know the secrets fully were a group called the Safekeepers, who passed much of their knowledge to my master."

The old man paused and stared distantly for a moment before blinking away the trance and urging his student, "Go on, close your eyes and try again."

Urietsin nodded and musingly watched the old man walk back toward the nearly completed dwelling. He closed his eyes and cleared his mind. His breath moved in and out slowly. He concentrated on that, letting it distract him from all other thoughts. In came fresh air, out went spent air. The Swift One focused on the sensation of air rushing in through his nostrils, down his windpipe, and filling his lungs. He paid equal attention to the opposite process of exhalation. He imagined the air as a liquid filled with swirling clouds of tiny particles so that he could see it moving in response to his breathing.

As this imagery coalesced within his mind's eye, he realized that he was watching the air move inside him as though he were transparent. He clearly saw it flow into his lungs, and even change color, just before it was expelled. He also noticed the pattern of the air all around him. Time seemed to slow down or speed up. Whatever it did, time did not really seem to be a factor. Countless breaths were all he had to mark the time he watched the air dance around him.

Within this meditative dream he saw the trees swaying in time to his breathing. He watched this in awe for several moments before it dawned on him that the trees were not swaying; they were breathing. As he breathed out they breathed in. He watched particles from his exhale disperse into the air and get slowly sucked up by the surrounding plant life. Urietsin began to feel like he was unable to breathe. He inhaled sharply and opened his eyes. He was startled by Kiusu standing before him, eyes closed.

"What did you see?" the old man asked.

"The air," was the student's simple response.

Kiusu nodded and opened his eyes. "Why did you stop?"

Urietsin shook his head. "It may sound foolish, but I felt like the trees were taking my breath away."

"Taking it, but giving it back," Kiusu explained. "You will find that existence is filled with many such relationships. Some simple, but most complex. The trees breathe our air, and we breathe theirs. We could not exist without one another."

The young warrior looked around at the many trees that surrounded them as he had several times before, but now he saw them with much respect and wonder. As his eyes played over the area, they came to rest on the hut, which was now completely finished. In the time that Urietsin had been meditating Kiusu had thatched the entire roof. "How long was I...?"

Kiusu chuckled. "A few hours," he replied. Indeed, the short shadows of noon had waxed to the full shadows of early evening. "Come, Swift One, let us eat," the old man said, helping his young student up. Together they went into the hut where a simple dinner sat ready. Urietsin was again amazed at the abilities of his mentor. A thatched roof and freshly hunted meat in a few hours with no sign of fatigue. There was even a small bowl of rice for each of them. How Kiusu had managed to obtain rice on this mountain was beyond even his imagination.

Urietsin bowed. "Greater is my debt, *seishin*," he said in the tradition of his family, and of most of those in the empire. Seishin was a title that meant 'master of the household' and was often used by guests in one's home, but was also commonly spoken by students to their teachers. The entire phrase was most often uttered before a meal as a show of gratitude toward a gracious host.

Kiusu bowed in return and replied, "Pay with a clean plate, *gru'iohin*," as this was the proper response, referring to the recipient as 'humble guest'. The two then began to eat, and although the meal was simple, they savored it. Such was as it had been for the two men for the past few weeks and for Kiusu for the past two decades.

Urietsin ate silently, but his mind was bustling with thought. Though he was excited about his meditation today, he felt a twinge of guilt. Three, maybe four, men would not be able to know the joys of new discoveries like this. They would not know the feeling of being homesick and the subsequent feeling of relieved satisfaction of their homecoming. Their families would never again know that latter same happiness. The Swift One had to admit that being here with Kiusu was fascinating, and he definitely wanted to learn more from the old man, but every thought that brought him closer to moving on from the tragedy of the brave men that had followed him on the mountain haunted the young warrior incessantly. He would not insult the memory of those honorable warriors by simply carrying on as though their losses were nothing. He would not carry on as though he could not have saved them from their terrible fate.

* * *

Tilon smiled as he watched the group of young elves dance. They practiced their song with serious effort, but as was always the case with young ones, their voices carried the lilting, carefree joy that went with childhood. The eldest of the group was his own son, strong and proud. He watched the boy lead the dance with purpose, placing each step flawlessly in time with their song. These children, the few of their realm, were the reason he was fiercely protective of his home. Out of the corner of his eye, Tilon saw his sister striding off purposefully with her bow and quiver slung over her shoulder. This, he knew, did not bode well.

"Marui!" he called to her.

The elven maiden turned and waited for Tilon to approach.

"Where are you off to?" he asked with concern.

Marui gave a slight sigh as though she had hoped to avoid this encounter. "I am going to guide some of General Etrusin's men through the mountains," she said honestly.

Tilon let his expression speak his disapproval.

"They are merely scouts, Tilon. I will help them find their way through to see if they might glean some useful information about the danger that is coming," she explained.

"Let me save you the trip, my sister. They are the danger," he grimaced.

Marui looked at him with the utmost disappointment. "I thought you had moved beyond this. When will you let the past go? You are clinging to things that happened in our parents' generation."

"It is in their nature," Tilon shrugged. "They will betray us again."

"They did not betray us!" Marui shouted. "It was Teomin that did so, and that only after we prevented him from betraying his own people."

"Which is why we should not interfere now."

Marui looked at him with disgust. "How can you possibly be so sure? Etrusin's men are the first humans you have ever met, and they have been nothing but friendly to us."

"How can I be so sure?" Tilon repeated. "Do you forget what father taught us? 'Be wary,' he said, 'for those whom you trust can most easily take advantage.' Even as we speak more humans are trampling through the forest, more soldiers of their army. Should we just sit back and leave ourselves vulnerable? Should we assume there is no ill intent?"

His sister sighed. "I remember well all that father taught us. I remember also that he told us humans have been the friends of elves since Felishan grew them from the earth."

Tilon had no response to this. He simply narrowed his eyes stubbornly at her.

Marui shook her head. "Tilon," she said softly, "let go of this. Hate is not natural for a Shionen. You do yourself, our father, and all of elvenkind a great dishonor to clutch at it so irrationally."

"Irrationally?" her brother repeated. "Marui, what about the signs? 'Fire from the east', the elders say. What more evidence do you need?"

"'And darkness from the west,' they say as well," she said, correcting the selectiveness of his memory. "The fire from the east is simply a reference to Teomin's ancestors. Even if it meant something more sinister, this is all the more reason I should join them. The last time our people stood idly by as a city was destroyed. Let us not make that mistake again."

It was clear from the firm set of his jaw that she was making little progress. Marui looked around in exasperation. She saw her nephew, dancing with the other elves. In him she saw a younger Tilon: inquisitive, graceful and headstrong. She truly hoped he would grow to be as strong as his father and his grandfather.

"You know what the signs foretell as well as I do," she said to her brother finally. "If we do not ally ourselves with the empire, we will find ourselves on the wrong side of this conflict. Etrusin is a good man, and he leads his soldiers for what he believes is right, which is nothing more than the defense of his home and his people. Look past your fears, and you will know the truth. If we leave him to fall to this darkness, we will be in its path when it rolls through our own home on its way to the empire, and it will not be stopped, neither by your bow nor your son's innocent face."

Marui could tell that she had struck a chord. His change in expression was slight, but it was enough to tell her that he would not soon have a rebuttal. With that she turned and walked away, leaving her brother to think about where he wanted to place his trust. She hoped it would be in her.

* * *

The eastern horizon glowed dimly as the sun neared its hour of rising. Five silhouettes stood by the edge of the camp carrying traveling packs and some weapons. Six horses stood nearby, pawing the ground occasionally and grazing on the grass. Komeris glanced at each of his companions with a grim expression. Pei-Shi stood as still as stone, hands resting upon the pommels of the two blades at her hips, calmly waiting. Next to her paced the bulky Reniu, muttering quietly and glancing sidelong at his captain, impatience evident in his eyes. Denlin, a tall, thin soldier with a shaven head, leaned upon his staff and stared at nothing in particular. Standing slightly apart from the group was O'eintsu, dressed all in black and watching Reniu's endless pacing without emotion.

The captain knew two of his companions well, for he had served with Reniu and Pei-Shi for many years, but these other two were new recruits. Komeris did know them by reputation, however, as both came from very well-known families within the empire. Denlin was from the house of Kou-Ioushin, which was so large it had virtually been its own tribe before the unification. The family boasted one of the most effective fighting styles in the empire and often took in students from other families to study at their secluded shiodu many miles east of the palace. Denlin was a master of the staff. Indeed, he had made it an extension of himself and was never seen without it.

The other soldier, O'eintsu, had also come from a family with its own shiodu, but no students from other families were allowed to join that school. The Lihou family was very secretive about their style, and it was rarely ever seen in public. Rumors had long spread throughout Kesitul, even before the unification, that all the male children of Lihou were indentured to their shiodu and were forced to undergo a harsh, lifelong training program that included extreme manual labor and sparse living conditions. The Lihou were masters of stealth, and if they donned their hoods, they were invisible in the shadows. Their only weapons, beside their limbs, were the small, flat, four-pointed *chiun*, star-shaped missiles that signaled eternal night for their victim.

Although the quiet Lihou soldier was more than a decade his captain's junior, Komeris had felt intimidated at their first meeting. But the captain had not gotten where he was in life by being timid, and he quickly recognized that he was more unnerved by the mystery surrounding this man's family than he was by the man himself. Knowing the nature of his own people, he also understood that the mystery and rumors of the Lihou shiodu had likely become exaggerated in the telling.

The horizon brightened a bit more, and Reniu's loud sigh broke the captain's thoughts. "Where is she?" he growled.

Komeris put up a hand to calm him. "Patience, Reniu, we are early. Remember?" Indeed, the five warriors had been restless all night, and each of them had come out to the agreed meeting place well before dawn.

"Not sure why she's got ta come along in the first place," the big warrior huffed in reply. "Not as if they ever leave their precious forest."

"On the contrary," came a sing-song voice from behind the soldier, "I think you will find we are much better traveled than even the most adventurous of your people."

Reniu turned slowly and scowled sheepishly at the approaching elf, and despite the difficult nature of deciphering the big man's expressions, Marui seemed to understand and accept his unspoken apology.

"Welcome, Marui," Komeris said with a bow. The other soldiers mimicked the gesture.

Marui nodded to each of them. "Good morning, my friends. No doubt Komeris has told you of me, though I do not know all of you."

Komeris caught the hidden request and briefly introduced all of his companions. Not wanting to waste time, he immediately pressed on. "Please forgive my haste, but we should begin."

Their new elven companion nodded her assent. "Yes, we shall proceed without delay, heading southwest. There is an easier path to the lands beyond the mountains that lies near the southern cliffs. Barring any recent natural catastrophe, the path should still be clear, though other dangers may wait along the way."

"For those, we will be ready," spoke up the otherwise quiet O'eintsu.

Marui gave him an appraising stare. "Very well," she said.

* * *

Su-Ni breathed a sigh of frustration as the group moved away from the camp. She had awoken early, grabbing the small pack of light supplies she had prepared the previous night, and snuck out to wait for the soldiers to gather. She scolded herself silently when she discovered that it had not been early enough, as they had all already assembled on the edge of camp. She was in the process of creeping around the tents when she saw Marui join the company.

The young diplomat cursed under her breath at the addition of the elf and the presence of the horses. This would all make it much more difficult for her to follow unnoticed. She strained to listen to their conversation, all the while making sure to be absolutely silent. She did not so easily forget the elves' keen hearing. As the group departed, the young woman debated with herself over the wisdom of following. It did not take long for her curiosity to win out, and she hurried off to try to get herself a horse. At least she knew the general direction they were heading. She was confident enough in her riding abilities to believe she could easily catch up with them at least by the time they got to the mountains. From there she would have many places to hide.

Sneaking off with a horse turned out to be easier than she expected, as few guards were actively walking that side of camp. And while she felt guilty about the theft, she didn't let it talk her out of what she was about to do. She thundered off in the early light of dawn, setting a steady pace to gain on her quarry, if perhaps not too quickly. As the sun broke the horizon, she felt very smug at having set out undetected after the group who had thought they'd been so careful. She wasn't really sure what she would do once they reached their destination, but she had the whole journey to work out the details.

It was clear to her that this group of battle-hardened warriors needed the presence of a level-headed diplomat, and she was going to make sure it was her. Ninei and Ini'io would never have understood. They would have insisted that this was not part of their original mission. That didn't really matter to her. What really mattered was that their empire was about to make its first contact with other humans for the first time in living memory. It was simply too important to be left to a bunch of soldiers.

The morning pressed on, and Su-Ni spent most of it imagining what lay at the end of this journey. She practiced several speeches aloud, one for if she was caught, one to make peace with their supposed enemy, and one to graciously accept the praise of the emperor upon her return. She was oblivious to the way her voice shuddered with every hoof beat, and she hardly noticed when her horse slowed down to rest before galloping off again. She only half watched for the scattered signs of the group's passing.

But by late afternoon, the young diplomat's cavalier manner faded, and she began to worry. Though she had wanted to catch up with the party gradually, she realized that night would be upon her soon, and she wasn't too sure about being alone in the wild. Her wisdom was returning to mock her curiosity. She began truly searching the ground ahead of her more closely for some sign that the group had passed this way.

The sun eventually began to set, and Su-Ni rode on, desperately searching for an indication that they had stopped to make camp. But she saw no campfire spring up on the horizon, and all she could do was continue in the direction she had been riding all day and debate turning back.

Hours passed and the moon had just begun to peek over her shoulder when a campfire did finally spring up not far in front of her. She brought her horse to a halt and practically dropped to the ground. She immediately felt foolish as she realized that, though she was surprised to find she was so close, it was unlikely that any of the warriors could see her in the darkness beyond their campfire. She did note with pride that her sense of direction had been completely accurate, as the fire had popped up directly in front of her.

Gratefully stretching her muscles, sore and buzzing from a whole day of riding, the woman unpacked a blanket and spread it out upon the grass. But before she lay down, she thankfully rubbed down her horse and apologized for pushing him so far today. The horse grazed wearily, but seemed pleased with the attention she was giving him. Finally, the young diplomat relaxed. She lay upon her blanket propped up on her elbows and facing the party's campfire. In this comfortable position, she realized how very relieved she was to be resting this night. She was weary from the day's travel, and soon her eyelids drooped, and her head nodded.

A well-waxed moon hung overhead when she awoke to find herself slumped over her arms, which had folded under her as she slid into a deep slumber. She couldn't imagine how she had managed to sleep in such an awkward position all this time. She rolled onto her back, stiff from the ride, and clenched her tingling fists several times to regain the circulation in her forearms.

Sitting up, Su-Ni looked to her unwitting companions' campfire. It was burning low, though she knew someone must have still been awake, keeping watch and tending the small fire. The young diplomat took comfort in the tiny yellow light in the distance, and she sat watching it for several minutes until her eyelids once again became heavy.

Somewhere to her right, a cricket chirped, and her eyes snapped open. A little in front of her, another cricket answered. She realized that the small insects had likely been playing all night, and it was her stirring that had momentarily silenced them. She continued to sit still as the whole grassy earth around her slowly came alive with a crescendo of the natural music. Normally the repetitive, high-pitched noise would have aggravated her and kept her awake, but her weary muscles and heavy eyelids took that away. The cricketsong was a lullaby, and she was succumbing to its magic.

Her eyes snapped open again.

The sudden silence roared in her ears. She flinched and looked around cautiously. Perhaps she had begun to fall back and caught herself or her horse had shifted and the sudden movement startled the crickets. She peered into the darkness all about her but could not see beyond ten feet in the light of this not-quite-full moon.

Su-Ni froze as a light patter, almost imperceptible, issued from her left. It seemed as though the sound darted quickly to somewhere in front of her. The distant campfire blinked out of her sight for just a moment. She knew something was out there now. Her horse sensed it too, as he snorted nervously. Something was circling them. Not ready to panic yet, she wondered if it might be someone from the camp investigating the area.

"Hello?" she ventured, but not too loudly. "Who is there?"

Something flashed in the darkness, low to the ground. Four little circles appeared and disappeared quickly just out beyond the dim light. The young diplomat recognized the reflection of the moonlight in the eyes of some animal.

Or animals.

It seemed to her that it had to be more than one, for she had seen two pairs of eyes flashing in the dark. She peered out all around her, squinting slightly at the effort. The pattering came again, followed by another flash of eyes. Her horse began to stamp restlessly. Su-Ni started to worry that a pack of hungry wild dogs had come upon them in the night and saw them for what they were.

Easy prey.

Su-Ni cursed herself for bringing no weapons with her on this journey. Not that she was skilled with any weapon, but she certainly would have felt safer now with some kind of dagger in her hand. She glanced over at the faintly glowing campfire in the distance and wondered if they would hear her if she screamed and, more importantly, if they would arrive in time to save her.

She gritted her teeth against that thought. She was not even sure if the creature, or creatures, were dangerous. She would only reveal herself if she perceived a greater risk in doing otherwise. Of course, she wondered again if there would be enough time to save them when she finally perceived that risk.

A low chittering sound broke the silence, causing Su-Ni to jump and her horse to let out a strained neigh. She got up quickly and cautiously stepped over to the horse, patting him reassuringly on the neck. She looked all about, trying to catch another glimpse of their stalker. She tried to control her breathing and strained to hear over the pounding of her heart in her ears. That sound was surely not made by any dog.

Out of the corner of her eye, she saw another movement, and she turned to look. Something stepped into the circle of low light offered by the moon.

She could see that it was some manner of quadruped, but she was confused by strange shadows waving near its head. The creature ventured closer, seemingly smelling the air and looking from side to side. As it stepped toward her and into a bit more light, Su-Ni's confusion melted into tentative fascination. The wavering shadows were made by an extra set of long, jointed forelimbs that grew from its well-muscled chest. She was also shocked to see that the two pairs of eyes she had seen belonged to only a single creature. It turned its head again to focus on her with the other pair of lidless, glittering black eyes.

Though the rest of the creature's brown fur-covered body was dog shaped, the four eyes and the two extra limbs, which now started to unfold and probe the ground in front of it with large, black, single-clawed tips, made it seem almost spiderlike. It chittered again, and Su-Ni noted the massive black beak from which it had issued the sound.

She marveled at the enigmatic looking creature. It seemed to be a mix of the most unlikely animals she could think of. She also thought, though it did nothing to quell her uneasiness, that the creature had a rather comical face. A bony ridge set high on its flat head made it look a bit surprised to see her. She knew better than to be at ease as those two taloned limbs now pawed at the air.

The creature chittered once more in an almost quizzical tone.

An answering chitter came from behind Su-Ni. At that unexpected sound, her horse gave a terrified cry and bolted. Now, she was definitely feeling panicked. She heard an unfamiliar screeching from the direction her horse had run. She looked back and forth between the two beasts that were creeping toward her while at least one more chased her horse. As they came closer, it seemed that their tapered bodies crouched lower, especially in the rear, where their thickly-built back legs twitched eagerly.

Su-Ni did not doubt the imminent danger, but she was too stunned to find voice enough to scream for help. The way the two creatures padded forward, more with those powerful rear legs than with their front, told her that she needed to be ready. Each inch that they crept closer brought the prominent ridge of their spines arching even higher.

The two creatures leapt at her with terrifying speed, using their rear legs to push them off the ground and their extra limbs to provide impetus. It was purely her instinct that had Su-Ni dropping to the ground at just the right instant. She had barely hit the dirt and started rolling out of the way as they crashed into each other in midair. They fell to the ground and fought with one another, trying to disentangle their limbs, snarling and screeching simultaneously. The sound chilled Su-Ni to the bone, but she wasted no time gaping at the struggling beasts. She jumped up and began running toward the low campfire in the distance. Out of the corner of her eye, she saw a third creature take up the chase, screeching loudly.

Now she screamed.

She was running full speed, yelling for help as loudly as she could. The fire that had moments ago seemed comfortably close now looked as though it were miles away. She looked back over her shoulder, hoping that the creatures had decided she was too much trouble. She looked just in time to see a sleek, fur-lined body flying at her.

Again Su-Ni ducked, but it was not fast enough this time. She was hit with a force that knocked the air from her lungs and pushed her to the ground. She screamed again as the creature's claws dug into her sides. She threw her arms up defensively against the wildly stabbing talons of its forelimbs. The beast's screech tore through the night air and left her ears ringing so that she could not hear the others bounding up fast to join in the kill.

She knew they were coming anyway, so she continued to scream and tried desperately to roll out from under the beast while still attempting to defend herself. The creature merely screeched louder and dug its claws in deeper. Its talons tore deep gashes in her forearms, which began to lower as Su-Ni tired and as muscle was cut down to the bone. Her screams became weak, pleading sobs. Tears mixed with blood.

Suddenly, the creature on her lurched, and the pitch of its screech increased to a surprised squawk. It jumped back and continued squawking loudly, its forelimbs flailing before it wildly. Su-Ni had to blink several times before the blood and tears cleared enough for her to see what caused the commotion.

An arrow protruded from one of the beast's four shiny black eyes. The other creatures skittered back uncertainly, turning their heads from side to side to consider their injured companion. Another arrow thudded into a second eye and went even deeper than the first. The creature flopped onto its back and writhed around violently, forelimbs desperately clawing for the painful missiles. One of the limbs did hit an arrow, but it did little to ease the creature's pain, at least at first. After a few more wild thrashes, its limbs shuddered sickeningly, then twitched a few times, then lay still. Both arrows had embedded deep within the beast's small brain. Needing no further prompting, the other creatures bounded out of sight in a few quick leaps.

Su-Ni dropped her head back to the ground and continued to sob quietly, holding her lacerated arms against her chest. She jumped slightly when a figure appeared in her tear-filled vision, but she was relieved to note that it was more human shaped. She sniffled a few times and took a few deep breaths to try and calm herself, but she was very shaken by her brush with death.

"Odd prey for the *meilif-danar*," a familiar voice said. "I doubt they are accustomed to diplomat, a delicacy to be sure."

Su-Ni sat up and shakily wiped her eyes. "Marui?" she asked.

"Yes," answered the elf, offering the woman an open hand.

Su-Ni looked at that hand, but did not take it. She could not bring herself to take her arms away from her chest, though keeping them there did little to lessen her pain. Moving them, it seemed, offered only more pain, so she simply rolled onto her thigh and bent her legs under her. Marui slung her bow over her shoulder and knelt to lend a steadying hand.

"Thank you," the diplomat offered, then after a thought, a more heartfelt, "Thank you..."

Marui nodded, but grimaced at the young woman. "You are fortunate it was my watch," she said. "If one of your kin had been at that duty, more than your horse would have perished tonight." Her voice was scolding, though in truth, even if it wasn't the elf's watch, she would have heard the struggle in the quiet meditation that served as her race's sleep. "Why have you come out here?"

Su-Ni hung her head, her sobs returned at the loss of the horse. "I was following you," she admitted shamefully.

"Obviously," came the reply, but Marui didn't question any further. She understood that the young woman was not in much of a condition to talk. "Come. We must tend to those wounds quickly. You are poisoned, but fear not, I have the remedy," she explained.

The two of them walked as quickly as they could manage to the camp, elf supporting human. They spoke no other words as they walked, for Su-Ni was lost in the contemplation of what the consequence of tonight might be, and Marui simply let her think. That knowledge, the fact that she would not have drawn another breath, and the fear that it inspired would be all the punishment the diplomat needed. The gashes on her arms were painful, but they would heal, and those scars would be a poignant reminder of the hard lesson she had learned today. So thought Marui, and it helped her to feel some measure of sympathy for the frightened woman.

She brought Su-Ni to the camp and bandaged her wounds tenderly. She administered a small sprig of some herbs to the young woman to help her sleep, though she was clearly exhausted, and to help counteract the dangerous poison that the meilif-danar exude from the tips of their sharp talons. Once the woman was resting soundly, the elf fed a few twigs into the fire and sat watching for the rest of the night, not bothering to wake anyone else in the camp. Let them rest, she thought, they would need the strength.

* * *

A quarter of the distance from the heart of the wetlands back to Niele'itio was through that plant-choked and treacherously muddy ground that made up the bog. Any man, no matter how road hardened, would have spent at least as much time navigating the swampy mire as traveling the longer open plain straight to the dark city. But Agucho was no man, and he walked and slithered and hopped his way through those lands he had known as his home for so many years of his life. He did not wish to so quickly be away from home again, but he knew better than to tarry. He knew the consequence of denying Orbein and his queen both.

So, the shapeshifter hurried through the saturated earth that felt so good against his feet, by the shelter of the plant life that made him feel so safe, and out into the sun as easily as if he had been walking on open ground. As soon as the ground became firm beneath him again, he ceased ambulatory travel and took to the sky, knowing that he could be back in Orbein's city before the closing of the next day if he flew rather than walked. Indeed, before he had been gone even a week, he saw the looming pillars of the temple gate of Niele'itio rising before him.

Flapping his wings to pick up some speed, Agucho circled the Dark City and saw the masses of Vethisir's army still training on the field of Ionotu.

He watched them roll up one of the three small catapults and fire it. He saw another more massive siege weapon being assembled not far off. The huge counterweight identified it as an impressive replication of the trebuchet design that the shapeshifter had also given to Orbein. He grinned at the surprising efficiency of the general's men. In the week since he had last seen him, Vethisir had gotten his army to assemble three siege engines, and they were well on their way toward completing the fourth.

Satisfied with the progress he witnessed here, Agucho turned toward the palace. He circled briefly. Then, seeing an open window, he flew in. The occupants of the room, two young women draped in sheer fabric, both obviously concubines of Orbein, jumped at the sudden appearance of the large bird. They paused in their obviously private moment of feeding grapes to one another in lewd and suggestive ways to gape at the intruder.

The shapeshifter heeded them not, as he found human women to be featureless at best, hideous at worst. He simply flew out into the corridor and continued making his way to the king's chamber, though he knew he would just as likely find him along the way.

And so he did, quite literally, bump into the king as he turned a corner. He bounced off Orbein's chest and fluttered to the ground, shifting instantly to his normal shape, already prostrating himself at the ruler's feet.

"Your pardon, highness," he begged.

Orbein sneered at the groveling Fiu-Het. "Get up, fool," he commanded.

Agucho stood and looked up at the king. "I have returned, highness."

"So I see," the king said dryly. "Follow me, we must speak." With that, he stepped off down the hallway at a brisk pace.

Agucho realized they were headed back the way he had just come, and in short order, they entered the room where the two women waited. They had obviously already forgotten about the shapeshifter's odd entrance, as they had resumed their activities. They jumped again as the king entered, but this time they smiled seductively at Orbein and patted the large bed upon which they were stretched.

"You, you," he said pointing to each of them, "out." The two women pouted briefly, but they quickly exited the room when Orbein snapped, "Now!" He went to the doors behind them and slammed them shut. He stood at those doors for a moment, then turned to Agucho, a telling gleam in his eye. He walked over to the bed and sat down.

"Tell me, Agucho," he said eagerly, "what news from the swamps?"

Agucho bowed and licked his eyes briefly before starting. "I saw my queen, highness. She has agreed to send allies to fight at your side, though she is suspicious. She does not entirely believe the reasons I gave her, but she knows there will be great danger to her should she choose to wait this battle out," he explained honestly.

Orbein smiled. "I see that you have interpreted the situation quite well. And when should we expect her warriors?"

"She is rallying them as we speak and will send them at my request," Agucho replied.

The king grimaced. "She will send them at my request," he corrected the Fiu-Het. "In fact, I am very disappointed that they were not immediately behind you."

Agucho's skin began to ooze. He once again moistened his eyes. "Highness, you must understand. She yet needs to send out the call. We are scattered thinly around the wetlands. We do not gather together in dense cities as you do," he defended.

The king's eyes narrowed. "Well then, you should have waited to return to me. I am very disappointed," he said again.

The shapeshifter bowed low. "I humbly beg your pardon, sire," he groveled.

Orbein grinned amusedly and said, "Perhaps, but there is something else that weighs upon my mind, my friend."

Agucho caught his breath. He had never heard the phrase 'my friend' uttered so insincerely. "Yes, my lord, what is it?" he asked hesitantly.

"I fear my castle must be an incredibly dull place compared to your swamps and bogs," the king said wistfully. "I wonder what you do in my kingdom when you are not by my side dealing with the tedium of court life."

Agucho felt he knew where this was headed, and he eyed the king warily. "I am not bored in your court, highness," he said slowly.

"Ah, of course not," he said with a chuckle. "Not when the training field of Ionotu is so close by. Tell me, Agucho, do you feel some sort of kinship with the only other foreigner in my city? Or do you perhaps envy him for the excitement he finds among the ranks of my army?"

"Laernus," reasoned the Fiu-Het.

"Yes, the seer," the king replied. "Perhaps, there is another reason you go to visit him."

Agucho grinned in spite of the situation. Truly, he thought, Orbein should have just come right out with it, rather than taunting the shapeshifter. He did fear the king, but his sense of self preservation was a much stronger force. As the ruler sat there trying to play on his fears, Agucho had perfected the lie he had been working on since he first met with the seer. "Yes, highness, I have visited Laernus on the field of Ionotu and have held private conference with him," he said honestly.

Orbein raised his eyebrows. "Do tell," he said smugly.

"You cannot deny that the seer has a valuable skill, especially given our current plans. Though he has a foul attitude and a tendency to be uncooperative, it seems a shame to let that skill go to complete waste.

Besides, he has learned some humility among the merciless soldiers of Vethisir," Agucho explained.

The king listened with a growing look of interest upon his face.

"Though I still say," Agucho went on, becoming more confident, "keep him where he is. He may yet have lessons to learn with his new comrades. But let us not ignore him. He has made it clear that he will not obey you, and were it not for his talent, I would say kill him. Let us instead glean what benefit we may from his talent and be rid of him when he is no longer useful."

Orbein's expression had now completed the change from accusation to intrigue. "I take it you have already begun this process," he stated more than asked.

"Yes, sire, I have," the shapeshifter said with a twisted grin, "and with the information given to me at our first meeting, I understood my people would join us on the battlefield long before I spoke with my queen. It will be a great force gathered for the march to the east, greater than any seen since the days of your ancestors."

Any lingering doubt in Orbein's mind about the shapeshifter was banished at this vision of supremacy. The man stood and gave a great cheer and ran for the doors. He pulled them open and yelled for the women. Wisely, they had not gone far and came running into their king's arms at his call. He kissed both of them lustfully and pulled them into the room.

"Would you like one?" the king asked Agucho, giving both girls a tap on the bottom.

Unlike the two women, the shapeshifter hid his disgust well. "Nay, highness, I have other business to attend to."

Orbein laughed loudly. "What's wrong, girls, don't you know what our friend Agucho is? He is a shapeshifter, a Fiu-Het. He can be anything you want him to be!" And with that statement he pushed both of them toward Agucho.

The shapeshifter noticed that the statement only increased the look of revulsion on one of the girl's faces, but the other walked up to him with a look of suggestive fascination. "Anything?" she whispered seductively.

Agucho eyed her warily and sent his sticky tongue out over those eyes even as she stared, hoping it would unnerve the woman and send her away. To his chagrin, it seemed to have the opposite effect. "I must be going," he said tonelessly, stepping around the excited woman.

Orbein laughed all the louder and said to the women, "But why would either of you want anything more than me?" and to Agucho, "I'll allow you this reprieve. Go to our seer friend on the field of Ionotu. See what benefit you can glean from his talents."

The Fiu-Het bowed deeply, then hurried out of the room, the king's boisterous laugh and the giggles of the two girls following him out. Heaving a huge sigh of relief, Agucho stepped quickly down the hallway, grateful to put that room far behind him for more than a few reasons.

* * *

Standing on a tiny hill, no more than a natural mound of dirt, Laernus looked out upon the construction of the enormous trebuchet. It seemed to be going well, but the seer was worried. The mishap with the third catapult was not far from his mind as he watched this larger and more complicated engine being assembled before him. The supporting structure, with heavy beams that went well into the earth for stability, was in place, and even the counterweight had swung freely in a preliminary test that had the men jumping and cheering. But Laernus knew that once the large throwing arm was secured, and ammunition was loaded into the sling, their mastery of physics would be put to the test. With an image of the catapult crosspiece almost crushing a soldier flitting through his mind, the foreign wizard glared sternly at the hammering, lifting, and sweating workers. One of those workers, a man hammering iron plugs with a large mallet, stopped his labor for a moment and looked over at the hill. The mallet fell to the ground, and his jaw hung open.

Laernus turned his glare to the man and scowled. "You there! Get back to work!" he yelled. Then, his keen intellect catching on, the seer understood the only possible reason for the man's agape expression.

"Good afternoon, Agucho," he said without even turning to confirm the shapeshifter's presence.

"Laernus," was the Fiu-Het's reply, punctuated by a serpentine hiss at the end. "It seems you are much better off than when last I left you."

The seer gave a smug chuckle. "It seems strange to me that I feared these men. Now I see them for the inept fools that they are," he said.

"Inept?" Agucho asked curiously. "It seems not long ago they were not so inept to you, when you stood bruised and battered in their midst." Laernus shifted uneasily at that. "I do not see many fresh bruises. Could it be that you have learned the way of the sword so quickly to put the fear of Laernus in them?"

Sticking out his chest, the seer grinned. "I have, indeed, learned the way of the sword."

The loose skin of Agucho's face tightened in disgust. "Or could it be that they fear something else? Yes, I think that is it. No matter how attentive a student, no one can so quickly learn to earn a man's fear or respect. If they thought I had no use for you, they surely would have killed you by now."

The blank stare on the face of Laernus told the shapeshifter that, not only was his assessment correct, but it was also the first time it had even occurred to the seer. So, once again had the Fiu-Het taught him humility. But that look was quickly replaced by something else: angry determination. Agucho had helped him survive his stay thus far. He had even given him an opportunity for advancement by getting Vethisir to agree that the seer should supervise the building of the siege weaponry, seeing as how he was the only one in the army familiar with the machines. This day would mark the end of that dependency. Laernus decided from that moment on, every gain he made in Vethisir's army would be by himself, for himself, and to spite the smug creature that now scowled at him.

Agucho recognized the set of the seer's jaw and its general implication. He smiled, the expression a nightmare of flesh in broad daylight, and said, "Good! I think you see my designs for you clearly now. Take your anger and harness it. It will be a powerful tool for you in the future."

Laernus snickered and looked back at the trebuchet. "The future..." he said.

The Fiu-Het clapped his hands. "Ah, yes!" he exclaimed. "That reminds me. If you could spare a few moments away from your duties."

The look the seer gave him now was quite different. He seemed pleased. "I believe I could be convinced." And with that he moved to follow Agucho.

A short distance away from the hill they met Vethisir. The general stood in their path with his arms folded across his chest and several large soldiers behind him. The man seemed to be in a foul mood. "Hold!" he commanded.

Agucho bowed to him. "I must ask you, good general, to step aside. I have pressing business to attend with this soldier."

"Business?" spat the incredulous Vethisir. "Any business you have with this soldier is my business and the business of the king!"

"Yes, indeed," Agucho replied without missing a beat. "Unless the king does not wish it to be your business."

The general sputtered out the beginning of a few responses before he finally came up with, "Then I suppose the king would not be at all surprised if I went and asked him of this right now?"

The shapeshifter waved a dismissive hand. "Please, go quickly. The sooner you leave my sight the sooner we can proceed with the king's business. In fact, you will find him in a private room far down the east wing corridor of the upper level. I told him to expect you." This was a dangerous game, Agucho knew, but one he could not help but play. He almost laughed out loud as the general instantly stormed off toward the castle. Without Vethisir there, the other soldiers quickly dispersed at the shapeshifter's frightening glare. With no further impediments, the two walked on to their conference.

General Vethisir fumed into the castle through a private side door that faced the field of Ionotu. He stomped loudly up the stairs and made his way quickly to the east wing. In truth there were several corridors in each wing, but they all had one main corridor from which they broke off to lead in many twists and turns that made each section seem much larger than it really was.

The general was virtually running down the main corridor in the east wing now. He came finally to a set of double doors, the last in the hallway. He clearly heard the king's voice through those doors. Vethisir almost pushed right through those doors, so furious was he, but then he remembered himself. He rapped three times loudly against the polished wood and stepped into the room.

"Who else has come to join us?" the king called out, but his voice died away.

Vethisir stood frozen. The king lay on volumes of satin and sheer sheets between two naked women. It really didn't appear as though he had been expecting the general.

"Your pardon, sire," Vethisir mumbled and turned to leave.

"Halt!" called Orbein. "Obviously something important brings you to disturb my relaxation. Speak your mind, general."

Vethisir turned back, but kept his eyes lowered. "It is the shapeshifter, highness. He meets with the seer again."

Orbein heaved an irritated sigh. "Vethisir...go back to your field. Count yourself as fortunate to have erred before me on a very good day."

The general stood there in shock for a moment, then turned and walked slowly out of the room, closing the door gently behind him. How had he been so foolish? He saw now that he should have recognized the trick as the shapeshifter had set it in motion. He had let his anger blind him, and that was not a mistake he would soon make again when dealing with Agucho. Vethisir may not have been the wisest of men, but he was reasonably intelligent. The Fiu-Het had struck the first significant blow of a personal war with the general, and it was one that he would pay for. The tactician who had gained leadership of the Dark City's army would see to it.

14 AWAKENING

Standing a few feet apart and facing one another, both Urietsin and Kiusu breathed deeply, their eyes closed. They were as still as the mountain upon which they stood, but their stances were relaxed. A long moment of silence was punctuated by nothing more than the almost imperceptible motion of the air. The two men seemed to be in some form of synchronous meditation.

Suddenly, Kiusu's fists were in motion, or must have been because in one moment they were one place and in the next another without seeming to have ever been any place in between. First a right, then a left to Urietsin's chest, both of which were picked off cleanly by the Swift One's equally fast parries. The right fist came in again, but upward toward Urietsin's jaw in an uppercut meant to knock a man unconscious, but again the young warrior proved the swifter, leaning just out of reach. Kiusu kept the momentum of the fist going up and then around to his shoulder to shoot straight out at Urietsin's face. The Swift One waved the attack away with his deflecting forearm. Again the old man continued, this time with the momentum of the inside block, to bring the same fist around in a backfist. Again, Urietsin sensed the tactic and continued leaning his body out of the way of Kiusu's seeking fist. Not ready to abandon the use of his right just yet, the elderly master shot out a double front punch aimed for his opponent's chest. Both of the Swift One's hands shot up and in between Kiusu's arms, continuing upward; the punch sailed harmlessly over Urietsin's head.

Kiusu decided to change his tactic. With both of Urietsin's incredibly fast blocking hands up high, the old man brought his leg up, bent at the knee, then thrust his foot out in a straight kick aimed for the Swift One's gut. To his credit, the young warrior managed to exhale completely and tighten his stomach, bending quickly to absorb some of the impact.

151

Ultimately, the kick was true, and Urietsin was sent stepping backward to maintain his balance.

Urietsin opened his eyes, which had remained closed since the beginning of the lesson. He frowned at the old man staring back at him, rubbing the slight sting he felt upon the skin of his abdomen. "You cheated," he defended.

Kiusu raised an eyebrow. "Indeed?"

"You kicked me," the younger man explained.

Kiusu nodded, but his look was still doubtful. "Do you think that men do not kick in a real fight?" he asked.

"Well, no," the Swift One admitted, "but neither do they fight with their eyes closed."

"There are many times when your sight may not be available to you, though I am confident that such instances will not prove a significant challenge for you." Kiusu meant the compliment sincerely.

Urietsin merely responded with a slow nod.

"Truly, much of your skill lies within your instincts. They are so finely tuned that one might mistake them for future sight!" the old man beamed. "I remember receiving many more such hits from my master in that exercise."

The Swift One's eyes softened as he imagined a young and inept Kiusu. "Well, regardless," he said, his expression now jokingly suspicious, "the lesson was to stand in one spot while we sparred. You lifted your foot."

"And yet here I am, still in the same position. Standing on one foot is still standing. My kick did not require me to move away or forward. I did not jump, nor did I crouch. I stood here and defeated you fairly," Kiusu explained. "Let us not forget that I made six offensive moves prior to that kick. How many had you made?"

The question was clearly rhetorical, but not boastful. Yet still it stung the Swift One's pride. He knew the value of a well-placed counterattack. He regarded his mentor sheepishly. "Your strikes came too quickly. I needed to focus my energies on defending myself," he said.

The old man shook his head. "You are very fast, Swift One," he began, emphasizing Urietsin's nickname. "As fast as any young warrior I have ever seen, and I have seen many in my long life. If you spend all of your energy solely on defense, you will tire before you can mount any offense. To what good will all that defense come if you are still defeated in the end?"

Urietsin looked down. He nodded slowly.

Kiusu grinned. "Come, strike me," he commanded.

The young warrior stepped toward his master, his arms at his sides in a relaxed position. He stood staring into the old man's eyes for some time. Urietsin didn't build up to the strike. He didn't wait some predetermined time to execute it. He simply let the moment happen, letting it be as much a surprise to him as it would be to Kiusu. In this way he could attack without giving his opponent any advanced warning. The pupil's left arm twitched, and his fist was there, seeking the face of the man standing opposite.

Kiusu's left arm, likewise, rose to meet the strike. The well-practiced master met his attacker's wrist with the side of his palm and pushed the fist aside, stepping away and letting Urietsin's momentum carry him beyond balance. As the Swift One's arm neared full extension, Kiusu's palm rolled fully onto his student's wrist. He gripped it and turned it toward himself. Urietsin's arm was now fully extended and locked uncomfortably into a position that forced him to turn his body away, but he did not need to look to feel the old man's right fist planted against his elbow. A strike that, if properly executed, would have shattered the joint and rendered his arm useless.

Kiusu released the young man and watched him step away with a look of comprehension. "You see?" he asked. "You can easily turn many defensive moves into offensive ones, even using your opponent's own momentum against him."

Urietsin nodded. Of course he understood. He even remembered using a similar tactic against Reniu when he had fought the big man as a new recruit in the imperial army, blocking the man's eager kick and holding the leg up to strike the felling blow. Of course, Reniu's thick limbs did not move nearly as quickly as his master's. The Swift One bowed reverently to Kiusu.

Kiusu returned the bow, offering as much respect to his student. "I must know, Swift One, how you perceive my strikes without your sense of sight," he said, indicating that the young man should walk with him.

After a long pause, during which Urietsin looked down deep in thought, he replied, "It is difficult to explain. Without my sight it is as if all my other senses are heightened. I hear the sound of your strike whipping through the air. I feel the air move as your strike cuts through it. And it may sound strange, but I am certain that I can sense your intent to attack. It's almost as though all my other senses work to form a second sight."

The master smiled at his student. "Exactly," he said. "You see, Swift One, using your other senses to compensate for lack of sight is a broadening of your perceptions. Such a broadening gives you a much clearer and truer sense of the interactions that occur in existence. You have proven yourself skilled at this with your physical senses, but there is so much more. If you go beyond the physical, you will begin to see that the possibilities for those interactions are boundless."

Urietsin listened quietly. He was coming to understand Kiusu more with each exercise. When the old man waved for him to follow, he went willingly, curious to see what his next lesson would be.

The two continued walking until they came to a small clearing. A large flat boulder sat within a circle of stones. It was the meditation spot that Kiusu came to frequently. Urietsin noticed a broken pole at one quarter of the circle. The other half, lying several feet away and topped with a scorched ring, piqued his already heightened interest.

The Swift One watched as his master entered the circle without a word and sat upon the boulder. Seemingly from nowhere, the old man produced a small pebble and placed it before himself. As Urietsin looked on, he recognized that Kiusu was now falling into a deeply meditative state. He was sitting cross-legged, his eyes were closed, and he was breathing deeply.

Several minutes passed, but Urietsin watched patiently. Eventually, Kiusu's eyes opened. The Swift One looked around curiously. He was about to ask the old man if he had missed something, when he realized that the lesson was not yet ended. Kiusu stared at the pebble, and immediately it rose into the air. It hovered for a moment, then slowly began to circle the master's seated form. Speeding up, the tiny rock wove tighter and tighter patterns around his body until, all at once, it stopped right in front of Kiusu's face. Slowly, it sank down to his lap, and once again, he closed his eyes.

After a few short moments, Kiusu stood. He noted the look of incredulity upon the face of his young student. He chuckled. "A mere trick?" he asked the young man.

Urietsin shook his head slowly and went to make several responses, but failed entirely. In his time with the old man he had seen some amazing things, but nothing for which he couldn't find some kind of explanation. Surely Kiusu had performed seemingly impossible feats of strength, but Urietsin realized the truth of ultimate focus. This seemed somehow beyond even that. That Kiusu had manipulated this pebble without even lifting a finger stunned the young warrior. This appeared to be real magic.

"To do such things," began Kiusu, "requires that you understand this one fundamental truth. Your body is merely a physical tool that your spirit uses to interact with the corporeal world. Transcending the bonds of your physical being, you will come to perceive that your spirit is an integral part of all that is. Because your spirit is connected to the essence within every tiny piece that makes up the universe, you have the ability to manifest change in the physical world by altering that which you perceive from the spiritual world."

Still in awe, the young warrior stepped into the circle of stones. If he had heard the explanation that Kiusu had just given, he made no indication. His eyes were locked on the small pebble that now sat upon the boulder. The old man moved aside and allowed the Swift One his inspection. To his surprise, Urietsin climbed on top of the large stone and sat down before the pebble. Kiusu grinned and stepped backward out of the circle to observe this necessary, and likely revealing, moment.

Kiusu watched the Swift One close his eyes as he went deep into his own meditation. He looked on curiously, but with great hope for his student. He knew that it was not reasonable to expect Urietsin to succeed on his first try. The old man wished he could let it happen on its own, if for no other reason than to see if the talented young man could do it. But Kiusu did not have the luxury of time, as he did when he was younger and a student himself. Beating back the rising guilt that he had been feeling since Urietsin's arrival, the master went within himself and was quickly swimming through the strands of infinity. He reached out to the Swift One.

Urietsin opened his eyes and regarded the tiny stone with them, as well as with a spiritual sight that had nothing to do with any physical organ. He keenly sensed all that truly existed around him, as he had begun to do frequently in meditation. His spirit reached out for the pebble, wrapping all of his thought around it until he thought he or it would explode from the pressure.

Kiusu could feel the spirit of the Swift One all about. It was strong and energetic, so much so that he feared his own spiritual presence would be discovered. He reassured himself, insisting that he was merely helping Urietsin to see, not to do. The old man ignored the tiny voice within that told him there were no shortcuts to these lessons, and he radiated his understanding of the multiverse to his student's spirit. He could feel a rise in tension in the surrounding atmosphere and realized that the young warrior was nearing the moment of truth.

Things far more detailed than anything Urietsin had yet experienced rushed past him in a flurry of indiscernible colors and shapes. They played in the periphery as the young warrior's focus on the pebble intensified. He was desperately curious about the pervasive understanding he knew was swimming all about him, but he was even more desperately determined to accomplish the task at hand. Just as he felt his being intertwine with every part of the tiny stone, three familiar faces shimmered in and out of the infinite swirling. Three warriors looked on sadly.

Suddenly, the moment was gone. Kiusu could no longer feel Urietsin's powerful spirit. He saw the young man's form slump considerably. The Swift One looked up at him with forlorn disappointment. Then, unexpectedly, Urietsin fell backward off the stone, unconscious before he even hit the ground.

When the young warrior opened his eyes, he found himself lying in his makeshift bed in Kiusu's hut. He could smell dinner cooking nearby. A few moments later, the old man approached holding a small cup of fresh tea. He offered it to the Swift One.

Urietsin sat up and quietly accepted the steaming cup, though he made no move to drink. He simply looked at it thoughtfully. After several minutes passed in seemingly uncomfortable silence, the young warrior finally spoke.

"Seishin?" he asked.

"Yes, Urietsin, what is it?" Kiusu returned hesitantly.

"How does death fit into this multiverse you always speak of?"

The old man nodded and heaved an almost relieved sigh. "Death is a part of an ongoing cycle. Without death, life would not be possible. Death simply means a part of something that was once living becomes a part of something else that is alive, which will in turn fulfill the cycle and become part of something else living once it's spirit has passed from the corporeal universe."

Urietsin pondered this. "What of the spirit? What happens to that?" he asked.

Kiusu smiled. "The spirit is a small piece of the infinite energy of the multiverse. When it leaves the physical body, it returns to that energy to be used again for all life in the multiverse," he explained.

While this was generally reassuring to the Swift One, there was something about it that still left him feeling empty. Surely, life needed energy from existence, which made death a necessity, but the good that came from such loss was little solace when men's lives were stolen in their prime. And the beauty of the cycle of birth and rebirth did little to alleviate the lingering guilt of one who felt even remotely responsible for such loss.

* * *

Though the year was beginning to wane, and the cool months were fast approaching, the weather showed no signs yet of giving up the warmth of summer. From the moment of dawn, the comfortable, if cool, temperature of the evening quickly rose to that of an early summer's day and continued to hold well after dusk. This did not make it incredibly uncomfortable outside, but under the dark hide of his tent, in the camp by the Shionen forest, General Etrusin of Kilelu felt a stifling heat. The daylight beat upon the outside and bothered him as surely as if the sun had come out of the sky to pound literally upon the tightly pulled flaps. The invasion of the sun's actual light through those flaps, however, seemed to agitate the general even more than the racket of the heat. He spent most of his time shut away in the privacy of that tent, no matter how hot it became, staring at the faint outlines on his map of the eastlands. But no man could withstand the sweltering temperatures within that small shelter day after day. Thus it was this day, when Etrusin finally emerged from his tent, albeit for a few short moments. When he reentered, he left the flaps, thus far so tightly drawn, open.

The soldiers in the camp were relieved at first to see that their commander was out and about, but quickly resumed their concerns as they noted his appearance. The general was a bit disheveled. He was unshaven and looked quite scruffy with uneven patches of scraggly hair growing on his chin and an almost full, but untrimmed, moustache. The hair on his head looked little better, sticking to his scalp and forehead with the salt of dried sweat. His koje and formal breeches were wrinkled and creased. He seemed to have just woken up from a month-long nap.

So, despite the fact that Etrusin's tent was now open to the camp, few soldiers approached. They all went about their business, training on the open ground and maintaining the site. The veteran soldiers gave the newer members their orders, and things went about as usual. But even those veterans were unsure about disturbing the general, who seemed constantly preoccupied by something. It was a visitor to the camp who finally entered through those flaps without hesitation.

Tilon marched out of the forest in full Shionen battle regalia, followed by a huge contingent of soldiers. The elf did indeed look regal, with a tall but light headdress of entwined gold and silver that crested forward and accented his angular features. He wore a complete suit of intricately-detailed leaves, shaped out of some metal that glittered brightly from each perfectly reflective curve. All of the soldiers who looked on from the camp, even those who were seasoned warriors, could only gape at the spectacle that was Tilon Enshei. By the time they regained their wits enough to wonder if they should take up their weapons, they realized that the force that followed the awe-inspiring elf was made completely of humans. It did not take them long to understand that these young warriors, clad in armor so familiar to them, were new recruits from the empire.

Tilon turned and called out to the men, "Go! Join now your kinsmen, soldiers."

The crowd that had come out of the forest dispersed quickly into the camp, and the low murmur of chatter quickly filled the air. Several officers attempted to approach Tilon for an explanation, but he merely brushed passed them straight toward the general's tent.

"Good afternoon, general," the elf said as he walked in.

Etrusin eyed Tilon warily and noticed the look of surprise upon the bedecked Shionen's face.

The elf recovered quickly and continued, "I have led to you a mighty gift from your emperor. Eight hundred new men to train at your camp."

The general's expression did not change. "Eight hundred?" he echoed in a hollow voice.

"Yes!" cried Tilon, who was already beginning to doubt again his sister's faith in the man.

"When did Tilon of the Shionen become concerned with how many men I will lead?" the general asked distantly.

Tilon looked down for a moment. "When I began to understand that those men would be helping to protect my land as well as their own, whether they knew it or not," he admitted.

"Protect..." echoed Etrusin as his eyes trailed along his map.

"General," prompted Tilon, trying to keep the disbelief from his voice, "what have you been doing here? You look terrible, and not at all like the man who marched here proudly with half an army behind him."

Etrusin laughed hollowly. "Yes, half an army, to defend half an empire against," he pointed to the map, "half an enemy? I started out so certain, but now that I am here. I cannot help but feel that we are ill prepared for whatever comes next."

Tilon could feel something strange inside. It was sympathy, much to his surprise. He had sat and thought long and hard after Marui had spoken to him. He realized, as he reviewed his youth and the things their father had told them, that his ill will towards the humans was nothing more than fear. Fear had kept him from seeing that his father did not resent humans, rather he regretted having to fight them because of one foolish leader.

The elf knew that he had to rely on the descendants of Teomin's empire, as they had to rely on the elves. But, looking at the general as he stared at his map, he could hardly bring himself to rely on this particular man in his current condition. Something was definitely distracting the general from his priorities, and it was not natural. Tilon decided drastic action was needed.

Moments later, the general jumped out of his seat as a shockingly cool sensation washed over his body. He looked out from under his dripping hair to see Tilon standing there with an empty bucket. The coolness of the water was only momentary, however, as it was quickly replaced by the heat of rage. He glared dangerously at the elf.

"Go wash yourself," Tilon suggested easily.

Etrusin seriously considered rushing the elf and pummeling him into the ground, but as the water ran down his body and pooled below him, it seemed to take with it some of the emotion that had been dragging him down. That emotion, he realized, was self-pity. He pushed his wet hair back and chuckled to himself, realizing how foolish he must have looked.

"I apologize," the general said sincerely. "I don't know what came over me."

"You are yourself again," remarked the elf. "Go cleanse yourself of the thoughts that have clouded your mind these past days. I bring more than the reinforcements from your emperor. We have much to discuss," he added.

It was almost an hour before Etrusin came back to his tent to speak with Tilon. He had spent considerable time rinsing off the dried sweat and dust, but the haze of the past few days as well. As he washed, he thought, and slowly he came to realize the strangeness of his attitude since his arrival at the camp. Several times he almost felt ashamed, but he quickly amended those thoughts as he recognized that they were not so dissimilar from what he had been feeling in the solitude of his tent.

After cleaning himself, the general went to the mess tent to get some much needed food. Once he was full, he walked about the camp, nodding to the soldiers as he passed. He knew they were all curious as to what he had been doing in his tent all this time. Actually, he wondered about that himself.

When he finally got back to his tent, Tilon was there waiting patiently for him. The sun was beginning to set, and the indirect light inside the tent revealed to Etrusin the true nature of the elf's armor. Out in the daylight, his mail shone brightly and made him stand out, but in the dim, early evening light inside the tent, or under the forest's canopy, he imagined, the elf simply disappeared. Each tiny, polished leaf so perfectly reflected the surroundings that, with the aid of a little Shionen magic, no doubt, it was the perfect camouflage. Had Tilon not turned to greet him, Etrusin probably would have missed him altogether.

The general bowed to the elf. "Good evening, my friend, and thank you," he said.

Tilon simply nodded. He indicated the seat across from him. "For centuries before this day, millennia even, we have been neighbors," the elf began. "We have lived next to one another, and this fact alone has fulfilled the definition of that word. But while our physical distance has not been great, we might as well have lived on opposite sides of the earth.

"Once, many years ago, my people and yours were great friends," he continued, "but time changed the nature of that relationship. Time and many mistakes on the part of both our peoples made us neighbors only in the strictest sense. It has been many lifetimes of your race that we called one another friends. It is too far back for the short memory of your culture, but barely more than a generation has passed for my people. There are many still alive who have not forgotten.

"Now we wish to lay aside the mistakes of the past and leave them in those days far away. It is unfortunate that it has taken a dark turn of fate to open our eyes, but we will not deny the opportunity while it lies so clearly open to us!"

The elf stood up quickly as his voice sang with hope. This was the moment he would redeem himself. In a motion that at first seemed completely foreign to him, he bent down to one knee and looked up to the general, who wore a look of quizzical bemusement. "The Shionen wish to offer their swords and bows in service of defending our two countries, and their friendship for the peace that must follow. We have only seven hundred warriors who are ready to join you, but I assure you they are the finest."

Etrusin stood and helped the elf back to his feet. He immediately bowed low. "Thank you again, my friend. They shall all be welcome," he said respectfully.

The Shionen smiled sincerely and nodded again, feeling more comfortable. The two sat once more, facing one another. It was silent for many minutes thereafter, but comfortably so.

"Tell me," Etrusin said finally, his curiosity having got the best of him.

"Yes?" asked the elf.

The general glanced once more at his map. "Of the times before. Of our ancestors," was his reply.

A dark look crossed Tilon's face. "Not all of it is pleasant," he explained.

"I believe you," Etrusin reassured him.

The elf heaved a long sigh, wondering how to tell the story with his new perspective. "Very well," he said.

* * *

"No less than four thousand years ago, when the elf who would bear my grandmother was little more than a baby, our two peoples roamed freely about the whole of this land," Marui began tentatively, capturing the attention of even the warriors who had been sulking at the discovery of the new addition to their scouting party.

Su-Ni had been too weary to even notice the scowls pointed in her direction, as her body fought the poison of the meilif-danar along with the help of Marui's antidote. So, she had engaged the only receptive member of the scouting party in a conversation that had led to this, a unique glimpse into her ancestors' past.

"There was a great, bustling city where your emperor's palace is now," the elf continued, "and it spread out for many miles in every direction. So many humans, and a few elves, lived there, and magnificent buildings and towers reached for the sky. It was a place so rich and diverse that it would not be unusual to see a Kundur craftsman or a Hahfdi merchant wandering the streets with wares."

"Wait," interrupted O'eintsu with a mixture of wonderment and confusion upon his normally expressionless face. "Kundur? Hahfdi?"

Marui grinned at the young soldier, and though it was in amusement, it seemed wistful also. "Races that have not been seen in this land for far too long. Both are shorter than humans or elves in stature, but there the similarities end. The Kundur, also called dwarves, are hard and gruff, whereas the Hahfdis are soft and gentle. Do not be fooled by the dwarven demeanor, though, for their hearts are forged of gold. Kundur have great strength and mine for metal or stones, with which they craft some of the most beautiful and clever creations the world may ever know. The Hahfdis are glib and dexterous. Actually, they are akin to elves in many ways. Their voices are musical, and they are skilled at almost any task they undertake, however they do have a lifespan closer to that of a human than an elf. Kundur live to be quite a bit older, though again not quite as old as elves.

"Both of them," she went on seeing that she already had the entire group enthralled, "would come with elves and men from lands far away to the glorious city of the east. It was the center of trade and culture for the entire continent. That is, until...the Cataclysm."

Pei-Shi gasped and whispered, "'And half the earth fell into the sea...'" a quote from a story told to all the children of the empire.

"Not into the sea," Marui corrected the warrioress, "just separated. It was an enormous mountain far to the north that vomited up ash and molten rock, so my grandmother told me when I was small. It covered much of the surrounding sky in blackness. The land all the way south to the shoreline cliffs became impassable. Thus were the eastlands, our home, severed from the rest of the continent. What has happened to the people beyond the great scar, I do not know. My father says they live still on the other side of the wetlands that sprung out of the destruction, but we have never heard or seen any sign of them in all these long years.

"I hope this is true," the elf added thoughtfully, "because it would mean that both of our races have kin somewhere in the wide world. Someday, perhaps, we shall all once again see visitors from those faraway lands, and go there ourselves. I lament the relative shortness of your lives as humans. I know that if such days do come again, I might still be alive to know the joy of seeing our cousins. For your people, that joy may have to be for your descendants long after you have passed."

Marui heard a choking sound and saw that Su-Ni's eyes were wide and filled with tears. The wise elf knew that the diplomat had keenly felt her mortality at this last statement, especially after her recent brush with death. She gave the young human a reassuring smile.

"It seems, however, that another joy may have come to you within your lifetime," she said hopefully. "Though it may be difficult to see it, for it comes wrapped in bad tidings."

"What do you mean?" asked Denlin leaning closer upon his staff.

The burly Reniu, who had thus far been standing nearby with his arms folded across his chest, pretending not to listen, stepped forward and chimed in. "She's meanin' the battle we're about ta fight."

Denlin looked from Reniu to Marui with an even more quizzical expression.

"He is right, young warrior," the elf explained. "It is no longer a secret to any who are here gathered that something is about to happen. We are about to be called upon to defend our lands from an unknown enemy, or perhaps one not so unknown."

She could feel their intrigue rising with every word, and even if they did not physically move toward her, she felt as though they were all closer, so focused were they upon her story.

"After the cataclysm," Marui continued with her story, "the eastlands had to become self sufficient. The people left here had to work together for their survival, and they did so with great success. Kesio'itio, the place you now call Kesitul, and Iono'itio, which I believe later became Iono'itul, grew to be the greatest cities the east had ever known. The Golden City and the Gleaming City were both well-named. Kesitul held the wealth of gold, provided by Iono'itul's miners, while the Gleaming City itself held the wealth of knowledge. Of the two valuables, gold is ever the one to inspire greed in men.

"Thus was Teomin, Determined One, first emperor of Kesitul, inspired. A lust for power over the city from whence came all his riches drove him to his destruction and ripped asunder friendships that had been forged for centuries. When Iono'itul denied his power, Teomin marched his army through our forest to conquer them."

Marui gave a pensive pause before she went on. "Teomin reached too far for Iono'itul and did not take care of what lay in between. We could not allow him to claim sovereignty upon a place that would know no ruler."

"You attacked them?" asked Pei-Shi with a look of astonishment.

Marui did not become defensive, she simply shook her head. "No. We had been friends of humans since well before living memory. We do not turn against our friends so quickly."

It seemed to Su-Ni that the elf had uttered this last statement a little too sourly. At a glance, none of the others seemed to notice, so she listened on, figuring that she would find out the source soon enough.

"We did not attack Teomin's men," Marui continued. "Instead we closed the path through the forest behind them as they made their way to the Gleaming City. My father tells me they went on to crush the city mercilessly, slaughtering innocent people in the streets, but when they turned back to their home, they found the way blocked. They never found a way back and eventually gave up and made Iono'itul their home."

"What did Teomin think of this?" Komeris asked, an amused smile upon his face.

Marui did not share in his mirth. "He did indeed find out what we had done, eventually. So displeased was he that he marched a force out to challenge us, but still we would not fight him. It was not long before his patience was worn thin, and he ordered his men to take up torches and burn down our home.

"No man left the battlefield alive that day," the elf said coldly, "not even Teomin."

All of the humans gathered around Marui were deathly silent. They were barely drawing breath, so shocked were they at the outcome of this story. A few legends about why the ancient empire had dissolved circulated throughout Kesitul for centuries, but none of them included the intervention of the Shionen.

Not that any of the humans before Marui could blame her kin for defending their home. Every one of them here listening to her story silently agreed that it had been the only course, though this was a drastically different characterization of Teomin than they were used to. Once everyone was breathing normally, and no harsh judgment was forthcoming, the elf pressed on.

"But here we are today, hopefully allies again. Therein lies the joy I mentioned. If we are fortunate, this new danger will prove to be the fate that binds us in friendship once again. Together we may also learn the fate of your lost brethren. We may find the descendants of your ancestors who marched through the mountains. Perhaps we will find that they, as you, have forgotten the mistake of Teomin and have become peaceful as of old."

Reniu snorted, "More likely that's who were goin' ta fight."

Marui grimaced. "I do fear that," she admitted, "but perhaps not. Perhaps we three peoples will be united against a foe that threatens all of the eastlands."

"I guess that is what we are going to find out," said Su-Ni, a determined look on her albeit weary face.

All eyes were on her now. Even Marui cast a doubting glance in the diplomat's direction.

"We?" asked Komeris.

Su-Ni turned to look at him with a panicked expression. "Surely you cannot think of sending me back to the camp," she pleaded.

"No. We cannot afford to tarry another day," explained Komeris. "We have already lost a day from your adventures, and we will lose no more. You may either go back to camp yourself or continue on, but make no mistake. If you choose to continue, know that we will not slow for you to catch up."

"You won't need to!" the young woman shouted indignantly. She stood up quickly and took up her blanket and headed for her pack.

"Let us continue right now," she muttered along the way. "I will no longer be such a burden. I will ride beside you with no complaint. I will..."

All of them heard her voice trail off, but only Reniu noticed her swoon. He ran up behind her and caught her as she fell backward. She looked up at the big man with a ghostly pale visage and tears streamed down her temples.

"I don't wish to be a problem," she said weakly. "I'm sorry..." Her voice trailed away again, and her eyes closed.

Reniu shook her gently. "Oh no you don't," he said. "Wake up, girl." But she did not. The strong soldier lifted her up and brought her to Marui.

Marui quickly reassured him. "It is alright, Reniu. She just overexerted herself too quickly. The antidote for the meilif-danar poison will cure her, she just needs to rest a bit more. I promise that tomorrow she will feel much better. She can ride with me."

The big man seemed relieved. He laid Su-Ni down gently and placed her blanket over her with care that almost seemed comical given the soldier's constant stern expression. He turned to face his captain. "With all due respect, sir, I'm thinkin' you might've been harsh on the girl.

Komeris raised an eyebrow. "You cannot deny that she has delayed us unnecessarily," he said incredulously, though his concern was more for the diplomat's safety than their travel time.

"If it had been one of us, would you be thinkin' it so unnecessary?" asked the big man seriously.

"One of you could have easily defeated the creature," Komeris argued.

Reniu shrugged. "Never seen a meilif-danar. Never seen a gotori either. Who's ta say how easy it would've been?"

"Marui," the captain replied easily, though he did wince at the mention of the gotori.

"That Shionen's mighty fine with a bow," Reniu came back. "Better than anyone I ever saw in the empire."

Komeris simply nodded.

About an hour later the scouts were gathered around a rather large portion of venison cooking over the fire. Marui had set about preparing the hide of the skinned deer for curing; she had refused to let any portion of the animal go to waste. Su-Ni slept fitfully nearby, jerking every once in a while away from something that hunted her in her dreams.

"How're we gettin' through these mountains?" Reniu asked, finally breaking the silence. "How'd they do it so many times in the old days?"

Marui looked up from the deerskin. "As I have said, there is a path, or there was in the days of my parents' parents. We are currently camped at the opening to that path. It will take us near the southern cliffs of Ikiu'iu, where the ocean beats upon the feet of the rock a long way below. The land along this path is not so uneven. We will have a much easier time traversing it than crossing directly through the mountains themselves."

"We will see Uselu'ikio?" asked Denlin, his young eyes wide with wonder.

"The Big Water should stretch out from the cliffs as far as even my eyes can see," the elf replied, "but our path may be far from the edge of the cliffs, and the ocean may only be visible from the highest point on that path."

Denlin wore a disappointed frown. "Never have I seen the ocean. My father told me he used to fish on the eastern shore years before I was born. I have always wished to see it, but I have always placed my dedication to my studies far above that desire."

Komeris, who was sitting nearby, reached over and patted the young soldier on the back. "Well, now it seems that it is those studies that bring you closer to that desire."

Denlin looked to his staff, realizing how much he depended upon it. It and his studies had been the driving force throughout most of his life thus far. He grinned. "Yes. Even if I do not see Uselu'ikio on this path, I know that my destiny will bring me to see it someday," the young warrior said.

"Pray that it is many years from now," spoke the usually quiet O'eintsu, "for if it is, it means that we have survived this mission and what is to follow."

With that sobering comment, the circle of scouts went silent. The only sound to be heard for some time was the crackle of the fire, the sizzle of cooking meat and the scraping of bone against deer hide.

* * *

A small, lone shelter, no more than a single-room cabin, sat among the thick trunks of the wooded area between the Ionotu training field and the castle of Niele'itio. It was far enough into the woods that it was not visible from the road, and its existence was known to few in the city. It was a secret place where General Vethisir could meet with some of his higher ranking officers and where some of those officers could spend leisure time with their women, or with the same woman if that was all they had available. As was often the case, two figures sat in the dim light of a single candle that flickered in the darkness. The purpose for this gathering, however, was neither recreational nor official.

"It is a great force that rallies around Orbein," Laernus said in a hoarse voice. His eyes were wide, but whether that was because of his awe at what he saw or the nature of gazing into the inky bowl could not be easily discerned.

Agucho sat, deep in thought, trying to pick his questions carefully. After several such meetings with the seer, he understood that some things were still too uncertain to be foretold. "How many of my people do you count among that force?" the shapeshifter asked.

"Many," was the initial response. Then, "Almost a third," the seer elaborated.

Agucho nodded. "Do they walk in the front?" he asked leaning forward.

"No," came again a single response, one that relieved the Fiu-Het, but then Laernus again expanded upon his simple answer with, "Most of them take to the sky."

The shapeshifter nodded again. "Scouts. Do they come upon anyone?"

Laernus squinted as if trying to see something very small or far away. "They strike the first blows of the coming battle," he said.

Agucho sat back. His lidless eyes felt so dry he thought they might crack. He shot out his tongue and massaged soothing moisture into them. "So, we are to be Orbein's fodder, as I thought," he said after his eyes were sufficiently wetted.

Laernus looked away from his gazing and considered the Fiu-Het inquisitively. "Do you so fear for your people?" he asked.

The shapeshifter regarded Laernus with incredulity. "Of course! How could I not?"

"From all that I understand about your people, it is Orbein's enemy that should be afraid," the seer clarified.

"You understand little about my people," was Agucho's harsh reply.

"I understand that the Fiu-Het are very effective at inspiring fear."

Agucho let out a loud and hollow laugh. He stopped abruptly and turned a menacing look on Laernus.

The seer's mind was suddenly awash with horrific imagery of the shapeshifter shooting out several sharp tentacles that stabbed straight through his body and tore him into pieces. He jumped back and shrank into a corner, covering his face with his hands.

"Effective," agreed the Fiu-Het, "but those fears are false and temporary. Once a human recognizes the trick, he will not fall victim to it again so easily."

Laernus crawled away from the corner, still a bit shaken from the abruptness of the visions imposed by Agucho. He stood and unconsciously patted down his clothing, feeling a bit sheepish about his reaction.

"Yes, yes, but you must have some ability that will aid you in the battle, aside from this distraction," the seer prompted.

Agucho grinned slyly. "Indeed. Need I remind you of your induction into Vethisir's ranks?"

Laernus scowled. "No."

"Our shifting abilities are useful for much more than disguise," Agucho explained. "In defense as well as offense. A man with a blade is almost useless against a Fiu-Het warrior, unless he is incredibly fast. If the cut from his sword does not sever, the wound will likely heal in very short order. We fear fire the most. Nor do we underestimate the wielder of a club, but again he must be very adept and very swift. Most humans are too clumsy and slow, and we can easily shift our bodies away from their blows."

"An impressive skill, indeed," the seer remarked.

"Indeed," repeated Agucho.

"So, why do you fear...?" Laernus trailed off.

The shapeshifter shook his head slowly. "Orbein will put us in the forefront of this battle, do not doubt. He will claim, of course, that he is letting us have the pleasure of taking revenge on those that are responsible for the death of Gayossha for ourselves. In truth, he will be protecting his own subjects by sending us to die before them.

"And we will die, many of us," he continued. "It is inevitable in war. I shudder to think what will happen to my home if many of our warriors are dead while Orbein's army is still strong. I do not need your seeing abilities to tell me our future should that be the case."

"You intend not to let that be the case," stated Laernus knowingly.

Catching the tone in the seer's voice, Agucho considered him with dilating pupils. He was impressed that Laernus had come to understand him so well in such a short amount of time.

"I do," was the Fiu-Het's simple reply.

* * *

General Vethisir stood in the throne room before his king with an uncertain look in his eye. He had grown accustomed to this expression, and he wore it easily of late when conferring with Orbein. Perhaps a bit too easily. Vethisir cleared his throat and tried to look more controlled.

"Are you certain you wish to leave so soon, sire?" he asked in the least doubtful tone he could manage. "The winter months soon approach."

Orbein sneered at the general. "I am not a fool. I am well aware of the seasons and the order in which they follow one another."

"Of course, highness," Vethisir amended. "I only meant that the men..."

"The men will march, and they will not complain!" the king interrupted. "The cold weather will keep their pace brisk. If the men of your army are strong, they will perceive no challenge in making it through the southern pass, where not even a single flake of snow has been seen in years. The ocean keeps the winter mild on that path. If there is one among your men who cannot endure such a simple trial, then better that he should die on the road."

Vethisir smirked. "There is one," he said.

Orbein's expression darkened even further. "Vethisir, I share your dislike of the seer, but let him be."

The general scowled. "So that he may conspire with that sniveling wretch?"

"Yes," the king replied easily, "because when they conspire, Agucho gleans valuable information for me."

"Forgive me, highness, but how can you trust him?" asked the general.

The question was met with a wicked smile. "Agucho is my puppet, though he may not know it." At that comment he stroked a small ring that sat upon the little finger of his left hand. The same makeshift ring he had placed there when he had sent the shapeshifter to the swamp to enlist the help of his queen, except it was now entwined with a thin band of gold.

"This ring binds his will to my command," he explained to the intrigued general.

"Magic," Vethisir whispered.

Orbein almost slapped away the general's foolish expression. It was a simple charm for the king, and the technique was far less interesting than the outcome.

"Yes," said the king, "I am sending him back to his homeland to bring to us what aid his people can spare."

If he wanted to, Orbein could have knocked the general over with one finger. Vethisir moved his lips voicelessly for some time, trying to find some manner of language to respond. He realized that he shouldn't have been so surprised at this news. After all, the king had been hinting at something like this ever since Agucho's addition to the court. The general had been subconsciously denying it, hoping that such a circumstance would never come to pass.

"How many?" Vethisir managed.

Orbein shrugged. "We will know when they stand beside you on the field."

Vethisir shuddered in spite of his efforts to recover from the shock of the king's declaration. He followed up with the next logical question, "When?"

The king cocked his head slightly and simply said, "As soon as possible."

15 DIFFICULT LESSONS

The small pebble held steady in the air. It was so still that it almost seemed to be a natural fixture in space. Were it not for the fact that it was simply hanging there, with no apparent support, an onlooker could have easily overlooked it. One onlooker was, indeed, taking note with bated breath. He watched with no small amount of fascination and respect as the pebble began to move around in a circle, then in more complex shapes. The tiny stone carved spiraling sculptures of air.

He felt very much the student then, watching the expert manner in which a tapestry of twisting patterns was woven before him. The ease with which every deft loop was executed impressed him greatly, even though he had seen much of the same thing for days now. He had never learned this so quickly. Of course, he had never had the kind of help this student had now.

"You demonstrate much control, Swift One," said Kiusu. He meant the compliment, but he had also spoken to see what effect it would have on the younger man's concentration. When it seemed that it would have none, the old man tried once more. "You've become adept at this exercise much faster than I ever did."

Urietsin was pleased at hearing the encouraging information, but he kept his excitement in some place far from his consciousness. He would not let himself become distracted. His focus was complete and would not be otherwise until the exercise was over. With a few more helical flourishes, he brought the pebble to rest before him upon the flat surface of the boulder. Then, closing his eyes, the young warrior took a few deep breaths and descended quickly back to his normal state of consciousness.

Upon opening his eyes, he grinned at his master. "Thank you, seishin," he said in reply to Kiusu's compliments.

The old man nodded and returned the smile. "I am truly impressed, although not entirely surprised," he added.

"Why not surprised?" Urietsin asked.

"We all have these abilities deep within us, Swift One," he explained. "They are natural, but as humans strive to separate themselves from what they perceive to be the untamed wilderness of nature, of our nature, they bury these abilities under the obscuring veil of a mundane consciousness. At one time humans were much like the Shionen, able to conjure up what we have come to call magic at will. It is magic to us because we have separated ourselves from it, and it has become mysterious to us, sometimes even frightening. Few humans still know that these talents are no more mysterious than the ability to see or touch. They are a more direct way of manipulating the universe in which we live than those limited physical functions.

"I say that I am impressed but not surprised because you are young and still cling to the open-minded innocence of your childhood. You have not yet completely covered up that other part of yourself, like so many others have by your age. There are not as many self-imposed obstacles in your way as there were in mine when I began my training. You impress me because my experience has shown a much slower expectation for progress, but you fail to surprise me because all of our race should be able to do what you have done thus far...and more," Kiusu finished, hiding no small amount of discomfort. While everything he had just said was true, the old man was stricken with guilt for leaving out what was to him a glaringly large detail: his own part in the Swift One's rapid advancement.

"More?" Urietsin asked, intrigued.

The elderly master blinked away his uncertain thoughts and stepped into the stone circle. He reached over and picked up the pebble. He held it before Urietsin for him to see, and with a twist of his hands, the tiny rock seemed to transform into a light, downy feather. A tuft of soft barbs waved as they caught the slightest current of air. Kiusu waited for a few moments and looked as though he were listening for something. Eventually, he placed the feather down in front of the Swift One where the pebble had been only moments ago. Then, with an encouraging gesture, he stepped back out of the circle.

The air was fairly quiet, but tiny little strands of feather still undulated in the imperceptible currents. Urietsin regarded it, and then Kiusu, with a perplexed expression. "What is the purpose of this?" the young student asked.

Kiusu shook his head slowly in response.

"But surely, if I can move a pebble, a feather will be no challenge to me. If I am to progress in my learning, then shouldn't my exercises become more difficult?" Urietsin said insistently.

Kiusu shrugged wordlessly.

Just then, a breath of wind, no more than a tiny motion of the air, came by. The feather grasped onto the current and rode away. Urietsin stared after it blankly.

"I suggest you go get it," the old man said.

Urietsin jumped up from the stone and took off after the errant feather. He could see it dancing on the breeze several feet away. He caught up to it easily, but when he tried to reach out and grab it, a sudden change in the wind sent it sailing away. He tried this several more times, only to be thwarted again by the cunning zephyr. He was beginning to think that the wind was toying with him when he finally snatched the floating tuft of down out of the air. The Swift One marched triumphantly back to the boulder with feather in hand.

Kiusu looked amused. "Do you still believe this will be so simple an exercise?" he asked smugly.

Urietsin stared at his master suspiciously for a few moments, then turned and hopped up onto his perch and sat. Waiting for the air to become still again, he held the feather against the smooth stone surface in front of him. When he could no longer feel any motion in the air, the Swift One let go of the feather and sat straight. He closed his eyes and began to breathe deeply.

With his student's first exhalation, Kiusu saw the down feather shiver on the waves of air sent out by Urietsin's breath. Within seconds of closing his eyes, the Swift One had sent the feather rolling forward, but not with the power of his mind. When a slight wind began to blow again, Kiusu had to stifle a chuckle.

Urietsin was not so amused.

Shortly thereafter, the elderly master left a flustered Urietsin to his exercise. And this time, he truly left him. Kiusu would not help him this time. While the old man feared time as he never had before, he insisted to himself that the young warrior would do this alone, no matter how long it took. He had to have confidence in the skillful warrior. It was not likely that Urietsin would succeed today, but Kiusu knew he would eventually. He had to.

Indeed, the Swift One did not complete the lesson that day. The early evening had brought a weary and frustrated young student back to the small hut, clutching the down feather between his fingers. But Urietsin was determined, so the next morning found him back at the circle to try some more. He was no more successful that day than the day before. Still, he would not be discouraged. Every morning he awoke early and went straight to his meditation. Once in a while Kiusu would come to check on his progress and to offer the occasional insight.

The resolute young warrior did make some improvement, though limited. After about a week, he was able to sit on the boulder all day without chasing after the feather. He had come to sense the currents in the wind, and whenever one strong enough to carry the feather away approached, he simply placed down his hand and held it in place. This did not turn out to be as beneficial a development as he had originally thought. Sitting on a hard boulder all day without getting up to stretch was not gentle on his body. Every morning his backside hurt as though he had slid down to the very foot of the mountain upon it. Aside from that, reaching out to catch the feather before it flew away was just as distracting to him as running off after it. None of these things, frustrating though they were, kept Urietsin from waking at first light and going at the exercise with a fresh perspective and that indomitable resolve.

Days slipped by into weeks as the young warrior practiced over and over again. It was a cool day in late autumn that broke the monotony of his daily routine. The air was unusually still, and Urietsin sat before his feather with the distinct intuition that this would be the day. He would master this lesson now or never.

Staring at the feather, he noticed that it barely moved at all, quite a departure from the past few weeks. He closed his eyes and breathed deeply, the customary beginning to all his meditations now. This struck him as strange, now that he thought about it. He always used to meditate with his eyes open and focused on something. Kiusu had taught him to internalize that focus by closing his eyes and concentrating on his breathing. Now it occurred to him that it might be to his advantage to combine the two methods.

Urietsin opened his eyes and looked again at the feather. He took a deep lungful of cleansing air and focused on the little tuft of down before him. Inhaling, he followed the breath inward to find that part of himself that was so much more aware than his conscious being. As he exhaled, he watched the soft barbs frolic in the currents of his breath. He centered on the random undulation of those little tendrils and how they reacted to his breathing. Entranced by the interplay, the Swift One eventually found himself fully aware of the nature of the interaction between the feather and its environment. He could see the tiny particles of his exhalation bouncing against the surface area of the down and how it caused the light material to react accordingly. He felt as though the feather were another part of himself, and he was experiencing all of the associated sensations of such an extension.

He gradually became conscious of something that had been bubbling just beneath the surface of his comprehension. The feather really was a part of him, as was everything in existence. He was connected to it and all else by virtue of being a part of the multiverse. With this realization he suddenly understood the other way this lesson was different. With all the other lessons, especially the ones where he reached out with his mind, there had been an endless call all around him from every channel that ran through existence. He had not heard the call in this lesson until just now. His consciousness pleaded with him once again to take advantage of this interconnectedness in an infinite number of ways. He blocked out the enticing distractions of infinity and held his focus only on the feather. He knew he was close now, and he would not let anything deter him.

He easily moved this object of his determination and recent frustration up into the air to float before him. He was almost surprised at how effortlessly this was coming to him, but such surprise would have been another distraction. He held his concentration and continued to move the feather around playfully, making it dance this way and that. He noticed, as it danced around, that its barbs would flail wildly depending on how quickly he moved it through the air, and this brought another idea to him.

He brought the feather before him again and watched it. He could see it reacting still to the subtle currents of his breath and the occasional slight motion of the mountain air. Reaching out with nothing but his thought, he froze the waving barbs where they were. Though he knew that air was still moving around it, the feather held perfectly immobile, as though suspended in time.

At this point, he could not help but feel a bit excited about his progress, and in that moment of celebration, the feather was gone. He felt something else there. Three sorrowful voices rose up above the calls of infinity and a pair of concerned eyes gazed upon him from the interconnectedness. He started to feel light headed, and he understood that he had gotten too distracted. As much as he wanted to seek out the spirits of the voices he heard and experience all of existence, he had to regain control and shift his perception back to normal on his own terms.

He opened his eyes to see Kiusu standing before him with his fist out. He was beaming. The old man turned up his hand and opened it. Lying on his palm was the feather. Just then, the wind started up quite abruptly. Kiusu closed his hand around the downy tuft.

"You were doing well," he praised the student excitedly.

Urietsin nodded. "I became distracted, though," he replied.

"Yes," the old man agreed, "but do not be discouraged. You have made much progress today. The more you practice, the better you will be able to disregard distractions."

His student looked pensive. "I felt something, seishin, just then, in my meditation," he said.

"What was it?" Kiusu asked uncomfortably.

Urietsin thought about it for a moment. "We are all one."

A chill went up the old man's spine. His relief was immeasurable. "Yes," he replied.

"What comes next?" the young warrior asked with an eager seriousness.

Kiusu chuckled. "Patience, Swift One. You have worked very hard on this exercise and have only just begun to understand its subtleties. There is yet more you can take from it."

"Oh," came the disappointed reply.

The old man patted Urietsin on the back. "Come. Let us have lunch," he suggested.

Urietsin's stomach grumbled in agreement. He hopped down from the stone and followed Kiusu to go get some food. Though he was disappointed that there was no new exercise, he was pleased with his progress today, and he let his gladness distract him from the memory of the voices. He wondered if tomorrow morning the wind would hold its breath as it did today. Regardless, he was confident that he could achieve similar results, considering the headway he had made. Let the wind blow tomorrow. Let it gust and howl. Urietsin would not be fazed.

* * *

Komeris and Reniu rode slowly through the valley, keeping near the trees whenever they could. According to Marui, they were very near the end of the path through the mountains. Indeed, for the first time since they began this journey, they could see no more mountains rising up behind the ones between which they were currently riding. On either side of them craggy peaks loomed, the last guardians of this mountain pass.

As the rounded what seemed to be the tallest peak of the whole chain, Reniu put out a hand. The two men came to a stop.

"What is it?" asked Komeris.

Reniu pointed. "There, captain," he said.

Komeris peered into the distance. On the horizon, he spotted what had caught Reniu's sharp eye. It was the corner of a stone wall. The captain nodded to his companion as they both continued cautiously ahead, pulses quickened by the thoughts inspired in them by this first glimpse of civilization since setting out.

They rode for several more minutes before the curve of the mountainside had pulled far enough to the side to reveal what seemed to be the edge of a city. It had, perhaps, once been surrounded by the stone wall, but all that remained now was the crumbled corner they had first seen. If not for the thin lines of smoke streaming from chimneys, the two men might have thought this city abandoned.

"We should get higher," Komeris suggested.

Reniu nodded in agreement and the two men rode into the foliage that crept up the mountainside to their right. Deciding that it would be faster to climb on foot, they left their horses to graze and started up the rocky incline.

It was not long before Reniu had made it far enough up the face to see over the thickening copses of trees that spotted the plain below. He was about to turn to check on the captain's progress, but he glimpsed something that froze him in place. There, in a wide open area outside the city, was a sight that brought upon him a mixture of excitement and despair.

"Captain," he whispered down as loudly as he dared, "You'll be wantin' ta see this."

Komeris pulled himself up to Reniu's level and peered in the direction his companion was gazing. "Minotros, protect us," he gasped.

In the clear plain beyond the trees, thousands of soldiers trained in the mid-morning sun. The two men stood agape at the sight for several minutes, watching the unmistakable movements of troops preparing for combat. Though the training field was yet some distance away, these two warriors had been part of such preparations countless times, and they knew without question what they were witnessing.

"We must get back to the camp," Komeris said. "I do not think it would be wise to tarry here."

* * *

Su-Ni leapt back defensively. She held high her broadsword just quickly enough to hear the clang of her opponent's blade meeting it. The jump was supposed to back her out of range of that wickedly cunning edge, but her challenger had met the move expertly, keeping the distance constant. The young diplomat had no choice but to continue parrying at a pace that was almost too fast for her to keep track of.

Left, right, high, low the blades rang out over the valley. Su-Ni's rival launched a blinding combination of cuts and slashes with the occasional thrust thrown in, but she matched them all with a desperate chain of blocks and parries. She was beginning to get tired. She knew she would have to take the offensive soon or the battle would be over. She tapped aside a fairly straightforward thrust and sprung ahead, inside the range of the parried blade. Her arm shot forward and pulled her entire body behind it and into a lunge.

It was a brilliantly executed maneuver that would have run most other opponents through. Her skilled adversary, however, had easily read the diplomat's intent and had employed a well-practiced sequence of footwork to step just out of range. As Su-Ni reached full extension, she felt her blade meet only the metal of her opponent's. Suddenly, it seemed as if her sword was somehow stuck, and she felt her arm pulled aside. The force was so great that she could not keep her grip, and the sword flew away. Her opponent advanced, and she fell back, away from the blade.

Pei-Shi lowered her sword and stepped up to Su-Ni, offering her hand to the prone diplomat. "You fought pretty well," she praised.

Su-Ni grimaced, but took the female warrior's hand. "I lost," she replied dejectedly.

"There's no shame in that," Pei-Shi reassured the diplomat. "To try and fail is courageous; to not try at all is cowardly."

"So, should I always try no matter how afraid I am?" Su-Ni asked doubtfully.

Pei-Shi thought for a moment. "Fear is healthy," she decided. "Reasonable fear is no more than logic. It helps you to wisely choose your battles. Courage isn't a lack of fear but of cowardice. Cowards let their fears decide their every action. The courageous also take into account the greater good weighed against their fears. Only the foolhardy rush into battle without that consideration."

The young diplomat nodded and bowed. She truly respected the warrioress. In the weeks since she had joined the small scouting party, Su-Ni had somewhat apprenticed herself to Pei-Shi. It was something of a mutual decision between everybody in the party. They had all decided that it would be safer for everyone, the diplomat especially, if she learned to wield a weapon.

It had been slow going at first. Su-Ni was a healthy young woman, but her life thus far had not been overly filled with intense physical activity. She was sore enough just from the days of unending travel, and now she was taking up swordplay. The diplomat had probably hindered their progress by at least a week in all, and she did feel very guilty about that, but none of them seemed to blame her. Now that they were almost through the mountains, according to Marui's estimation, they could all see the progress she was making. Day by day she was becoming faster and stronger.

Pei-Shi walked over and picked up the sword she had lent to Su-Ni for her training. When she gave it back to the diplomat, she was met with a curious expression.

"How did you do that anyway?" the young woman asked.

"Do what?"

"How did you take the sword from me? It felt like you grabbed the blade and pulled it right out of my hands, but it looked like only a parry from where I stood," Su-Ni clarified.

Pei-Shi chuckled. "That's what we call a bind or swordlock. Here, attack me slowly with a straight thrust," she said, adopting a defensive stance.

Su-Ni gripped the hilt of her sword firmly and brought its tip slowly toward the blademaster, mimicking her earlier lunge. It came in fairly close before Pei-Shi moved to block it. When she did she met the oncoming blade with what seemed to be a simple inside parry, but she then angled her sword around causing Su-Ni's blade to slide up and hit her crossguard. The tip of the swordswoman's weapon then swept down and out, bringing the diplomat's sword with it.

Since the move was done in slow motion, the force was not great enough to break Su-Ni's grip on the weapon, but she could easily see why it was called swordlock. The tip of her sword was held firmly against the inside of Pei-Shi's guard by the outside of her blade. The diplomat tugged on her sword, but Pei-Shi's blade bound it tightly. The expression on Su-Ni's face was a blend of puzzlement and intrigue.

"I shall have to remember that," the young woman said.

"It's not an easy move, and the opportunity to employ it does not occur often, but it's effective and surprising," Pei-Shi explained.

The diplomat was just about to ask if she could practice the technique with the blademaster when Marui called out, "Hoofbeats approach!"

Denlin and O'eintsu, who had been watching the women spar for most of the morning, leapt to their feet and ran quickly behind a pair of trees, ready to jump out at a moment's notice. Marui, Pei-Shi and Su-Ni, stood casually out in the open, hiding their weapons behind them.

Everyone relaxed when they saw the familiar forms of Komeris and Reniu astride their horses. Their relief soon faded back into tension when they noticed the pace and posture of the two men. As they came close enough for their expressions to be read, it was clear that something was amiss.

"What did you find?" Marui asked urgently as they dismounted their panting horses.

"There is a city," explained Komeris quickly, "about two hour's ride from here."

"Is that all?" Denlin prompted, his tone suggesting he knew the answer.

"No," Reniu chimed. "There's an army."

Su-Ni gasped. Everyone exchanged looks of apprehension.

"How many soldiers?" Marui asked.

Reniu shrugged. "Not sure. Maybe five thousand."

Everyone silently processed the news. Of course, this information was the reason they had come out here, but now that they knew something concrete, it was a bit disconcerting.

Marui broke the silence. "Well, even if there is an army, there's no need to assume they are a threat. They haven't started marching yet, have they?"

Komeris and Reniu glanced at one another.

"Well," the captain said, "they aren't marching at the moment, but it certainly looks like they'll be ready to soon."

"Perhaps we should observe them more closely," suggested the elf.

Komeris looked behind him toward the west. "Perhaps. I think for now we should move our camp into the trees. We can discuss how to proceed from there. Maybe tomorrow we can get a better glimpse."

The group efficiently picked up their things and moved off to the cover of the nearby wood. There they discussed for hours what their next move should be. Though they were trying to remain objective, as Marui had advised, they suspected they were now in enemy territory. As evening approached, they would have preferred not to light a fire for fear of attracting a passing sentry, but with the cold season fast approaching, and the temperature dropping lower and lower each night, this was not an option. They kept the flames low and huddled around it wrapped in their furs.

* * *

Though the scouting party had been wisely cautious in moving their camp, there were things that they could not be prepared for. Agucho of the Fiu-Het was one such thing. The party was still many miles from Niele'itio and the training field of Ionotu, and thus well out of sight of anyone in Orbein's dark kingdom. But they could not completely obscure themselves from the overhead flight of the shapeshifting servant of the king, even among the trees.

Agucho circled well above the camp and noted with glee the tiny spot of light between the treetops below. It was just as Laernus had said it would be. He glided lower to see if he could make out how many figures there were. From his vantage point, he thought he could see seven. But with the darkness, and especially the pine canopy over their heads, he could not be certain. He veered off and headed northwest.

Minutes later, he fluttered into the midst of a similar group huddled around a low, crackling flame. Five of Vethisir's soldiers and the seer Laernus stood and watched eagerly as the shapeshifter reassumed his native form.

"All appears to be as you said." Agucho directed his confirmation at Laernus.

"How many?" one of the soldiers asked hungrily.

"Seven, I believe," the Fiu-Het said, grinning at the seer.

The soldier snorted, "You believe?"

Agucho eyed him dangerously. "If you think you can scout better, go find out for yourself. You should have more faith in Laernus. He predicted they would be here and how many. If you had been listening, you wouldn't even have to waste our time with such questions," he spat.

The soldier bristled at the shapeshifter's words and looked as though he was about to spring upon him, but one of the others intercepted. "Let's save this hostility for our enemy. They await. By all the information we have, we're evenly matched, though we have the advantage. How likely do you think it is that as many of their number are well-trained warriors as we?" he asked with a wicked grin.

Laernus cleared his throat forebodingly. "Do not make such assumptions," he warned.

"What do you mean," the first soldier asked. "Have you seen that we will fail?"

"No," the seer said. "I just mean that the future is not immutable. If I could see our victory against these 'enemies', as you call them, I would not say. By ensuring your triumph I might give you a false sense of confidence. You might enter a battle thinking yourself invincible. I assure you that none of us are invincible. It may be that we all die tonight."

Only the slight breeze rolling lazily through the valley could be heard. Everyone stood silently contemplating the wizard's words. No longer did anyone seem impatient to set out.

Laernus sighed and rolled his eyes. "I only said that it may be, not that it will be. If we are intelligent about this, then we will all live. The first thing to do is make a plan. Gather nearer to me and I will give you my idea."

For several minutes, the quiet, accented voice of the seer laid out a plan to approach and attack the nearby camp. The soldiers listened, entranced by the wizard's surprising strategic skill. When he was done explaining, every one of them felt confident again that they could not lose this battle. After everyone quickly recited his part in the plan, they set out in the direction indicated by Agucho.

* * *

It was late, and Su-Ni was quite weary, but the cold of the night had her shivering so severely that she could not get to sleep for very long. Every once in a while she would open her eyes and look over their small fire to Marui, who sat in what seemed to be an alert meditative state. She had only ever seen one other person meditate in such a way. She mused about the young Urietsin, who she had not known for very long before he was lost. It seemed such a waste for such a man to die so young. She still held out a glimmer of hope that death had not found him.

The young woman blinked her sleepy eyes and watched the elf for a few more moments. She noted a strange expression on Marui's face and opened her eyes wider. The elf caught her gaze and put a finger to her lips. Though Su-Ni knew that Marui had simply moved her lips voicelessly, she heard a quiet whisper in her ear say, "Someone approaches. Be still."

The young woman could tell that the elf was relaying her message to the others as well by the way they either cocked their heads or gripped their weapons nonchalantly. Pei-Shi, who lay nearby, slowly slid one of her swords over to Su-Ni. The diplomat, suddenly very awake, reached out carefully and wrapped her hand around the hilt, pulling it to herself. The only one of the group who was not reaching for or gripping a weapon was Marui. She was simply staring ahead unblinkingly and sitting completely still.

Suddenly, the elf was on her feet with an arrow nocked in her bow, which seemed to materialize with the quickness she had drawn it. "Identify yourself!" she called over Su-Ni's head.

The diplomat twisted and was terrified to see a large, well-armored man approaching from behind. He did not seem to be heeding Marui's call. In response the elf let loose her arrow to fly dangerously close to the man's head. It was a warning shot, and the soldier stopped for a moment to consider his next action. That action was to draw out his sword and charge the few steps he had left to the closest of the group, Su-Ni, crying out something that sounded familiar, but was incomprehensible.

He barely completed his first step when an arrow and two tiny metal star shapes seemed to sprout from his face. He fell back forcefully and did not move again, his battle cry silenced permanently. Su-Ni pried her gaze away and looked back to the elf, who was again pulling taught her bowstring. Nearby stood O'eintsu with a chiun, a throwing star, in each hand. The young diplomat could hardly catch her breath. She jumped up, sword in hand, turning around quickly to see if she could see anyone else emerging from the darkness.

The camp erupted into action. Figures did, indeed, leap out of the shadows, but the scouting party, well-warned by Marui's whisper and the foolhardy actions of the overzealous soldier, sprang to quick defense.

Two soldiers, armored as the first one in metal-plated hide scales and a simple helmet, rushed toward Komeris and Reniu brandishing swords. The veteran warriors met the charge with blades of their own. Reniu and Komeris had fought together for many years, and they knew how to compliment one another's moves against multiple opponents. Each of them wielded two curving broadswords that were much lighter than the longswords carried by these hostile fighters.

Both of the foreign soldiers lunged at Komeris and Reniu, dividing their efforts against them. The first stabbed toward the captain's bronze-covered chest, but quickly had to get his heavy blade under control as Komeris deflected its course with minimal effort and brought his second blade slashing horizontally. The enemy barely avoided being disemboweled, and then had to execute a series of blocks that quickly tired his forearms. He had never seen anyone swing a single sword so quickly, never mind two.

Reniu's opponent came on with wide, alternating slashes. He was a bit more skilled than his comrade, so it was a moment before the captain's bulky ally could attack, but it was only a moment. Reniu's blinding bladework was made more spectacular by his considerable size. The big man twisted his wrists deftly and worked his swords in graceful, flowery circles around him. The whipping edges of those blades came at his opponent, threatening to shred his face if he did not act quickly.

The impressive bladework of the two veterans was a bit more than their foes had suspected, but they were completely unprepared for the next stage of their cooperative strategy. Reniu's opponent attacked. The momentum of his weapon was redirected with a flick of the big man's wrist. Reniu dipped to the side, placing himself between his captain's opponent and his own. Another sweeping circle of his sword whipped against the armor of Komeris's enemy.

The captain grinned. Months ago the young Urietsin had defeated Reniu in hand to hand combat. He couldn't help but wonder if the outcome would have been different had they used swords instead. Komeris's opponent seemed distraught from the sudden attack at his side, and the captain took advantage of this. He pressed ahead, swords twirling.

Reniu set the next step in motion, as his footwork brought him further around his rival. Once more his other weapon reached out and smacked the captain's challenger as he stepped by, this time on the shoulder. Still the big man was able to hold off his own enemy as he taunted the captain's. Suddenly, he lunged, both swords slashing downward. His foe leapt back, swinging his longsword desperately. He successfully blocked Reniu's attack, but yelped out as the captain's blade came from the side and slashed through a seam in the hide of his armor.

Suddenly, the two soldiers found themselves defending against the opposite attacker as Komeris and Reniu switched opponents. They began to wonder if attacking this camp had been such a wise move after all.

While the captain and his partner gave their enemies a harsh lesson in swordplay, two other rivals presented themselves to the two younger warriors, Denlin and O'eintsu. Though they were younger, and had not yet developed a cooperative fighting style, their foes found no easy challenge in them either.

Denlin's challenger ran up swinging the same heavy sword that all the attackers seemed to carry. The soldier could not possibly have been prepared for the younger man's skill with his staff. The hard, wooden weapon had a much longer reach, and Denlin immediately swung around and, using his leading hand as a pivot around his body, he brought the staff sweeping across to clang hard against the soldier's wild swipe. The sword went wide, and Denlin advanced and brought his staff over his head and down in a strike that cracked loudly over his opponent's helmet. Heavy though the piece of headgear was, it dented inward at the hit and the man collapsed. Denlin raised his eyebrows in surprise at the effectiveness of his attack.

O'eintsu's man did not go down so quickly, but that was no indication of the dark soldier's skill. The mysterious, black-clad son of Lihou launched over his challenger's head as soon as he approached and had the man spinning to defend himself against some well-placed kicks to the back of his knees. The armored, sword-wielding soldier could hardly believe that this apparently unarmed man was attacking him, never mind that he had just flown over his head. O'eintsu, however, continued to confuse and surprise his foe. The soldier swung diagonally at the young fighter, who seemed to vanish at the strike. He understood where he had vanished to a second later when his feet were knocked out from under him by a powerful sweep. He rolled desperately to get away from the young man. Weapon or no, he knew he could be easily defeated if he lay prone.

To his credit, the soldier did make it back to his feet, only to feel an excruciating pain tear through his gut. He looked down and saw two small, shiny pieces of metal embedded in the abdomen of his scale hide. The wounds were painful, but the armor had kept the chiun from being fatal. He looked back up at O'eintsu, who was advancing toward him lightly. The soldier leapt forward and stabbed at the slowly approaching young man.

O'eintsu again dodged the strike, but instead of crouching down for another sweep, he leaned aside letting the blade stab past him and reached forward under the blade with a reverse grip around the soldier's wrist. Now the soldier was overbalanced, and all the young fighter had to do was turn in the opposite direction, using the momentum of the attack to pull his opponent over his thigh, slamming him against the ground. O'eintsu wrested the sword from the soldier's grip as he fell. With a deft twist in the air he brought the blade plunging down into its owner's chest.

Su-Ni and Pei-Shi both noticed the directions that these enemies had come from and realized that the group had tried to surround them and face them all evenly. So, they were not surprised when their horses cried out and another attacker emerged from the shadows toward them. But this one was different.

The man approached in a well-fitted set of studded leather armor. He was a bit thinner and smaller than the soldiers, but he wielded the same type of sword. Most unusual, though, was that he seemed not to be watching the two women brandishing their own swords in defense, rather he stared somewhere beyond at some indeterminate spot. Pei-Shi ran up to meet him with a quick downward swipe, which he easily defeated with an overhead block. The warrioress grinned at the challenge and slid her sword off of his weapon and swung it around for a diagonal slash. This too was met with resistance as the man parried easily.

Su-Ni stood back, watching but ready, in case Pei-Shi needed her help. She was impressed as she watched the two fight. Especially at the man, who never seemed to actually look at his opponent, but still he blocked all of her moves flawlessly. It took her a while to realize that, though he was an impressive defensive opponent, it appeared he was hesitant to attack. After several blocks, parries, dodges, and a host of other evasive maneuvers, the man had not taken one offensive move toward Pei-Shi.

* * *

Laernus jumped back and swung his heavy blade across, blocking the deadly jab that had just come at him. It had been the most haphazard block he had made through this entire fight. He was beginning to tire, which was more dangerous to him than to any of the other warriors here tonight. He held tight to his concentration, however, and continued to defend himself with his weighty sword.

Staring ahead, he saw the female twist her blade around in the air once, twice, thrice, then came the downward chop. In the same spot, her double did the same move seconds behind the first. Laernus brought up his own blade to defeat the real move. The first woman whipped her sword back and down to rotate under and up. The woman's twin followed exactly as the first and again Laernus barely escaped death by jumping back, the only defense against a strike that would have gone into his gut and driven upward to his lungs.

Though the soldier-wizard was tiring, he still had a great advantage. He was seeing Pei-Shi execute her moves seconds in advance. His future sight helped him to meet an attack before the woman even made it, hence his double vision. For anyone else this would have been incredibly disconcerting, but Laernus had developed this tactic against the cruel soldiers of general Vethisir and had become an excellent defensive fighter. Most of the time, he could easily tire his opponent and wait for an opening, which came soon enough. This woman was a bit more of a challenge. It seemed that she took advantage of his constant defensive stance by raining a nonstop flurry of strikes upon him, and with her lighter blade she did not tire as quickly as the large men of Ionotu.

Again the woman twisted her sword in the air, this time switching from one side to the other with each rotation. It was clever technique that looked very flowery, but was in reality very effective. The constantly changing location of the blade made it difficult to know where a strike might occur while allowing the wielder to easily defend herself from an attack in any direction. Against Laernus, however, it was not so helpful.

Watching the twirling blade, the seer knew that he needed to take advantage of this opening or flee. He saw the woman bring her sword back across her body and down a split second before she actually did. As the momentum brought the weapon down too fast to bring it back of for a parry, Laernus lunged forward and stabbed.

Amazingly, the woman did reverse the direction of her swing more swiftly than the wizard could ever have imagined. That, coupled with a quick dodge, kept the strike from being fatal. The attack did land, however, and raked a deep gash in her shoulder. She leapt back and clenched her jaw. Laernus could see that she was in pain and rushed ahead to take advantage of the situation.

He heard a yell and saw a movement out of the corner of his eye. The younger woman, who had been standing by, rushed forward and intercepted the seer. He cursed himself for letting his excitement break his concentration and brought his sword up for a wild block. It was not even close, and the sharp blade sliced into his leather tunic and opened a small wound in his side. He stumbled backward as the woman rushed on determinedly, swishing her sword diagonally at him. He was practically running in reverse to get away from the dangerously close swipes of that wicked edge. Even with his broken concentration, it did not take him long to see the rhythm of the young woman's attacks. She was apparently not as skilled as the other one. With this in mind, he sprung forward with a stabbing thrust like the one that had injured the woman's older partner.

Quite shocked was Laernus when he felt his sword pulled aside as the woman parried. The force and surprise of the strange twist he felt in his wrist caused him to release the weapon, and it went flying away. He stood looking at his new opponent, who stared back at him with as much awe as he. Weaponless, the wizard was not quite sure what to do. He looked around and noticed quickly that two of his comrades were obviously dead, and one was severely incapacitated. Clearly, the odds were no longer even. This had not gone anything like his plan. He turned and ran.

* * *

Su-Ni watched the strange man run off. She was stunned that he had been so easily defeated by her after he had put up a fairly good defensive fight against Pei-Shi. Furthermore, she was surprised that she had so easily disarmed him with the move that her mentor had taught her only this morning. She looked back at the swordswoman, who gave her a pained grin. Su-Ni went to her.

"Are you alright?" the diplomat-fighter asked with concern.

"I'll be fine. Let's see to the others," Pei-Shi replied as she turned to take in the campsite.

Komeris and Reniu were chasing off their attackers, Denlin and O'eintsu, like the two women, were surveying the outcome of the battle, and Marui was peering into the darkness with her bowstring taught. Nearby, the soldier that Denlin had struck was half stumbling, half crawling away from the camp. The fight appeared to be over, and when all the surviving attackers were well out of sight, everyone in the camp moved toward the elf, who was still aiming her weapon into the night.

"What's out there?" Denlin asked quietly.

"Something," Marui replied cryptically. "Something familiar."

They all stood squinting into the blackness beyond their small fire, but could see nothing. Marui scanned this way and that with her bow, a deadly arrow there, waiting to fly. She saw nothing out there, well past even the keenest eyesight of any of the humans. Slowly, the strange feeling of familiarity ebbed away, and she lowered her bow and stowed her arrow.

"We must leave this place now," she said ominously.

"To go where?" asked Su-Ni, least familiar with the specific orders of this mission.

"East. To the general's camp," explained Komeris.

"Do you not think there is more we can learn?" asked the quiet O'eintsu.

Komeris shook his head. "Our orders were to return at the first sign of conflict. We have only minor injuries now. If we wait for them to bring back their brethren on that field beyond the pass, we will not survive," he reasoned.

"But they are so close. Perhaps if we hid more effectively," the young warrior insisted.

"We have learned all we need to know," Marui stated firmly.

"What makes you so certain now?" O'eintsu challenged.

"The first man to fall cried out, 'Die, dogs of the empire' as he charged. Mark my words, our fears are confirmed. The enemy is nearby, and now they will be on the lookout for us. We must turn back. They will be coming soon, and we can no longer move so quickly." With this last statement she nodded in the direction of the horses.

One of the poor creatures was sprawled upon the ground, a deep wound in its side. Another limped along the side of the campsite, blood flowing down its front leg. The mood quickly went from tense to somber. The situation had so suddenly turned out of their favor, and though they all felt there was much more that could be learned, they knew it would be too dangerous. As they headed back to the east with their remaining horses in tow and the moon sinking low behind them, they prepared themselves for a wearying journey. They knew it might be a while before they would actually have a restful night.

* * *

"They sneaked off in the night without my permission! I've lost two good men, and another will probably not be fit to fight for the rest of his life! And for what? Nothing! It was a wasted adventure that ended in disaster!"

Vethisir continued raving, as he had been for the past ten minutes, pacing to and fro before Orbein's throne. The surviving members of said adventure were standing behind him, hanging their heads. Certainly it was an unfortunate incident, but the general had a flair for the dramatic, especially for anything that involved Agucho and Laernus. Vethisir was furious, and he wanted retribution.

"And you!" he shouted at the shapeshifter. "Coward! You stood in the distance and watched my men get slaughtered! You deserve punishment more than any of them. At least the wizard actually fought his enemy, while you lurked like the scum that you are!"

Agucho hissed and shouted back, "Bite your tongue, fool! You were not there; you could not possibly know what happened. That witch with the bow was an elf! Had I approached, she would have shot me down where I stood."

"And better off we would all be if she had," Vethisir replied easily.

The sound of a metal blade sliding against a sheath silenced the room. King Orbein pointed his dagger at the general and the shapeshifter. "I will gladly decide this argument for both of you. Unless, of course, you would all like to shut up," he said evenly. He stood and stepped down from the dais and gave them all an unsettling grin.

"It seems that none of you have been paying attention lately," Orbein continued. "So, allow me to refresh your memories as to my aspirations. Our great city rose from the ashes of destruction rained down upon us by the very people we are descended from. Our ancestors abandoned us to the refuse left over from their greedy exploits. Now I have deemed that the time has come to reclaim our home of old and find the empire that had forsaken us so long ago. You see, this is a sign. It is an omen that our desires are vindicated."

The king went on, but as if talking to himself, "Strange people wander into our land; where did they come from? Over the mountains is the only logical answer. Our foes come to show us their mettle. Very well then, we will rise to the challenge. Vethisir!"

"Yes, highness," the general replied, a bit fearful of the gleam that shone brightly in his king's eyes.

"Ready your men."

"When do we march, sir," Vethisir asked.

"That all depends. Agucho, when can your reinforcements get here?" Orbein asked with another devious grin.

The Fiu-Het shifted nervously. "No more than a week, highness," he said timidly.

Orbein spun on the shapeshifter with a scowl, gesturing with his dagger. "Is there a problem?"

"The elves are a dangerous foe, sire," Agucho answered.

"Which is why we will need your help," the king explained on no uncertain terms. "Go now," he added to the rest of them.

Everyone turned to leave. "Except you." Orbein pointed at Laernus.

The others filtered out slowly, looking over their shoulders at the seer with something resembling pity. For several moments after they left, a cacophonous silence pervaded the entire throne room. Orbein stared at the wizard, and Laernus simply stared forward in response. When the king finally broke the silence, it nearly startled the both of them.

"You've made quite a reputation for yourself in Vethisir's army," Orbein scoffed.

"Thank you, highness," Laernus said blandly.

The king laughed coldly. "Yes, I suppose I am the one to thank. I put you there."

The seer badly wanted to interject that it was Agucho's idea to send him to Ionotu, but he simply nodded instead. He had finally learned better than to contradict the king.

"And now," Orbein continued, "here you are. One of the first to engage the enemy. Really, the architect of the whole situation. It was your plan to go out and find them, was it not?"

"Yes, sir," Laernus replied quickly.

Orbein nodded. "Because you foresaw their coming?"

"Yes," was the seer's reply.

The king shook his head slowly. "Tell me why, Laernus, why, when such a morsel of information would have overjoyed me greatly, did you deny such insights to me when I sought your counsel?"

The wizard likewise shook his head. "I cannot control everything that is shown to me. Patience must be employed by those seeking to know the future, especially to know those things far in the future. To force it would be like trying to change the shape of clouds."

His explanation was met with an inscrutable squint from the king. "You should know by now that I have no such patience," he said. "Which is why I think it is better that you work unexpectedly from within the ranks of Vethisir's men, and with Agucho. The battle is no longer so far in the future, and I'm sure more fruitful information will come to you. But this time, if you foresee something, you will report it to me immediately."

Laernus had to try hard to stifle a grin. "Yes, sir," he said with enthusiasm.

Orbein stared at him for a few moments longer, then dismissed him.

The seer gladly returned to the ranks of Vethisir's army; he was even excited. The battle was about to be underway, and soon he and Agucho would make their play for freedom. When he got out to the field, he could hardly hear the general barking out orders over the fantasies that played out in his mind's eye. But even with that distraction and the constant activity of getting ready for the journey through the mountains, the week seemed interminable. On the fifth day since he spoke with the king, the sky darkened with thick clouds of flying creatures. He nearly fainted with excitement.

They rained out of the sky by the hundreds, landing in neat formations on the field next to Vethisir's stunned troops. The soldiers watched agape as two thousand shapeshifters transformed, mid-landing, into their native Fiu-Het appearance. A few men with less willpower ran screaming from the field, terrified at the volumes of creatures they had thus far only seen one at a time. Most of them, however, stood frozen in horror or uncertainty. Some of them were reassured by the arrival of their king, but the majority couldn't help but fear that their doom was near.

Orbein rode onto the field on a heavily-armored black war horse. He truly looked regal and terrible astride the powerful animal. Both human and Fiu-Het marveled at the sight of him, and he basked in the attention. He looked out over the lines of soldiers, his soldiers, before him. Never before in his rule had he felt so powerful as this.

"Defenders of my kingdom!" Orbein called out with an unnatural, booming echo. "Hear me! We stand now upon the precipice of destiny. One step will bring us to doom or glory. It is up to us to decide which it will be. Our enemy in the east has made the first strike against us, showing that they desire this meeting as much as we do. And as they desire it, so shall we bring it to them!

"Now is the time for you to stand with me, man and shapeshifter, to defend our homes that the ambitious men of the east do not overrun us as they have in the past. Let us bring the fight to them, and when they are dead or cowed at our feet, let us take back the lands of our ancestors. Believe not in fate, except that which we will make for ourselves. Believe in the fate that we design and take up in our hands with our swords! Believe in our victory!"

Seven thousand soldiers of Ionotu rose up in a riotous cheer at this climax of Orbein's speech. They were worked into frenzy at his words and looked as though they were ready to march to war. The shapeshifters did not seem to share their enthusiasm. They stood quietly, regarding the humans with queer expressions.

The king rode toward the Fiu-Het ranks, stopping beside Agucho, who also seemed both awed and repulsed by their allies' reaction. "Say something to them," Orbein commanded.

Agucho stared at the king blankly for several moments before shrugging. "Very well," he said.

The hunched shapeshifter ambled forward, away from the horse that was so many times larger than he, and held up his hands. "Hearken, brothers and sssisters!" As he called out, the serpentine hiss in his voice was quite evident and the whole field went silent as even the humans listened closely to the series of hisses and gurgles that came forth from his mouth.

"As I have told you all before," Agucho began in his own tongue, "we are here today for so many reasons, not the leassst of which is our own protection. We stand now beside the great army of this king ssso that, like them, we can prevent the same kind of aggression that they fear. I need not remind you of our dear prince Gayossha, and his fate out here, serving our people. In Gayossha's last words he revealed to me his killer. On the field of battle I will find that man for you, and when I command, you will kill him and all that follow him without quessstion. We will not be caught unawares, and we will have our vengeance!"

These words, while meaningless to Vethisir's men, roused a great reaction in the Fiu-Het. The roles of moments ago were reversed. The soldiers of Ionotu were terrified at the insane looks of glee upon the already frightening faces of the shapeshifters.

Orbein motioned to Vethisir, who ran over immediately. "Sound the march," he said to the general and Agucho.

"Yes, sire," Vethisir said, giving a proud salute to his king. He turned and called out to his soldiers and began to set a rapid pace to the southeast.

As the great training field of Ionotu emptied of human soldiers, Agucho bellowed out orders for the shapeshifters to follow quickly. He was pleased that the march was beginning with the humans taking up the lead, but he knew that before they met with any violence, many of his own people would find themselves in that unenviable position. He shook the thought away and concentrated on the road ahead. Many things were about to transpire that he knew would be for the best. It was likely that he was sacrificing many of his people, but he understood that it was necessary to avoid an even worse outcome later. The shapeshifter urged on the soldiers with sincere enthusiasm. They were reaching toward their destiny and grasping fate. The march had begun.

16 CHANGE OF PLANS

A single pole stood about man-height on the south side of the circle in which the familiar meditation stone lay. The pole was capped with a large metal ring, over which was stretched the hide of some animal. Urietsin was in his typical seat upon the boulder, facing the pole. His attention was on the feather that hung in the air before his gaze.

He was already in a deeply meditative state, concentrating as intensely as he could upon the tiny piece of down. His spirit was as intimately linked with it as it was with his own body. He felt every barb as an extension of himself, and he was completely aware of every molecule that made it up. Focusing on those miniscule building blocks, he pulled them into tight formation, just as he would flex his biceps.

The feather reacted instantly to this manipulation. Every little tendril, right down to each barbule that protruded from its surface, straightened out perfectly and spread apart equidistant from one another. When it was done, the feather resembled something more crystalline, like a spherical snowflake. Unlike a snowflake, this crystal would not so easily melt or break.

Controlled by the Swift One, the feather-crystal began to turn, slowly at first, but then faster. It twisted and turned this way and that, faster and faster until it blurred into a flawlessly rounded ball. There it hovered in front of Urietsin, looking like a tiny marble hanging motionlessly in thin air.

Suddenly, it was gone. It simply seemed to disappear. Urietsin shifted the focus of his physical eyes to the ring-capped pole. The hide that was stretched over the ring now had a perfectly round hole directly in its center. Even though this had been his intention, the Swift One was still astounded by the effect. That something so small and soft as a feather could be transformed into a deadly accurate missile was amazing to him. Reigning in his excitement, he called to the feather, which was spinning somewhere just

190

beyond the pole. It came to him instantly, and he stopped its impossibly fast rotation. As it levitated before him, he admired it briefly, then set it down in front of him on the boulder.

Without even closing his eyes, Urietsin pulled his spirit back to himself and refocused his perception of the multiverse. Even from within the confines of his mortal coil, though, he could feel it out there. Infinity called to him, and he had become more and more aware of it as he spent these months here training. But infinity was a lot to be aware of, so Urietsin understood why he had to go back to the limited perceptions of his physical body. The stress of always perceiving existence in all of its form was far more than someone with his inexperience could handle. Indeed, the Swift One wondered if any amount of experience could prepare one for a lifetime of feeling everything.

Urietsin looked down and blinked. The feather lay there before him, but still in its stiff, crystalline form. He reached down to pick it up and withdrew his hand quickly; it was quite sharp. More gently, the Swift One retrieved his creation and turned it over in his hands. Cupping it between his palms, he jumped up to go find Kiusu.

Urietsin came upon his master while he was performing a slow and graceful routine that was meant to be a sort of moving meditation. He waited patiently as the skilled old man flawlessly stepped through each careful action. Soon the young student let the thoughts of his recent session slip way as he watched in awe the impeccable sweeping moves executed by the man. Like the waving of trees in the wind and the flutter of a butterfly's wing, his technique was flexible, powerful, and beautiful, the perfection of nature in motion.

Kiusu finished the routine in a bow and stepped over to his student. He noticed the Swift One's expression and asked, "What is it?"

Urietsin bowed deeply. "I aspire to someday acquire a level of skill that even resembles your own," he said humbly.

"First step," the old man replied quickly. "Do not be so quick to compare yourself to others. You should improve because you wish to be better than yourself, not some other man. Your best competition is within."

"Yes, seishin," Urietsin said with another bow.

Kiusu smiled. "How did you do today?"

"Ah yes," the young student grinned offering his creation up for inspection. "Take care, it is sharp," he cautioned.

The old man paused mid-reach to give Urietsin a curious look. He gingerly picked up the tiny crystalline object. Rolling it around in his hands, his expression shifted from curious to fascinated.

"This is your feather?" he asked.

Urietsin nodded.

From no place that seemed apparent to the young warrior, Kiusu produced a small pouch and gently placed the crystal into it. He handed the pouch to his student. "Save it. At least as a memento of this day, for you seem to have truly mastered this lesson," he congratulated with a bow.

The Swift One returned the bow with an even deeper one. "Thank you, seishin."

"Which means..." the old man continued.

Urietsin could not help but smile, "A new lesson?"

Kiusu gave a slight nod, but one that indicated to his student that he was only half right. "Let us see you apply what you have learned," the master said slyly.

The Swift One began to inquire Kiusu as to his meaning when the old man suddenly flew at him with his fist extended. Urietsin barely dodged out of the way and turned to face his master. He understood clearly what was happening and took up a defensive posture. He gestured, inviting the next attack.

That attack came on as a flurry of sidekicks to the Swift One's head. He backed away from each kick, stepping just far enough away as Kiusu hopped ahead, one deadly foot leading. After several kicks, Urietsin decided to put a stop to them. He reached up with his leading hand to snatch at Kiusu's foot as his leg fully extended, but that foot abruptly disappeared. Before the Swift One could comprehend what was happening, Kiusu had advanced forward and grasped his student's blocking hand and pulled it down. A quick punch to the chest had a startled Urietsin stumbling backward.

The young student rubbed the spot where Kiusu had punched him and regarded his teacher with a bewildered expression. The old man was not paying attention. Urietsin had to duck as Kiusu sailed over his head with another kick. Clearly his master would not be pulling any of his punches during this match, or kicks for that matter. With this in mind, Urietsin rushed ahead to get on the offensive.

His master was ready for him. The student launched a two punch combination, each strike flawlessly blocked by Kiusu. The front kick that Urietsin followed up with was no closer to hitting home. It was pushed downward with such force that the Swift One almost fell forward. Instead, he fell backward as his master continued down with the block and kicked up into a handstand that lasted only a moment as one of his feet smacked Urietsin in the face.

Kiusu leapt back into a ready stance and looked down at his prone student. "Perhaps we should call you the not-so-Swift One," he chuckled.

Urietsin growled as he kicked up from the ground and landed, ready to defend not only his body, but also his pride. The old man's strikes came on in a whipping, whirling fury, and his footwork had him stepping in circles around his student, but Urietsin kept a shield of blinding defense with nothing more than his limbs. Every so often he would try to find even a tiny break in the unending stream of attacks to send an offensive move hurtling at his master, but no such opening could be found. Every time he thought he saw something, he would have to quickly turn his intended strike into a block.

Changing his tactic, the Swift One began blocking Kiusu's attacks with heavy counterstrikes against the offending limbs, which he immediately followed with a number of random kicks or punches. It quickly became obvious that Kiusu was much too clever and powerful a fighter for such a tactic to work. He seemed to be aware of every move that Urietsin intended to make even before he was, and his strong limbs, conditioned by years of training and experience, were as hard as stone. Every counterstrike affected the young warrior more than they did the old man.

Urietsin became frustrated and momentarily lost his focus on the fight as he wondered what he could possibly do to even present a challenge to his very skilled master. The distraction proved to be a mistake that the Swift One did not need in this fight as he went flying back from a double front punch to the chest. He hit the ground with a thud and immediately propped himself up on his elbows and shook away the dizziness that had suddenly come over him.

"You fight better with your eyes closed, *Urishe'etsi'in*," Kiusu called out with a laugh.

Urietsin cocked his head curiously. His master's reference to their previous match seemed significant to him. "...apply what you have learned," the old man had said at the beginning of this fight. An understanding grin spread across his youthful face. This time he rose with a look of confidence rather than anger, which was somehow much more intimidating.

The young warrior did not have to strain to hear infinity's call. He faced his master with his eyes wide open, not that his eyes had much to do with how he saw things now. His senses spread out to take in the entire battlefield; his spirit was surveying the arena.

Kiusu rushed at him suddenly, but the Swift One could feel the disturbance in the environment the moment the old man's muscles twitched. As his master came within reach, Urietsin jumped up and flipped effortlessly over his head. He landed into a sidekick that just barely grazed Kiusu's back, but still added to his forward momentum.

The old man stumbled a few steps, then turned swiftly to eye his student a bit more cautiously and respectfully. It seemed now that the fight was truly on in full. Kiusu came on then, a blinding flurry of whipping limbs. Urietsin met his charge with a blur of defensive moves and counters. The two men danced their way around the sparsely wooded area and uneven terrain as if it were a dance floor. The percussion of their strikes provided the musical accompaniment.

Many steps into their dance, Kiusu managed to back his student up to one of the thin trees that dotted the area. Urietsin was clearly aware of the trunk behind him, as he continually tried to sidestep away from it, but Kiusu would allow no such evasion. Whenever his student stepped sideways, the master would circle him so that his back was again almost brushing the smooth bark of the tree. The old man feinted with another double front punch, which Urietsin was all too eager to block. But the adept student was more completely aware than even the most attentive warrior. So, when Kiusu's foot swung up from the side seeking the Swift One's temple, it found only the hard wood of the tree.

Urietsin dove under his master and rolled to safety.

Kiusu winced, not in pain, but in sympathy for the tree that had just received a huge dent from his kick. He did not waste any more time than that, however, and spun to face his opponent. He had to dodge aside immediately as Urietsin's fist sailed past. A loud crack rang out as the student's punch connected with the hard wood.

"Be careful of the tree!" Kiusu wailed, noting with lament that the Swift One's strike had left a similar scar to his own.

Urietsin looked apologetic, but he did not let it distract him from the fight. The two men faced off and were about to leap at one another when a creaking groan turned their attention elsewhere. They both dove away from each other as quickly as they could while the tree around which they had been fighting came tumbling down between them. When the dust cleared, the two sat up and looked over the trunk at one another.

"I think, perhaps, we should postpone this test," Kiusu suggested dryly.

Urietsin nodded slowly in response.

Together the men retrieved some cutting tools from Kiusu's rebuilt hut and got to work chopping each and every part of the tree into wood that they would use later. They both were saddened that the healthy tree had been prematurely knocked down by their own actions, but they thanked it for its sacrifice and vowed to make use of every scrap. By the time they were finished and had packed the wood in their ample winter store, it was early evening, and there was a slight chill in the air. They retired to the hut to have a quiet and simple dinner, rice and some type of fowl.

That night, Urietsin's sleep was restless with many dreams. He found himself surrounded by violent foes that attacked him ferociously. He fought desperately to keep them all at bay, but he seemed always on the verge of defeat. He could hear Kiusu's voice somewhere calling out to him, urging him on, but as from far away. The voices of three fallen warriors echoed across the dreamscape as well, but he couldn't see anyone he knew. Instead he saw volumes of fierce men and other creatures clawing and swiping at him. Morning found the young warrior sluggish and bleary eyed, as if he had actually spent the whole night fighting.

"Are you feeling well?" Kiusu asked when he saw him that morning.

"I am tired. Strange dreams..." he said absently.

"Will you be well enough to continue our little match?" the master asked with a curious expression.

"Perhaps," shrugged the Swift One. "We shall see."

Kiusu nodded and watched the young warrior walk off into the foliage.

Urietsin went to his traditional spot for his regular meditation, but unlike most days, it was quite some time before he could quiet his mind enough to hear the multiverse calling out to him. Even then, his trip through the great interconnectedness seemed fraught with turbulence. He wondered if his weariness was the cause, and with that thought his mind came alive with a thousand other distracting thoughts, pulling him again away from his concentration. Eventually, he was able to find some peace drifting upon the tide of infinity, and it was very restful. By late morning he was able to make his way back to the hut feeling refreshed, the strange feeling of this morning fading into memory.

"Better?" Kiusu asked when the Swift One stepped up more lightly than when he had left.

"Much," Urietsin nodded.

"Good," was the old man's response, which he immediately followed up with jumping toe-kick to his student's chin.

Urietsin's reaction was completely instinctual. He reached up with both hands and turned the kick away with such force that Kiusu landed with his back to his student. The Swift One's rapid sidekick caught his master across the shoulders, and Kiusu went rolling away. The young warrior chased after the tumbling form of his master, who suddenly stopped and twisted around in a low sweep. Urietsin was ready for the move, though, and he jumped over the old man's seeking leg. From the failed sweep, Kiusu lunged forward with a rigid spearhand, which was parried effortlessly by the student. Urietsin followed the block with his knee.

Kiusu tried to fall away to absorb most of the hit, but the Swift One's knee was true and landed a solid hit on the lunging master's jaw. It was a jarring strike, but one that the old man recovered from quickly. Rolling backward and leaping to his feet, Kiusu pressed ahead against his ready student. A high kick to the head, fast one-two front punch to the solar plexus, and a head butt were all blocked or dodged expertly by Urietsin. The old man could see that today was going to be very telling about his student's progress.

The Swift One weaved around his master's strikes with hardly any effort. He could feel himself slipping deeper into his meditative state. Kiusu seemed to him to be moving in slow motion, so apparent were his moves to the ultimately focused Urietsin. The young warrior saw an opening, and with all his concentration he struck at his master, advancing with a deadly backfist.

No stranger to the enticing call of infinity, Kiusu recognized that he was no longer fighting the Swift One's physical being alone. The old master had been forming his own connection with the multiverse since the fight had begun. He could see his student's fist coming at him with a force that went beyond the capabilities of mere muscle. The old man knew that there was no physical block he could offer that would stop that strike. In a split second Kiusu had to decide whether to counter or dodge.

He countered.

The area around the two men lit up with a blinding flash and shook as a loud boom echoed out over the valley below. The light faded quickly, and they found themselves lying on their backs several feet away from one another. It took a few minutes to shake off the daze that followed.

Kiusu got to his feet and stepped up to the Swift One and bowed deeply.

Urietsin stood and mirrored his master's bow.

The old man shook his head slowly. "I begin to wonder if there is much more I can teach you."

The young warrior's expression shifted between surprise and pride. "Can it really be this easy?" he asked curiously, wondering how long it had truly taken his master to learn as much as he had.

Kiusu's expression suddenly changed; he seemed almost upset. "No, it is not easy," he said quietly. He then turned and headed back to his hut.

Urietsin watched him go, stunned at this strange reaction. Never had he seen Kiusu look unhappy, but it seemed something he had said to the old man had disappointed or saddened him. For the first time in more than a month he thought about home and felt the longing rise up in him more powerfully than ever before. Along with the homesickness returned a stinging sense of guilt. His studies had been distracting him from the memory of his fallen comrades, although it seemed many things had tried to remind him. He admitted to himself that he had been looking for a distraction from that painful memory.

Now that he was thinking of it, nothing could stop the flow of the other thoughts that logically followed. He understood now that he should go home soon. Kiusu had buried the soldiers that had fallen to the gotori, so Captain Komeris and the rest of the empire's soldiers probably had no idea what had happened to them. Unless, of course, the fourth man had escaped. Even so, the fallen warriors' families should at least know where their sons were buried.

Urietsin felt ashamed. He did not even know where Kiusu had buried them. He had let his guilt keep him from honoring their sacrifice to the empire.

Suddenly, the Swift One felt like all these thoughts were twisting around in his head faster and faster until they became an overwhelming whirlwind. He didn't understand the dizziness that came over him, and he could not shake it. He blinked and looked around, but his surroundings seemed to be dissolving before his very eyes.

With eyes still open, but staring sightlessly, the young warrior toppled limply to the ground. As the last bits of what he knew to be reality fluttered away, Urietsin found himself in completely unfamiliar surroundings. He stood next to Kiusu on a wide battlefield. Men and other creatures lay lifeless or dying on the ground. Above them a dark cloud whipped by and cast an ominous moving shadow over the already gloomy setting. The young warrior looked up at the cloud curiously; it all seemed so surreal.

Impossibly, the cloud turned in the air and came back, swooping threateningly over the massacre. Urietsin ducked, and when he got back up, it seemed to him that the cloud had turned into a huge, featureless monster. Beside him Kiusu stood passively, as if nothing were out of the ordinary. The Swift One again looked up at the demon cloud, noting with dread that it was soaring back in his direction. As it dived toward the two men, it broke into thousands of flying creatures, all screeching terribly.

The creatures descended upon the young warrior in torrents, and somehow he managed to fend them off. His limbs were an impenetrable blur that sent the rain of beasts scattering, but that hardly stopped them from coming on. Through the cloud of pelting creatures, Urietsin could see his former master standing there, unaffected by the downpour. The old man made no move to defend himself, and the flying demons did not attack him. The Swift One was dumbfounded at this, but did not dare to stop swinging.

But despite all his efforts, Urietsin could not hold out indefinitely against a near unending stream of attacking creatures. They overpowered him and wrestled him to the ground and covered him so completely that he saw nothing but blackness.

"Do not fear Urietsi'in," Kiusu's voice echoed in his mind. "Death is but a new beginning."

Slowly, the Swift One's vision faded back in. He realized that he was in Kiusu's hut, but it was dark except for a small fire burning in the hearth. He ached all over and felt very ill, though he could not discern exactly what it was that did not feel right.

"What happened?" he asked groggily.

Kiusu gave him a curious expression. "Perhaps you should tell me," he said mysteriously.

"What do you mean?"

The old man shrugged. "I found you lying on the ground unconscious.

For days now you have been tossing and mumbling restlessly. Tell me what you saw."

"Days?!" the Swift One exclaimed in disbelief. He sat up quickly, but his head swam, causing him to seek his pillow once again. "How long?" he asked weakly.

"Almost a week now," Kiusu explained gently. "Tell me, Swift One. What did you see?"

Urietsin swallowed in disbelief. "A week..." He paused, trying to adjust his mind to the passage of time. "Well, I saw a field. Many lying dead. And these beasts, terrible things, attacking me..."

Kiusu nodded slowly, leaning closer in intrigue, eyes wide with bemused fascination.

"...and you told me not to be afraid," the Swift one added, closing his eyes as he tried to remember. "For some reason, they could not hurt you."

The old man blanched visibly, even in the dim light. Kiusu wiped away the beads of sweat that were forming on his forehead. He knew now that the time had come. "Urietsin," he said slowly, deliberately, "rest well. When you are feeling better we must be ready to leave this place."

Urietsin tried to sit up again. "Where?" he groaned as he wisely lay back down.

"Home," the old man replied distantly.

* * *

The day was dreary with thick clouds blocking out much of the daylight. General Etrusin crouched down behind a rock and looked over his shoulder to the men waiting behind him. He signaled back to them, and they nodded, turning to tell the others. The general again peered around the boulder to the valley below.

A river of men wound its way through the valley beginning directly under Etrusin's hiding place and stretching back as far as he could see in the dim light. It was a large army, but he and his men had an advantage. They were lying in wait to surprise them from the high ground. Etrusin stood and shouted out a call that echoed back and forth between the mountains. His men bounded up behind him, answering with a deafening charge.

Several soldiers ran up next to the general and helped him push his boulder free of its perch. It bounced down the side of the mountain toward the head of the army below. To their horror, the rock slammed hard against the jagged edges of the mountainside and broke up into smaller pieces, which in turn broke apart as they hit the hard surface again. Soon there was nothing left of the boulder that still rolled downward.

Etrusin and his men looked at one another with slightly worried expressions, then joined the rest of the soldiers that were charging down the mountain. Below they could see a flurry of activity as the other army reacted to the general's charge. He couldn't hear over the noisome rush of his own men, but Etrusin knew that orders were being called out as the men in the valley broke formation and hurried into position to meet the enemy.

Arrows sailed overhead and dove into the valley aimed for the ranks below. Etrusin could not make out more than a few hits as he ran on. He wished he could get down there as fast as those arrows had. Now that he thought about it, hiding a bit further down the mountainside would have been wiser. He shook his doubts away and plunged ahead.

With great dismay, Etrusin watched as several of his own soldiers found the loose rock left by the broken boulder. They tumbled down the mountain, some headfirst, others sliding and rolling. He saw many of them flailing in an attempt to grab onto something and stop their descent. Others, however, bounced limply down into the valley. As the enemies gathered around those men who were the first to reach the bottom, the general prayed that they were already dead.

Although the charge had gone poorly thus far, Etrusin still hoped to press their advantage. He called out for men to watch for loose rock and for them to fire another volley of arrows. The missiles again whistled over them and down into the valley. As the general watched their course, he noticed that the army below seemed to be gathering around what looked like several large wagons.

Etrusin continued to watch, confused as his enemies lit fires on top of the wagons. It became clear to him very quickly that his estimation of the situation was grossly inaccurate. The fires lit on the wagons below launched into the air, and Etrusin could only stare as balls of flaming pitch rained out of the sky onto his army. His men had no determined direction in mind once they saw the approaching fire; they simply ran. Regardless, the balls of pitch fell and splattered outward onto the soldiers of Kesitul, covering them in a gooey, burning mess.

Chaos ensued. Etrusin watched helplessly as his soldiers, brothers and sisters of the empire, came tumbling down the mountain in flames. Some ran. Some were already dead and simply rolling to their final resting place in the valley of their enemy. Although not all the soldiers had been hit, at least not fatally, the general knew without question that the battle was lost. He shouted out the call for retreat.

His order was lost in the hectic screams and bustle of the scene around him. He saw soldiers stumbling by, barely able to walk, horribly disfigured by the fire. Some of them were covered in blood from falls that had not been merciful enough to kill them. His army now looked like a gathering of walking dead. He briefly thought, in this moment of defeat and desperation, that if they all ran down in this condition, they would scare off their foes. The thought humored him in a macabre way, and he almost laughed, but a dreadful sound echoed out from below. The second volley of pitch was already in the air.

The approaching balls of fire arced in slow motion, and general Etrusin took one last look over his troops. A line of soldiers, once the proud army of Kesitul, now stood pitifully on the mountainside awaiting their doom. They looked up at the fiery death in the sky, and it reflected in every one of their eyes. The general couldn't shake the idea that they looked evil, many of them deformed from their injuries and their eyes glowing with the reflection of flames. The scene somehow looked so familiar to him. Then the fire hit, and his was a world of pain and light.

A terror-stricken scream rent the dark silence of the bedroom as emperor Geilo awoke from his nightmare. It took him a moment to realize who and where he was, but for that moment he knew only the fear of death. He sat up panting heavily and nearly jumped out of his skin when two guards rushed in through the door.

"Sire, we heard a scream," one of the guards explained.

Geilo held up his hand and nodded gratefully. "Thank you," he said, "but it was only a dream."

The guard nodded. "Then, if you are certain you are well..."

The emperor nodded and waved them out of the room. When the doors were closed, he heaved a weary sigh. In fact, Geilo was not certain he was well at all, even though he reassured the guards night after night when they rushed in after he awoke screaming from one of his nightmares. Between the dreams of being Etrusin in his last moments and the dreams of wasting away from the poisonous stab of a bejeweled dagger, he was quite certain something was very wrong.

He sat in his bed, as he did after every nightmare, and pondered its meaning. Why would he be having these same dreams over and over again? Obviously they had to do with his recent decisions regarding the empire. This, however, confused him to no end. Had not Minotros himself told Geilo to go forth? Had the God of Fate not reassured him that the aggressor would fall?

"Go forth, Geilo. Brandish your sword. Your enemies cannot stand against you. Know this: the aggressor will fall..."

Geilo muttered to himself, reciting the counsel of Minotros. As he did so he mentally stepped through the dreams he had been having lately. Despite the seemingly reassuring message from Minotros, he could not figure any of it to come out to some kind of positive message. He thought of Etrusin, the disastrous ambush that had played out in his dream, the fire falling from the sky. He remembered thinking that his own people, the army of Kesitul, looked evil in those last moments, like an army of demons with dark clouds raining fire around them.

A chill traveled up Geilo's spine, and every hair on his body stood straight up. It had been a glimpse of his very first vision. As he thought back to the things that he had seen, the faces of those he had called demons all looked chillingly familiar to him. In that moment, he realized his folly. He did not understand why the God of Fate would have misled him, but he had deciphered the hint hidden in those divine words. He knew what he had to do.

Geilo leapt out of bed and ran across the room to the doors. He burst through them, startling the guards waiting outside. He left them behind stuttering confused questions. Wildly he bolted through the palace, causing a stir whenever he happened to pass someone. He rushed down some steps that led to a side exit near the stables. He nearly ran over the poor stable hand that was tending to the horses that night.

Minutes later the emperor, still clad in only his nightclothes, came pelting around the palace on his hastily-saddled and bridled horse. As the sound of pounding hooves faded west, several guards hurried out of the palace. One of them stomped up to the stable hand, who was looking quite bewildered.

"Which way did he go?" the guard asked gruffly.

The boy pointed.

The guard looked back to his comrades. "One of us will have to go after him," he said.

They all exchanged looks of uncertainty. The smallest of the group of large men stepped forward. "I will be able to ride the fastest," he volunteered.

The rest of them nodded. They looked over the horses quickly. They all silently agreed that the emperor must have gone mad. He hadn't even taken the fastest horse. This fact did not bring them much comfort, as they knew that Geilo, the master horseman who had defeated Reisothin, would manage to bring out the best in the animal. The smaller guard climbed up on the mount they had chosen and kicked the stallion into the fastest gallop he could.

"Good luck, Weipo!" the other guards called after him. "Bring him back safe!" When he was out of sight they all glanced at one another. Even after all these years, Geilo was still the finest rider in the empire. They knew it was not likely that Weipo would catch up to him at all.

* * *

A line of sharp elven arrows pointed up at an angle, seemingly aimed at some distant spot in mid-air. Each glinting, metal tip held steady, awaiting the call to fly free toward its target. That call came, and each bowstring was loosed in unison, propelling the elegant missiles in perfect projectile motion. Up and forward they went, climbing until gravity overtook their ascent, then down they came. Every one of the perfectly-crafted arrows thudded into the distant practice targets that had been set up on the training field.

Tilon noticed with pride that almost all of the arrows were either in or just outside of the center circle. That each target had exactly five arrows in it reassured him that the accurate aim was not simply chance; he had assigned five archers to a target. In little more than two months he had taken the best archers Etrusin's army had to offer and finely tuned their skill to a degree not likely known by many humans. Though none of them were consistently as good as even the worst elven archer, they were definitely able enough, in Tilon's estimation, to provide the army with a formidable weapon that would help swing the battle in their favor. With the added assistance of expertly-fashioned elven bows and magical elven arrows that bit more fiercely than their human-made counterparts, few would be able to stand in defiance of Kesitul's line of archers and their Shionen allies.

A commotion from across the camp captured the attention of the training archers and their instructor. While the humans strained to hear the calls that echoed from just beyond the camp, Tilon heard them perfectly and smiled. The normally reserved Shionen warrior dashed off toward the sounds.

Approaching the camp from the west was a small band of man-sized figures. Tilon suddenly burst into a Shionen melody that started out powerfully, but then shifted to a more subdued song that drifted on the wind gently. Although he did not sing the entire song loudly, indeed at times it was little more than a hum, the entire camp could hear it as clearly as if the elf were standing beside each person. Every once in a while, Tilon would pause, and a feminine voice could be heard on the air continuing the song. Together the voices mingled and entranced every man and woman who could hear it. All throughout the camp there was a palpable sensation of returning home, and it left everyone feeling joyful and reassured.

Indeed, the melody was a Shionen homecoming song, though none of the humans in the camp could have known that from the words. The emotion of the voices that drifted through the air and the magic of elvensong transcended the barrier of language. Thus no one was surprised when the distant figures came close enough for familiar features to be discerned, and it was revealed that the voice that joined Tilon's belonged to Marui.

From out of the crowd that had formed behind Tilon stepped General Etrusin. The proud commander grinned broadly at the approach of the scouting party. That grin became even wider when he counted all of those that left on the journey almost two months ago, including a couple that he had not known about.

"Su-Ni!" came the cry of Ninei from the crowd. The diplomatic advisor rushed out and ran toward the group while Ini'io, Ninei's other student, watched Su-Ni's return with disbelief.

The scouting party stepped onto the campground and was greeted happily by the awaiting crowd. Komeris walked up to general Etrusin and bowed deeply. Etrusin pulled him into a big hug, slapping him on the back happily. Su-Ni was inundated by questions from Ninei, who was hugging her in relief, and Ini'io, who still could not believe that she had come back alive. Tilon and Marui also embraced as kin who had been apart for some time, even though the journey had been short relative to the Shionen lifespan.

The mood in the camp quickly turned celebratory, and plans were already being laid for a party that night. Before the revelry, however, there was business to attend to. Etrusin motioned to Komeris, who nodded and turned to gather together the scouts. The general moved off to his tent, and everyone who had gone through the mountains followed soon after. Tilon joined them. They left the crowd to their plans of the festivities to come that night. So caught up was the camp in its excitement, that the homecomers were hardly missed.

In Etrusin's tent, the mood was a stark contrast to the one outside. Though the scouts were happy to see their kin again, the message they returned with was hardly a hopeful one. Several minutes went by before anyone spoke. It was Tilon who broke the silence.

"What do you have to report?" the elf asked somewhat impatiently.

Komeris sighed heavily. "I believe we have discovered that which emperor Geilo fears," he said gravely.

"The enemy?" Etrusin asked almost rhetorically.

The captain looked around at the rest of the scouting party. "Well, we have discussed it much on the return journey and we have agreed that, given all the signs, there can be little doubt."

The general leaned forward eagerly and pushed his woefully incomplete map across his table. "Tell me," he urged, his voice nearly a whisper.

"Well," began Komeris, "we made our way through the mountains by traveling a pass that runs across the southern part of the chain." He ran his finger along the southern coastline of the map.

"Did you see the ocean?" Etrusin asked.

"Alas, we did not," the young Denlin moaned sadly.

Komeris nodded in agreement and continued. "The pass is about a fortnight's travel on horse through to the other side, though it took us a bit longer. It was there where we spied our enemy."

"You saw them?" the general with intense interest.

"Yes," confirmed the captain. "Reniu and I rode out ahead before the others broke camp to see if we were close to exiting the pass. Just beyond the mountains was a city and a training field. On the field were about five or six thousand soldiers. They seemed to be preparing."

"Preparing?" Etrusin asked.

Komeris shrugged. "We never had the chance to get a closer look. We went back to camp to decide how to proceed. We moved into the trees and set up camp for the night. We had planned to return as a group the next morning, but that night we were attacked."

"Attacked?" exclaimed the general.

"By whom?" Tilon demanded.

"Men, six of them," replied the darkly clad O'eintsu.

"Seven," corrected Marui, "or six men and one other being that was too cowardly to show itself. I could sense it, though, hovering just beyond the battle."

"Magical?" Tilon asked his elven kin.

Marui responded with a simple nod.

"Was anyone harmed?" Etrusin asked.

Pei-Shi stepped forward. "One horse was killed, and another was made unfit for riding, which is why our return took so much longer. I received a fairly deep cut on my shoulder, but fortunately my new student was there to defend me," she said proudly, indicating Su-Ni.

The general raised an eyebrow at the former student of diplomacy. Many questions ran through his head about the young woman, but they would have to wait. "What of your attackers?" he asked the group.

"Two died, one by my bow. As he charged, he cried out, calling us 'dogs of the empire,'" Marui answered.

Etrusin leaned back in surprise. "How did he know you came from the empire?"

Komeris shook his head, unable to offer an explanation.

"The seventh," said Marui, "the one I mentioned that hid in the shadows. It felt very familiar." She turned to Tilon. "Remember that 'magician' in the forest when we were tracking Komeris and his party?"

The elf nodded. "The shapeshifter."

"Yes," Marui responded, "I believe he was spying on us. More specifically your people, general," she directed at Etrusin.

"But spying for who?" the general asked.

"The descendents of your own ancestors," Marui replied.

"Iono'itio," the general whispered in realization.

"You know of the Gleaming City?" Komeris asked in surprise.

Etrusin nodded. "Tilon has told me much in your absence, as I imagine Marui has done for you."

"Yes," the captain confirmed.

"If they are the brood of Teomin's lost army, and have sent spies and attacked our scouts, then I do not doubt what emperor Geilo has foreseen," the general stated with a deep sigh.

"The signs of our people too tell of conflict," agreed Tilon, "which is why we have offered ourselves as your allies."

The entire scouting party stared incredulously at the elf, but it was Marui who seemed the most shocked. "Tilon, is this true?" she asked.

"Yes!" answered General Etrusin happily. "Ranks of Shionen archers have joined us in training. Tilon himself is teaching my best archers how to refine their skill. With the addition of their brave warriors and more coming from the empire almost every day now, our numbers have swelled to over six thousand."

The look Marui gave her brother now was one of admiration.

The general continued, "With these soldiers, and the knowledge of what is to come, we will have a great advantage in this battle."

Everyone nodded in agreement.

Etrusin noticed that there was one among the party who had not said one word during this entire meeting. "Reniu, you have not yet offered your input. What say you to all this?"

Naturally, the burly man scowled. "I'm agreein with you, sir. It'll be an easier fight for us, knowin' what we're knowin'. In fact, this whole time I've been thinkin' of somethin' that's been in my head since we started headin' back."

"What is it?" the general asked with genuine interest.

"Well, the pass we went through the way there and back was pretty easy, as the captain said, but especially for a small bunch like us. There are a few places where the mountains crowd in, you know, and it'd be mighty hard for an army to march through 'cept a few men across," Reniu explained.

Etrusin's eyes glinted with comprehension. "So, we could move our army into these tight spots and lie in wait for our enemy. This way we could strike at them before they could even get to us," he mused.

"Yes, sir," agreed Reniu. "I think yer followin' me just fine."

General Etrusin stroked his chin thoughtfully while everyone praised Reniu's cleverness. It was a good plan, and the finer details were forming in Etrusin's mind as his scouting party began to take on the mood of the camp outside. It sounded as though it was shaping up to be a huge celebration, one which the scouts now felt like they could enjoy. The general dismissed them gratefully and went out to join in the festivities himself, though he knew he would have to order an early night. Tomorrow they would begin setting their plan in motion.

* * *

Like so many blades of grass did the seven thousand human soldiers of Ionotu's army appear as they stood waiting for their king's next command.

Every once in a while, the lines of men would ripple in waves as word made its way back through the ranks. The way ahead was narrow, and they would have to march through in a different formation. At least, that seemed to be the explanation at first.

Laernus had easily managed to work his way toward the back of the formation early in the march. He was the only one to communicate any information to the two thousand shapeshifting allies who were taking up the rear. None of the other men seemed too concerned about shouting back the calls that came from the forward lines. Now the seer stood beside Agucho, the commander of the Fiu-Het army. The two stood there watching Vethisir's men shifting uneasily.

"They say he is riding back," Laernus informed the shapeshifter.

"The king or the general?" Agucho asked.

The wizard warrior shrugged. "Likely both."

"What is the purpose of this?"

"The way ahead is not very wide," Laernus answered. "We will have to narrow our formation."

Agucho rolled his eyes. "So glad the king thought that was worthy of a visit."

"Do not despair, my friend. Our time is almost at hand," the seer reassured.

"Scheming together as always!" The shout came from the mounted Vethisir riding next to his king.

Laernus grimaced at the irritating general, but Agucho's expression was inscrutable. "Scheming is a word not oft used of allies," the Fiu-Het commander retorted.

"Allies," Vethisir spat.

Orbein shot them both a dangerous glare.

"To what do we owe this pleasure, highness?" Agucho asked with a haunting grin.

"We will have to lengthen the line to navigate the terrain ahead," the king replied.

"While we appreciate the time you took to ride back here, it was not necessary to do so. We would have gotten the message," Agucho told him.

Orbein bared his teeth. "We also have a...request," he said, though the meaning of this last word was obvious.

Agucho raised what, for his race, served as an eyebrow. "You have but to ask," he said smugly with a bow.

"Given your race's talents," the king began, "it would be best if you led the way. The general and I will, of course, guide you. This way some of your soldiers can fly ahead to scout the area and make sure that we don't meet with any unexpected resistance."

The shapeshifter shot Laernus a sidelong glance and stifled a wry laugh.

The king sounded ridiculous, making this sound like a noble assignment. It was really an order for the fodder to get in its place. Agucho knew that the show was merely for the rest of his race, who believed Orbein to be a true ally. He bowed again and turned to shout the orders to his troops. The king and the general rode back to the front without another word. Agucho, Laernus, and the rest of the Fiu-Het were not far behind.

It took a few minutes for the hundred score Fiu-Het to get into position. When they were done, Orbein nodded approvingly. He paused when he noticed Laernus standing beside Agucho. "Do you keep counsel with him?" the king asked with amusement.

Laernus nodded abruptly and eagerly answered, "As you desired."

Orbein was a bit surprised at the wizard's brazen confidence. He had hoped that Vethisir's army would break the seer; instead it seemed to have made him even more headstrong. He glanced questioningly at the shapeshifter, who merely shrugged. The king laughed out loud and shook his head. "You've hidden yourself from me long enough, Laernus. It's a good thing you have value, else I would have been rid of you by now."

Though Laernus had learned, somewhat harshly, the value of holding his tongue, he could not help but test the king in this difficult setting. He grinned and bowed. "Then it is, indeed, fortunate that I am 'of value'," he responded.

Orbein scowled and clenched his jaw. Regardless of the illusion of himself that he presented to the Fiu-Het, he would not stand for such defiance. He reared his horse and trotted dangerously close to the seer, kicking out as he rode by.

Laernus flew to the ground. He sat up holding his fattening lip, which had tasted the king's boot.

Orbein called back to the seer, "Of value, for now..." He rode off quickly with a chuckling Vethisir in tow.

When they were out of earshot, Laernus swore under his breath. "So much for marching beside us," he added.

"Do not despair, my friend. Our time is almost at hand," Agucho said, mockingly repeating the seer's earlier sentiment.

Laernus scowled at the shapeshifter. "What, have you been deceiving me all this time?" he asked.

"No, it is true," Agucho confirmed. "I just wanted to demonstrate how unreassuring it sounds."

The seer nodded repentantly and spit out some blood as his shapeshifting conspirator gave orders for a few scouts to take to the skies. It was going to be a long march, and Agucho was right. 'Almost at hand' was not very reassuring at all.

17 REUNION

For the first time in months, Urietsin looked out from the mountainside and did not see more mountains. Mostly flat land stretched out for miles, and in the distance, almost imperceptible to human eyes, was the green line of the forest. It seemed so far away to the young warrior, physically and in time. He had only been with Kiusu for little more than a season, but in some ways it felt longer. When he thought about home, it seemed like he had been away for ages, but his time with Kiusu felt like no more than a week. Though a part of him yearned for the land he had known in his childhood, he had grown comfortable in that tiny hut on the western side of the mountain. So it was with some excitement and a bit of uncertainty that Urietsin made those first steps down the mountain beside his friend and master.

Uncertain didn't even begin to describe the many layers of Kiusu Tho-Shoishu's emotions toward leaving his home of twenty years. He had not been around anything resembling civilization in two decades and, though the Swift One had helped to readjust him, he wondered how he would feel when surrounded by his own people again. The rational side of Kiusu that had used these years of his life to gain a better understanding of his higher self, tried to reassure him that all was well. The other side of him that had controlled all of his thoughts and actions for most of the other ninety-two years of his life was terrified.

The wizened master simply reminded himself that change was a crucial part of existence, and one that maximized experience. In the back of his mind, though, insecurities that he had thought long expelled from his very being resounded loudly. He began to wonder how much wisdom he had truly gained in living alone for almost a generation of his kin. He did not doubt that they would happily welcome him back; rather he was afraid that he would be far too happy to be welcomed back. For there was one fear that surpassed all others. It was the fear of what lay at the end of this journey.

"Are you alright, seishin?" Urietsin asked with a touch of concern.

Kiusu smiled and nodded. "Yes, Swift One, quite. You should be more worried for yourself. It was you who was not well recently," he reminded the young warrior, though that was another confusing emotion in the bundle that he had packed for the trip.

The Swift One adopted a faraway look. "Yes..." he said quietly. He shook his head and blinked away the trance. "You look troubled, though," he insisted.

"Long has it been since I walked among my people...our people," the old man admitted with a shrug, leaving out the other half of his feelings. He wondered if he could ever tell the young man that he had hidden him from his rescuers, that he had forced the speedy completion of his lessons. It had been easy to justify these things in the solitude of the mountain hut, but on the road back to the empire, they worked their way to the forefront of his thoughts.

Urietsin patted his shoulder. "Don't worry, I'm sure they have missed you in your absence," he said with a reassuring smile.

Kiusu nodded. "Yes, and I think I have underestimated how much I've missed them." He returned the young warrior's smile with a wistful one of his own.

"Well, come on then!" the Swift One cried cheerily. "Let us speed our return!" And with that he bounded as carefully down the mountain as he could, Kiusu in tow.

They reached the foot of the mountain in relatively short order and rested long enough to eat an early lunch. They were both eager to be moving, so they were quickly headed east again. They were grateful of the distraction that their fast-paced travel provided. From the base of the mountain it was a two-day walk to get to the forest's edge, but the two companions were determined to arrive sooner. They had traveled all day and well into the night when they saw pinpoints of light spring up on the horizon in front of them. Though they were tired, they pressed on, and it was almost dawn when they came upon a sprawling campsite.

"Halt! Name yourselves!" called out a stern voice.

Urietsin and Kiusu stopped walking. A large soldier, wielding his sword cautiously, stepped toward them. Urietsin held up his hand in greeting. "Hail," he called, "I am Urietsin of Retso and my companion is Kiusu Tho-Shoishu. We are both your kin of Geilo's great empire."

The soldier lowered his sword. "Tho-Shoishu?" he echoed. "I know that name."

Kiusu nodded. "I have been away for many years, alone in the mountains. I hope to know my people again," he said with a sad smile.

Sheathing his weapon, the soldier bowed in welcome. "I wish this reunion could be during happier times. As things are, we still are glad to have our own here at the general's camp."

"Urietsi'in?" came another voice.

"Ninei!" the Swift One called back. He went over to the diplomatic advisor and bowed. "It is fine to see a familiar face again."

The diplomat grinned and bowed in return. "What happened to you? We were certain you were dead."

Urietsin nodded. "For a time, I thought so as well. I have Kiusu to thank for my survival," he explained, indicating the older man.

"Kiusu," Ninei said blankly as she offered a respectful bow.

"Ninei," the old man answered. "I know you, though I have not seen you in many long years."

The diplomat looked at him with a perplexed expression. "I am sorry, sir, I do not remember you."

"I am Kiusu Tho-Shoishu. My master and I fought beside your emperor against the Abomination."

The look of confusion on Ninei's face was washed away by one of shock. She immediately bowed again, more deeply. "My apologies, master, I did not recognize you."

Kiusu reached out and patted her shoulder, then displayed as much respect for her as she had for him. When he came up from his own bow, he smiled reassuringly. "Do not concern yourself. I am simply a man."

"A great man by any account," the diplomat insisted.

Urietsin grinned as Kiusu waved away the attention. "Is the captain here at the camp?" the young warrior asked.

Ninei's brow furrowed. "No. He has gone with the general. They have taken the army, as it is, to the southern pass in the mountains. Through there lies the path to those who threaten our way of life."

"Army?" the Swift One asked, though the answer played out in his head before Ninei explained it to him.

"I forgot you have been missing since all of this really got started," she began.

Urietsin held up his hand. "There will be time for that later."

The diplomat seemed confused, but did not proceed. "You two look tired from your journey. Come rest and tell us of your travels. Breakfast is being prepared now, if you are hungry."

The two men nodded gratefully and followed Ninei to the mess tent where the scent of breakfast waited to invite them in. For Kiusu it was a little unnerving. He had lived by himself for twenty years, and now, even though most of the camp was empty, he found himself surrounded by people. He could keenly feel every single person around him, and the thoughts that left him with made him question again the past two decades.

As he entered the tent with Urietsin and Ninei, he was presented with another distraction from the uncomfortable workings of his mind.

Urietsin entered and had almost run into the young woman who now stood before him speechless and agape. "Su-Ni," the Swift One murmured breathlessly.

The young woman, clad in a much different style than he had last seen her, found her voice again. "Urietsi'in, we thought...I mean, I didn't, but..." She stuttered over some explanation of her shock, but gave up and pulled him into a powerful embrace.

Urietsin laughed in surprise and hugged her back. "What are these clothes? They hardly seem fitting of a diplomat," was the only response he could think of.

Su-Ni beamed at him proudly. "I have learned to wield a sword. I am a soldier now," she said showing off her ringmail and leather tunic.

Something about that image made the Swift One's heart pound a little harder. "Why are you not with General Etrusin and his army?" he asked in a voice that belied his suddenly increased interest in the young woman.

At that question she pouted. "I have been left behind with all the other soldiers of lesser skill."

"I'm sure you're not as bad as all that," Urietsin chuckled.

Su-Ni was about to agree when yet another somewhat familiar voice called out, "If this isn't a time for unusual happenings."

The Swift One recognized the taller of Ninei's protégés, Ini'io. He bowed in greeting and asked, "What do you mean?"

"Su-Ni returns from the mountains a warrior, the rider from two nights ago and now you and the legendary master Tho-Shoishu appear at our camp," the young diplomat explained, failing to return the Urietsin's bow.

"Rider?" the Swift One asked curiously.

"There was a rider that came to the camp two nights ago," Ini'io went on. "One of the Shionen sentries spoke with him. He came out of the forest on a horse that was near death with fatigue. The sentry said he was in his nightclothes and claimed to be carrying a very important message for the general. When he found out that Etrusin had already gone, he became very distressed and insisted on taking another horse."

"His nightclothes?" asked Urietsin. "Did he say who he was?"

Ini'io shook his head. "No, he would say nothing else, or so the elf said. He simply got on the new horse and rode away like he was the emperor himself."

"How strange," said Su-Ni with a raised eyebrow.

"Indeed," agreed Urietsin. "I wonder what could have been so important. I shall have to ask the general when we get to the southern pass, or wherever he is when we join with him."

"You are going to the army?" asked Su-Ni, eyes wide in wonderment.

Urietsin nodded.

"You must let me come with you," she said assertively.

The Swift One regarded her, unsure of how to answer. "It...it may be dangerous."

Su-Ni rolled her eyes. "Don't you think I know that!" she exclaimed in exasperation. "I am not a silly little girl."

"Of course you aren't." Urietsin bowed in apology. "If you wish to come, I cannot stop you. I-we shall welcome your company."

Ini'io spoke up. "I, however, must protest. Su-Ni, despite your little adventure, you are not a warrior. You have known nothing but diplomacy for much of your life. I advise against you sprinting off on this foolish quest to become a champion."

Urietsin gaped at the man in surprise, but his reaction was nothing compared to Su-Ni's. She marched up to him, and though she barely stood taller than his shoulder, leaned toward him in a manner that could only be interpreted as intimidating. "If Urietsin could not stop me, then you would have no hope to."

In spite of his obvious physical advantage over the young woman, he backed down with a look of awe. She turned immediately and stomped off, nodding to Urietsin as she exited the tent. Ini'io glared at the Swift One, shook his head and, likewise, left in a huff.

Urietsin found himself standing alone by the opening of the tent with a bemused expression. He looked around for the two he had come in with. He spotted Ninei and Kiusu sitting and talking quietly at one of the large tables. He began to make his way over to them when his stomach growled loudly enough to startle him. He decided it would be best to get a plate of breakfast before he joined the table.

When he did finally join the table, he brought with him a plate that was overflowing with food. He sat and immediately dug in, hungrily savoring foods that he had not enjoyed in months. About midway through his meal, which was not very long after he had taken his seat, he noticed that Ninei and Kiusu were staring at him with amused expressions.

"My apologies," the Swift One amended. "Are either of you hungry?"

Kiusu waved the offer away, and Ninei informed him that she had already eaten. They continued to watch him virtually inhale the rest of the contents of his plate. When he finished, he leaned back in his chair and rubbed his stomach in satisfaction.

"That was quite good. Are you sure you're not hungry, Kiusu? You have not eaten since yesterday," the Swift One reminded.

The old man nodded reassuringly. "I know. I am fine. Besides, I think you've eaten enough for the both of us," he chuckled.

They all shared in a brief laugh at that, and the mood became very relaxed. Even Kiusu, who had seemed a bit tense since he walked into the tent, looked to be back to his usual, placid self. Together the three of them chatted for well over an hour about news and the empire. Mostly Ninei was filling Kiusu in on all that he had missed in his years of solitude. Every once in a while, Urietsin would interject with memories that offered a different perspective on events. By the time the conversation had drawn to a close, both the Swift One and his former master were very tired. The weariness of their trip had finally caught up to them, and they requested that Ninei take them to a place where they could rest. She brought them to a tent not far from the west edge of camp where they had arrived. Already there were bedrolls and blankets on the floor, and the two men had hardly laid their heads down before they were asleep.

Several hours later, they awoke to the sound of voices passing by their tent. When they exited, they found that people seemed to be gathering at the center of camp. At first, the two men thought it was some kind of line to get into the mess tent for dinner. They soon came to realize that the people were crowding around a very tired looking man in a palace guard's embroidered koje. They were questioning him, and he answered impatiently and seemed very eager to be elsewhere. Urietsin spotted Su-Ni on the edge of the crowd and walked over to her, Kiusu following close behind.

"What's going on?" the Swift One asked quietly.

When Su-Ni looked back at him, the expression on her face spoke volumes. "He says he is Weipo, a palace guard. He raced here by horse on the heels of the emperor himself! That was the visitor to the camp the other night. Weipo says he rushed out of the palace in his nightclothes and jumped on a horse and rode it through the forest without stopping. That was five nights ago," she explained.

"Five nights ago!" Urietsin exclaimed. "That means is took the emperor three nights to get through the forest. A ride like that would kill the horse!"

"It nearly did," Su-Ni agreed. "That's why the emperor changed horses here."

"Why would the emperor be so desperate to get to General Etrusin?" the intrigued young warrior asked. With no obvious answer forthcoming, the Swift One looked over at Kiusu. "We must go after him. At his pace he is probably already there, I would imagine."

"The entrance to the southern pass is a little more than a full day's ride," Su-Ni confirmed.

"We must still go after him," insisted Urietsin.

"I am ready to go," Kiusu replied.

"I have been ready since this morning," agreed Su-Ni. Indeed, she already had a pack slung over her shoulders.

"Then let us go," Kiusu nodded.

The three of them sneaked away from the distracted crowd to where the few horses left in the camp were tied. Each of them quietly led a horse away and made their way around the outside of the camp. Minutes later, they were pounding out over the open grassy land between camp and the mountains. Su-Ni was in the lead and brought them in a southwesterly direction, tracing the route she had made following the scouting party. As she had on that night two months ago, she displayed an uncanny natural sense of direction and led the group true.

They rode well into the night, and the moon climbed high into the sky. The light from the virtual fullness of that moon was helpful to the group, as they could easily see one another while they rode. The ground below them was also well lit, and it was Urietsin's sharp eye that caught an unusual glint as they rode past. His horse reared and neighed as he pulled on his reign.

The other two heard Urietsin's horse and quickly turned around. As they trotted up, they saw the Swift One jump off his mount and kneel down. He seemed to be investigating something on the ground.

"What is it?" called Kiusu.

Urietsin stood, and in one hand he held a bit and bridle just like the ones outfitted on each of their horses.

"Where did that come from I wonder?" Su-Ni realized how silly it sounded as she uttered it.

"Well, what happened to the horse that wore it?" Urietsin salvaged her question.

"It might not even be the emperor's," the young woman suggested. "Many more horses passed this way with the army."

"This bridle is perfectly good. Why would anyone leave it behind?" the Swift One reasoned.

Kiusu offered, "We must search the area."

Su-Ni nodded in agreement. She pulled off her small pack and produced three torches from within. "Here, each of you take one of these." She handed one to each man and produced some flint. After a few tries, she got all the torches lit. "This way we can split up, and as long as we stay within sight of each other's torchlight, we should not get lost," she explained.

"Yes, but let us not spend too much time on this search," advised Kiusu. "If it is not Geilo's, we may be wasting our time."

"Yes," agreed Su-Ni, "and there's no telling if the emperor met with some danger further down the road." A chill went up her spine as she recalled her encounter with the meilif-danar.

The three of them rode out away from one another. They circled around and tried to cover as much ground as they could while remaining roughly equidistant from each other. They searched the ground around them up to the edge of their vision and then moved on, looking back every once in a while, each making sure that there were still two other torchlights bobbing around in the darkness. Almost a half hour of this pattern went by without a single sign of anything unusual.

Su-Ni's horse plodded along slowly as she peered into the dim circle of light offered by her torch. She held the light high and a bit behind her so that the bright flame didn't obscure her sight more than it helped it. Regardless, she found nothing in this spot also and moved her horse forward. This search was clearly fruitless, and she was becoming weary of it. She barely stopped her steed at all and simply continued along halfheartedly.

The young woman sighed deeply and was about to turn around and call out to end the search when something odd caught her attention. As she turned her head, she could have sworn she saw a dark shape just beyond her circle of light. When she looked in the direction she had seen it, only darkness was visible to her. She looked off to the side a little, and there it was in her peripheral vision again, a shadowy shape close to the ground. Her chest began to thud with the pounding of her heart. She strained to hear, but only the sound of the blood in her veins rushed in her ears. She began to move cautiously in the direction of the shape.

As she came closer, the shadows retreated, and she clearly saw something large and dark on the ground in front of her. She quietly got off her horse and drew her sword. With the torch held behind her and her blade in front, the young woman stepped slowly toward the shape, afraid that at any instant it might jump up and attack her. It was only a few feet in front of her now, but though she strained and squinted, she could not make out its exact shape in the dancing light of her torch. She was inching forward and stretching out her sword, gripping it so tightly that her knuckles shown white. She came just a little bit closer and leaned in until her sword touched it lightly. When no reaction seemed forthcoming, she stood straight and brought her torch forward to see what it was that lay before her.

"Urietsin! Kiusu! Come quickly! Here! Here! Come here!" Su-Ni called out as loudly as she could while she waved her torch frantically in the air.

Within seconds the two men came galloping to her. They leapt off their horses and gathered around the shadowy shape lying on the ground. They all shared a surprised, perhaps slightly unnerved look.

"A horse," Kiusu said finally breaking the stunned silence.

"What could have done this to it?" Urietsin asked in awe.

The horse, or what was left of it, lay on the grass staring lifelessly into the night. There were several large, gaping holes on its flanks and midsection. Its corpse was riddled with several smaller holes and random raking gashes. Kiusu was stepping around it carefully and investigating all of its visible wounds.

"Whatever it was, it did this recently. This horse has not been dead for much more than a day," the old man informed the other two.

"Regardless of what it was," piped the Swift One, "if this was the emperor's horse, then where is the emperor?"

"We must continue our journey," responded Kiusu. "If Geilo escaped, we may find him along the way. If he did not..."

"...then he is surely dead," finished Urietsin.

The two men quickly got back on their horses and turned to leave. Su-Ni, however, who had been silent since Kiusu and Urietsin arrived, simply stood and stared at the lifeless equine body before her. The younger of the men called out to her, and she blinked with a start. She mechanically walked back to her own horse and climbed onto it.

"Are you alright, Su-Ni?" the Swift One asked her delicately.

She nodded, and the hint of a grateful smile passed briefly over her face. "Let us waste no more time," she said determinedly.

The young woman rode out hard with her companions, but in her mind she still stood near the decomposing corpse of the animal that had bore the emperor. Its terrible wounds flashed in horrid detail in her mind's eye. She shuddered as she played out the last moments of that poor creature's life in her head. Haunted by these images that seemed eerily familiar, Su-Ni had little hope that the emperor had escaped with his life.

About an hour later, it was Urietsin, once again, who spotted something ahead, though a bit off their course. This was something that was not so difficult for the others to see as they rode up to it. Considering their search an hour ago, they were hopeful and terrified as they came upon a roughly man-sized shape lying in the cold, dew-clad grass.

Urietsin and Kiusu dismounted and approached the shape. It was the Swift One who bent down to turn over what was definitely a man lying face down in his nightclothes. There was a slight moaning sound as he did so, and a face that he recognized as the emperor's looked up at him blearily.

Geilo was deathly pale and as cold as the grass he lay in, but he was not quite dead. He looked from Kiusu to Urietsin and smiled. "The dead have come for me," he whispered weakly.

"Nay, highness, not yet," Urietsin reassured. "Su-Ni, give me some water."

The young woman reached into her pack and drew out a waterskin and tossed it to the Swift One. He unstoppered it quickly and poured some of the cool liquid into the emperor's mouth. Geilo began to drink, but was soon coughing and sputtering. As Urietsin pulled the skin away, the emperor retched and vomited up the water he had just consumed.

The Swift One looked up at Kiusu sadly. "We must get him back to camp," he said, though his voice revealed no hope with that statement.

"No!" the emperor yelped with surprising fierceness. "I must get to

Etrusin."

"Emperor, you are not well. We must get you help as soon as possible, and the camp is the closest," Urietsin explained.

"My throne will be empty," Geilo said hollowly. "There is no help for me. I must get to Etrusin, or there will be no help for the empire!" This last statement seemed to be too much for him and he slumped into unconsciousness.

Again, Urietsin looked up to his former master. "What should we do?" he asked.

Kiusu looked down at the man he had once known. The strong rider who had led his people to victory against Reisothin. It was that strength that kept him alive now, and Kiusu knew that if he died before his message was relayed, the results could be catastrophic. He intimated as much to Urietsin.

"Perhaps one of us can continue on with Su-Ni to relay his message while one of us rides back to camp with the emperor," the Swift One suggested.

Kiusu shot him a doubtful look. "Perhaps you would like to ask him what his message was," he said, indicating the unconscious Geilo.

"He is poisoned," called out Su-Ni suddenly, "and I know that Marui has the cure. Many of the Shionen probably do. Let us not ride back to camp when there is a chance that it will end up with the emperor dying in vain. Take him, with his message, to Etrusin. If Marui can help him, we will all be blessed. If not...then at least the emperor will die proudly, knowing that he has saved the empire once more." Tears welled up in the worried woman's eyes.

Kiusu and Urietsin looked at one another and nodded slowly in agreement. "Let him ride with you, Su-Ni," the older man said. "You are the lightest."

Su-Ni nodded and shifted as they lifted the emperor onto her horse's back. "Will you be able to hold him?" the Swift One asked her. Again she nodded and reached around Geilo's limp body and gripped the reign tightly. "Tell me if he becomes too much for you to carry," Urietsin reassured her.

In seconds their horses' hooves beat the ground again as they rode like the wind to the southwest. The moon was setting, and the horizon behind them was getting brighter, but their only focus was on the way ahead. They did not stop to rest, and they drove their horses as hard as they dared. Though the temperature was cool, even after the sun rose, the animals were lathered in sweat, and the riders felt no better. They were all experienced riders, but none of them rode regularly enough to make this an easy journey.

Su-Ni was having the worst time of it, trying to hang on and keep the emperor in place as well. While the past several weeks had done wonders for her fitness, she was still not nearly as well-built as her two male companions. Her arms burned, as did her legs, and because of the way she was sitting toward the back of her horse to make room for Geilo, she feared her teeth would be rattled right out of her head. Every time Urietsin looked back at her, though, she grit her teeth and forced a reassuring grin. She was determined to make it to the end of this journey without holding up her companions. She would get the emperor to Etrusin even if her limbs fell off doing so.

* * *

A red sunrise greeted General Etrusin as he woke from his brief and intermittent sleep. He sullenly watched the sun continue its upward path as his army bustled around him, clearing the camp and getting ready to march. More than one soldier glanced furtively over his shoulder at the ill omen on the horizon. Few armies marching to war have ever welcomed the red sunrise. As Etrusin stood pondering the possibilities that the day might present for good or ill, Komeris and Tilon walked up behind him.

"The Shionen know the news that the dawn brings," Tilon said, his glittering armor taking on a deep golden hue in the red light of the morning sun.

"Fear it not, general, it may be for our enemy," reassured Komeris.

Etrusin nodded, but still he stared at the brightening horizon. "Rarely is the red dawn for one side only. The fighting will take its toll no matter how many or how few soldiers fall," he said soberingly.

The captain and the elf were silent. They agreed that the general was right, but both of them had known and accepted their possible fate at the end of this march. It was the price they were willing to pay for the safety and freedom of their people. Komeris spoke this sentiment aloud as Tilon nodded his approval.

General Etrusin turned away from the sunrise to look at the captain. "You are right, of course," he said with an appreciative smile.

Komeris returned the smile and asked, "When shall we give the order to march?"

"Immediately," Etrusin responded.

"General," Tilon interrupted, "riders approach!"

Etrusin spun and peered in the direction that Tilon was pointing. "I see nothing," he admitted after a long pause.

"Three of them," the elf insisted.

Komeris and Etrusin continued to squint in the direction indicated by the elf, but it was still some minutes later before they recognized the three blots on the horizon that were moving toward them. By this time, Tilon was able to make out one more detail.

"One of the horses carries two," he said.

They stood and waited and wondered who could be riding in from the camp, as that was clearly the direction from whence they had come. Soon the riders were close enough that the three onlookers could faintly hear the pounding of the horses' hooves carried on the wind, although it was Tilon who heard them long before the other two. Indeed, many of the elven archers among the army perked up their ears at the sound of approaching horses. Those who paid attention could sense an urgency in the riders' pace. It did nothing to quell the unease that had come with the dawning of the sun.

Shock did not even begin to describe the reaction of the three that stood to receive the riders when they finally galloped up and stopped short. All three were surprised to see Urietsin, the man they had thought lost forever on the mountainside, but not nearly as surprised as Etrusin and Komeris were to see their emperor slumped in front of Su-Ni in his nightclothes. They all simply stood there agape for a moment before they remembered themselves. Then all at once, they sprung into action, running to the riders and asking the obvious questions.

"See to the emperor!" Su-Ni shouted to all of them.

Etrusin hurried over to her horse and gently took the emperor's unconscious form in his arms. If he had not been worried before, he certainly was now as he noted with fright how light Geilo felt. He carried him away and shouted orders for a canopy to be put up.

"What has happened to him?" Komeris asked of the three riders.

"He was attacked by something. We believe he has been poisoned," Urietsin answered.

"Why have you brought him here?" the captain continued, the confusion evident on his face.

"He was already on his way," explained Su-Ni, who looked very road weary. "A guard from the palace said that the emperor rushed out and galloped away on a horse as fast as could be. He made it through the forest in three days."

Komeris's eyes widened.

"We came after him," Urietsin went on. "We found his mutilated horse, then later the emperor himself. He insisted that we take him here. He said he had and urgent message for the general."

"Why would he come himself? And by himself?" Komeris wondered aloud.

"The message must have been very important indeed," the Swift One offered. "He knew he was the only one who could have ridden so fast."

"Hopefully it was fast enough," the captain said with a look over to where Etrusin and Marui were looking after Geilo. He went to walk over to them, but paused briefly and called over his shoulder, "I don't know how you are still alive, Swift One, but it is truly good to see you."

"Thank you, sir," he replied sincerely.

Kiusu tensed in spite of himself. He recognized Komeris as the man who had come looking for Urietsin after the gotori attack.

"Your mounts look tired, as do you," Tilon said. "Let me get someone to tend to them."

"Thank you," said Su-Ni, truly grateful for that offer. She went to climb off her horse, but she could not hold on well enough to steady herself, and she tumbled to the ground.

Urietsin leapt off his horse and was by her side in an instant. "Su-Ni! Su-Ni, are you alright?" he cried.

The young woman looked up at him as tears streamed down her temples. "I can't feel my arms, Urietsin," she moaned.

The Swift One took her hand and lifted her sleeve. Huge purple bruises covered the entirety of her forearms, which he also noticed were heavily scarred from some previous injury. "Su-Ni, why did you not tell us? One of us could have taken him," he said plaintively.

"My horse had the lightest load," she responded. "I did not wish to slow us."

Urietsin grimaced and lifted the young woman and carried her over to where the emperor was being tended. He saw Etrusin standing by impotently as Marui administered what care she could. Busy though she was, the elf did acknowledge Su-Ni's condition. The Swift One laid the former diplomat down and said, "Fear not. I will go find someone to tend to you."

"No," she pleaded. "Stay here with me, Urietsin. Marui will see to me when she is done. My wounds are not so grievous. Please don't leave me alone."

Urietsin paused, then nodded.

Kiusu remained seated on his horse and watched the wave of curiosity and confusion wash over the army as they wondered what all the commotion was about, then realized the answer. A young soldier, looking very disconcerted, stepped up to him and offered to take his horse. The old man jumped down and gave the horse a grateful pat on the neck as the soldier led it away. He went back to looking at the throng of kinsmen that were crowded around the canopy where the emperor lay. It was sobering to see Etrusin's army rebuilt, especially when he considered that the last time he had seen so many people was when he had been part of the original fighting force that had glued the empire together.

"I know you," came the voice of Tilon, shattering Kiusu's reverie.

The old man considered the elf for a moment before answering, "You may, though it has been many years since you saw me, no doubt."

Tilon nodded. "Yes, my people have a fine memory, especially for that which is unusual to us. Few who are not our kin may walk through our forest without being noticed. Where were you going all those years ago?"

Kiusu shrugged and shifted his focus to somewhere beyond. "I was not sure then, and I don't believe I am all that sure now. I felt I needed solitude, though I fear I have had more than my fill," he decided.

"It is strange to be among your people again?" Tilon asked, though it was more of a statement.

The old man nodded in confirmation. "Strange. Strange because I regret being away for so long, now that I see them. I have lived many more winters than most men, and though my master was many more years older when he died, I fear my reunion with my people may be a short one," he lamented.

"Life is only as long as you live it," the Shionen elf said matter-of-factly.

Without pause Kiusu, again, nodded in agreement and looked back out at the crowd. Though he knew Tilon was right, the old man started to feel the way he had when he and Urietsin had entered the general's camp near the forest two nights ago. How could he feel so alone with so many people about?

General Etrusin looked over Marui's shoulder, feeling powerless, though he was surrounded by over six thousand warriors that were at his command. He stared down at his emperor, the man who had bestowed this power upon him, lying there close to death. He watched Marui as she unwrapped the cuff that Geilo had balled into one of his hands. The green color of the infection that oozed out of the puncture wound in that palm nearly made him sick. Etrusin was not normally a man possessed of a weak stomach, but standing here watching his emperor die, knowing that in moments he may be the most powerful man in Kesitul, wreaked havoc with his constitution.

Marui dabbed at the wound, clearing away as much of the pus and blood as she could. She produced some herb from a pouch and wrapped it against the wound. She informed Etrusin that it would need to be changed every few hours, though the look in her eyes said that she doubted it would need to be changed once. With one last sympathetic and sorrowful smile to the general, the elf walked away to aid Su-Ni as she could.

Etrusin took Marui's place by the emperor's side. He looked down at the pale, drawn face and could hardly recognize the strong man that pulled the empire together. It saddened him greatly to think that the man who was so loved by all the empire was expiring in a field in the middle of nowhere by the Ikiu'iu mountains. The man who he had ridden beside, and to whom he had pledged his sword in allegiance and friendship, Ushisorein, Most Beloved Emperor, his old friend, was soon to be only a memory. At this General Etrusin of Kilelu began to weep.

"Do not lose hope, sir," Komeris said comfortingly. "He is not gone yet."

Yet, still, at these hopeful words, Etrusin could not hold back the tears that surprised even him. At either the sound of his sobs or the tender touch that the general gave to Geilo's uninjured hand, the emperor stirred.

"Sire?" Etrusin called to Geilo. "Emperor, can you hear me?"

The emperor opened his eyes weakly, though he did not look at anyone or anything in particular. "Etrusin?" came his rasping, shaky voice. "Etrusin, my friend, are you here?"

"Yes, sire!" he cried, taking up Geilo's hand in his own to confirm his presence.

"Oh, Etrusin, I am so glad I have found you," the emperor whispered haltingly.

"Please try to rest, sire, you need to save your strength," the general urged.

Geilo shook his head, though the action seemed to pain him. "No, my friend, there is no strength left in me but that to deliver this message..."

"Nay, emperor, your end is not here." Etrusin wanted to believe it, but he heard the doubt in his own voice and it almost overwhelmed him.

Again the emperor shook his head, but smiled weakly. "Please, Etrusin. Call me by my name before I die, like in the days long past."

"Yes, si-, Geilo. Geilo, my old friend." Etrusin smiled as well, though tears rolled down his cheeks.

The emperor's smile returned again, and he seemed to gain a bit of strength for the moment. He tilted his head up and looked directly at the general. "I know what you have planned, my friend, and that is what brings me here," he paused to take a few breaths. "I beg of you, do not be the first to attack. I know it seems prudent, but by the word of Minotros, the aggressor will fall. I have seen..."

Etrusin gave the faltering emperor a helpless look. "What shall we do?" he asked.

Geilo's head fell back, though his eyes remained open. The only sign that he had not yet passed was the loud rasp of his breath. "Promise me!" he said in a cracked voice. "Promise me you will not attack first!"

"Yes, Geilo, I promise," Etrusin assured him desperately, hoping the promise would somehow renew him and wipe away his injury.

Once more, the emperor smiled as he continued to stare upward. He squeezed the general's hand briefly, and his wheezing gulps of air slowed and faded away far too quickly.

"Geilo?" Etrusin called. "Geilo! Emperor!" He called several more times and stopped only when Komeris laid his hand gently upon the general's shoulder. He looked up at the elder captain, his eyes no longer wet. For some inexplicable reason, he felt like that which gave him emotion had flown away with the emperor's spirit. How he wished that he,

Etrusin, held the lower rank instead of Komeris. For just a moment, he considered relinquishing his title and walking off forever.

The captain gave Etrusin a few moments and did, himself, pay his respects to the emperor. "What will your orders be, sir?" he asked the general quietly.

"Prepare the emperor for his return home."

Komeris knelt down beside his general. "How shall we prepare him, Etrusin? We are ill equipped for anything but war," he said solemnly.

Etrusin put his face in his hands and remained that way for several minutes. He did not shake, or sob, or give any indication that he was mourning Geilo's passing with tears. When he finally looked back up, he no longer seemed sad, rather a determined fire burned in his eyes. "Bury him here," he said easily. "Bury him on this very spot."

The general stood up fiercely and called out to all who were gathered around, "Weep not for Geilo, Emperor of Kesitul!"

Word of the emperor's passing had filtered out very quickly, and several in the crowd managed to look incredulous, while still others wept openly, seeming not to have even heard the general's command.

"Weep not!" Etrusin insisted, "Rather cheer for the man who has, once again, saved us. Geilo gave his life so that we may continue to live. We may yet fight, and many may die, but only to save our empire and our way of life! Though our beloved emperor has left us here on this field, he will be with us always, if we remain united in remembrance of him.

"Here let us build Geilo's tomb, the place of eternal rest for his body. And let our people journey here throughout the coming centuries so that we may never forget his spirit. And let us never allow, on this ground hallowed by his death, those who would strive to erase his memory and his people. We are his people. Let us never forget him! Let us cheer for Geilo, greatest of men!"

The gathering had fallen silent, every being's attention trained on Etrusin, entranced by his impromptu eulogy. Now they did indeed let out a great cheer. They clapped, and they yelled, and they waved their fists in the air, though their cheeks were still wet with tears. Even the Shionen joined in on the unexpected celebration. They cheered not that Geilo was with them no more, but that he was now with them eternally, in a way that meant more to them than they could ever fully express. Though Geilo had been truly loved by all of his people, that love was now strengthened and renewed by his last act of selflessness for them.

"What are we to do now?" Komeris asked Etrusin. "What of this army? What of the hostile men we met beyond the pass?"

The general gave him a look that sent a chill up his spine. "We will wait, forever if we have to. I will only move to defend the empire against imminent attack, as I promised Geilo. As such, I want sentries on the mountainsides along the pass. If someone does come, I want us to be ready. We will make camp at the mouth of the pass and stay there as long as we must."

Komeris nodded and thoughtfully watched Etrusin walk away. The captain found himself at a crossroad of emotions. He could not decide whether he wanted the fight that they had all been expecting to come and be done with it, or for this all to be just one big mistake so that they could all go home and finally rest. Never before had he felt so old as he began to feel in these few moments the emperor had been dead. He had ridden beside Geilo and Etrusin, and they had all been relatively young then. Geilo had been the eldest, Komeris the second and Etrusin the youngest. But that was twenty years ago. It may as well have been a lifetime ago, when three young companions saved a people and built an empire.

* * *

"So tell me, when are we going to do this?" Laernus hissed impatiently as he glanced furtively around the single standing stone to the ranks of resting men and shapeshifters that lay no less than fifty paces away.

The tip of Agucho's tongue coiled around one of his eyeballs, but it did not appear to interfere with his response. "Be patient, my friend," he said quietly.

The seer grimaced and stared unnerved at the Fiu-Het's tongue as it steamed in the cold air of early morning. "Surely you don't plan to march all the way to 'the enemy' before setting things in motion."

Agucho eyed his co-conspirator uneasily, switching his tongue from one eye to the other. He took a deep breath before answering, "I think that might be best, actually."

"What?" came the expected incredulous response, "Have you not even given these...your people any hint of your plan?"

"I could not!" Agucho whispered fiercely. "When I went to my queen to ask this of her, and so many times since then, I have tried, but I feel the will of the king surge up, and I cannot. Besides, I do think it might be best to do this while the king and his army are otherwise distracted."

Laernus nodded his concession of the point, but his response showed a change in his focus. "So my charm did not work."

"Not completely, but I believe it did somewhat. Orbein's power over me is not absolute, else we would not be having this conversation," the Fiu-Het pointed out.

"Do you know what his device is?" the seer asked.

Agucho nodded. "I believe so. He wears a strange ring on the small finger of his left hand. It looks like cloth secured with gold."

Laernus sighed. "My skill has never been prominent in much magic beside divination."

"Clearly not even in that," came another voice that startled them both. From the other side of the stone behind which the seer and shapeshifter hid stepped Vethisir. "Bit of an early start, don't you think?"

Laernus's heart was beating so hard it nearly ripped through his chest. He wondered how long the general had been standing there and how much he had heard. Even in the cold air, sweat beaded on the seer's forehead. His companion, however, seemed unruffled.

"If it isn't too early for you to be sneaking around, then clearly it isn't early enough," the shapeshifter shot back.

"Watch yourself, beast," warned Vethisir. "If anyone can be said to be sneaking, it is you two."

Agucho snorted, "Laernus concentrates best without distraction. This was the best place for him to retrieve more council that I may relay to the king."

The general did not catch it, but Laernus saw the shapeshifter hold his breath in uncertain expectation of the general's response.

Vethisir looked from Agucho to the seer and back. "Council..." he sneered. "It is more likely that the two of you came here to conspire against the king."

The shapeshifter made a good show of bristling at that comment. "You have no evidence of that, so stop wasting our time," he said making a shooing gesture at Vethisir.

The general narrowed his eyes at the pair, then looked over his shoulder at the sleeping army behind him. When he looked back at them, his eyes gleamed wickedly. Slowly he drew out his sword and took a step toward Agucho. "The way I see it," he said in a low, hoarse voice, "the king no longer has need for either of you. We are already on the road to victory, and you two are merely extra baggage. Once Orbein realizes this, I will be the one to cut you both free...happily."

The way Vethisir jabbed the sword forward with the word 'cut' made it clear that neither of them would enjoy the freedom that followed. Agucho and Laernus exchanged nervous glances, and both were afraid that the general was about to run them through then and there. Instead, he whipped his blade away and sheathed it forcefully. He said not a word, but glared at them one last time before turning to stomp off.

Once Vethisir was out of earshot, Laernus took a deep breath. "Do you suppose he heard anything?" he whispered shakily.

Agucho grimaced. "No. He was bluffing. If he ever did kill me, he would have all of the Fiu-Het to contend with," he decided confidently.

"What if he killed me?" Laernus clearly thought this the most likely possibility.

"Never mind about that," Agucho said dismissively. "Let's just keep our focus on what we have to do."

The seer nodded absently, but he continued to think about Vethisir's blade penetrating his chest. Though skilled in divination, there were limitations to his power. He could not, for example, meditate on the circumstances of his own death and see exactly what they were. As such, he had no idea when or how he would die. He didn't even have any idea about how this march was going to end or if he or Agucho were going to live past the battle that was surely approaching. In fact, the battle was about the only thing he knew was going to happen for certain. It was this that made him suspect that he would not survive. For now, he had little choice but to trust in Agucho and go forward with their plan. At least if he died, he would die fighting.

The sunrise came, and the human and shapeshifter army awoke to a red sky filled with small and puffy, but dark, clouds. The horizon looked like a wide, deep wound cauterized by the fiery sun. The men of Ionotu grumbled among themselves about the omen while the Fiu-Het regarded it stoically, thinking of the significance of their position in the ranks of this ambulatory force. Most of them were unsure why they were here backing up the humans, especially when they were backing it up by taking the front line. But they had orders from their queen, and every one of them knew of Gayossha's sacrifice.

In the very lead of the gathered force were Agucho and Laernus. They had been up since their meeting that morning and were taking in the dawn with no small amount of trepidation. They didn't need the wizard's power of foresight to know what the sunrise signaled, though both of them wondered why he had not seen the coming of such a sign. It was Agucho, however, who was most curious about it.

"Can you see anything more than I in such an omen?" he asked the seer.

"No more than the wild speculations of my overactive imagination," he replied nervously.

Agucho gave a wry snicker of agreement. He turned away to take in the army behind him and gave an irritated sigh, "Here they come."

Laernus did not need to ask what the shapeshifter meant. Indeed, he did not even turn around to greet them. He simply stood there and continued to watch the horizon and listened to the sound of the hoofbeats growing louder. He prayed that they would just keep riding past them and onward, away from the army and off the edge of the world, but they did not.

"Tell us, seer, did you not foresee this?" came Vethisir's sarcastic call.

"Didn't you?" Laernus snapped back. "We are, after all, going to fight a war, are we not?"

"The red dawn is for our foes, who await us somewhere on the road ahead," Orbein said, staring at the horizon.

'Clearly...' thought Laernus sarcastically, though he kept his lips, still swollen from his last encounter with the king, pressed tightly closed.

"And with such a fortuitous sign of my impending victory, let us begin our march!" the king shouted these last five words loudly, and they echoed back and forth across the pass so that the whole army heard them.

With a unified deep breath, the soldiers took the first step of the day toward the rest of their march. This had been one of the few rests they had taken on the journey, as the king seemed to be tireless in his quest to find his enemy. So, they did not doubt that it would be one of the last times they would camp before the battle. They were well into their fourth week, and according to Orbein, they were almost through the mountain pass. From there he was not sure where the enemy might lie, but he reassured them that it would not be far.

So, on the army of Ionotu marched, and as the day grew brighter and the sky became clearer, it brought on a bright blue ceiling, free of clouds. By midday, the fears of that morning's red dawn were forgotten as they trudged along the hard earth of the mountain pass. They had lunch on their feet, and some groups joined in marching songs to take their mind off the long journey ahead of and behind them. Sometime around late afternoon, though, their march was halted.

A flock of low flying birds came on squawking loudly and cutting maneuvers in the air. No one was surprised when they landed before the king and shifted into a small group of Fiu-Het. The leader of the group stepped forward holding some sort of bundle.

"Greetings," Orbein said importantly. "What have you there?"

The shapeshifter let go of the bundle with one hand, and as it unfurled, two severed human heads tumbled out onto the ground. Orbein and Vethisir pulled their horses back as the heads rolled to a stop in front of them. The general looked disgusted, while the king appeared enchanted.

"An army isss there. Beyond the passss," the lead shapeshifter said with a heavy accent. He apparently did not have as firm a grasp on the language as did Agucho.

"An army? How could they have known?" the king mused aloud. "How big is this army?" he asked the shapeshifter.

"No big," the Fiu-Het explained. He struggled to find the words to indicate the force he saw, and when he could not, he turned to Agucho. "*Ssskt tck ehht't shssst.*"

"He says not much more than six thousand," translated Agucho.

Orbein grinned. "And how, pray tell, did he come upon these two trophies?"

Agucho relayed the question to the flock leader, who responded in the odd hissing gurgle of his people's language. "He says they were wandering toward the pass on their own. He thinks they were sentries," Agucho explained.

"How far?" He asked the leader the short question directly.

"Two daysss walking," the shapeshifter answered.

The king briefly adopted a pensive look, then he turned to Vethisir. "General. As we discussed earlier," he said as he turned and rode back toward the human end of the army. To everyone's surprise, he called for another camp to be set up.

General Vethisir hopped down from his mount and walked it over to Laernus. "Take my horse," he commanded, handing the reign to the seer.

Laernus took the reign uncertainly, but did not otherwise respond.

"You, you, come with me," the general said, pointing to Agucho and the leader of the scout group.

The two shapeshifters followed him uncertainly. Agucho shot Laernus a curious look and a shrug as he walked away with Vethisir in the wake of King Orbein. They walked most of the way to the human ranks when they were met by two of the general's soldiers. With very little conversation, Vethisir turned the group back around, and the five of them headed back to the front line. Agucho and the other shapeshifter whispered to one another in their own language until they reached the spot where the wizard still stood holding the horse's reign.

"We are going to go out ahead," the general explained to the perplexed seer and the small group that followed.

"Oh," Laernus answered dumbly as he began to hand the reign back to him.

"No," said Vethisir raising his hands. "You take care of my horse while we are away. We should return in four days time."

"Why not just send out the shapeshifters again as birds?" the seer asked.

The general shook his head. "I must see this army for myself so that I may make the attack plan. Apparently they knew of our coming, which gives them an advantage. I plan to take that advantage away," he said wickedly.

"And you need him with you?" Laernus asked nodding toward Agucho. He was clearly unnerved by the turn of events.

Vethisir bared his teeth with a grin. "If he was brave enough to take part in the little escapade that cost me three good soldiers, then surely this will be nothing for him."

"Let me go with you, then," the wizard offered.

"I think not," was the general's simple response. With that he turned and walked off with the other four in tow, leaving Laernus and the army behind.

Agucho was not sure what to make of this most recent turn of events. He plodded along warily behind General Vethisir and watched suspiciously as he asked the other Fiu-Het which direction to go. Though he believed that Vethisir had been bluffing that morning when he threatened him, this all seemed a little too convenient. He decided he would definitely keep his wits about him and flee at the first sign of danger. He had to make sure he was present when his people met with Orbein's enemy. He had to make sure to put his plan into effect before the Fiu-Het found themselves entrenched in a battle where they were caught between two sides that cared nothing for their well being.

So, Agucho tried to prepare himself mentally for any possibility. In doing so he found himself concentrating so hard that he hardly noticed the passage of time. He realized that he was spending more time imagining what might happen rather than paying attention to what was actually happening. He tried to reign in his imagination, but he found himself wishing more and more that he had been more expressive to his people about how much he and Vethisir disliked one another. By the time he regained focus, the sun had long since set, and everyone had his weapon out and was creeping along carefully.

The shapeshifter looked at the three humans, two of which were brandishing the typical heavy longsword of Ionotu's soldiers, including Vethisir. The third human hefted a large mace decorated with dully pointed metal studs. Agucho's kinsman wielded his traditional Fiu-Het dagger, almost sickle-like in its sweeping, curved blade. Seeing that dagger made him think of his own, and he drew it out silently. He wondered if he should try to get his kinsman's attention and somehow indicate his suspicion to him.

No sooner had he taken out his dagger when, to his alarm, the human with the mace whipped his weapon across to land heavily against the side of the other Fiu-Het's head. The one who had led the flock of shapeshifting bird-scouts stumbled sideways, a thick knot already swelling on his temple. Without missing a step, the human advanced and swiped the poor creature again, hitting almost the same spot.

"What is this?" Agucho exclaimed, finally finding his voice, though his surprise seemed out of place even to him.

Vethisir stepped up to him and viciously swung his sword. It was quick thinking and a bit of luck that saved Agucho from a cut as he shifted and formed a hole in his body right around the blade as it passed through him. The general blinked disbelievingly as though he had just attacked a ghost. Agucho wasted no time in turning to run, as he had planned to do in just such a situation. Instead, he toppled to the ground as the mace-wielding soldier rushed at him from the side. He heard a tremendous clang as an intense pain exploded on the top of his head.

Somehow Agucho managed to roll away and struggle to his feet. His ears rang, and black spots bubbled before his eyes. He tasted blood in his mouth and was certain he had bitten off his tongue. He tried to blink, to clear away the black spots at least, if not the pain. He heard Vethisir's voice say, "Leave him, he is mine." Agucho was able to clear the spots just in time to see the general's blade sweeping toward his neck, then there was complete darkness.

Vethisir watched gleefully as the shapeshifter's head fell back unnaturally, severed by his estimation. Nothing more than the thinnest strands of muscle and skin held that head to the body, but it was enough to sway the momentum of the Fiu-Het's descent as it fell on top of the dangling head. The general threw back his own head and laughed, and the other two men joined in.

"That was easy," the mace wielding soldier said jovially. "One would think you hardly needed us."

"Actually, I did," Vethisir said soberly. Without another word, or even any effort, he stuck out his sword and slid it into the unsuspecting soldier's gut. "I am sorry," the general offered lamely as he pulled the blade across and disemboweled the unfortunate man.

"What is this?" the other soldier repeated Agucho's last sentiments.

Vethisir turned to the other soldier, brandishing his bloody sword dangerously. "You see, it would seem a bit suspicious if only the shapeshifters were killed in an ambush," he explained.

"I see," the soldier said uncertainly. He watched the general cautiously, not sure if he would be the next to meet his fate on that wet edge. When Vethisir did not make any move toward him, he added probingly, "Then will we head back to camp now, or should we wait a day? Or did you actually intend to scout out our enemy?"

The general responded with a hollow laugh. "We are not going anywhere. It will be only one of us that returns to camp alive. If it is you, I hope you will return with the same story that I intend to."

"I will not fight you, sir," the soldier said earnestly.

Vethisir sneered. "Then spare me the effort of fighting and slay yourself upon my blade."

"Is there no other way?"

The look in the soldier's eyes was clearly desperate. He frowned at the young man and held out his sword, shining with fresh blood, in a ready stance. He had gone this far; he would leave no one behind. This fight was happening whether either of them liked it or not.

The soldier had other ideas. He bolted sideways and took off running at top speed, desperately trying to put as much distance between him and the general as he could. After sprinting several steps without hearing the general's pursuit, he felt a burst of confidence. He leaned forward and pumped his legs and ran like the wind, not daring to look back.

Suddenly, a crippling pain tore through his right calf, and he misstepped and went flying to the ground. He slid face first into the hard, gravelly earth before he could even comprehend what was happening. His head was buzzing as he sat up and shook it to clear the daze. He looked down at his calf and saw something shiny and metallic sticking out of it as blood oozed out and ran down his leg. It was the end of a tiny throwing dagger, embedded quite deeply into the muscle. He looked up at the slowly approaching shape of the general, his wet sword glittering in the moonlight. It would be the last sight he ever saw.

* * *

"Someone approaches!" the call reverberated across the valley and over the quiet camp, causing it to stir like a great, slumbering beast. It had been only a day and a half that the small group of scouts had gone out, and they were not expected back for another three days at the earliest. The news of someone approaching so soon had everyone chatting curiously and straining their eyes toward the eastern opening of the pass in the hopes of glimpsing a moving figure.

Laernus, who had been sitting nervously ever since the group faded from sight, hoped against hope that the sentry had been mistaken and that it was actually five someones approaching. Or, perhaps, four someones with a tragic tale of Vethisir's accidental demise. As he squinted at the horizon, however, he began to make out a solitary blob twitching in the distance. The pace of his heartbeat quickened as he imagined Agucho's uneven trudge in the rhythmic motion of that blob. He tried not to imagine that the shapeshifter was returning alone, fearing that the thought would rule out the possibility of it being true.

After several minutes of eager staring, it became clear that the figure drawing near was too large to be the natural form of a Fiu-Het. Several hushed whispers suggested that it was a limping man. This caused the seer's heart to beat even harder, though now it was a return to nervousness rather than hopefulness. He had little doubt who the limping figure would be. He even sat down and stopped watching the approach.

A few moments later, King Orbein trotted casually by him on his horse, though it was clear to the wizard that his proximity was intentional. He briefly looked up at the passing king and was rewarded with a malevolent grin. At that moment, he seriously thought of walking into the mountains to whatever fate he could find; anything had to be better than what was undoubtedly in store for him now. As he sat debating the merits of running away and trudging through the mountains for the rest of his life, he could hear the murmurs of the soldiers around him. They sounded awed and excited, but he could not make out what they were saying. Eventually, curiosity got the best of him and he stood and turned to see what the commotion was about.

"Did you miss me?"

Laernus jumped back, startled. Vethisir's face had been just inches from his as he turned around. The general looked terrible. His face was covered in dirt and streaked with blood. A thin red line went from one side of his neck almost to the other. He held his hand against his thigh where a trail of dry blood was caked down to his knee. He didn't waste much time intimidating the seer. He had stopped just long enough to deliver his rhetorical greeting, then he continued on with the king toward the back of the camp.

Vethisir chuckled as he limped back with Orbein. Other than that chuckle, the two walked silently, though each step was punctuated by questions from human and shapeshifter alike about the companions who had gone with the general. None of the questions were too insistent yet, as those who asked could see that Vethisir needed to rest and, perhaps, to be bandaged a bit.

Orbein, however, was insistent once they entered his tent. "What happened?" he demanded before the general even had a chance to sit.

"They are all dead," Vethisir replied quickly.

"Were there complications?" the king asked.

"No," said the general.

"Where are the rags?"

Vethisir stared blankly at the king for a moment. "Oh," he said suddenly, reaching back to something tucked into the back of his belt and producing two sets of tattered rags. "The shapeshifters' clothes."

"Excellent," Orbein said, practically salivating over the cloth he had snatched from Vethisir's hand. "Now we also have Agucho's death to empassion his people to our cause."

"Indeed," said the general, a wide grin spreading across his face.

"We must also get the seer away from the Fiu-Het," the king added. "Pull him back to your ranks. Tell your soldiers not to let him out of their sight."

"Yes, sire," Vethisir said.

Orbein tossed the shapeshifters' rags to the ground and pulled off the small gold ring he wore and dropped it among them. "Have these things burned," he commanded.

The general chuckled, seemingly to himself.

"What are you laughing about?" the king asked.

A wicked gleam sparkled in Vethisir's eyes, and it seemed to take away the bedraggled look that he had returned to the camp with. "Oh, it's just funny how things have worked out so far," he said conspiratorially.

Orbein gave him a sour look. "Well, it had better continue working. It won't if you sit in here guffawing triumphantly to yourself all day."

"Yes, sire," Vethisir said with a solemn expression. Taking the hint, he stood and followed the king outside to face their armies.

18 WAR

Early afternoon cast virtually no shadow as the sun slowly crossed a cloudless sky on an unusually warm day in early winter. Two young soldiers sat against a huge, flat stone, on top of which lay a large pile of kindling that overlooked the valley pass through the Ikiu'iu Mountains. They ate their lunch at a leisurely pace, though they glanced around the stone periodically to see if anything unusual was happening below. Thus far, neither of them had seen any concrete sign of the enemy that their emperor and general had warned them about, but that did not mean that they doubted the approaching danger. Had Captain Komeris and his scouting party not met their enemy face to face on their journey through the pass, they might not have felt the imminent sense of peril. Still, they were not expecting to look into the valley and see an army marching through anytime soon.

There was one other unnerving point to consider. Two other soldiers had been sent out by the general as scouts days ago and still had not returned. The camp passed many interesting theories around as to their whereabouts. The most popular explanation, that the enemy was closer than they thought, was the current topic of conversation between the two young warriors as they ate.

Two birds fluttered down out of the sky and landed before the sentries.

"Look," said one of the warriors, a young woman. "They're probably starving. Why haven't they flown away for the season?"

The young man who sat beside her shrugged. He tossed some of his rice cake toward them. When they did not immediately hop over and peck at the cake pieces, he shook his head. "Foolish birds," he sighed. He jumped up and went to shoo the birds away.

The woman watched in horror as one of the birds raised its wing, which transformed into a blotchy gray and pink arm that seemed far too large for the bird to support it. Between the fingers of this appendage was a sickle shaped dagger. The weapon glinted briefly as it was held aloft, then it cut through the air blindingly fast and embedded in the young man's forehead. He reached for it, but the moment he clutched the handle, he fell over with a twitch and did not move again.

Shaking her head as though trying to wake from some terrible nightmare, the other soldier pressed herself against the rock and rose slowly, never taking her eyes from the strangely endowed creature. Her disbelief and confusion multiplied as the one-armed bird increased in size quickly, and its feathers and beaked sank into its skin and left behind an even more terrifying beast.

Behind it, the other bird likewise morphed, and it brandished a curved dagger of its own. She froze and could only watch as the two things approached her. The pace of her breathing increased, and she could feel her heart trying to escape the confines of her chest. As they got within a few feet of her, she blinked and felt like she was in control of herself again. She reached for her sword and began to creep around the stone and back away.

Suddenly her mind was awash with horrible images of these creatures pulling apart her mangled body. Bile rose in her throat, and she retched as the morbid imagery played out. She began to shiver and could feel all of her muscles tightening, but she continued to fight against the terror.

The poor woman, for all her training, and for all that Etrusin's shiodu had taught her, nothing could have prepared her for a foe like the Fiu-Het. They were like monsters out of the nightmares of a demented mind, worse than her own imaginings could conjure. Her body did not respond in time to her demands to leap out of the way as both of the shapeshifters leaned back, then shot forward with a whiplike ripple that seemed impossible. They were on her in an instant, twisting around her and thickening like constrictors. She tried to scream, but one of them had wrapped around her neck and was squeezing too tightly. She felt the pressure building in her extremities. Her temples pounded painfully. Her eyes bulged. The last thing she could comprehend before the darkness took over was the sickening crack of almost every bone in her body.

After her tense body gave up the struggle, and they could feel her heart beating no more, the two Fiu-Het slithered off her. They shifted back to their natural state and surveyed the scene. Like all of the other spots they had been to along the pass, it was a simple station. A pile of dry wood was heaped upon a flat surface and guarded by two humans. The two shapeshifters chuckled at the efficiency of their work thus far.

"Stupid, humans," one of them gurgled in their native tongue.

"Vengeance for Gayossha and Agucho," hissed the other.

At that they changed form once again and took flight in search of the next sentry post. The apparent readiness of their enemy would be disrupted here. When they emerged from the mountain pass, it would be the forces of the west that had the advantage. These two Fiu-Het would see to it.

* * *

The day was overcast and cold, a drastic change from the previous day. Etrusin's soldiers and many elves huddled together around fires as their breath misted in the air. Every so often several of them would look up as if expecting snowflakes to come fluttering down out of the sky at any moment. In between skyward glances, they conversed about the weather and agreed that yesterday was the last warm day they would see for the rest of the year. The humans compared weather knowledge with the elves, and together they tried to predict how cold the winter would be. At some campfires the question was raised of whether or not there would be any fighting before the cold season passed. There were skeptics among them, but none of them thought that a unified force to protect the eastlands was a bad thing.

On the western edge of camp several warriors stood on guard watching the mountain pass. Somewhat apart from them, but carrying out the same function, sat Urietsin and Kiusu, side by side. They stared westward in a meditative state and were absolutely still. Though they seemed expressionless and calm, their minds were alive with activity that made them a little anxious. Neither of them was completely certain, but they felt something foreboding on the winds of eternity. Both of them could tell that something was about to happen that was a significant intersection of all their destinies.

The young warrior Urietsi'in saw the world partially as other men saw it and partially as it truly was. Intermittent flashes of the vision he had on the mountain before he and the old man had left overlaid themselves on everything he saw. The dark swooping cloud cut through the sky, sometimes looking like a huge demon, sometimes looking like many tiny ones. As he sank deeper and deeper into his meditation the cloud persisted more and more, until it no longer disappeared from his vision.

Urietsin blinked.

There was a strange feeling that told him something was amiss. He concentrated as much as he could on the corporeal world, willing himself to see through his physical eyes. The dark cloud still persisted, though it was not as close as it appeared in his vision. Just there, in the sky beyond the pass, a dark blotch among the blanket of clouds. As he watched, it got larger, much larger. At this the Swift One leapt to his feet.

"What is it Urietsin?" Kiusu asked.

The Swift One turned to tell not only the old man, but the humans and elves behind them. "To arms! To arms! Our enemy approaches! Quickly, take up your bows!" he yelled.

The response was instantaneous. Every man, woman and elf jumped up, grabbed the nearest weapon and ran to the western front. Etrusin, Komeris, Tilon and Marui made their way through the excited bustling to stand beside the Swift One and the old man.

"Where are they," demanded the general squinting toward the pass. "Where do you see them?"

"There," said Urietsin pointing at the western sky.

Then they all saw it. Spread out above the mountain pass was a dark cloud that was speeding toward them. "It's nothing but a flock of birds migrating for the winter," suggested a soldier from the ranks.

Tilon and Marui exchanged significant glances, as did Urietsin and Kiusu.

"These birds are a season late," Tilon shouted with authority.

The approach of the dark cloud was marked by an uncanny silence. As it got close enough for the army to see that it was indeed made up of hundreds, possibly thousands, of smaller flying creatures, presumably birds, they expected to hear a roaring chitter as large flocks tend to make. There was no such chitter, however, as the cloud grew larger and loomed overhead. Then, suddenly, it dropped, and the sound began.

Arrows rained up as birdlike creatures rained down, screeching as they came. Urietsin noted with a chill the coordinated way in which they dove at the army. He saw them swoop over the whole encampment. Some of them went all the way to the ground with an elven arrow protruding from their small, squirming bodies, while others swung back into the air, leaving behind warriors clutching their bloody faces. One group of the avian forms had latched onto an unfortunate soldier, carrying him high into the air, only to drop him screaming on several others below. A couple of soldiers were injured as he crashed onto them, but for him the fall was fatal.

Then came the wave of fear.

While many of the warriors on the field were operating on varying levels of alarm, it was nothing compared to the sheer terror that suddenly descended. Soldiers looked up and screamed uncontrollably; some began to run away. Even those who were not gripped by an all-consuming dread found themselves feeling a bit out of place, confused. The flying enemy took advantage of the distraction, clawing and pecking at the disoriented. Things quickly looked very dim for the forces of Kesitul.

Then a cheer went up, and a low sound reverberated over the field. It was answered by a higher pitched chant. The Shionen men called out again and were, again, answered by their female counterparts. It was a rousing battle call, as ancient as the language in which it was sung. The few elves who were stumbling from the effects of the fear found themselves able to shake it away and join in the cry. Slowly, all on the field began to feel the invigorating effects of the elvensong. Before long, the mysterious fear was dispelled.

As Urietsin ran into the fray, he could hear the chanting of several priests somewhere nearby, punctuating that of the elves. After their foe had made a few passes, Urietsin realized that some of the birdlike creatures were combusting spontaneously. The Swift One guessed that this was the high priest's contribution to the battle, but while the fire seemed to end the creatures' flight for good, it did not seem to affect nearly enough of them. Though there were many squirming on the ground, and some charred remains as well, the bulk of them still flew overhead, and when they swooped down, they left carnage in their wake. It seemed to the Swift One that they were somehow slashing wide cuts into soldiers as they dove, and they were much more effective in their attacks than their targets were at countering.

Overhead the sky darkened further as the clouds thickened. They transformed from a sheet of endless gray to a boiling morass of blackness. Urietsin prayed that the sudden change in weather was only a coincidence.

Fortunately, it was not. The young warrior noted, as he looked around, that some of the chanting Shionen were not fighting physically. The part of him that could still see beyond the perceived reality of his physical senses witnessed waving tendrils of energy that flowed up from the elves and into the clouds. He wasn't sure what they were doing, but it surely could not hurt.

Focusing back on the battle, the Swift One decided to see what these 'birds' were made of. In their next pass, he leapt into the air and plucked one of the creatures from the flock. He received many slashes along his forearm for the effort, but he managed to hang on to the thing as it flapped and struggled against him. When he landed, he saw that the bird had one excessively long hooked claw, and as he tried to keep it from lacerating him, he felt the bird getting thicker and heavier. He dropped it, startled at the sudden and seemingly impossible change, though he had suspected as much since he saw this airborne army approaching. Within moments, a hunched creature a bit shorter than a man stood before him brandishing a curved dagger.

Urietsin crouched and looked the ugly beast in the eye. It seemed to almost laugh at him in a gurgling sort of way and came at him with a sweeping swipe of its dagger. The Swift One leaned slightly toward the approaching weapon and shot out his open palm, gripping the creature's wrist and redirecting its momentum. His intention was to pull the creature forward and trip it over his leg, but he had underestimated his foe. No sooner had Urietsin grabbed its wrist when the shapeshifter utilized that ability which came so naturally. Its wrist shrank and wriggled through the

Swift One's viselike grip, sliding the sickle-shaped blade along his fingers.

Urietsin pulled back his bloody hand. Three of his fingers were sliced almost to the bone. It had been a painful lesson, but one the Swift One picked up on quickly. He approached this fight with a bit more caution, scrutinizing his enemy for any revealing information.

The shapeshifting creature seemed very pleased with the battle so far. It wore a terrifying grin and mimicked Urietsin's stance and circling steps. It was toying with him. By its estimation, it could end this at any time. In fact, it decided to end it now.

The Swift One leapt back as a pair of tentacles shot out at him from random places on his foe's body. He could not jump far enough, though, and found himself entwined in the tightening appendages. He gripped them and tried to pull them or twist them off, anything to free himself, but it was like trying to grab water. His hands passed right through the tentacles with a wet sensation, while they very solidly squeezed him. He tried to push his hands into those living bonds to find something to clutch, but all in vain.

It was becoming clear to Urietsin that he would have to think of another way to free himself. He tried to pull his hands away but found that they too were now held fast, and the slimy flesh of the tentacles was oozing up his forearm. He had to duck as best he could as the swarm of creatures overhead took another dive. At this point, most men would have begun to panic. Urietsin, however, realized that panicking would not help him find a way out of his current situation. Instead, he relaxed and focused.

The shapeshifter felt its prey loosen and thought for a moment he was losing consciousness. As it squeezed its tentacles even tighter, it realized that he had not passed out; rather he simply released all the tension in his body. It gurgled out a chuckle as it came to the conclusion that the human had simply surrendered to his fate. A few more tentacles sprouted from its body to completely envelope the human's chest as well.

Urietsin was trying hard to ignore the suffocating pressure around him as he concentrated. He reached out with his mind and called to the tiny feather in his pouch, holding down the urge to smile triumphantly. That urge fled quickly as he realized that nothing was happening. He tried to relax more and called to the feather again. When there was again no result, Urietsin tried to feel his surroundings with all of his senses. When this failed, he found it difficult to hold down a rising sense of desperation. He suddenly became painfully aware of how impossible it was to breathe.

His opponent's laugh had become a screeching cackle. It squeezed with crushing relentlessness as it felt its prey's struggle returning, but by now it was too late. The creature's watery flesh was creeping all over the human, and the victim's panicked writhing only urged it on.

Suddenly the pressure around Urietsin's body released, and the blackness that had been growing inward around his vision receded. It cleared just in time to see the creature's headless body topple. Behind it, one of Etrusin's soldiers was turning to face another foe, giving a stunned Swift One only the slightest nod of acknowledgement.

Meanwhile, up in the sky, the clouds swelled ominously. A low rumble was barely heard above the battle. A red flicker, almost imperceptible at first, lined the dark clouds with an eerie glow. A spidering bolt of red lightning erupted from the dark sky, taking to the ground dozens of shapeshifters. The defenders of Kesitul howled triumphantly, and the chant of the elves grew louder, provoking another rumble from the sky.

Kiusu had stood on the edge of battle just long enough to watch Urietsin rush in, but he noticed, as the young warrior had, the chanting of the priests and its relatively ineffective results. He rushed off toward the sound, which was soon almost completely drowned out by the sounds of the soldiers trying to swat foes from the air and the elves' own powerful chant. He came upon the six holy men crouched in a circle around a very large ivory horn.

The old man recognized that horn instantly. It was almost the size of a small man, and twenty years did nothing to diminish the chillingly wicked image of the face it once adorned. Even if he had never seen the beast, he would have recognized the aura of dark energy given off by this pointed artifact. It was the horn of Reisothin, the magical focal point of the fiend's malicious powers. Seeing it standing free on the ground gave Kiusu the impression that the priests were crouching on the dragon's forehead. For a moment he expected the ground to come alive and toss the men in the air and swallow them up. He had seen the Abomination devour several men, one of them his master, and these six would have been no more than a light snack.

The ground remained still, however, and the priests seemed to want to be as close to it as they could without lying down. Kiusu could see that they were afraid, and though none of them broke their circle or their chant, more than one of them broke their concentration by looking up at the twisting cloud of dagger-clawed creatures and the darkening sky above.

Kiusu understood their fear, but he knew that the power of such an item as they wielded was cunning. Because Reisothin had used it with such evil purpose, some of that purpose remained within the horn as part of its energy. Such residual sentience often finds ways of manipulating the wielders of relics like this horn. The old man knew that he had to help the priests to find their focus and thus increase their effectiveness and decrease their susceptibility.

The priests' chant was a simple plea to the energy within the horn to make itself known to the enemies of Kesitul. Kiusu began to chant a variant of this, more a command than a request, and insinuated himself into the circle. The two men whose hands he had grabbed were startled nearly to panic, but when they realized that Kiusu was not an enemy, they quickly resumed their chant. The old man increased the volume of his voice in the hopes that the six others would pick up on the alteration he had made to their words.

The chant became a mantra to Kiusu as he began to perceive more and more with his spirit. As he ascended to this higher state, he realized that the horn was slowly growing larger in his physical eyes. After many minutes, it grew to fill his entire field of vision, and his chant seemed to almost go mute in his own ears as his focus was drawn to the wicked remain of Reisothin. The horn was subtly trying to dominate Kiusu's will, but the old man would not be fooled so easily. He screamed back at it with all of his strength.

The effect was drastic. The horn shrank away, while the world and the universe came back into focus. Out of the corner of his eye, Kiusu saw the red bolt of lightning. He could hear the cheer of the army around him and urged the priests into a louder chant.

The holy men complied, though their confidence in Kiusu's technique was starting to flag. So far, nothing significant had happened since the old man had inserted himself into their circle. Suddenly, there was a roaring explosion and a wave of heat as a ball of fire expanded out of nowhere right in the middle of the swarm of shapeshifters. Nearly four score charred, vaguely bird-shaped forms plummeted from the flock. The priests were stunned, but Kiusu, apparently unfazed, continued to chant, and his tone urged the six of them to continue as well.

Halfway across the field of warriors, Su-Ni gave an exasperated look to her companions Denlin and O'eintsu. Just before the battle had begun, she had gone searching for Pei-Shi in the crowd of soldiers, hoping to find reassurance from her most recent mentor. The two young warriors that had been on the scouting mission with her were all she could manage to find before the attack. Now the three of them were waiting for the next dive to swat the air in the hopes of injuring one of their infuriating enemies.

Between them they managed to catch a few, especially Denlin with his long staff. He swung the wooden weapon high in the air and always seemed to knock a bird-shaped form to the ground, sometimes two. As the rest of them soared up and away for another pass, he would beat the ones on the ground with a dazzling sequence of jabs. He was so skilled with his weapon that, though the three of them were in fairly close quarters with one another and the rest of the army, Denlin never hit anything beside an enemy.

O'eintsu was the next most effective with his chiun. Regardless of whether the creatures were flying toward or away from them, he would throw the little metal stars with uncanny accuracy. Not for his lack of skill, though, the creatures seemed generally unaffected by his attacks. Sometimes he would throw a chiun directly at his target, but it would seem to pass right through without harming it. Other times he hit, but it seemed to do no more than incur the beast's wrath. Already he had a long gash from his right eyebrow to his left temple. He did bring a few from the sky, though most did not fall as near as those struck by Denlin.

Su-Ni felt the most impotent of the bunch. Her sword was not nearly as long as Denlin's staff, and she certainly could not throw it. When she wasn't swiping ineffectively at the swooping storm, she was watching the elves' arrows cut through the air with envy. She did like her sword, but right now it didn't seem to be doing much good. She made a mental note that if she lived through this war, she would have to take up archery.

They all flinched as red lightning shattered the sky. Handfuls of foes fell to the ground, and the three warriors could not help but yell out happily. Then another explosion engulfed a portion of the sky, and a wave of heat blasted toward them. Once again, several scorched lumps of previously living shapeshifter rained onto the soldiers. The army of Kesitul cheered on at the work of the elves and the priests. The creatures that were not hit by the blasts scattered momentarily, then rejoined and dove angrily. Su-Ni, Denlin and O'eintsu set aside their brief celebration to steel themselves against the fresh attack.

Whatever the sources of these magical attacks, the shapeshifters did not like them. They sped toward the soldiers, cawing and screeching wildly. Su-Ni and Denlin had to flail their weapons, more to beat away several attacks at once than to bring down any of the beasts. O'eintsu, who had run out of chiun, was doing his best with only his limbs. He punched, leapt into the air and kicked. He even grabbed two of the creatures and smashed them together. Despite all of their best efforts, they each received several wounds from the slashing claws of their foes.

The attack went on like this for many more minutes, which contrasted with the hit-and-retreat method the shapeshifters had been using for almost an hour now. A glance out over the army showed virtually no one without blood on his face or arms. If they made it through this alive, most of this generation from Kesitul would be marked by the physical scars of this battle for life. The army was focusing so much of its attention on keeping the taloned monsters at bay that they hardly noticed a second and third fireball erupting from nowhere, and several more flashes of lightning from above.

This time when the shapeshifters regrouped for the attack, they did not remain in the air. Chaos ensued as the birdlike creatures transformed, landing right in the midst of Kesitul's army. Su-Ni almost lost sight of her two companions as the crowd thickened with enemies. She found herself blocking multiple attackers. This was more than she had ever trained for.

Three shapeshifters in her immediate vicinity, two directly in front of her and one to her left, advanced toward her. She eyed them cautiously as they spread further apart to flank her. She held her sword before her and stepped back, trying to keep all three of them within sight. They saw her creeping backward and decided to close the gap quickly. They all shot forward and attacked her. She swiped her blade in front of her from left to right and heard two satisfying clangs as two daggers were turned aside while the third, poorly timed and poorly aimed, flew wide of the mark. They went at her again, this time a little more discordantly than the last. The one directly in front seemed to stretch out its arm impossibly long for an overhead attack, which Su-Ni defeated with an overhead twirl of her blade. Her block came down to the left in time to catch a slashing attempt from the one on that side. She took a bruising hit to the ribs as the right opponent failed to get through her armor with his weapon. Su-Ni retaliated by swinging her sword into its face.

The effect her successful hit had was not one she would have entirely expected. Though it seemed her sword was embedded halfway into its head, the creature merely leapt away howling and seeming no more inconvenienced than she was by the hit it had dealt her. For her clever hit she was rewarded by the other two with a series of fervent hacks and jabs. The one in front of her knocked the wind from her lungs while the other searched for a weak spot in the leather under her ringmail. When she finally brought her blade around to deter these two, the third sprung toward her and slashed at her leg.

Searing pain almost toppled her. She cried out and fell to one knee, swinging her blade out defensively. The three shapeshifters seemed to be making a snickering sound as they went to descend upon her. She suddenly wished desperately that someone in this throng of battle would come to help her, but all her allies seemed much occupied. She could not see Denlin or O'eintsu through the shapeshifter in front of her. There was a light trickling down the front of her thigh as her wound pumped out a bit of blood with every throb of her heart. She gritted her teeth, relaxed her focus to take in as much of the periphery as possible, and she waited.

The one on her right twitched first, and her sword was there. She did not turn her head to focus her attention on the block, she simply trusted her instincts. Adrenaline was thick in her veins as she reacted to the instantaneous motion of the other two shapeshifters. Her sword rang off the dagger of the right one, then twirled under to come diagonally up to meet the attack from the left. She finished what seemed to be a single, flowing move with a straight cut across from left to right that intercepted the opponent directly in front of her. The shapeshifter had been attempting to use its natural abilities again to attack in a way impossible to most other races. The move ended in the creature pulling back a dripping stump.

Su-Ni did not let her attention be drawn to the appendage that fell to the ground, which was especially fortunate because she would have been distracted by the way it simply melted away into nothing. The shapeshifter that had lost the hand seemed most distressed about it. It backed away horrified, and the other two gave it a momentary glance, though they were not too eager to take their eyes off the warrior who had just done this to their comrade, and for whom they had just gained a measure of fearful respect.

With a surge of strength and confidence, Su-Ni pushed herself back onto both feet and brandished her sword threateningly, but paled when she saw the injured shapeshifter grow another hand right before her eyes. She noticed that the flesh around the hand was a bit lighter and that the creature still seemed none too pleased, but these facts did nothing to help catch her fleeting optimism. She looked worried as it and its companions advanced on her again. Adopting a more defensive stance, she steeled her expression and tried to force herself to maintain her confidence. After all, the fight had gone well so far.

As it turned out, Su-Ni did not have to force too hard. Suddenly, the middle shapeshifter pitched forward face first into the ground. With the chaos around her, she hadn't heard Denlin's staff crack the back of the creature's skull. Before the beast even hit the ground, the young warrior had swung the butt of the staff under his right arm and brought the length of it whipping toward the face of the creature on that side. It went flying back as he twirled his weapon overhead to reverse direction and mirrored the move on his left. He stood in a crossover stance with the staff still out to his left. His eyes flitted from side to side. He was ready to spin around and level anything that wasn't human.

O'eintsu stepped around him, giving the master staff wielder a wide berth. When he came within Denlin's eyesight, he raised an impressed eyebrow. Coming from O'eintsu, that was a strong reaction. He called out above the din, "Save some for me!"

Denlin looked around at the battle. "There are plenty!" he retorted and sprung off to assist more allies.

Su-Ni got a quick nod from O'eintsu, and she noticed the slightest hint of a grin on his lips as he ran into the fray after Denlin. It was clear to her that the two were very much in their element. She looked down at the three shapeshifters that lay in a heap at her feet and wondered if she should make sure they were dead or run in after her companions. Despite the fact that she understood the consequences of hesitation in battle, she could not bring herself to pull back the head of one of the unconscious and defenseless creatures to slit its throat. She decided to find a more mobile enemy, one that would give her immediate justification to kill it. There was certainly no shortage of that; all she had to do was take a few steps.

On the western front, not far from where Urietsin had experienced his brush with death, the most elite group of senior officers were holding their own. Reniu, Pei-Shi, Komeris, and General Etrusin formed an impenetrable ring of bladework. The first two officers, Reniu and Komeris, each wielded two of the curving broadswords that were so common in Kesitul. The captain and the Pei-Shi, however, each brandished two of the more traditional blades of the empire, still curved, but much more narrow and elegant. Between them their eight blades wove a blinding, intertwined defense. The motion confused their enemies, and most did not see the attack when it shot out randomly from the blur of metal gleaming in their eyes.

Though the four warriors fought tirelessly, and were very successful at hitting their opponents, they did not seem to be very effective at disabling them. While many shapeshifters received various slices and cuts, none of them really seemed bothered by the hits. In fact, by the reckoning of the experienced officers, the number of wounds they were noticing did not seem to match up to the number of hits they landed. Also, the longer the four fought, the more their talent seemed to attract the attention of the enemy. As the battle progressed they each found themselves faced with multiple opponents, and the ring around them was thickening.

They all understood what was happening. The shapeshifters could tell that this small group of warriors were among the most skilled, and thus were likely to be one of the bigger problems out here on the field of battle. They were concentrating their focus on these soldiers so that they would not have to deal with them later, once they were tired from facing the many easier to kill humans. It was Pei-Shi, however, that first noticed that it was not just the crowd around them that was thickening.

"I think they are getting bigger!" she shouted to the other three.

Komeris kept up a brilliantly twirling defense as he tried to pay attention to the size of the creatures. He noticed that one seemed to leap onto the back of another, and the next thing he could see was that the beast did seem to be slightly larger. "They're joining together!" he exclaimed more to himself than the others.

It quickly became apparent to all four of them what was going on. In a matter of a few minutes, they had gone from fighting a crowd of these nasty creatures, to ducking the swings of a few massive monsters. Five of these giants, gray and faceless, towered eight to nine feet over them and blocked out most of what little light the day had to offer with their thick, stooping bodies. Fortunately for the four elite, it took a bit of adjustment in coordination for the shapeshifters to control such a formation. They took the brief opportunity to break out from the circle where, had they stayed, they would have waited to be crushed like bugs.

They all had to run in somewhat separate directions, but Komeris was able to join back up with the general almost immediately. They ran together a few steps and heard heavy pounding behind them. They looked back and saw three of the huge shapeshifter giants beating after them, while the other two trampled into the crowd of fighting warriors, presumably on the tail of Reniu and Pei-Shi. The two soldiers looked at one another and silently agreed that they could not take on three of the creatures by themselves.

That problem was answered momentarily by a reverberating roar of many strange voices behind them. They stopped dead and turned to stare agape at one of the giants, completely engulfed in flame. The flailing thing seemed to come apart as individual shapeshifters struggled to get away. The other two enormous creatures backed away in horror, not wanting a stray ember to land on them.

As the giant disintegrated into its separate parts, another sound rose from the crowd. It was difficult to make out at first, but as it spread across the field, it became louder with the sound of many voices.

"The Shionen," Etrusin realized for the third time this battle.

Indeed, almost every elf on the field were echoing the same chant. The two other giants that had been so eager to get away from their companion were struck from above by crackling bolts of crimson electricity. Both of the juggernauts exploded as each individual Fiu-Het separated from the formation forcefully. They were either dead or momentarily paralyzed. At this the entire shapeshifter army's morale plummeted. Unnerved by the continuous and effective Shionen chanting, not to mention the fiery demise of so many of their brethren, they decided to flee. Most of them took to the sky, while some others near the edge of the battle sprouted additional legs and galloped or sprinted off.

Many of Kesitul's soldiers tried to follow, but as they could only ever be bipedal, wingless creatures, they could not keep up. They gave a triumphant roaring cheer as they chased after their fleeing foe in vain. They stayed for a long time after, watching the last of the strange creatures fade from sight, and they were slow to return as they congratulated one another on a well-fought battle. They seemed reluctant to turn their eyes back east, away from the soon to be setting sun.

"That was too easy," Komeris remarked to the general as he watched the men and women plod back to the field where the battle had been.

Etrusin looked to where many elves were tending the seriously wounded and lamenting the dead, both human and elf. "It was hard enough," he returned with a firm jaw. "Get them to help the Shionen, then meet me in my tent."

Captain Komeris watched sympathetically as his general stalked off. He understood that Etrusin was keenly feeling the loss of every soldier, human and elven, that had fallen today. It could have been considerably worse, and would have been if the battle hadn't ended so quickly. Komeris knew his general was not thinking that way. He knew that, after Reisothin had been slain, he hoped that any soldier still alive would only die of old age and not at the hand of another enemy of the empire. The captain tried to feel reassured that Etrusin would not blame himself for those premature losses, and he prayed that the battle really could have been that easy.

* * *

Dusk brought on the frantic return of the Fiu-Het to the waiting army of King Orbein. At first the humans watched excitedly as they saw the quickly darkening sky fill with the shapeshifters in bird form. Their excitement turned to foreboding as their allies landed. They could sense the tension and fear in the frightening creatures. They scurried back and forth, murmuring to one another furtively and did not approach any of the humans with an explanation. It took Orbein's imposing presence and powerful voice to still them.

"Fiu-Het!" he boomed at an unnatural volume. When they froze almost instantly, he continued at a normal level. "Tell me what has happened."

A rather large shapeshifter with a hump on his back that accentuated his race's normally hunched stance stepped forward. This one seemed to have taken over for Agucho and was definitely very much more suited to the position of leadership. "You said they would be easy prey," he spat fluently in the king's language. "You sssaid they would be terrified of us and flee at the very sssight!"

Orbein grimaced. "From your mutterings I will assume they did not," he replied dryly.

"We had them in the beginning," the shapeshifter sneered at the human, "but then balls of fire erupted from the sssky and swallowed many of us. They used some sssort of magic on us. Between that and the biting arrows of the elves, we could-"

"Elves?" Orbein interrupted curiously. So, the mythical race had joined them, as Agucho had said.

"Yes, and I'll wager they had a lot to do with the fire and lightning that drove us away," the Fiu-Het said angrily.

"No!" another voice shouted from the ranks of the shapeshifters. A much smaller one of their race ambled forward and added his own testimony in an accented and somewhat squeaky hiss. "It wasss men who made fire. Old man with gray hair helped them. They could not make big fire without him. Elvesss helped later."

"He's right," said another, more capable speaker. "A group of wizards of some sort stood around a large, decorated...cone. I heard them chanting, but I didn't believe they were causing the fire. I began to suspect after the old man appeared and it got worse. I was certain when the elves joined in the chant and ran us off."

"Old man?" the king repeated significantly. He seemed to be thinking very hard. "It couldn't be the same," he almost whispered.

"You know this fiend?" the current leader of the Fiu-Het army asked disbelievingly.

Orbein looked up with a snap. Behind his eyes the gears of his mind cranked lightning fast. He forced himself, with much effort, to keep a grin from spreading across his face. Instead, he furrowed his brow and pasted on a look of concern. "Gayossha's murderer..." he said dramatically.

There was a mixed reaction of surprise, awe and anger among the shapeshifters. The king had to bite the inside of his lip to keep from smiling. "In Gayossha's final breaths he revealed his killer. I am sure Agucho would have pointed him out to you, but sadly he met the same fate as your prince. Thus, I am sorry to say that it must be me to tell you what he could not. Your prince, as he lay with blistering scorch marks on his back, screamed for the retribution of his death. He called for the destruction of the wicked empire and the death of the old man of Eastmountain!"

It took a few moments for the shapeshifters to convince themselves of the connection. Those who spoke the king's language translated the revelation to those who did not. In minutes the whole lot of them looked as angry and ready to kill as they had when Vethisir told them about the supposed ambush that had led to Agucho's death. Their unexpected defeat of earlier was forgotten in a fresh wave of fury toward the empire that had taken so many from them. Orbein's plan had worked brilliantly.

"My allies," the king shouted. "I know you must be tired, but come with me. Let us go now together to this enemy and vanquish them once and for all. Surely they will not be able to best us while we are united."

"No!" shouted the large Fiu-Het commander. "Give us until sunrise, then we will join you on your march."

"But under the cover of night we will-," Orbein began.

"No!" the shapeshifter yelled more insistently. "In the morning."

The king bristled at the interruption. But, he reminded himself, lashing out in anger at these beasts was not likely to inspire loyalty from them. Realizing that he would not change the shapeshifter's mind, and knowing that his patience would pay off, he nodded. "Very well," he relented. "I understand. You must rest."

"We need no ressst," the big shapeshifter hissed. There was a calmness in his voice that would have frightened any other man. "When I return in the morning, we will all set out. Then we will see how the battle faresss." With that he stepped away and several other shapeshifters followed in his wake.

'Even better,' thought the king slyly.

* * *

It was unusually quiet in the encampment where the soldiers of Kesitul rested after the day's battle. Many of the warriors, tired from the endeavors of the day, slept soundly. Some, for whom the adrenaline still quickened their pulses, sat awake and alert, but quiet, as if straining to hear the slightest sound. Yet others assisted the Shionen with the wounded and prepared the dead, who were fortunately relatively few. The quiet mood did not make it feel like a field of victory. Rather it was somber, with an air of watchfulness.

Kiusu sat, as he often did since he and Urietsin joined General Etrusin's warriors, on the edge of camp in a deeply meditative state. He had been this way for several hours, which was also not unusual. Moving with the flow of existence, the old man was releasing the fatiguing negativity that came with handling the horn of Reisothin. He was finally beginning to feel relaxed when Urietsin stepped up with an uncertain expression.

"What is it, Swift One?" Kiusu asked without even looking up.

Urietsin sighed hesitantly. "Seishin, something was not right today. I..." The young man sat and put a hand on his head as if to coax out the difficult thoughts.

The relaxation Kiusu had managed to achieve fled quickly. "What was it?" he asked, concerned.

"I don't know," the Swift One admitted with a frustrated shrug. "I was in a bad situation, fighting an enemy. I felt sure I could get out of it, but when I tried to reach out with my mind, nothing happened."

Kiusu's eyes were wide and the color had gone from his cheeks. Guilt had been nagging at him slightly for the shortcuts he had taken with his student, but the more he had seen Urietsin in action, the less he had let it affect him. He had thought the young man ready for the challenges brought on by the real world, but what the Swift One told him now revealed the truth. Kiusu had never stopped helping him. Even in their contests with one another, the master had subconsciously reached out and opened up his understanding and experience to his student. Actually, he hadn't really been helping his student at all; he had been cheating him.

There was only one solution. He had to tell Urietsin what he had done. He had to tell the Swift One everything. How and why he had hidden him from the search party, how he had guided the student's progress more closely than the young man may have thought. He wasn't sure how this could resolve the situation now, but he knew it had to be done. Urietsin had to know so that he could learn to do these things on his own and so that he wouldn't be caught unawares in the middle of battle again.

"Swift One..." the old man started resignedly. The sound of approaching footsteps interrupted his confession.

The two men looked up at eight soldiers who stood frowning down at the both of them. "What is it?" Urietsin asked them with a start. "Is there another attack approaching?"

All eight of the warriors just stood there and stared, as though not hearing or not comprehending Urietsin's queries. After a few silent moments, one of the soldiers grinned, and suddenly a curved dagger flashed into his hand. He lunged for Kiusu, and all of the others did the same.

The aptly-named Swift One didn't even have to rise to spring into instinctual action. He rolled forward onto his back and swung his legs out into a sweeping circle that tripped two of the would-be assassins. He kicked himself up to his feet, dodged around the two fumbling attackers and kicked the dagger away from a third.

Kiusu, a swift one himself, rolled backward from his sitting position onto his feet and into a handspring. The well-placed trajectory of his foot deterred a strike from an oncoming blade.

It was on in full. All eight of the soldiers kept trying to focus their attention solely upon Kiusu, but Urietsin made that impossible. At least the Swift One's fighting prowess was truly all his own. His quick sequences of wide ranging attacks abruptly taught them that they would need to divide their efforts. Within seconds, each of the two men found themselves surrounded by four attackers.

All of Urietsin's opponents attacked at once, thinking that the young warrior could not possibly block them all. It was surely a surprise when he leapt into the air and spun full circle with one leg out and accurately maneuvered the move to kick aside two of the four curved daggers and dodging the others. Two of the enemies on opposite sides of the Swift One recovered first and came at him, one sweeping the blade low, the other stabbing high. With a preternatural sense of his enemies' proximity, Urietsin leaned back and swiped aside the high attack that came from behind while his counterbalancing foot pelted the low attack off course. Instantly he snapped his body in the opposite direction and sent the opponent behind him staggering away with a reverse kick while the one in front was presented with a fist to the face.

The two attackers to the left and right saw their brief opening as he executed this impressively fast move and lunged at him. The Swift One, however, was hardly caught unawares, and as the other two fell away from him, he again leapt into the air and kicked left and right simultaneously. He brought his legs down slightly from his midair split to absorb the impact of landing, but went back into a full split once he was on the ground as he ducked the returning attacks to his front and back. He whipped his right leg around and rolled onto his shoulders as he allowed the momentum to bring his leg in a complete circle. He spun the other one after it and his legs windmilled out as the rest of his body pivoted on his shoulders and arms. Each of his opponents got hit at least once by this whirling fury and backed away, either of their own wisdom or from the force of Urietsin's brilliant acrobatics.

Kiusu's defense was a bit more discordant than his younger counterpart's. He sprung first toward the one directly before him. His leap brought both of his feet level with his opponent's face. His left foot snapped forward, then his right as his leap kept him moving after the staggering attacker. He landed on the opposite side of the fallen foe and took off running as the other three pursued and the fourth wobbled to his feet.

The old master seemed to be fleeing as he took several sprinting steps away from his enemies. Suddenly he jumped and stretched his feet forward. His landing looked completely off balance as he skidded forward and fell onto his behind, but the move was not as uncoordinated as it may have seemed at first. He continued to roll back and over his shoulders, flipped to his feet, sprung backward onto his hands, continued the rotation so that his legs could propel him into a twisting backflip that spun him in the direction of his pursuers.

The reversal was so fast that none of them realized what Kiusu was doing until his flip landed him inches from the leading attacker. A fist backed by all the impetus of the old man's gymnastics flattened him, and Kiusu continued by, rolling between the other two, who could only watch with surprise as he whipped past before they realized that they should stop running. The roll took the old man to his feet, where he instantly brought his hands and leading knee up, then swung them down as he lifted himself into a spinning, jumping crescent kick that rammed into the staggering foe that he had originally attacked. He landed with a half twist to face the two he had passed with his roll and invited them over with a wave of his hand.

One of Urietsin's opponents was rolling around on the ground moaning and holding his head. The other three, however, were still attacking the Swift One with inhuman zeal. They slashed at him with the gleaming edges of their daggers or stabbed with their dangerously sharp points. He kicked at the one behind him and snatched at the wrists of the other two. The skilled young warrior brought his right leg up so that his toes extended beyond his own height, then he bent it at the knee and heel kicked the elbow joint of his right opponent, which gave a resounding crack. The one on his right made the enemy's first successful attack on him with a swing of his fist into the young warrior's ribs. Without lowering his leg, Urietsin extended his foot again. He repaid the talented adversary with a toe kick to the face, after which he reversed direction again to heel kick the one on his right.

The Swift One let go of his two foes as they stumbled backward, and not a moment too soon. The third was approaching from behind again. He was about to swivel around and issue a sidekick, when a whistling sound cut the air beside him and he felt something pass by his head. When he looked at the attacker behind him, there was an arrow protruding from his eye socket. Slowly the enemy's human form melted away to reveal the not completely unexpected countenance of a shapeshifter. Urietsin looked the other way to see the two that had been stumbling away from him; they were running at Kiusu. With the commotion that suddenly appeared at the edge of camp, the assassins knew that their time was up.

All pretense was dropped as the six shapeshifters who were still capable of focusing on their target decided to redouble their efforts. They dropped their human forms as a few more Shionen arrows zipped past them, or through them. The shapeshifter on the ground behind Kiusu sprouted several whiplike tentacles that lashed around the old man. Similar appendages were emerging from the skin of the other five as they rushed toward their target with reckless abandon. With all of their attention now on Kiusu, they had to stop watching for the arrows that were arcing toward them. Those whose backs were exposed to the archers found them quickly riddled with feathery elven flights.

Urietsin made for his master immediately, feeling for a small pouch at his waist. He pulled out his small crystalline feather and focused, desperately hoping that whatever had affected him on the battlefield today had passed. He closed his eyes for a moment and took a deep breath, but it was no use; he could not concentrate. The moment his eyes were shut, his mind screamed at him that Kiusu was being crushed by the creeping tentacles. He cried out and ran at the group of strangling creatures with a flying kick.

He crashed into the closest shapeshifter with his foot and fell to the ground. He could see that it had been affected and was trying to keep its balance, but its tentacles were still winding around the old man. Kiusu could barely be seen inside the cocoon of slimy, twisting limbs. Urietsin leapt to his feet and began to pound on the creature he had kicked. There was no grace or technique to these hits; he was simply pummeling the beast as hard as he could, in any way he could. Within a few seconds the shapeshifter was only still standing because its tentacles and Urietsin's fists held it up. Once the young warrior realized this, he stopped and went for the next one in line.

He paused.

A faint glow was radiating from the center of the mass of slick appendages. It grew brighter, and the tentacles seemed to expand for a moment. Urietsin could hear a snapping sound, and the few creatures that had not yet been hissing or gurgling in discomfort were doing so now. To his apprehensive relief he saw some of the tentacles unwrapping and falling to the ground as they dissolved away. Kiusu's face was, once again, revealed. His eyes were closed, but his jaw was firm. The light suddenly flashed to an almost blinding brightness, and the six shapeshifters flew back.

Urietsin's master stood, fists clenched by his sides, a look of concentration etched on his face. He opened his eyes and stepped lightly toward the Swift One and gave a weak smile.

"The reinforcements are here, seishin. I think it's time you rested," the young warrior suggested, returning the old man's smile.

"Urietsin," Kiusu said with a strangely strained voice.

A mysterious chill went up the Swift One's spine. "Yes, seishin?"

"You have thus far proven yourself to be a skilled student, but I fear I have wronged you in my teachings," the old man said, pausing to take a deep, shaking breath. "See your own reality, not mine."

Urietsin's eyes grew wide, but not because of Kiusu's words, rather he noticed the bit of blood trickling from the side of Kiusu's mouth. "Seishi-," he began with an increasing feeling of panic, but the old man put up a hand to stop him. Kiusu's next words were almost a whisper. "Do not fear, Urietsin...death is but a new beginning."

"Kiusu..." was all the Swift One could manage.

The old man bowed deeply, and Urietsin almost jumped back in horror at the five curving daggers that were embedded into his master's back. Kiusu did not rise from that bow. He toppled to the side and laid there, still.

The Swift One clenched his jaw and returned the old man's bow, his tears dropping freely from his eyes and onto Kiusu's lifeless form. It was almost as if he could feel his master's spirit retreating. He wished very much that he could reach out and stop it, but he knew that he could not. So, he remained in that position, feeling that to come up from that bow would bring an end to this moment and finalize Kiusu's death. His mind denied with all its power by believing that if he held this last action toward his master, looking upon the old man who still wore an expression of focused determination, then he would never truly die.

When the elven archers had edged all the way forward, and even after Etrusin, Komeris, Reniu and Pei-Shi broke through the thickening crowd of onlookers, Urietsin was still in that low bow. Torch and starlight still glinted through his tears. His young, strong form, bent in sincere and profound respect, so captured the attention of the gathered men and elves, that none of them noticed the dissipating corpses of the six shapeshifters or the urgent retreat of the other two as they slithered off in the shape of badly-injured serpents.

* * *

Urietsin opened his eyes. His heart raced with the possibility that it had all simply been a vision. After all, hadn't he been meditating next to Kiusu on the mountain just moments ago? While it may have been a disturbing vision, it would have been better than it being reality. Then again, perhaps it had been a dream. He sat up and looked around. The blank hide walls of a tent stared back. He had just been asleep, hadn't he?

Then it all came rushing back. How Kiusu's body had been carried to its place with the rest of the dead awaiting burial. How Komeris had practically had to drag him back to camp. How he had sat in this very tent and stared until he fell back in weariness and grief. The beating of his heart became a slow twisting of his insides until all of the emotion from last night had been wrung out of him. A feeling of emptiness overcame him.

How could it be that Kiusu was dead? The memory of it made him shudder. In his mind's eye, he saw the old man's final bow, and it made him ill. Tears welled in his eyes. If only he had been faster in dispatching his enemies. He recalled with sickening clarity how he had actually been enjoying the fight until its final turn. He played over each moment in his head and revised it in ways that saved Kiusu's life. He could have done it. Why hadn't he?

Light poured in as the tent flap was pulled aside. Komeris poked his head in. "Swift One," he said lightly. "Come out. You should eat something."

"I am not very hungry," Urietsin replied coolly, wiping his wet eyes.

"You should eat anyway," the captain insisted.

The Swift One remained seated for several more minutes. Eventually, he decided to stand, but a noise from outside made him pause. They both listened as the call sounded out again. Komeris withdrew his head from the tent and looked out. He stuck his head back in with an expression of urgency.

"Something approaches from the west," he relayed, and though it seemed like something important enough to require his full attention, he still waited to see Urietsin's reaction.

The young warrior's brow was creased, and he stared down with eyes wide. The expression quickly became a scowl, and he looked up at Komeris. Taking no notice of the captain's bemused expression, the Swift One pushed past him and bolted from the tent. He continued to run and forced his way through the rows of soldiers that had already lined up to prepare for whatever the day might bring. He emerged and ran a few steps away from the army of his kinsmen and neighbors. He stood alone ahead of the line of soldiers to watch the approach of something very large on the horizon. He imagined line upon line of armored shapeshifters coming to finish on the ground what they could not do by air. Rather than frighten him, the thought simply drove his fury higher. The minutes dragged on agonizingly as he waited to confirm his suspicion, as he waited for them to get closer.

Though there was little doubt in Urietsin's mind as to the identity of the approaching figures, for it was many figures, they did not get close enough for him to get a good view. It looked like thousands of them to him, but they stood just beyond his ability to make out each one, and their forms blurred with their bustling motion. But this did not cause the Swift One to question his assumption that they were, indeed, his enemy. It was as if they were standing just outside his reach and taunting him. As he listened to the questioning murmurs of the soldiers behind him, he decided that he was going to take control of the situation.

"We must attack them!" Urietsin demanded. When no response seemed forthcoming, he pushed his way back through the crowd and found the priests who stood watch over the horn of Reisothin. Upon seeing the relic, the Swift One knew he was right. He could not explain it, but a sudden sense of confidence was welling up beside his anger. It was as if Kiusu was somewhere nearby, whispering to him. It was not he who should take the blame for his master's death; shapeshifters wielded those daggers.

One of the priests looked at him sadly. "Your master...he helped us to control the horn. We would be honored if you took his place today," he said hopefully, bowing to the young warrior.

The Swift One blinked and paused uncertainly, but then gave a grim nod and led the holy men and their powerful weapon to the front line. He stopped only briefly, taking in the horizon of moving shapes. They were his enemy. Even though he could not make them out clearly with his eyes, in his mind they sneered at him triumphantly, the killers of his master. He stepped forward.

"Urietsin!" shouted general Etrusin with apprehension in his voice.

The young warrior did not ignore him; that would have required effort. He simply could not hear the general. He walked on toward his foe. The priests, seemingly enchanted by his hypnotic focus, followed him. It was a slow, determined march at first, but it picked up speed with each step.

General Etrusin knew he would not be able to stop the young warrior, but he was certainly not going to let him face the enemy alone. As Captain Komeris trotted up alongside him on his own horse, Etrusin nodded to him.

"Forward!" the captain called out powerfully. As one, nearly six thousand humans and seven hundred elves moved westward.

They caught up quickly with the Swift One and the priests, who were weighted by the horn. With these first steps the general felt an upwelling of relief. They were defenders of their lands. They were not seeking to destroy and conquer. Their foe had taken the initiative thus far, making them the aggressors. Any doubt he had ever had dissolved away with each second that brought them closer to their destiny. Then, for a moment, it came rushing back. His eyes widened.

Spots of yellow, seeming tiny and faint at first in the daylight, shot up from the western horizon and quickly grew larger and more defined as they neared. Etrusin tried to call out, but it was too late. Several balls of flaming pitch slammed into the middle ranks, splattering the sticky, fiery substance everywhere. Cries went up as humans and elves were engulfed in flames, and others attempted to put out small fires that quickly spread as they tried to wipe away the viscous, scorching death.

* * *

"Excellent!" Orbein cried happily. "The volley could not have landed more perfectly. I commend you, Laernus." He chuckled at this last statement.

The seer glared darkly at the king, who was far too fascinated with the effect of the siege weaponry to notice. Laernus tilted his head uncomfortably, trying to relieve the irritation of the thick rope that bound his hands to his neck. The rope trailed to a lead that General Vethisir held tightly as insurance of the wizard's loyalty.

"Ready the catapults!" the king shouted eagerly. The trebuchets had shown their deadly range. Now the catapults, which did not fire quite as far but were faster to load, were prepared for their battle debut. Orbein watched impatiently as his enemy regrouped and continued their charge.

"Shall I ready the men to meet them, sire?" Vethisir asked eagerly.

The king held up his hand in a signal of delay. "Wait," he said with a smile. "Let the machines of war do their work. If our enemy is so fond of fire, we shall give them fire."

Laernus noticed that the general seemed disappointed at this, then he shot the seer a sly grin. The wizard scowled back at Vethisir resentfully. It revolted him to think of how much pleasure the general no doubt took having him in such a vulnerable position. On the one hand, Laernus wanted to close his eyes and foresee what this day might bring, but on the other he did not want to know. It all led to a sense of distraction that would have made it impossible even if he could make up his mind. He just tried to accept that he would know by the end of the day what fate awaited him.

* * *

Etrusin shouted out orders, trying to organize the ranks around the still burning fires. For a while it was chaos. Scorched warriors lay motionless on the ground, or stumbling painfully through the crowd. Flames leapt from the bubbling masses of pitch on the ground. The whole scene seemed eerily like the aftermath of a battle with Reisothin. The image chilled him to the bone, but he did not let it pull his attention away from his duty.

Order began to be regained as the remainder of the army marched around the fire. Some of them stopped to aid the injured. Etrusin and Komeris rode through the ranks quickly to make sure that the bulk of their force did not lose their focus on what lay ahead. As they coordinated the help to the wounded, Komeris came upon Urietsin, who was assisting an elf with a badly singed soldier.

The Swift One looked up at the captain with an anguished expression. Komeris knew what thoughts plagued the young warrior. Urietsin felt responsible for the scorched woman he helped the elf drag away from the flame, for he had started this march. Even if she survived, the severe burns covering her body would drastically change her life forever. There were many such brave warriors lying in the blackened grass. Urietsin keenly sensed all of their pain.

"Come, Swift One," the captain called firmly, having accepted that to overcome such emotions was a valuable lesson for a warrior. "We will need you in the battle."

Urietsin sadly looked down at the woman, then apologetically at the elf. The Shionen nodded his head reassuringly. The Swift One left the soldier in the elf's hands and marched off to find the priests. For the second time today, anger displaced his sadness. First they had taken his master, now they savaged his people.

These enemies would pay.

When he found the keepers of the horn, they all rejoined the march. The Swift One watched with a mounting sense of purpose as he saw other priests kneeling in prayer for the healing power of their god. With them were a few elves, healers in their own fashion, and other soldiers to tend to the fallen and the dead. In total, five score fewer soldiers pressed on, though many who had rejoined the ranks were injured. It had only been minutes since the rain of fire, but it had all played out so slowly in Urietsin's mind. The sluggish pace of time continued as the Swift One forged ahead within the ranks of Kesitul's army.

* * *

The restoration of order became clear as Orbein watched the approaching line. Such excitement welled within him as he had never felt before. The fools were coming ever closer and into a greater danger than they faced from the trebuchets. He and practically his entire army held their breaths as their enemy came closer to doom.

"Light the volley!" the king called out eagerly.

"Sire," Laernus said with caution.

Orbein leveled a threatening gaze on him.

The wizard's sense of self preservation reared. "I beg your forgiveness, highness, but they are yet too far for the catapults," he said, hoping the king would heed, and be grateful for, the good advice.

Orbein glanced back at the advancing line. They had picked up speed even in just these few seconds. To him they seemed tantalizingly close. A surge of hatred swelled up within him. He had seen the catapults perform their tests. They were close enough. He could wait no longer. "Fire!" he boomed unnaturally loudly.

The missiles sailed over their heads, and they watched the balls of fire spread in the air on a path toward their target. The fire hit the ground and sent up plumes of smoke. Orbein squinted into the distance, uncertain of the damage. It took a few moments, but when he finally saw activity on the horizon, it became clear to him that this volley had not been nearly as successful as the first. It seemed that flaming pitch had different aerodynamic properties than small boulders. He cursed loudly.

With a hint of lament, Laernus intoned, "As I said, too far."

The king's face contorted in rage, but his voice remained calm. "What was that?" he asked the seer.

Laernus swallowed. "I only meant, if you had waited a moment longer...the next volley will devastate them, highness, I assure you," he amended.

Orbein's expression relaxed. "Ready the next volley!" he called out. "But leave one bucket empty."

The general and the seer both looked at the king quizzically.

"Vethisir," Orbein said evenly, "take Laernus to test the range of these machines firsthand." A wicked grin spread across his face.

* * *

The army of humans and elves spread out in a wide formation at Etrusin's command. By the general's estimation, the enemy could probably only get one more volley off before it endangered its own troops. He wanted to quickly close the gap, but he understood that increasing the distance between soldiers would decrease the damage taken from the devastating weapons.

As the warriors fanned out, the general led the charge onward. As expected, there came another set of fiery lights from the enemy. "Here they come!" shouted Captain Komeris, riding far to Etrusin's right.

Larger holes opened up in the rows of soldiers as they fled the approximate area of impact. One roiling missile struck close to the front line, and Etrusin just barely galloped away from the explosion of sticky flames. He called out a battle cry, long and loud. They were too close to stop. Whatever casualties had been taken from this last attack would have to be tended to later. Now there was only one focus: the imminent battle before them.

Fortunately, there had not been many casualties. The soldiers had heeded Etrusin well, and their instincts had saved them. A few were hit by splattering pitch, some seriously, but the rest of the army charged ahead. If these soldiers died, it would not be in vain. Those who witnessed the fall of their comrades were determined to survive so that they could honor the fallen as heroes. This promise to themselves added strength to each pounding step that brought them to their foe.

They raced across the field, screaming as their last few steps brought the enemy looming before them. Suddenly, there was a chorus of clanging as weapons and armor met one another. The two sides rushed together, and the melee was on in full. Soldiers on both sides, trained in styles very distinct from one another, abandoned those styles in the confusion of bodies and metal that began the fight. Each warrior lost himself in the sea of opponents.

* * *

Vethisir watched from behind the line of catapults as the battle was joined. The cacophony of war echoed over the field, but was somewhat muted from his position. He watched as soldiers in the rear tried to position themselves closer to the fight. Behind him the Fiu-Het army stood still, watching the humans and elves fight one another.

"What are you doing?" Laernus asked in confusion. While he was certainly grateful not to have been loaded onto the catapult, he was not at all certain how much longer he would remain alive. Every once in a while he could make out Orbein, riding just out of reach of the real fighting. Sooner or later he would notice them back here. Then he and the general would probably both be dead.

General Vethisir gave the seer his sly smile again. He drew out his sword and pulled on the rope that bound Laernus. Slipping the sword through the bonds, he cut the man free and handed him the weapon. "I believe our time," the general said in a voice that was not his own, "has finally come."

Laernus gaped as Vethisir's form became fluid and rippled into a familiar shape. "A-Agucho!" the wizard stuttered.

The shapeshifter hobbled past the shocked seer. A thick scar ran across his neck where General Vethisir had almost decapitated him. Fortunately, the small strip of skin that kept his head attached had saved him. As he had once indicated to Laernus, it was not so easy to kill one of his race with a blade. It had felt good to stick his own curved dagger between Vethisir's ribs just as the general finished murdering his last soldier on their farcical scouting mission. The Fiu-Het knew something else that would feel even better.

"My people!" Agucho called out in his own language. Hidden pockets under his chin ballooned out weirdly, amplifying his hissing screeches. "I told you once that I would show you the killer of our Prince Gayossha." The shapeshifter pointed at King Orbein and the army of Niele'itio. "Go now and take your revenge on him and those that follow!" he cried.

* * *

Urietsin joined hands with the priests around the horn. A ring of soldiers stood around them, protecting them as they concentrated. The priests prayed to Minotros for strength and guidance, while the Swift One went within himself. He was surprised at how easily it suddenly came to him, given the hectic circumstances and his failure yesterday. Reaching out with his very spirit, he felt the true untapped power of the horn.

The young warrior had been disappointed to see that the foes waiting for them on the other side of the field were human, but if they were allied with the shapeshifters, then they would feel his wrath as well. The Swift One wondered how to best use the power of Reisothin's horn against them. Humans did not fly, so fireballs in the sky would not be so effective.

As Urietsin focused on the nuances of the horn's power, the priests started to chant as Kiusu had bade them the previous day. The rhythm of their chant swept up the Swift One in a mesmerizing swirl of energy. He could feel the vastness of infinity, and Reisothin's horn was one large pulsing light among many. The young warrior drew his spirit closer to it and saw it looming before him, as bright as the sun, as large as the very mountains themselves.

But the Swift One did not let the magnificent sight hold him in awe. He reached out with his will and commanded it to obey. As he exerted his influence, it seemed as though the bright energy changed. It seemed to be a trick of perspective; the size of the pulsing brightness was a matter of his focus. Suddenly, it seemed small enough to fit in his hand. He could see tendrils of energy that spiked off of it in rapid, twirling bursts. It reminded him of his crystalline feather.

As he had done with the feather, he manipulated the sphere of energy by simply perceiving it where he wanted it to be. Like the feather, it obeyed. Urietsin reached out and felt the enemies that were attacking his people. He moved the energy toward them.

* * *

"It seems my skill in divination has somewhat declined," said Laernus, still amazed by Agucho's presence.

Agucho offered a grin that was more grotesque than the one he had given as Vethisir. "I am glad you did not know," he comforted. "It made things much more convincing."

The seer looked out at the battle. In the distance he saw Orbein trotting back and forth nervously on his horse. He had noticed the press of the Fiu-Het from the other side and did not look so smug anymore. "It's a shame," Laernus finally said with a sigh. "I would have enjoyed killing him myself."

Agucho gave him a long hard look. "I do not care," he said, his eyes gleaming, "as long as he dies." With a leap he took to the air, wings sprouting from his back.

Laernus watched him glide over the battle. The excess skin under shapeshifter's chin expanded with air again, but the seer could not hear his screeches over the din of the fighting. A few more Fiu-Het took wing and ascended to Agucho's side. Together they circled above King Orbein's head.

The king saw them and waved his sword threateningly. His mouth moved and a streaking light came from the tip of his weapon. The hovering shapeshifters scattered as the light burst into a shower of sparks. They wavered in their flight, but only for a moment, then they dove angrily. Long tentacles descended ahead of them and wrapped themselves around Orbein.

Laernus watched in awe as he was reminded of the king's rarely seen magical skills, but was even more impressed at the ease with which the shapeshifters captured him. The seer was still blinking in disbelief as they carried Orbein through the air with a swoop and released their tentacles. The king fell a painful distance and landed with a thud before the seer.

Orbein got to his feet slowly and dusted himself off. He eyed his captors warily as they fluttered to the ground and surrounded him and Laernus. With a sneer he spat blood from his fattening lip at them.

"So, Laernus," the king said still glaring at the Fiu-Het, "I see I underestimated you."

The seer shrugged.

"Come," Orbein said, "call them off. Together we can defeat the army of this wicked empire, as I planned. At the end of this battle awaits riches and glory you cannot imagine."

Laernus laughed, something he had not done in some time. "Highness,

I could not call them off even if I wanted to. They are not under my command. And I think you might be surprised at what I can imagine."

The king scowled. "I see. So, am I to fight you then?" he asked, assessing the situation.

Again, Laernus shrugged.

Orbein laughed. "It's a shame we shall never know if you could have defeated me in a fair fight," he taunted, indicating the waiting shapeshifters.

The seer smiled. "I ask," he said to the surrounding Fiu-Het, "that you do not act until the contest between me and the king is decided."

From behind him Agucho spoke. "Do as he asks."

Given the expression on his face, Orbein had clearly only just noticed Agucho's presence. The king simply shook his head, unable to find words bitter enough for this betrayal.

Laernus took a preparatory stance, his sword up. "Ready?" he asked rhetorically.

The king answered with a rapid gesture in the seer's direction and the shout of a word none of them recognized. Suddenly, the sleeveless, studded leather tunic that Laernus was wearing began to constrict in the most uncomfortable way.

Understanding that more magic was afoot, the seer tore desperately at the side buckles of his armor. Meanwhile Orbein rushed at him. Laernus got his sword up at the last moment, though it pulled at the leather that was already squeezing his throat. The seer ran back and quickly undid the strap on his shoulder. His tunic practically popped off. Now he stood with no protection on his upper body, only a simple shirt.

Orbein threw back his head and laughed.

* * *

O'eintsu pointed to the sky. "Shapeshifters!" the normally quiet warrior called out.

Denlin nodded grimly as they watched the flying creatures dodge a small explosion of sparks, then dive with extended tentacles to carry off the mounted man on the opposition's side. He gripped his staff anxiously. He and O'eintsu were among the ring of warriors protecting Urietsin and the priests. They had yet to see any fighting, which was the cause of young Denlin's anxiety, but he knew how important his current position was.

The two warriors, and much of the battlefield itself, gaped at the sudden appearance of a flaming prominence in the sky. A serpentine rivulet of fire snaked down from the clouds and wriggled its way into the enemy's ranks. Both Denlin and O'eintsu were too young to have seen Reisothin with their own eyes, but the dragon had been described in detail to them in stories. This was surely the Abomination's ghost, albeit a bit smaller.

Even over the sound of the battle, they heard a great cry rise up from the other side as the fiery apparition slithered over the enemy lines. The two warriors looked at each other, then over their shoulders at Urietsin, who was standing serenely with his eyes closed. Even the priests around him stopped chanting to boggle at this latest miracle.

From deep within himself, Urietsin could hear O'eintsu's shout. Indeed, his spirit sensed the presence of the shapeshifters as he expanded his influence outward. A twinge of anger rippled through his inner self, but it did not break his focus. He guided the spirit of the dragon through the sea of enemies that immediately endangered his friends and allies.

"But look at them," a voice inside him whispered. "Look at what they are doing."

It did seem strange to the Swift One that the hostility the shapeshifters emanated seemed to be directed at the same foes his own kin were fighting. He wondered if perhaps the army of Kesitul had been mistaken in their target. But then, there were the volleys of burning pitch that had descended upon them as they charged.

"They betray their own allies," the voice within explained. "Their dishonor knows no bounds."

Urietsin's rage surged again. This time, it had the opposite effect of what he would have expected. The anger made him feel even more powerful, and he poured that energy into the task at hand. Out on the field the flaming serpent thrashed. A tall wave traveled its length, and its tail snapped into the air like a fiery whip. The tip of it came down and flicked at the edge of the shapeshifters' front line.

* * *

Komeris galloped across the battlefield, directing his horse to trample a prone enemy when he could. He glanced eastward to see if he could spot any of his old friends in the fray. He suddenly realized that his quick glance had lasted too long as his horse suddenly pitched forward. Reacting quickly, Komeris rolled with the fall. The back of his head struck the ground roughly, and his sword pressed into his left bicep, leaving a superficial slice. It disoriented him to say the least, but he quickly leapt to his feet at the ready. In front of him his horse lay, kicking frantically, a spear protruding from its ribs.

Komeris looked around angrily. A few feet away stood his opponent, unsheathing a thick longsword triumphantly. The captain glared at him and walked with purpose in his direction. His confidence in the situation faltered, however, as four more men ran up beside the killer of his horse, all of them intent on the captain's advance.

Reniu and Pei-Shi had been shadowing the captain as best they could throughout the battle. It was a difficult task, given the constant flow of enemies and the fact that Komeris rode a horse. But he had fought beside them many years ago, and they were not about to leave their brother in arms to face destiny alone. They beat their way across the field at a frantic pace when they saw Komeris's horse hit the ground. Panting, but ready to fight, the two veterans came up alongside the captain just as his enemies decided to press their advantage.

The five longsword-bearing soldiers of the western army lunged at the three friends, still of the belief that the odds were in their favor. Two of them slashed at their original target, Captain Komeris. A second sword flashed into the captain's free hand as he drew it from his side and defeated both attacks with a swift, glancing strike on each blade. Another opponent on his left stumbled as one of Pei-Shi's delicate weapons raked across the side of his head below his helm, practically taking his ear.

The female warrior worked her first blade in alternating rhythms, easily keeping the challenger directly in front of her busy as her other sword reached for the enemy in her peripheral vision. She dodged right as the angry opponent she had just struck came at her. With swords flashing she met the two soldiers' attacks with gusto. When they simultaneously lunged at her with extended blades, she swiped the longswords outward and leapt between them, slashing their shoulders as she passed.

The enemy on Pei-Shi's left doubled over as another blade slid along his waist, leaving a gaping hole in his armor and a nasty wound in his side. The strike had come from Reniu, who seemed now to be focusing only on the fifth challenger, much to the injured soldier's surprise. He went to exact retribution on the big man, but another strike bounced off the hide scales covering his other side, reminding him that Pei-Shi had not forgotten him.

Reniu glanced to the side to see how successful his sneak attack had been. His attention was quickly redirected as a heavy longsword dented his breastplate and poked into his pectoral muscle. With a scowl and a snapping slash he stopped his foe's strike before it could go any deeper. The weapons clanged as the snarling soldier's strike was turned away. The enemy pressed ahead again, looking for another opening. He couldn't find one, and as Reniu worked a sword in one hand to beat off the attacks, his other sword flicked out and stung one of Pei-Shi's opponents again.

The soldier on Pei-Shi's right growled in frustration and turned his attention to the big man who kept hitting him. He delivered a deft slash across the back of the man's right shoulder and grinned wickedly as he noticed the strap on the Reniu's breastplate snap off. His grin left quickly as Pei-Shi's blade slid through the scales in his armor and into his belly. He leapt back quickly, barely saving his own life with the dodge, but he was badly wounded.

Komeris worked his blades furiously to fend off his two attackers. They were quite skilled, and it was only Komeris's faith in the abilities of his comrades that allowed him to keep his focus. That focus was almost lost when he noticed in his peripheral vision that more enemy soldiers were fast approaching to help finish off the companions. The captain swiped at the man on his left, whose parried weapon was sailing wide. The foe stumbled backward in shock, holding his neck as blood bubbled through his fingers and soaked his armor. Komeris had no time to celebrate the victory as he fought off the soldier on his right and another ran up to take the fallen man's place.

The press was becoming more difficult. Reniu now fought two enemies as his breastplate hung off only one shoulder. It was a hindrance, but he dared not pause to rip it off. To do so would bring his two foes upon him, and death would surely follow. With a scowl of frustration the large soldier noticed another enemy squeezing in to fight Pei-Shi. Her blades were a blur, and if any one of them could handle three at a time, it was her. But with more soldiers charging up to help, things were about to get out of hand quickly.

Somewhere very close by, a horse neighed loudly and the stamp of hooves could be heard above the cacophony of clanging. A white shape blurred by behind the companions' enemies. One of Reniu's opponents fell. Then one of Pei-Shi's followed. The white stallion that had ridden by reared up and General Etrusin leapt out of the saddle and to the ground. He cried out in triumph and jumped in beside Komeris and the other veterans and began taking on enemies of his own.

The four friends, fighting side by side again as they had for years, put up a wall of blinding metal as their swordwork wove together. Now, though they clearly outnumbered the senior officers of the empire, these soldiers from the Dark City no longer felt like they had the advantage. One by one they fell or had to pull back because their wounds became too grave to fight. Soon Etrusin, Komeris, Pei-Shi, and Reniu were standing among a circle of enemy corpses.

When the last man dropped, Komeris looked to his allies and grinned. "They were foolish to attack," he said to them over the sounds of similar battles all around them. "They counted four warriors instead of eight swords!"

Their momentary mirth was forgotten as yet another set of fresh enemies emerged from different parts of the general fray, oblivious to the copious bodies of their fallen allies. The friends faced them with looks of frightening determination. They were ready to bestow their harsh lessons on any foe foolish enough to challenge them today.

* * *

A group of Fiu-Het backed away from their victims as the fiery tail swiped through their vicinity again. They were eager to claim their vengeance upon Orbein's men, but they were wary of the unusual ghostly flame that occasionally lashed out at them. Though they did laugh in nervous glee whenever a soldier of Niele'itio was consumed by the fire.

One of these shapeshifters took a particular interest in this fire spirit. He looked to some of his nearby kin and gargled out a few words punctuated by a hiss. They all nodded in agreement, and the message was relayed to a few others. Within seconds, several Fiu-Het took to the sky in search of the suspected source of the apparition.

* * *

The fighting was getting louder. Denlin gripped his staff anxiously as he tried to peer over the line of defense put up by his kin and the Shionen. He could tell from the sound that the battle was edging closer. Soldiers from the other side were beginning to push their way through. It wouldn't be long now before he was part of the fray...or so he hoped.

O'eintsu tapped on his shoulder and pointed at the sky in front of them. Shapeshifters, about twenty of them, were gliding over the battlefield, swooping left and right, but generally heading in their direction. They seemed to be searching.

Suddenly, they scattered as elven arrows flew at them from below. None of the arrows seemed to hit the mark, but it was difficult to tell with these creatures. Still, the shapeshifters climbed a bit higher to get out of range.

Denlin and O'eintsu watched as the winged figures hovered high above for a few moments. Their shapes grew very quickly as they went into a sudden dive. Apparently, they had found what they were seeking.

O'eintsu threw a chiun straight up at a shapeshifter that was almost upon them. It hit the target. The creature practically reversed direction in mid air as it flapped instinctively, trying to flee the pain. It recovered quickly and went straight for its attacker, who appeared to have disappeared. The black-clad Lihou soldier seemingly materialized from behind an ally and leapt with a flying kick at the shapeshifter.

Somewhere nearby, Su-Ni watched the circling shapeshifters dive. She had found herself in the middle ranks with no one that she knew. Her thigh was bandaged tightly, and her wound was bothering her a little, but she would still be able to fight. She had been looking around desperately for anyone she could recognize. For some reason, the absence of a familiar face caused her confidence to waver. She figured Denlin and O'eintsu were in the thick of things. During the charge she had lost sight of Urietsin and the priests.

She was about to curse herself for this when she saw the shapeshifters. The logical connection in her mind was instantaneous. They had flown past the main fighting and had zeroed in on something. It could only be one thing. She began to run in their direction.

The ring of soldiers, and anyone else who was close, sprung into action as twenty shapeshifters landed in their midst. Denlin cried cheerfully and swung his staff around his body. With footwork that was almost like a dance he stepped into range of a few of the creatures. His staff twirled in front of him, then he passed it from one hand to the other behind his back. His other hand twisted it over his head, then thrust it suddenly at an opponent.

The firm but flexible weapon became a blur around him. It bounced off the face of the shapeshifter in front of him, and he guided its ricocheting momentum under one arm with both hands, half twisting his torso to smack a challenger who came up behind him. He continued to turn his body, lunging ahead and coming down with an overhead strike to a third shapeshifter. He straightened up and let the staff continue swinging down and under to poke a fourth.

These four shapeshifters were angry.

They descended upon him furiously, whipping out many reaching limbs that shot from various parts of their bodies. Denlin whipped the staff around himself, rotating it at the center and switching it from one side to the other, spinning on his feet to turn them all away. He was doing quite well until one of the shapeshifters reached along the ground and wrapped around his ankles.

* * *

"Focus...focus...focus..." a smaller voice whispered to Urietsin. It repeated that single word over and over again until he began to wonder if he was chanting it himself. He understood the wisdom in this word. He could sense the shapeshifters, especially the ones who were so close to him now, but he needed to focus on the bulk of enemies that threatened the army.

This logic kept him listening to that soft voice, but he was enticed by the possibility of laying waste to those who had killed his master. It was a subtle debate inside him that he had, thus far, kept mostly under control. Suddenly, his focus was shattered as Denlin's form came barreling into him.

The two warriors rolled to a stop. Urietsin jumped up quickly. Denlin did not. The Swift One knelt by him. He could tell that the young man was in considerable pain. He looked down and noticed an odd red glow coming from the injured soldier's side. It took him a moment to realize that he was actually seeing the injury itself, as it was beneath the skin. It pulsed red from heat as blood rushed to it in a blossoming bruise. Four of his ribs were cracked cleanly through. The young man moved his lips at Urietsin, but the Swift One could not hear him over the fighting. He held up the staff that he was still clutching. Urietsin took it as the warrior lost consciousness.

Urietsin rose and turned. Before him twenty shapeshifters wreaked havoc. Two priests lay motionless on the ground while the rest hid behind soldiers and prayed for divine intervention. Denlin was not the only warrior down either. The Swift One looked down at the staff and saw the strong wooden fibers that made it up. He even saw the small particles that composed the fibers. He saw the energy within waiting to be released.

He ran ahead, looking for an opponent. There were plenty to choose from.

* * *

Su-Ni navigated through the crowd of soldiers that stood awaiting an opportunity to join the fray. When she took in the scene, she could see why some of them were a bit hesitant. All of the twenty shapeshifters were still standing, but a few of the defenders had fallen. She saw Denlin laying a few feet from the fight. She swallowed back the sudden sense of panic that rose in her throat. There were many more warriors who were in need of immediate assistance before they found themselves in situations not so dissimilar from Denlin's.

She turned her attention back to the fighting. Catching sight of Urietsin, she gasped. He seemed to be almost glowing with some inner light. He swung a staff that she assumed was Denlin's. The way he moved was unnatural.

Urietsin swatted defensively with the bottom of his staff at the shapeshifter in front of him, flipping aside a dripping appendage. He flung out his open hand toward the creature. To the amazement of anyone who was looking on, the creature flew back as if it had been struck, though the Swift One's hand was too far away to have made contact.

Pressing his advantage, Urietsin shot forward, staff leading. His weapon snapped downward in an overhead swing that connected with a loud crack on top of the creature's head. He took another half step forward, swinging the staff back up to hit the slimy beast with the other end. Urietsin's rear hand, supporting the butt of the staff, went under his leading arm, which flung the staff straight out to the side and sent the creature spinning head over heels sideways.

Suddenly, Su-Ni shouted, "Urietsin, behind you!" She was too late, though, as a tentacle wound its way around the Swift One. The young woman ran into the chaos. As she pushed forward, sword leading, she found the way blocked.

A shapeshifter leapt in front of her. It grinned grotesquely and waved. She noticed its hand was a lighter pink than the rest of its skin. She only had a split second to wish she had killed the thing yesterday when she had the chance. It flung its arms and a few other spontaneous limbs at her.

She hacked profusely, successfully injuring the creature a bit, but it would not underestimate her this time. One tentacle got through her defenses and twisted around the wrist of her weapon hand. It pulled her sword aside and wrapped her in slippery tendrils of flesh. The tentacles tightened in opposite directions, making her feel like she was being squeezed to death and torn apart at the same time.

Reacting only on instinct, Su-Ni flicked her wrist around and slid her sword under the tentacle that restrained that hand. The shapeshifter, distracted by the glee in trying to wring the life from her body, did not react in time and lost the appendage. Taking advantage of the opportunity, the young woman swept her sword across and severed the rest of the slippery limbs around her. She stepped forward to take revenge upon the now frightened creature but almost immediately leapt back. The beast's mouth opened and a horrified screech poured out. Smoke slowly curled above its head. Its face began to take on a yellowish tinge that got continuously brighter. His head burst into flames, and a tiny white light flew out of the conflagration. The Fiu-Het toppled to the ground.

Behind him stood Urietsin. If he saw Su-Ni standing there agape, he made no indication. Instead, he turned to the next closest shapeshifter and extended his hand. His eyes were like fire. The same small white light came out of his hand and embedded itself into the creature's chest. It combusted almost instantly.

One of the other Fiu-Het noticed this strange phenomenon and expanded the pockets under his chin in a cry. All of the shapeshifters turned away from their opponents. With inhuman speed they converged on Urietsin. They threw themselves at him, stretching their bodies out to envelope him completely.

Within the prison of wet, constricting muscle, Urietsin could feel the movement of the shapeshifters around him. They tried to maneuver their daggers into his body, but he turned them away with a thought. For a moment, he looked on in fascination as he saw the secret behind the Fiu-Het's magical abilities, then the voice in his head spoke.

"Destroy them," it said much more loudly than anything else he had heard thus far.

With barely any mental effort, Urietsin supplied the particles that composed the shapeshifters with an enormous burst of energy. The particles quivered for a moment, then the ones exposed to the air outside began to react. The shell of shapeshifters that were trying to squeeze the breath of life from the Swift One's body dissolved in a haze of white flame. Like a phoenix, Urietsin emerged transformed.

"Destroy them all," the voice urged.

* * *

Laernus dove aside as the king threw the grass that he had just ripped from the ground at him. He had seen Orbein do this a second earlier with his gift of sight, but the information given to him by the magic was not very helpful. The king's spell honed in on him, and twisting vines sprouted from the air and wrapped around him. He tried to cut at them with his sword, but he only got hopelessly tangled.

Orbein laughed confidently, though the success of the spell was a great relief to him. He had not expected the seer to recover so well from his difficult start. Nor had he expected him to be such a skilled swordsman. Perhaps it had not been such a wise idea to send him to train in Vethisir's army. The king pressed the back of his weapon hand against the wound in his left arm. It stung a bit, and blood still oozed from it, but it was not serious. He approached the seer slowly, flicking the tip of his thin sword in front of him as he stepped. When he passed by the wizard's discarded tunic, he kicked it aside with a sneer.

"Let me ask you, Laernus," he said disdainfully, "is the fact that I will be dead in a few moments any consolation to you?"

The seer grimaced. "You wouldn't really care if it was," he spat.

"Ah, yes. Perhaps. But I am glad that my last deed will be to kill you," Orbein said. His face came within inches Laernus. Suddenly, he reached out and put his arm around the seer's neck, pressing the point of his sword against his opponent's chin. He turned to Agucho, gripping Laernus tightly. "Now, I propose a deal," he said, trying to sound cool and confident. "Let me go and I will spare the wizard."

Agucho considered the king dubiously. He had grown to respect the seer somewhat. He certainly wished for Laernus's victory over Orbein, but he didn't think his life was worth the king's escape. He was about to voice this last sentiment when Laernus himself spared the shapeshifter the trouble.

The seer sounded out an archaic word. Orbein flew back as a familiar yellow shield sprang up around Laernus. The ivy that bound the wizard disintegrated into nothing in the shield's area of antimagic. Orbein cursed in his prone condition.

"Don't be too disappointed, highness," the seer said, willing the shield away. "I don't think that deal would have gotten you very far." He walked up to the king, who hopped up and backed away.

But Orbein was disappointed. He wasn't sure how he was going to get out of this situation, but he did know he wanted this fight to be over. He was running out of useful combat spells, and though he was an excellent swordsman, he did not enjoy the challenge put forth by Laernus. The king's weapon was light and swift, which was usually quite advantageous against such a slower, heavier weapon as the seer carried. But Laernus blocked any strike Orbein threw at him. Magic had also been difficult because Laernus pressed him constantly. Aside from the first and last spell, the seer dodged everything with a preternatural sense that was exactly what it seemed to be.

Laernus lunged at his nemesis, thrusting his longsword forward. Orbein managed to parry the heavy sword deftly. The king flicked his wrist and moved his sword away from the seer's, ending in a straight jab to the heart. Laernus's second sight showed him this, and he reversed the direction of his own blade. His parry clanged hard against Orbein's weapon, jarring the king's arm as each strike had been doing for the whole fight. Orbein retreated a step, drawing the seer with him, then he jumped forward, working his sword back and forth in a dizzying array of feints and lunges.

Laernus had a bit of trouble keeping up. The king's future self twitched the blade one way, then his present self twitched it the other. Left, right, lunge, up, left, up, down, lunge...not unexpectedly, the seer lost track. Things resolved themselves quickly as a sharp pain tore through his shoulder. Orbein had finally scored a hit.

The king felt the contact and tried to push the sword deeper, but Laernus whipped his own weapon across and dislodged it. The seer backed away cautiously, trying to cover the wound as he did. But now that they were finally even, Orbein was not ready to give up so easily. He matched every one of the seer's retreating steps, his sword extended outward in a flurry of slashing that whistled in the air.

For Laernus, the stab in the shoulder had been an expensive wound. It was not deep, nor did it bleed profusely, but it had broken his hard-gotten concentration. Now, with the king advancing upon him, he could not get it back. He had learned to use the longsword by itself before he discovered how to meld magical skills with martial, but it was definitely the combination of the two that made him a formidable challenger. The one was not very effective without the other.

Orbein shot toward him again, and only the seer's desperate instinct saved him. The king's sword rang off his own, but swooped around to find another opening. Laernus brought the longsword to meet it, but it was not there. The king's thin blade poked into the side of his chest opposite his first wound. The pain caused him to jump back and fall to the ground, pulling away from Orbein's sword just before it went deep enough to become fatal. The king stood over him in triumph. He raised his sword and brought it down as fast and hard as he could.

But Laernus was not quite ready to die. He forced his sword over him with as much strength as he could muster and caught the tip of the king's weapon, throwing it off target. It stuck into the ground beside him, and he brought his longsword back around in an awkward circle. The force of the swing made his punctured chest tense in agony. He heard a loud pop from his shoulder, and he cried out painfully.

Orbein fell away from the seer. A deep cut on the side of his left knee bled profusely. The king tried to stand back up, but the pain was unbearable. He reached over and pulled his sword out of the ground, eyeing the rising Laernus warily.

It was difficult for the seer to get to his feet. He could not move his right arm without waves of pain. He sat up and grabbed the longsword beside him with his left hand and struggled to his feet. He saw Orbein kneeling there on his good knee, leaning now on his sword for support. Laernus stepped up to him, pointing his weapon unsteadily with his off hand.

Agucho gasped loudly and unexpectedly.

The two men looked over at the shapeshifter, then turned their heads to see what he was gaping at. In the sky over the battlefield behind them hovered a massive, twisting serpent of fire. It dipped and slinked through the air, and with a deafening roar, it flared brightly, sending great plumes up off its body. It was a terrifying sight.

Laernus half doubled over as Orbein's sword slid into his belly. It was the only thing that could have pried his eyes away from a sight he had not seen in many, many years. It took every ounce of adrenaline-fueled strength he had left to do what he did next. In his last act of defiance toward the king, he swung his heavy weapon before falling to the floor, motionless.

Orbein did not have time to react as the blade's momentum brought it to the bridge of his nose and across his eyes. It did not embed itself deeply into his skull, but it was deep enough. The king of Niele'itio crumbled, his body splayed over the legs of his killer.

* * *

The whole field froze in awe and terror as this enormous, flaming dragon slithered over their heads. If the apparition earlier had been a miniature ghost of Reisothin, this was surely the full-sized one. Veterans of the empire screamed at the manifestation of twenty years of nightmares, the reincarnation of their old enemy. Shionen wept at the malevolent power the dragon exuded with every fiery burst.

It snaked across the sky over the field in great, sweeping undulations that rained heat upon the onlookers. Its very real horn pointed the way as it moved from east to west. Through the transparent flames of its head, the unscathed form of Urietsin could be seen. He stood firmly on the insubstantial inside surface of the dragon, holding the horn in place over his head. The glow in his eyes projected outward to the dragon's, giving them a chillingly intelligent light.

Suddenly, it stopped.

From where he hovered Urietsin could clearly see that even the shapeshifters had stopped fighting to watch him. A hint of a smile came across his lips. This was the moment that would end all this chaos. These wicked beasts had come to destroy the empire, costing the life of his master, his emperor, and many of his people.

"They must all die," the voice reassured him.

Deep within him, something made Urietsin wonder if this was true. Within the swirling inferno of the dragon's head, a figure slowly began to appear. The Swift One's eyes widened as he recognized a wavering image of Kiusu.

"You know what you should do, Etsin," his master's soft voice said. Through the ripples of the mysterious image he could see the old man smiling. Behind him, the spirits of the three warriors that had fallen to the gotori nodded reassuringly.

There was a deep rumble that extended for miles as the dragon roared angrily, but its fiery form still hung in the air, its flames lessened in intensity. Within its head the form of Kiusu suddenly melted. Instead of the three fallen warriors behind him, there was only a cackling Fiu-Het holding a curved dagger, dripping with fresh blood.

"Wait not, Urietsin...the aggressor will fall," the deep timbre of the original voice said to Urietsin, just as it had to Geilo months ago. The will of Reisothin, locked within his horn, had managed to bend events to his desire thus far. After twenty years of slumber, it had inspired the emperor with fears of an unknown enemy. It had preyed upon the weak souls of Kesitul. Most satisfyingly, it had sensed Geilo's desperation and pushed him along on this path toward war, meanwhile sending out waves of wicked inspiration that had been grasped by Orbein's sympathetic ambitions. The foolish emperor hadn't even suspected as it impersonated Minotros, their god of fate. Geilo's death had been the revenge that the evil will had been plotting for two decades now. This war was the catalyst to execute those plans. Now, as it struggled to maintain control over this powerful young warrior, it was determined to continue exerting its influence. Now that Reisothin knew life again, he would not give it up so easily.

The dragon flared anew and began to circle in the sky. The shapeshifters below began to scatter. Urietsin barely heard the quiet whisper that repeated his nickname, "Etsin...Etsin...Etsin..."

"They must all die..." the voice of Reisothin urged one last time, drowning out the whisper.

The Swift One screamed in defiance.

The head of the ghostly Reisothin rose briefly, then turned straight down. It plummeted toward the center of the fleeing shapeshifters. The glowing, scaly body unwound from its coil as it followed the rest of itself down to the center of the empire's enemies.

The impact was followed by a blinding flash and a concussive boom that dropped everyone on the field. Even beyond the two armies, the sparse grass and dirt rippled away in the shockwave. Many of the shapeshifters found themselves lifted into a growing sphere of fire that vaporized them almost instantly. The rest of them were thrown violently in all directions and bounced sickeningly a few times along the ground as they landed. Many of Niele'itio's soldiers were severely wounded as they too flew away from the impact.

Within seconds of the explosion, everything on the field was still, except for the column of smoke that extended high into the sky. The silence was complete. Nothing stirred for many minutes, either because it was unconscious, or because it was terrified that the worst was yet to come. But, after two days of war and chaos, peace had finally descended upon the battlefield of Ikiu'iu.

19 AFTERMATH

Though the weather was cool, smoke still curled up into the air from the scorched earth of the previous day, especially from within the huge crater left by the dragon's impact. Figures moved through the hazy area, their heads turning this way and that. They were searching for survivors.

Tilon made his way over to Komeris. "Have you found anything?"

The captain squinted through the fog at the elf. Both of their faces were covered with soot, and underneath the black they were slightly red. "Nothing. It is as if the blast turned them to smoke," he said.

Tilon nodded in agreement. It was the only logical conclusion, given that no living thing could be found within the crater. The massive explosion had leveled the area and injured many of the soldiers of Kesitul, though fortunately they were far enough away that no one was harmed fatally. Anyone or anything as close as they were now, however, seemed to have been destroyed utterly. There was no sign of the shapeshifters, and no sign of the Swift One or the horn he had carried with him in his descent. Yet still they looked, just in case.

Tilon paused in his searching and regarded Komeris curiously. "What do you suppose will happen now?" he asked.

Komeris shrugged. "It's difficult to say," he answered honestly, still peering at the ground through the smoky haze. "The general has already called for Ninei to come with some of the few soldiers left at camp. I would guess that once things have died down, there will be another mission through the mountains, this time to negotiate with this Dark City the enemy soldiers speak of. We can only hope that this was the bulk of their army."

The elf nodded sympathetically. "And who is emperor now? Did Geilo have a child?"

Komeris shook his head. "Emperor Geilo never took a wife. The empire was his one love. The general is the next most powerful man in the

275

empire..." The captain trailed, only now realizing what he was saying and what it meant for his own destiny.

Tilon merely walked beside him in thoughtful silence.

"Over here!" a feminine voice suddenly called out.

Searchers came running from all directions toward the call. On the far side of the field, Marui and Reniu stood over two humanoid figures lying prone in the blackened grass. A crowd was quickly gathering, and Tilon and Komeris pushed their way through.

"What is it?" demanded the captain. "Have you found him?"

"No, sir," answered Reniu, his bare chest riddled with slashes and blackened with soot. "Neither of these're ours. One of them's dead."

Though the forms were covered in soot as well, it was clear that the two men were not of Kesitul. Oddly, from the position of the men and their weapons, they seemed to have been fighting one another.

"I know one of them," stated Pei-Shi, emerging from the crowd. "He gave me this." She pointed to the mostly scarred injury on her shoulder.

"He is one of the men who attacked you beyond the mountains?" asked Tilon.

The blade master nodded.

A spark of recognition registered on Marui's face as well.

"What about the other?" Tilon asked.

Pei-Shi shook her head uncertainly.

"Nor do I know him," confirmed Komeris. "His armor is very fine. Perhaps he was commander of the army."

"Come," said Marui pointing to the man she and Pei-Shi had recognized, "this man is badly injured. Help me carry him back to camp."

No complaint was heard among them as they hoisted the human, possibly an enemy, and carried him back to be tended. At the camp the elves cleaned and bandaged him as the captain and his warriors reported to Etrusin. By nightfall, the unconscious man was resting on a bedroll beside soldiers who might have killed him the day before.

Somewhere nearby, another young warrior stirred. Her injuries were not very serious, and she found little comfort in sleep. When she closed her eyes, painful images assaulted her. Though she knew her empire had won the day, to her there was no comfort to be had from that knowledge. She had trouble reconciling the cost with the outcome.

Su-Ni sat up and sniffled. Her eyes felt puffy with weariness and dried tears. She looked around and saw O'eintsu sitting nearby. His eyes were closed, but she suspected he was not asleep. Next to him lay an unconscious Denlin, who she had managed to drag away from the fighting yesterday. She sighed in relief that at least those two had survived. She stretched morosely and stood.

She knew that she would find no rest tonight. But she wished she could sleep. A dreamless sleep that did not remind her of the past few days. At one moment she felt foolish being specifically upset over the death of two warriors who she barely knew; in the next she was angry with herself for thinking she was foolish. And more than just those two warriors had died, should she not feel those losses as keenly?

Confused and lonely, the once diplomat, now warrior, limped away from the rows of injured soldiers that lined this healing pavilion, one of many such structures all across the field. She did not walk far. Off to one side of the camp were long lines of linen-wrapped objects upon the ground. A few men and elves stood guard over them. These carefully covered parcels were the prepared corpses of soldiers, twenty-one hundred humans and three hundred elves, waiting to be delivered to their final resting place. The sight of them made Su-Ni shudder, but she hobbled closer just the same.

"Halt," called one of the guards, an elf. "This is no place for you. You should be resting."

'This is a place of rest,' she thought morbidly. Only those who rested here would never awake. "Kiusu," she heard herself say. "Is he among these warriors?"

The elf shook his head. "He will have his place of honor as an imperial guard beneath the monument that will overlook the rest of the tombs. He lies now by the emperor."

"Where are they?" Su-Ni asked. "May I see them?"

The Shionen guard looked uncertain for a moment, then he smiled sympathetically. "Come," he said.

She followed him to a small tent and stepped inside. Within there were two tables. On one lay the shell of Geilo's spirit, carefully wrapped in a shroud. The other table was empty.

"Where is the body?" the elf asked rhetorically.

Su-Ni's mind turned over sickeningly.

"Someone put him out with the others," he said with authority, though his expression was not so certain. "Come."

"Wait," the young woman said. "Where are you going?"

"I am going to find out who moved the body and where," the elf replied.

"What if you don't?" she asked a little too forcefully.

Once again, the elf's expression was sympathetic. He came and put his arms on the woman's shoulders gently. "Come," he repeated, "it really is best if you get some sleep."

Su-Ni realized he was right. No matter how much she wished otherwise, Kiusu and Urietsin were gone. With that thought, she suddenly felt too exhausted to stay awake. She could not keep from weeping, but she did let the elf walk her back to the pavilion. She made her way back to her bedroll and fell asleep almost instantly, happy to leave her harsh world behind for a while.

EPILOGUE

The sun glinted faintly off the polished pommel of the shortsword that stood embedded into the top of the small cairn. It was not a bright light, but the lone figure that stared at it squinted painfully. This was a proper resting place for the old man who had once called this mountainside his home. Next to the mound of stones, three humps in the ground marked the place where the old man himself had buried three brave warriors. The figure standing nearby, completely clad in black so that only his eyes peeked out, bowed long and low before the graves. The action hurt every part of his body, but the pain was secondary to his respect for the men who lay buried here, especially for the one under the cairn.

The cold winter wind blew briefly, bringing a measure of relief to the always burning skin beneath the black shroud. The figure rose from his bow and relished the sensation of the cool breeze. A single flake of snow drifted down and landed upon his arm. He looked at the white flake. It reminded him of a down feather frozen in time. The heat emanating from beneath his black wrappings quickly melted the water crystal, but it was soon replaced by another.

Looking up, the figure noticed many such flakes falling from above. It was the farthest down the mountain that the snow had come thus far this season. He stayed for several minutes by the graves and simply watched, but he knew it would not be wise to remain and let his bandages become soaked by the melting snow. Slowly, he trudged back to the tiny wooden hut that now seemed so familiar to him. He was tired. It was time to sleep away the long winter. Urietsin was home.

ABOUT THE AUTHOR

Born in Massachusetts in 1978, Jeff Goguen is a software engineer and author who lives with his wife Denise on Florida's Space Coast. His interests include linguistics, martial arts and, of course, writing.

www.ingramcontent.com/pod-product-compliance
Lightning Source LLC
Chambersburg PA
CBHW071308170626
46809CB00001B/371